Praise for Beth Wiseman

"*Plain Promise* is Beth Wiseman's masterpiece. It's the story of two unlikely friends' journey toward faith and love. This heart-warming novel brings readers hope and paints a beautiful, authentic portrait of Lancaster County, Pennsylvania. Her characters are so real that they feel like old friends. Once you open the book, you won't put it down until you've reached the last page."

> — Amy Clipston,
> best-selling author
> of *A Gift of Grace*

"Beth Wiseman's *Plain Pursuit* is a charming work of fiction that beautifully paints the quaint picture of the simple ways of the Amish lifestyle. This novel, like its predecessor, *Plain Perfect*, really brings home a message of family devotion. This is wholesome entertainment that I can effortlessly recommend without any reservation. What a sweet romantic story."

> — word-up-studies.blogspot.com

"Wiseman's Christian romance novel is just 'plain' good."

> — *Fayette County Record*,
> La Grange, Texas regarding
> *Plain Perfect*

"*Plain Pursuit*'s story line will hit you in the heart almost from page one. As you keep going deeper into the story, it ceases being a "story" and begins to feel like you are an active participant in a group of people's lives. Learning the history of shunning in the Amish world and trying to justify what they believe in your world where anything would be done to save a child's life. When you witness where these two worlds collide, there is frustration, awe, and tears. [It] will take you from the thrills of a new love as Noah and Carley explore each other's pasts together, to the bottom of despair as the life of a child hangs by a thread."

— The Romance Readers
Connection

"I was kind of dreading reading yet another Amish novel as not too many of the more recently published ones measure up to Beverly Lewis or Wanda Brunstetter. However, *Plain Perfect* is the exception rather than the rule. And I couldn't help but keep reading the well crafted story. The characters could be real, with real life struggles, and even the Amish had issues to work through."

— Laura V. Hilton,
lighthouse-academy.
blogspot.com

"Beth Wiseman gives the reader a delightful glimpse into the life of [the] Amish [in *Plain Perfect*]. [Her] writing is truly inspired."

— *Schulenburg Sticker*,
Schulenburg, Texas

"The importance of finding peace and acceptance, especially within oneself, is a central theme in this book, the second in Wiseman's Daughters of the Promise series. Well-defined characters and story make for an enjoyable read."

— *Romantic Times* regarding
Plain Pursuit

"[A] touching, heartwarming story. Wiseman does a particularly great job of dealing with shunning, a controversial Amish practice that seems cruel and unnecessary to outsiders . . . If you're a fan of Amish fiction, don't miss *Plain Pursuit!*"

— Kathy Fuller,
author of *A Man of His Word*

"[*Plain Pursuit* is] a well crafted story with fully drawn characters and has nice pacing."

— LibraryThing.com

Plain Promise

Other Novels by
Beth Wiseman

Plain Promise

A Daughters of the Promise Novel

BETH WISEMAN

THOMAS NELSON
Since 1798

NASHVILLE   DALLAS   MEXICO CITY   RIO DE JANEIRO

Published in Nashville, Tennessee, by Thomas Nelson. Thomas Nelson is a registered trademark of HarperCollins Christian Publishing, Inc.

Thomas Nelson, Inc., titles may be purchased in bulk for educational, business, fund-raising, or sales promotional use. For information, please e-mail SpecialMarkets@ThomasNelson.com.

Publisher's Note: This novel is a work of fiction. Names, characters, places, and incidents are either products of the author's imagination or used fictitiously. All characters are fictional, and any similarity to people living or dead is purely coincidental.

ISBN 978-0-7180-1449-0 (custom)

Library of Congress Cataloging-in-Publication Data

Wiseman, Beth, 1962–
    Plain promise : a Daughters of the promise novel / Beth Wiseman.
      p. cm. — (Daughters of the promise)
    ISBN 978-1-59554-720-0 (pbk.)
    I. Amish—Fiction. I. Title.
PS3623.I83P576 2009
813'.6—dc22   2009027371

Printed in the United States of America

14 15 16 17 18 RRD 6 5 4 3 2 1

To Rene Simpson, my dear friend who refuses to settle for anything less than true love.

Pennsylvania Dutch Glossary

ab im kopp: off in the head

ach: oh

baremlich: terrible

boppli: baby

daadi: grandfather

daed: dad

daadi haus: a separate dwelling built for aging parents

danki: thank you

Die Botschaft: a weekly newspaper serving Old Order Amish
    communities everywhere

Em Gott Sei Friede: God's peace

Englisch or *Englischer*: a non-Amish person

fraa: wife

guder mariye: good morning

gut: good

haus: house

kaffi: coffee

kalt: cold

kapp: a prayer covering or cap

kinner: children or grandchildren

kinskind: grandchild

lieb: love

mamm: mom

mei: my

naerfich: nervous

narrisch: crazy, insane

Ordnung: the written and unwritten rules of the Amish; the understood behavior by which the Amish are expected to live, passed down from generation to generation. Most Amish know the rules by heart.

Pennsylvania *Deitsch:* Pennsylvania German, the language most commonly used by the Amish

rumschpringe: running-around period that begins when a teenager turns sixteen years old and ends when he or she is baptized into the Amish faith

schee: pretty

wedder: weather

wunderbaar: wonderful

ya: yes

1

THE DEN IN THE OLD FARMHOUSE WAS THE COZIEST room in the house, but a nip still hung in the air. Sadie pulled her sweater from the rack on the wall and tossed another log onto the fire, orange sparks shimmying up the chimney. She walked to the window, raised the green blind, and looked toward the guest cottage about a hundred feet away. She couldn't help but recall the hours she and Ben had spent restoring it five years ago, painting the whitewashed walls, installing carpet, and making it fit for use by the *Englisch*.

Sadie was glad when Bishop Ebersol allowed her to furnish the cottage with electricity last year for use as a rental property. Her current renter had come all the way from Los Angeles, his long, sleek automobile now crowding the inside of her barn. But she was grateful for the income. It had been difficult to make ends meet with Ben gone, though her Old Order Amish community never let her go without.

This time of year, men in the district made sure she had plenty of firewood and kept the snow cleared from her driveway. In the spring and summer, the womenfolk kept her supplied with fresh peas and corn from the family crops, but Sadie, a fit woman at age thirty, kept a small garden on her own. She grew tomatoes, peppers, strawberries, melons, and the like—produce easy to tend. In the fall, her neighbors brought her lots of potatoes. She also had plenty of meat stored in a locker in town, thanks to her best friend, Lillian Stoltzfus, and Lillian's husband, Samuel.

Her shop out front gave her a bit more income. She sold handmade Amish goods that fared well with the tourists. Other women in the district added their crafts to Sadie's, and they took turns tending the store, splitting the profits among them. She turned her head around and checked the clock on the mantel. Nearly seven. She straightened up, tucked loose red ringlets beneath her *kapp*, and bowed her head.

After she thanked the Lord for the blessings of this new day, she grabbed her black cape, bonnet, and gloves. Then she pulled on her calf-high black boots and braced herself for a blast of arctic air. She took a deep breath, swung the door wide, and closed it quickly behind her—gelid wind stinging her cheeks like a thousand tiny needles.

A frosty mix of sleet and snow dusted her cape as she made her trek across the front yard to the shop. How fortunate she was that Ben's old workshop was near the road and visible to tourists. She had cried when she'd given away her husband's tools and turned his favorite place into the shop, but her friends had worked by her side to transform the old building. Then, just two months ago, they opened Treasures of the Heart.

She glanced around at the snow-covered pastures, visions of Ben tending the land still fresh in her mind. Less painful, but still there. It had been four years since the *Englisch* car had sped around a corner of Black Horse Road and into Ben's buggy. She would never forget their crates of fresh vegetables strewn across the road, patches of red, green, and yellow dotting the black asphalt. She envisioned the toppled buggy, their injured horse, who would later have to be put down, and her Ben . . .

When she'd heard the commotion that day, she had run down Black Horse Road faster than she knew her legs could carry her. Jacob King was squatting beside Ben when she arrived, and she knew by the expression on Jacob's face that her Ben was gone.

A glimpse of movement to her right pulled her back to the present. She looked toward the cottage and saw her renter, Kade Saunders, retrieving wood from where she had placed it on the front porch. He was sparsely clothed for such weather, denim pants and a short-sleeved, white T-shirt. Sadie watched him hurriedly scoop two logs into his arms, then drop one before making it to the front door.

She heard him grunt loudly and say something that sounded like cursing. She wasn't sure, but it stopped her in her tracks. She watched him walk backward into the house, cradling the logs in his arms. She couldn't see his expression, but she waved anyway. He didn't wave back. Of course, his arms were full. He kicked the door shut and was out of sight. It was the first time she'd seen the man since he'd arrived three days ago.

She tucked her head to avoid the thickening snowfall and continued toward the shop. It was hard not to wonder what Kade Saunders was doing in Lancaster County for three months, so far from where he lived in California. When he had stopped by to pick up the key, he hadn't looked prepared for the twelve-degree weather—denim breeches, a black overcoat, and white running shoes not fit for two feet of snow. And the man didn't have a head covering. His wavy, dark hair glistened with icy moisture, and his hazel eyes shone with irritation. Shivering as he spoke, he had declined the maid service included in the rental cost but requested that his automobile be protected from the wintry elements. She could see it through the open barn doors.

She rubbed her hands together and recalled the phone call from Mr. Saunders's personal assistant. The woman requested the one-bedroom cottage January through March for Mr. Saunders, but only after insisting that his privacy be respected during his stay. Sadie had hesitated. Her previous renters had been couples and families. How would it look for a single man to be occupying the same property as Sadie for three months, even if they were under separate roofs? Would the bishop be displeased?

As if sensing Sadie's concerns, the assistant said, "Mr. Saunders is quite well-known, and I can provide you with any references you might need."

The woman also asked that the refrigerator be stocked weekly. Sadie's normal rental package didn't include groceries, but Mr. Saunders's employee assured Sadie that cost was of no concern. The fee they'd agreed upon caused Sadie to gasp, but she agreed, grateful for the additional income during the off-season.

Sadie learned that actually finding the products Mr. Saunders desired was a challenge. She'd never heard of Gruyère cheese, for example, so she substituted Gouda cheese instead. His exhausting list of flavored coffees, organic breakfast cereals, and gourmet pastries were also frustrating.

She did the best she could and also threw in some extras. He was, after all, in Paradise, Pennsylvania—the heart of Lancaster County. Wouldn't he want to try Amish favorites, like shoofly pie and chowchow? She provided these for him in an attempt to make up for the items she couldn't find. She'd also prepared him a hearty batch of tapioca pudding, along with a loaf of home-made bread, a meat loaf, and zucchini casserole, and had also included a few jellies and jams she had canned last summer.

But even Mr. Saunders couldn't distract her from thinking about her forthcoming visit from Milo Troyer, her Amish friend from Stephenville, Texas. They had been writing letters for over two years, and he called Sadie every Tuesday night at eight o'clock. They talked for fifteen minutes, a cold fifteen minutes out in the barn this time of year, but she was thankful that the bishop allowed telephones in the barn these days, a luxury that would have been unheard-of in years past. Sadie looked forward to Milo's call all week long, and this spring he would be riding on a bus from Texas all the way to Lancaster County. They decided he would stay with her friends Ivan and Katie Ann for his two-week visit.

With pictures forbidden, she hadn't a clue what he looked like, except what he told her. He was tall and slender, like she was, with dark hair and the customary beard after marriage. His wife died shortly after Ben, and Sadie's cousin had introduced them via mail.

His looks were of no concern though. Milo's heart spoke to her in a way she didn't think possible after Ben died. He under-stood the grief of losing a spouse, and their hours of consoling each other had grown from friendship into much more. She knew it was God's will for her to move on; it was customary in their community to quickly remarry. But she'd been a widow for four years, and there were no options for remarriage. Perhaps she'd been too picky, but she refused to settle for anything less than something comparable to the love she'd shared with Ben.

She could tell by Milo's letters and phone calls that they would be a good match, and her desire was to begin her life with Milo soon. Milo's correspondence was always upbeat, kind, and filled with hope for the future. He was a hard worker, like Sadie, and family was his top priority. Perhaps they would have the children that she and Ben never did, for reasons the natural doctor in town couldn't seem to explain.

She entered the gift shop, went straight to the gas heaters, and lit them both. Only the cottage had electricity. It'd be cause for a shunning if she connected to the outside world when it wasn't necessary or approved by the bishop. She rolled up the green blinds in each of the four windows. The sun was just starting to rise, giving only a hint of light, just enough for her to attach price tags to some of the quilted pot holders she'd finished the night before. Fridays were usually good sale days, even in the off-season.

If she lived to be a hundred, she'd never understand why the *Englisch* found their way of life so interesting. With less farmland and bigger families, many in her community worked outside the home; it had become a way of life. She felt blessed not to have to travel farther than her own front yard.

The bell on the front door chimed, and Sadie turned to see her friend Lillian walk in. Lillian's mother, Sarah Jane, followed behind her. Lillian and her mother now shared a close relationship. But it hadn't always been that way. Sarah Jane had left the Amish community when she was a young girl of eighteen, and she had protested when Lillian left to come live with her grandparents. But after a few months, Sarah Jane surprised everyone, returning to Lancaster County and being baptized into the faith alongside her daughter. Then when Lillian married Samuel Stoltzfus, a widower in the community with a son named David, Sarah Jane had made her home with her father.

Lillian hung her cape on the stand inside the door. "Whose Mercedes-Benz?"

Sadie ignored the question. She had a hunch the less they all knew about her mysterious guest, the better. "Where's Anna?" she asked instead. Lillian usually brought her daughter, a precious bundle who wasn't much over a year old.

"Anna is with Samuel's sister, Mary Ellen," Lillian answered. She rubbed her expanding belly.

Sadie noticed the gesture. "How are you feeling? Are you still having morning sickness?"

"No more morning sickness." Lillian moved toward the back of the shop and peered out of the window toward the barn. "That's a very expensive car," she said. "Who does it belong to?"

"Kade Saunders." Sadie joined Lillian at the window while Sarah Jane took over pinning price tags on various items. "I don't know much about him. His personal assistant told me he's from Los Angeles. I reckon it's *gut* to have a renter this time of year. These harsh winters tend to keep people away." A tinge of cold air seeped in from outside when her face neared the window. "He's leasing the place for three months."

Lillian pulled her head back and squinted her eyes. "*Ya?* What for?"

"Don't know. But that assistant lady asked me to stock the refrigerator with all kinds of strange foods every week. Some of them I couldn't even find at the market." She paused. "And he doesn't want any cleanup service. I reckon he'll have to wash his own towels and linens in the washing machine and dryer."

"Hmm. That is odd," Lillian mused, still gazing toward the cottage and the fancy car in the barn.

———————

Kade stared at the TV screen and wondered if he could survive without basic cable for the next three months. The antique antenna provided a whopping four channels. No CNN or other national channels, only local news that was fuzzy at best. But this is what he wanted, he reminded himself—away from everything.

He leaned back on the couch and propped his feet on the coffee table, trying to ward off his festering thoughts about Alicia. It wasn't as if she'd broken his heart or anything, but once again he'd let himself be used and fooled by a member of the opposite sex. One shiny new car, a diamond bracelet—and pretty much anything else she'd asked for—and then she was gone. Story of his life. Young, attractive women interested in his money, nothing more.

Kade glanced around at his modest accommodations. This was hardly what he had in mind when his friend Val had suggested he get out of Los Angeles to unwind. Val had brought his ex-wife here and said the peacefulness would help Kade clear his head. Though it must not have worked for Val—he and his wife had divorced shortly after their trip. Val never wanted to talk about what had happened, and he seemed to be mending his soul with travel. Kade could rarely get hold of him these days. But Kade understood. Kade's soul could certainly use some mending as well.

The roaring fire warmed the room, and his refrigerator and pantry were stocked, though he couldn't identify some of his host's offerings. Amish food, he presumed. He wished it wasn't so cold outside, but he didn't feel the need to venture out anyway. That would mean interaction with others, and he wasn't up for that. Besides, he found the simple cottage to be quite cozy. He'd hole up here and try to heal himself of all that ailed him. It was a long list.

For whatever reason, he thought of the Amish woman he was renting from. He couldn't remember her name. But he could recall her ivory skin, incredible blue eyes, and strands of wavy red hair spiraling against her cheek from beneath a cap on her head. She was quite lovely, even without a stitch of makeup on her face and clothed in a baggy dress to her knees. And she was tall and slender. Like Alicia. Kade's brows narrowed as he grumbled in disgust. *Blasted woman.*

Still. It was no reason to be rude to the Amish gal when he'd first arrived—demanding he park his car in the barn and hastily accepting the key before he retreated to his much-needed solitude. Perhaps he could have been a little kinder to the woman. Kade hadn't seen another soul on the property, except for a few women who entered the shop up front each day. He wondered if she took care of this whole place on her own.

He opened the refrigerator and took out the plastic bowl of tapioca pudding. Best pudding he'd ever had in his life. He grabbed a spoon from the drawer and finished the last little bit in the large container, then tossed the empty bowl in the sink, along with the past three days of dirty dishes. He would have been better served to have accepted the Amish woman's housecleaning services included in the rental. He wondered for a moment if he should reconsider but disregarded the thought. It would require a limited amount of conversation. He began to fill the sink with soapy water.

Thirty minutes later, he was back on the tan couch. He adjusted the volume on the TV, listened to a woman discuss a nearby animal shelter, and then he turned it off. And he sat—thinking.

He crossed his ankles on the coffee table and thought about how successful he'd become by following in his father's footsteps. At thirty-seven, Kade had more money than he'd ever spend in one lifetime. And, he decided, he couldn't be more miserable.

One thing would cheer him up, though—some more of that tapioca pudding from the Amish woman.

In the fading twilight, Sadie braved the below-freezing temperature and pulled two logs from the stack of firewood she kept in the barn, wishing she'd remembered to do it earlier in the day. Her boots heavy in the deep snow, she edged toward the farmhouse, glancing at the cottage lit up by electricity, smoke wafting out of the chimney. Something caught her eye on her renter's front porch. It was the empty plastic bowl that she had sent the tapioca pudding in. Why in the world would he set it on the front porch?

She put the logs down and trudged toward the cottage, the frigid air nipping at her cheeks. She grabbed the bowl, retrieved her wood, and then headed toward the farmhouse. All she wanted to do was climb into bed and reread the letter she received from Milo two weeks ago, to take refuge in his words and combat her dwindling hope.

Following a bath, she lit the lantern by her bed upstairs and pulled out Milo's note.

My Dear Sadie,

I am counting the days until we meet. I will come to see you when the winter weather has passed. I reckon the springtime is when I will come. The sound of your voice helps me to picture you in my head. You are schee, I know. If it is God's will, you will become my fraa and we will be together. The Lord will guide us.

I am reminded of a song from our Sunday singings—"We Have This Moment." The words make me think of you—"Hold tight to the sound of the music of living. Happy songs from the laughter of children at play. Hold my hand as we run through the sweet, fragrant meadows, making memories of what is today. We have this moment to hold in our hands, and to touch as it slips through our fingers like sand. Yesterday's gone and tomorrow may never come, but we have this moment today."

I want to share mei moments with you, Sadie. I will write you again soon.

In His name,
Milo

Sadie folded the letter and pressed it against her chest. She could only pray that Milo would be everything she longed for. While she'd grown accustomed to fending for herself, how wonderful it would be to have a man to help with chores, to hold her, to love her, to grow old with. Maybe God would even see fit to bless them with a child.

"We Have This Moment" was one of Sadie's favorite songs. She recalled another verse from the song—*"Tender words, gentle touch, and a good time sharing, and someone who loves me and wants me to stay. Hold them near while they're here and don't wait for tomorrow to look back and wish for today."*

Please God, she prayed silently, *bless me with companionship as I go forth in life to serve You.*

The ground was solid beneath Sadie's feet as she walked toward the shop, with no new snow since the heavy downfall yesterday afternoon. She wondered if the snow would keep tourists away, but it was Saturday. At least a few customers would rough out the weather. Today's schedule called for Sadie and Katie Ann to work, since Lillian and her mother had worked the shop yesterday. But Katie Ann was down with the flu, and Sadie declined Mary Ellen's help. There wasn't enough going on this time of year to require two women to run the shop. Sadie knew she could handle it on her own. Besides, Mary Ellen had a family to tend to. She, on the other hand, did not.

It was nearing eight o'clock when she lit the heaters and drew the blinds in the shop. Her day had started early that morning. She'd made another large batch of tapioca pudding, thinking her guest might have been requesting more when he left the empty container outside. It was no trouble. She also baked two loaves of bread for an elderly friend down the street, Lizzie Esh. Lizzie suffered with arthritis and had difficulty cooking these days, particularly considering the effort it took to repeatedly knead dough. She planned to run the bread to Lizzie after she closed the shop in the late afternoon.

The container of pudding sat next to her, and she peered out of the back window toward the guesthouse. One light appeared to be on. With her winter cape, bonnet, and boots still on, she decided she'd leave Mr. Saunders's pudding on his porch. Surely he'd come out soon for firewood and see it before it froze.

She was grateful for a pleasantly warmer day, approaching thirty degrees. Nearing the cottage, she saw that Mr. Saunders still had plenty of firewood stacked on the porch, which reminded her that she would need to cart some to the farmhouse for later. Then she heard the music.

Evidently he was awake. She plodded slowly across the yard and stopped at the bottom of the steps. A woman's voice belted loudly above an assortment of instruments. Sadie loved to sing and wondered what it would be like to sing along with actual instruments, something that would never be allowed in her district. Owning an instrument was said to bring forth unnecessary emotions.

This is like spying, she thought, as she held her position, beginning to hum to the rhythm. *Just a little longer.* How could owning an instrument that produced such beautiful sounds be wrong in the eyes of God?

Finally, she placed the plastic container with the tapioca pudding on a small table between two rockers. She turned to leave but hadn't even made it to the steps when the cottage door swung open.

Sadie spun around. Stunned, she faced Kade Saunders standing in the threshold. A flush rose from her neck, accompanied by a knot in her throat as she gulped back her embarrassment. The man was wearing what appeared to be pajama bottoms. He was barefoot, and he didn't have a shirt on. She instinctively threw her hands over her eyes, gasping, but unable to move.

"Wait right here." Kade held his palm toward her and backed into the house.

No problem. She couldn't move. She widened her fingers on one hand to have a peek. He stood in the living area, pulling a white sweatshirt over his head as if sensing her embarrassment at seeing him in such a way. The flush had overtaken her face, she was quite sure. She brought her hands down and began nervously twisting the ties on her black cape. *Pajama bottoms, for goodness' sake.*

When he returned to the door, she stammered, "I . . . I brought you some tapioca pudding."

Kade walked toward her, still barefoot. "Thank you. That was the best tapioca pudding I've ever had."

His shoulder brushed hers as he whisked by her to retrieve it. Her feet were rooted in place when he came back her way; then he stood uncomfortably close to her, facing her. He put one hand on his hip and tucked the pudding container against his side with the other hand. "Do you want to come in?"

"No. I do not." She wished right away that she hadn't sounded so shocked by his offer. He wasn't smiling, but at least he didn't have the irritated look on his face like he did the first day of his arrival. "Okay," he said, then shrugged. "Suit yourself." He turned to head back into the cottage.

Finally, she was able to move her legs and turned to head down the steps, promising herself she would never come back to the cottage until time to deliver more groceries, which she quickly calculated wasn't for another three days.

"Hey," he called out to her.

She had only taken four or five steps into the snow when she was forced to turn around and acknowledge him. "*Ya?*"

"What's your name?"

"Sadie." She offered a brief smile before turning back around.

"Hey, Sadie?"

Again she turned around. "*Ya?*"

"If you like listening to the music so much, why don't you

knock on the door and come in out of the cold next time?" he said. "You don't have to loiter on the front porch."

If only the earth would open up and swallow me, she thought.

"No, no," she mumbled. She gave him a quick wave and began stepping backwards.

She remembered falling. She wasn't sure what she tripped over, but as her legs buckled beneath her, she hit her head on the icy ground.

Sprawled out on her back, she recalled the image of Kade Saunders bolting barefoot across the snow.

2

"GOOD GRIEF!" KADE SPRINTED DOWN THE STEPS, THE frozen ground beneath his feet stinging his soles, a thought that quickly became secondary when he saw splatters of blood around the Amish woman's head. *Oh, man.*

He cradled his hand behind her neck and lifted her head. Not too much blood. But she was out cold. Kade lifted her into his arms in a clumsy, ridiculous way that he was sure would be uncomfortable for her if she had been conscious. His feet were numbing so much that he worried he'd fall with her in his arms. She wasn't fully in his grasp. Her left leg hung loose, her black boot dragging across the snow. Not his most heroic moment.

The icy steps proved challenging. He quickly gave up any hope for gracefulness as Sadie's left calf bounced off of each step. He cringed with each cumbersome movement, his feet practically anesthetized by the slick coldness beneath them.

The central heating from the cottage hit him while he was still on the porch and gave him the extra push to get inside. He wound around the coffee table and laid her on the couch. Kade propped a throw pillow behind her head and wondered if she'd be angry that he let her bleed on her own couch. He'd worry about that later. He wasn't sure Amish people got angry anyway. Kade crouched beside her and gently lifted her head. He fumbled with the string on her white cap, then gently pushed it aside. Strands of red hair escaped, making it difficult for him to see the wound.

Her blue eyes opened wide. *"Ach!"* she screamed, then pushed his hand away. He was startled, but not half as spooked as she was. Then with the power of an army, she thrust her hands against his chest and pushed him to a standing position. When she stood up, a round of dialect unbeknown to Kade followed.

I think she's angry, Kade thought, without a clue about what she was saying.

He stumbled backward. "Hey, hold up, lady. You had a nasty fall, and I rescued you." If you could call it that. She probably had a pretty banged-up shin that she didn't have before.

She was on her feet and scurrying toward the door, trying desperately to tuck her hair beneath the white cap on her head. Kade would've never known her hair was so long, hidden beneath the cap on her head. Now several strands cascaded below her shoulders almost to her waist, wavy and full.

Kade thought he saw tears in her eyes. "Wait," he said. "You banged your head pretty good. Maybe—"

She swung the door open, never looked back, and was gone.

Sadie's head throbbed, and she weaved from side to side across the snow. She made her way inside the shop, then reached up and touched a gooey mess on the back of her head. *Blood.*

The recollection of Kade Saunders leaning over her in a most inappropriate way was much worse than the pain she was in. She winced as she recalled the horror and embarrassment of it all.

She should've never agreed to lease to a single man from the city. He'd come to the door in long, flannel pajama breeches—with no shirt on. *Most improper, indeed.*

She was surprised to see Jonas Miller standing outside her shop. What in the world was Lillian's grandfather doing here, especially in his condition? He'd had the cancer for some time now and didn't get out so much as Sadie knew. Plus, it was a frigid day for a ride in the buggy. Sadie's eyes darted to Jessie. Jonas had had that old horse for as long as she'd known him.

Lillian. Was something wrong with Lillian?

"Jonas, what brings you out here on a day like this? Everything is all right, no?" She wiped her bloody hand on her apron.

"Is that blood?" Jonas pushed back the rim of his straw hat, squinted his eyes, and walked over to Sadie. He lifted her hand. "That's blood for sure." He dropped her hand, stroked his beard, and scanned her from head to toe. "Where are you hurt, child?"

"*Mei* head." She pointed to a spot beneath her prayer covering, which was absorbing the slow trickle of blood. "I slipped earlier."

Jonas tilted her head to the side, pulled back her *kapp*, and looked intently at her wound, his touch causing her to flinch. "I reckon you'll live," he said matter-of-factly, then stepped back from her.

That's it? I'll live?

Lillian's grandfather had a way with words—and people—that wasn't reflective of most Amish men she knew. Everyone loved Jonas, but you never knew what might come out of his mouth. And knowing that to be true, her heart skipped a beat when she noticed Kade awkwardly making his way across the snow. At least he was sporting some running shoes, but didn't the man own any boots? And he wore no jacket, only the sweatshirt he'd hastily thrown on.

"Who's the fancy fella comin' across the yard like he ain't got a lick a sense?"

"Kade Saunders. He's renting the cottage for three months." Sadie felt her heart quicken as she saw Jonas eyeing him with suspicion.

"Three months?" Jonas twisted his mouth to one side and narrowed his brows. "He rentin' it all by himself, or he got a *fraa* and *kinner* with him?"

"No. It's just him."

They stood silently as Kade came within listening space. *Please, Jonas . . . be good.*

"I wanted to make sure you were all right," he said to Sadie.

Sadie nodded and opened her mouth to speak. She supposed she should thank him for not letting her lie in the snow and freeze to death, no matter the awkwardness of the situation.

"She's mighty fine," Jonas interjected. "What brings a man like you to Lancaster County for three months in this *kalt wedder?* You runnin' from something?" Jonas stared the man down.

Sadie warmly reflected that if her father was alive, he would have the same question for a man traveling alone, especially a man Kade's age. Sadie figured him to be in his mid to late thirties.

"No . . . I'm not running from anything. I just . . ." Kade looked bewildered by the question.

Jonas stood a little taller. "I come by every day to check on Sadie."

Jonas, that is far from the truth. Sadie arched her brows and shot Jonas an inquisitive look.

"Just so ya know," Jonas added. He didn't take his eyes off of Kade.

Bless his kind heart. Sadie knew Jonas wouldn't be any good to protect her, even if Kade were a threat to her, which she doubted.

Kade folded his arms across his chest, shivered a bit, and smiled. He seemed amused at Jonas's display of chivalry. His dark hair was neatly parted to one side with a hint of gray at the temples. Sadie thought he looked very formal, until he smiled. His teeth were straight and white, but his smile crooked up on one side. It made him look nicer somehow.

But the smile was short-lived. "As long as you're okay." He held up his hand to bid farewell and turned to leave.

"Mr. Saunders?" Sadie realized she'd probably overreacted when she awoke on the couch. But it was so disturbing—his face so close to hers, his hands in her hair.

He turned around. "Yeah?"

"Uh, *danki* for helping me when I fell."

"You're welcome." He didn't smile. Whatever warmth she thought she saw earlier—gone. He was a strange man, that Kade Saunders. Seemed like an unhappy man.

Jonas kept a scowl stretched across his face as he watched Kade walk across the snow. When Kade was out of earshot, Jonas said, "Sadie, I don't know if it's *gut* for you to be out here alone with only him on the property."

"I'm sure he is of no harm, Jonas. The lady who made his arrangements said he has *gut* references." She paused. "I think he might be *somebody*. You know, like famous or rich."

"Well, he ain't nobody 'round here."

"Jonas, what brings you out here on a day like this? It's too *kalt* to be riding in a buggy today, unless you have to."

Jonas pried his eyes from Kade and turned toward her, a blank expression on his face. "What?"

"Did you need something? You didn't really come just to check on me, did you?"

Jonas stood taller, then raised his brows. "I reckon I must have." He paused, as if unsure. "And now that fella knows to mind his manners."

Sadie reached up and touched her head. The ache had lessened, but she was aware of it.

"You better go tend to that cut on your head," Jonas said. He tipped his hat in her direction, as if he was leaving. "You don't need no stitches. A *gut* cleaning oughta do it. And you're probably gonna have a big bump for a while."

Sadie nodded. Before she could say anything else, Jonas was heading back to his buggy. She couldn't help but wonder if Lillian and Sarah Jane knew he was traveling around in the buggy on a day like today. Sadie recalled when Lillian and her mother had frantically showed up looking for Jonas a few weeks ago. Apparently, he'd left without telling anyone, and daughter and granddaughter were worried sick. Sadie hoped this wasn't one of those times.

Kade warmed his hands in front of the fireplace and wondered why he kept foolishly walking out into these elements without his jacket. At least he remembered his shoes this time. He couldn't help but smile at the way the old man had tried to intimidate him.

He kicked off his shoes, then pulled off his socks and hung them on a hook on the mantel. Something he'd never done before, but being here seemed to call for it. But then his socks dangling in front of the fireplace reminded him of recent Christmas preparations with Alicia. They had hung stockings at his house for each other. He'd been foolish enough to think Alicia might want to take their relationship to the next level.

His thoughts drifted to the Amish woman, the petrified look on her face when she awoke on the couch. Why didn't she have a husband? She had to be close to thirty and was certainly attractive. Maybe she'd never had a man that close to her before. Kade shrugged. Their simple way of life—buggies, no electricity, the plain clothes—it all seemed so prehistoric in this day and time. Hard to believe people still lived this way.

But the woman had shoved him. Was that allowed by her people?

Kade paced around the small living room, questioning her aggressiveness, and suddenly he realized that for the first time in his life, he had no agenda. Nowhere he had to be. Nothing he had to do. And he could only think of one thing that mildly sparked his interest.

As he dove into the tapioca pudding, not even bothering to serve it up in a bowl, he feared he was a man on the brink of depression—binge eating like some of the women he knew. The thought didn't stop him from shoveling the custard into his mouth. He propped his bare feet on the coffee table and made a mental note: if he had to rescue a damsel in distress again, he would take the time to put some shoes on. He wasn't completely sure that he didn't have frostbite.

He was on the verge of devouring the entire container of pudding when his cell phone rang. He blew out a sigh of exasperation, set the pudding aside, and walked to the kitchen where he'd left his phone on the counter. He glanced at the number.

No, no, no. Not now. Talking to Monica was the last thing he needed. He hit the End button. Her calls were always upsetting—on so many levels.

Sadie opened the medicine cabinet in her bathroom and found something for her head. She parted her hair with her fingers and felt for the cut. The pain led her to it. She gingerly dabbed it with ointment then carefully wound her hair in a bun. After placing a fresh prayer covering on her head, she silently thanked God that it wasn't worse and headed back to the shop.

It was later in the afternoon before she had her first customer, who turned out to be her last customer as well. But the woman from Florida purchased a quilt for seven hundred dollars, two handmade pot holders, and four dolls. *It made for a fair day,* she thought, locking up the shop.

She walked to the road and checked the mailbox. Nothing. She had hoped for another letter from Milo. Disappointed, she headed back down the driveway, taking care with each step. Her eyes drifted toward the cottage. The *Englischer* was staring out the window—at her.

She put her head down and quickened her pace as she made her way to the farmhouse steps. Firewood was stacked neatly on the porch, piled against the house. Lots of firewood—that she hadn't collected. And the empty container of pudding sat on top of the logs. Instinctively, she spun around and squinted to see if he was still there. He wasn't.

She was thankful to have the firewood nearby, and she supposed another batch of pudding was a fair trade. She'd never known a man to eat so much custard. She took the bowl into the house, then remembered the newspaper's prediction of another temperature drop into the teens tonight. Before she kicked off her boots, she went back to the porch for two logs and glanced quickly toward the cabin. No sign of him.

Later that evening, she prepared a fresh batch of pudding, then placed it in her refrigerator. She didn't have anything else to do anyway. Loneliness began to creep in, the way it always did this time of day.

She headed upstairs for bed. It was only Saturday. Three more days until Milo would call. Until then, she'd have to be content rereading his letter. She considered penning him a note, but she'd already put two letters in the mail since the arrival of Milo's last correspondence.

After her bath, Sadie lit the gas heater in her bedroom, climbed into bed, and snuggled underneath a thick quilt, extra blanket, and flannel sheet. She reached for Milo's letter, and her bedside lantern illuminated the page.

When she was done reading, she put the letter back on the bedside table, feeling like it was somehow losing its impact. She tried to stay hopeful, and each letter carried her into another week until she heard the sound of Milo's voice on Tuesdays. But the letters seemed to have slowed down on his end. If she allowed herself to think too much, her heart ached. Two years was a long time to be writing letters back and forth.

She pulled the nightstand drawer open and took out her brush, as she'd done at bedtime ever since Ben died. Then she mechanically smoothed the tangles, careful of her cut. Sometimes, like tonight, her loneliness was beyond tears as she remembered the feel of Ben brushing her hair before bed, something he'd said he enjoyed doing. And, oh, how she'd loved the feel of his hands in her hair, the brush sweeping downward to her waist. She cringed, recalling that Kade Saunders had seen much of her hair when it fell from beneath her *kapp*. *So wrong*. Only a woman's husband should see her hair in length. She drew in a breath, blew it out slowly, and continued to brush, thinking about Ben, about Milo, and strangely enough . . . about Kade.

He was an odd fellow. Void of enough sense to protect himself from the cold too. *But one of God's children*, she reminded herself when judgment cut in. Still she speculated. Why was he here for three months? Why does he seem so angry one minute and then rather heroic the next? But was he? Heroic, that is. It had been unfit for him to be so close to her on the couch. But she was hurt and . . .

She twisted in the bed, pushed the covers aside, and examined her shin. She still wasn't sure how she had acquired the bruise.

Her mind played back and forth about Kade. He embarrassed her when he told her he knew she was listening to the music from the porch. So brazen when he'd said it too. She shook her head, decided not to give him another thought, and closed her eyes to pray.

It was only an hour later when Sadie was startled out of a deep sleep. It took her a few seconds to focus on the battery-operated

clock by her bed, illuminated a soft white. Nine o'clock. What
could all the ruckus be about? Four o'clock came early in the
morning. No one she knew would be visiting at this hour. The
noise grew louder, and it was quite clear that someone was pounding on the front door. Loudly.

She pulled her thick robe over her nightgown and headed
down the stairs as fast as she could, holding the handrail for support. She couldn't see a thing at first, but the cooler temperature
downstairs hit her when she neared the first floor. The fire was
still flickering in the fireplace, and the glow from the hearth
offered enough light for her to stumble her way across the den.
She reached for the doorknob but stopped when she heard *him*
yelling—hollering like a madman.

"Sadie!"

Only one thought came to mind, as silly as it seemed. *Serial
killer*. She'd read about people like that in the newspaper. He
yelled again.

"What is it, Mr. Saunders?" She was shaking all over.

"It's freezing out here! Can you open the door?" His tone was
agitated, and she wasn't sure what to do.

"What's the matter?" She fought the tremble in her voice.

"For heaven's sake, woman, please open the door."

Sadie reached for the knob. Then hesitated. "Is anything
wrong?"

"Yes. Something is wrong!" he yelled.

She heard him mumbling from the other side of the door. She
reached for a scarf hanging on a peg nearby and draped it over
her head.

"What is the problem?" She tossed one end of the wrap over
her shoulder and assumed she must look a mess.

"I need your help with a problem at the cottage. Can you please open the door?"

Silly, silly woman, Sadie thought. There is something wrong at the cottage, of course. She opened the door. "I'm sorry, I just . . ."

The *Englischer* scooted past her and went directly to the fireplace, stretching his arms near the dwindling fire.

"Don't you own a coat, Mr. Saunders?" Sadie folded her arms across her chest.

He looked down at his jeans and white sweatshirt, then shook his head. "I don't know why I keep running out the door without it on." He shook his head and returned his attention to the fire.

"What is wrong that brings you here at this time of night?" She held her place firmly by the door . . . just in case.

He turned to look at her. "Were you asleep?" He sounded shocked. "It's only nine o'clock."

Sadie prepared to defend her schedule, but he waved his hand as if to say never mind.

"I forget you people go to bed early and get up early."

You people? She pierced her lips together and narrowed her eyes at him.

"Sorry," he said when he saw her expression.

Sadie took two steps forward. "Mr. Saunders, what do you need?"

He sighed. "That phone in the barn is ringing nonstop, followed by the sound of an answering machine picking up. The barn is so close to the cottage, and, well . . . it's irritating me. Why don't you have the phone in the house?"

"The phone is ringing?" Sadie couldn't imagine who it might be. *Milo?* But on a Saturday?

"Yes. It's ringing over and over again. I walked outside to take the darn thing off the hook, but the answering machine had just picked up again. I decided I better come get you when I heard the message."

Sadie's heart flipped in her chest. "What was the message?" Occasionally, Milo left tender messages on the machine. She hoped this wasn't one of those times. A flush was building in her cheeks.

"She said her name was Lillian and that it was an emergency. She said for you to come quickly if you got the message." He paused. "And here's the part that really caught my attention . . ." Kade shook his head, a perplexed look on his face. "She said she needed *my* car."

"What?" Sadie turned and moved toward the door.

"Why would someone named Lillian need my car?" He was hovering right behind her.

Sadie tied the kerchief in a bulky knot under her chin, pulled her boots on, and swung her cape over her robe. Then she bolted out the door.

"Be careful! It's slippery out there!" he yelled as he followed her.

It was snowing again, and the bitterly cold wind blew through her cape as she hurried across the white powder. Lillian would never call this late. And she said it was an emergency. *If she needs a car, something is terribly wrong.*

When Sadie got to the barn, she was numb from head to toe. Her hand was shaking when she reached for the answering machine—another luxury that was unheard-of years ago. She pushed the button.

"Sadie, it's Lillian . . ."

Sadie could hear the *Mr. Saunders* coming up behind her in the barn. "What is it?" He paused, sounding out of breath. "Who is Jonas?"

She gripped her hands together, drew them to her chest, and took a deep breath as she listened to the rest of Lillian's message.

"Oh, no," she said, fighting tears.

3

KADE REMEMBERED HIS COAT AND GLOVES THIS TIME. He carefully backed the car out of the barn and wondered how in the heck he was going to drive in this weather. He was from L.A., for crying out loud.

Sadie waited on the front porch, bundled up like a snow bunny. The last thing he felt like doing was driving around, particularly in these elements, to find a lost old man. Not because he was a cold, heartless kind of guy, but because he'd been this route before. And the end result hadn't been good. Kade thought back to when his mother first told him about his father's Alzheimer's disease. Dad was such a young man at the time too. Not much older than Kade. According to the doctors, early onset of the illness accounts for 5 to 10 percent of those diagnosed, and his father fell into that unlucky percentage. Kade feared losing his mind more than anything else. And it seemed to run in his genes.

Oh man, oh man. The car slid sideways when he tried to turn the Mercedes around. Pulling forward, the tires spun in the snow. He glanced up at the porch and saw Sadie, who appeared irritated at his efforts. Did she want to give it a try? *You don't even know how to drive, and I'm doing the best I can.*

Finally the car inched ahead. When he stopped, she was already down the porch steps. She opened the back door and slid into the seat.

"What are you doing? Do you think maybe you should sit in the front seat and help me navigate?" She gave him a strange look, then exited and eased her way into the front seat. All his frustration washed away when he looked into her teary, blue eyes, reflective of the pain in her heart. *This old man must be very dear to her.*

"We'll find him," he said soothingly.

"I'm sorry about this." As they pulled onto Black Horse Road, Sadie turned to look at him. He seemed to be concentrating. "But they will need all the help they can get. And Lillian knew there was a car here, so . . ." It seemed strange to be sitting in the front seat with him. Normally, when an *Englisch* driver was called for a ride, she sat in the backseat. Unless, of course, it was a friend of hers. She barely knew her renter.

Kade leaned forward on the steering wheel and struggled to see past the falling snow. "How far down the road is it?"

"Not far." She shook her head. "Poor Jonas."

"Did your friend say how long he's been missing?" Kade turned briefly toward her, then steadied his eyes back on the road.

"Lillian's mother said Jonas left in the buggy after supper, which would mean he went home after he left my shop today. Lillian said her mother tried to talk him out of going for a ride in this *baremlich*—I mean, terrible—weather."

"What's that language you're speaking? It sounds like German."

"Pennsylvania *Deitsch*. It's rather like German, I suppose." She pointed to her left. "Over there."

"Thank goodness," Kade grumbled.

"I'm sorry," she said again. She'd rather not be going anywhere with him either.

"No, it's okay. I just don't know how to drive in these conditions. I'd hate to have an accident."

And mess up this fancy car. Sadie didn't say anything.

"Wow," he said when he pulled into the driveway. "I've never seen this many buggies in one place at one time."

"In our community, everyone helps everyone else, 'specially at a time like this."

"What's everyone going to do? Trudge around in the snow, looking for this guy?"

Sadie knew the look she shot Kade Saunders would have God frowning, and she tried to free herself of the bad thoughts she was having about this man. But even in the darkness, he evidently picked up on her dislike for him.

"I mean, I'll help look, but it's freezing outside, and—"

"We don't need your help, Mr. Saunders. You are welcome to sit in the car, if you see fit." She folded her hands in her lap.

"Of course I'm going to help." She thought he rolled his eyes before continuing. "And you can call me Kade."

Sadie didn't answer. She opened the door and headed toward the crowd of people on the porch.

"Thank you for coming, Sadie. And for bringing the car." Lillian hugged her.

Lillian's mother, Sarah Jane, was talking to the elders gathered at the other end of the porch. Even the bishop had come, and he had to be at least Jonas's age.

"Where do you want us to start looking?" Sadie asked. She scanned the porch. About twenty folks so far.

"Barbie should be here soon in her car. And she's bringing several other *Englisch* friends with cars. Noah and Carley will be here soon, too, in their car. But in this *wedder*, it will take them longer to get here." Lillian looked over Sadie's shoulder. "The *Englisch* man is walking this way. Is he friendly?"

Sadie shrugged. "He has a car."

"Hi." Kade extended his hand to Lillian. "I'm Kade Saunders."

"Thank you for bringing your car, Mr. Saunders." Lillian looked at Kade's running shoes, covered in snow. "Do you have no boots?"

"No . . ." Kade sounded embarrassed. "I wasn't very prepared for this weather. I'm planning to get some in town when the weather clears."

"You won't need them then," Lillian said with a smirk on her face. "*Mei daadi* has an extra pair of boots inside the house. I'll get them for you."

"Thanks," Kade said.

Sadie could hear Sarah Jane instructing the others where to go, areas Jonas might have gone. Her stomach rolled. In this weather, Jonas would freeze . . . She squelched the thought and turned her attention to Kade. He was shivering like a little girl.

"I hate the cold," he snapped as he wrapped his arms around himself.

"I told you, you can sit in the car."

Kade waved his hand in front of her, signaling silence. He'd done that before, and she didn't like it. "I want to help. I'm just not used to this weather. That's all."

Lillian returned with a pair of Jonas's boots and a heavy

coat. Much heavier than the lightweight overcoat Kade was wearing. "Here you go, Mr. Saunders." Lillian offered him the boots and coat.

"Thanks." Kade wasted no time putting on the coat, then pulled the boots over his tennis shoes.

Lillian grabbed Sadie by the arm and began pulling her away from the others. Kade stayed where he was—still shivering.

"The elders will divide up and search the back roads. *Mamm* will stay here, and everyone will be checking back on the hour. When other *Englisch* get here, we'll have several portable telephones to use. Does your friend have one? A cell phone?"

"He's not my friend. He's my renter. But I reckon he has one."

"Sadie, there's somewhere I need you to go, to look for Jonas. Somewhere I don't want the others to know about. I don't even want *mei mamm* to know." Lillian flinched and glanced toward her husband, Samuel, at the other end of the porch. "Actually, there are two places. Samuel will go to one of the spots with Noah and Carley in their car when they get here. Will you and Mr. Saunders go to the other place?"

Sadie knew that Lillian trusted her, and Noah and Carley, to be discreet. Noah was Samuel's shunned brother who had left the Old Order to become a doctor, and who ended up marrying one of Lillian's best friends. They were officially outsiders, but really weren't. The entire community adored them both. Noah's clinic was frequented by the Amish, despite the bishop's initial ruling that their district couldn't patronize Noah's health facility. But ever since Noah had donated one of his kidneys to Samuel's son, David, things had been different. The bishop now seemed to overlook things related to Noah and his shunning.

"Where is it that you want us to go?" Sadie asked.

Lillian frowned and leaned toward Sadie's ear. "There's a little pub down a ways on Lincoln Highway. I fear he might be in there." Lillian stood straight again and waited for a reaction from Sadie.

"Uh, do you mean a *bar* that serves beer and the like?" Sadie had never been in such a place.

"I hate to ask you." Lillian paused. "But once, I was driving the buggy to market, and I saw Grandpa's buggy parked outside the place. I know it was his, because it has that dent on the right side from when Noah backed his car into it one time." She shook her head. "I remember that Grandpa was fit to be tied when that happened. Anyway, I had the baby with me, so I didn't go in."

"What's the other place?" Sadie was wondering if she could choose between the two—if the other spot might not be as bad.

"It's a pub, too, further down Lincoln Highway. It's a little rougher, though. I figured Noah, Samuel, and Carley can take that one."

That answered Sadie's question. "Have you caught him in there before too?"

"*Ya*. I did. And that time I wasn't with the baby, so I went in and coaxed him out. He made me promise not to tell *mei mamm*, which I didn't. It was harmless enough. He was chatting with some *Englisch* men that he knew. But he had no business in such a place, so I kindly told him we needed to be on our way." Lillian's eyes grew glassy. "Sadie, I am *hoping* he's in one of those places on this night. If he's out in this weather . . ."

"We'll leave right now." Sadie turned to see Kade holding his position and making no effort to talk to any of the others. He looked out of place, and she dreaded having to spend more time with him.

"There's Noah and Carley." Lillian pointed to a car coming up the drive. Then she hugged Sadie. *"Danki."*

———

Kade was glad to reach the main highway. There was little traffic, and the snow plows were hard at work keeping the streets clear. Driving down Black Horse Road had been an effort. He sure hoped this Jonas fellow was indoors and not out in the weather. It had been just the opposite the day he found his father. Hot. Humid. Kade struggled to push the thought to the back of his mind.

"There it is." She pointed to their right. Looked like a hole-in-the-wall joint. "You don't have to go inside," she added.

"I was just about to tell you the same thing." Kade suspected Sadie wouldn't be comfortable going in such an establishment.

"No, Jonas knows me. I'm not sure he trusts—"

"Me?" Kade grunted. "Yeah, I got that impression earlier today."

"He's very protective of Lillian and all her friends," she said with pride.

Kade put the car in park. "Ready?" He certainly wasn't, but the sooner they got this over with, the better. "Hopefully, we'll find him inside."

She stepped out of the car and pulled the hood of her black coat over her head. Kade found a similar hood on his coat and pulled it on. It was a short walk to the pub, but the snow was coming down in thick blankets. He felt ridiculous in the black galoshes, but his feet were staying dry. He pulled the long, brass handle protruding from the wooden door. Cigarette smoke hit him in the face as he held the door for Sadie. He stayed close behind her.

About fifteen square tables were scattered about the place, each with a red and white-checkered tablecloth and four chairs. Small, glass vases housed worn silk flowers in the middle of the tables, surrounded by salt, pepper, ketchup, and steak sauce. At least it wasn't *just* a beer joint.

Only two of the tables had patrons. A long bar ran the length of the back wall, and it didn't take Kade long to spot an Amish man sitting alone—his straw hat on and a frosty mug in his hand.

"There he is." Sadie pointed. She sounded relieved and wasted no time moving toward him. Kade followed.

"Jonas!" Sadie snapped when she reached his side. "The entire community is looking for you." Relief flooded over her, despite her disciplinarian tone. "We have a car with us. Let's get you home. Thank the good Lord you are safe." She threw her arms around him. He didn't respond, and a chill ran up Sadie's spine. Perhaps he was angry with her for coming.

"Jonas?" She waited for an acknowledgment. He took a drink of what appeared to be beer from a tall, glass mug. Then he turned toward her, stared, and looked past her to Kade.

"Who are you?" He cut his eyes in Kade's direction.

"You saw him this morning, Jonas. His name is Kade Saunders." Sadie stepped back and made room for Kade, who extended his hand to Jonas.

"Nice to meet you, Jonas. A lot of people will be glad you're safe."

Jonas firmly took hold of Kade's hand, stared blankly at him, and then turned to Sadie. "And who are you?"

Sadie's mouth dropped. "Jonas. It's me. Sadie."

Jonas let go of Kade's hand and stared at her. "Sadie who?"

He was playing with her. He had to be. "Why Sadie Fisher, of course." She smiled hesitantly. Jonas didn't.

"Serve these folks a beer, wouldja, Hank?" Jonas said to the short *Englisch* man behind the bar.

"No. *Danki*," Sadie quickly said to the bartender. She knew Jonas's medications caused him to act out of character from time to time, but never anything like this. She glanced at the bartender, who was trying to get her attention with a wave of his hand.

"It's only root beer," the man mouthed in Sadie's direction when Jonas wasn't looking. Sadie nodded.

"Jonas, I don't want a *beer*. We have to go." She gently touched his arm. "Right now. Lillian and Sarah Jane are terribly worried, and—"

"I don't know why they'd be worried. I told Irma Rose where I'd be." Jonas took another drink from the glass.

What?

"Who's Irma Rose?" Kade directed the question to Sadie, but it was Jonas who answered.

"Irma Rose is *mei fraa*. She don't much care for me comin' here, but she don't make too big a stink about it."

"Well, if his wife knows he's here . . ." Kade said to Sadie in a whisper after Jonas turned and focused on the television behind the bar.

"His wife is dead," Sadie mouthed and stared at him.

"Oh, I see . . ."

She faced Jonas. "Jonas, Irma Rose isn't here—"

But Kade interrupted her by waving his hand in front of her again. "Jonas, what's Irma Rose cooking you for supper?"

Huh? Sadie glared at Kade. What was he doing?

Jonas turned to Kade and smiled. "A mighty fine meal it will be. Irma Rose is a *gut* cook. I reckon she'll have me a pot roast when I get home."

"Pot roast, huh?" Kade stepped closer, edging Sadie back a bit. "Nothing like a pot roast. Does she put potatoes and carrots all around it and let it cook all day? That's how my mom used to do it."

Sadie stood quietly.

"Your *mamm* sounds like a *gut* woman. That's exactly the way my Irma Rose does it. Makes for a fine meal indeed."

"Isn't it after the supper hour? I bet Irma Rose has that pot roast ready and is keeping it warm for you." Kade touched Jonas's arm, a gesture Sadie found endearing, considering the way Jonas had treated Kade earlier.

Jonas was focused on the television. A commercial. "Why would anyone cook food from a box?"

Kade kept talking. "I agree. Never as good as a home-cooked meal. I haven't had pot roast in a really long time."

Jonas turned his way. "Irma Rose always makes plenty enough. You wanna have yourself some pot roast tonight?"

"I'd love to." Kade smiled. "And I'm starving. Why don't we head that way?"

It's working. Sadie played along. "I'm hungry, too, Jonas. Can we go now?"

Jonas pushed a five-dollar bill toward the man behind the bar. "Hank, I can't let these two young people starve, so I reckon I'm heading to the *haus*."

"Okay, Jonas. You take care now." Hank winked at Sadie. "You folks be careful."

Once Sadie had buckled Jonas safely in the front seat of the car, she prepared to close the door. "I will see you at the *haus*."

"What?" Kade eyed her like she was a crazy woman.

"I have to take the buggy home." Did the *Englischer* think she'd leave Jessie and the buggy here?

"It's freezing out here. You can't drive that buggy home!"

"The boy is right, Lilly. Too cold for you. I'll drive the buggy home." Jonas unbuckled his seat belt, and Sadie ignored the fact he called her Lilly, his nickname for his granddaughter.

"Jonas, you stay put." Sadie slammed the door and began making her way to the buggy. Kade was quickly out of the car and walking her way.

"Just go back to the car and get Jonas home." She shook her head. "I've never seen him like this."

"I can't let you drive the buggy in this weather." Kade put his hand on his hip. "That's insane."

Sadie laughed. "*Ach,* I suppose you will drive it?" She paused, lifted her chin. "And I will drive your fancy car. It can't be that hard."

"Have you ever driven a car?"

"Have you ever driven a buggy?"

The car door opened, and Jonas stepped out.

"Go get him back into the car and take him home!" Sadie stomped her foot. "Please. It's not like I've never driven a buggy in the snow. Now, go!"

Kade drove slowly behind the buggy. He kept a safe distance while he watched Sadie maneuvering the buggy like she must have done her entire life. But it seemed wrong for him to be in the warmth of his car while she fought the elements. *She can be a little spitfire when she puts her mind to it.*

"You courtin' her?" Jonas asked after an awkward silence.

"What?"

"That woman. You courtin' her?" Jonas tucked his thumbs beneath his suspenders and turned toward Kade.

Not sure if Jonas knew who *that woman* was, Kade said, "No. We're just friends."

They were hardly friends. He barely knew her.

"Sadie is a special gal. I wasn't sure the poor girl was gonna survive after her husband died."

Kade was glad to see Jonas knew who Sadie was, and the old man had sparked his interest. "When did her husband die?"

"Several years ago." Jonas sighed. "I weren't sure we'd ever get her back to normal again. The girl had a hard time of it. But she's done a fine job tendin' to her farm."

"It's a lot to take care of for one woman."

"She has lots of help from the community. Just until she marries her friend from Texas." He paused and drew his mouth into a frown. "If that ever happens."

"Oh, she's engaged?"

"If you wanna call it that." Jonas shriveled up his nose. "How can you be writing letters to a fella for two years? Seems to me he'd have already made it a point to travel here. But I don't mention that to her."

"They've never met?" *Wow.* Two years was a long time to be corresponding.

"Who's never met?"

Kade assumed he was losing Jonas. "Sadie and the man from Texas."

"Oh. No. They've not met. He better be *gut* to that Sadie if they get a notion to marry. She is special. A *gut* friend to *mei* granddaughter too."

They sat quietly as they neared Jonas's house. Kade couldn't imagine how cold Sadie must be. He felt like a heel. But she was right. He didn't know how to drive a buggy, and she didn't know how to drive a car.

"Bet that pot roast is gonna be mighty *gut.* Hope Irma Rose doesn't fuss because I'm late." Jonas shook his head.

Kade just smiled. He was thankful this night had a happy ending.

His cell phone rang when he pulled into the driveway at Jonas's farm. He picked it up from the console and was surprised to see that it was Val. He glanced at Jonas, who was staring straight ahead, and flipped the phone open.

"Well, hello, stranger."

"Hey, partner," Val said. "I've got some news you're not going to like."

Straight to the point. "That's never a good thing to hear." Kade braced himself. "What?"

"Monica's on her way there."

"What? How does she know where I am?"

"I haven't a clue, Kade. I didn't tell her. I wouldn't do that. I know you need this time to regroup."

"Do you know when she's going to be here?" Kade's chest tightened.

"Any day. That's what I heard via the grapevine from the women at the country club."

"She called recently, but I didn't answer the phone. I didn't want to deal with her. But she didn't leave a message. I cannot believe she is coming here all the way from North Carolina. That's insane."

At least the old man was okay, he thought, putting the car in park. "I'll be there in a minute," he whispered to Jonas, who nodded.

"Kade . . ."

"Yeah?" The way Val said his name indicated there was more. "What else?"

"She's not coming alone."

4

ON THE DRIVE BACK, SADIE SOAKED UP THE JAZZY music filling the inside of Kade's car. She'd already thanked him for what he'd done, but he had waved her off with that bothersome gesture that irritated her more with each shushing movement. Didn't he realize how rude that was?

She breathed in the aroma of leather coming from the black seats in the car, commingled with a hint of Kade's cologne. More gadgets than she'd ever seen lined the console, and he seemed to be controlling the selection and volume of music from his steering wheel. The small confines of Kade's automobile gave her a glimpse into the luxurious way he lived. It all seemed very unnecessary. Did the *Englisch* really need all this to be happy? Kade seemed to need more than most.

She'd be glad to get home. The snow hadn't let up, but Kade seemed to have better control of his automobile as he steered onto Black Horse Road.

"What kind of music do you enjoy?" he asked when the silence grew awkward. "I hope this is okay. It's Dmitri Shostakovich."

Sadie turned toward him. "I mostly listen to country gospel when I have a chance." She paused and looked straight ahead.

"We can't own radios, but we listen to music when we get rides with *Englischers*, and sometimes we attend local festivals when there is a gospel concert—if it's a *free* concert in the park. The bishop doesn't like for us to buy tickets for such events." She glanced back toward him. "But I'm enjoying this music very much."

He smiled. "Do you sing or play any instruments?"

"*Ya*, I love to sing. When I was younger, I attended many Sunday singings. We sing in church, too, but only in High German." She sighed. "We are not allowed to own any instruments, though."

The car seemed to slow down. "What? Really? But why?"

"Owning an instrument would bring forth heightened emotions. It's not necessary to our way of life." She hoped that would end the conversation so she could enjoy the music.

"I don't understand. Singing brings forth emotion too. How can you be allowed to sing but not own an instrument?"

It was a valid point and one she didn't really know how to answer. She'd asked herself the same thing ever since she had first been introduced to instruments during her running-around period. Truth be known, most of the community couldn't remember why instruments weren't allowed. Like much of the *Ordnung*, rules to live by had been handed down from generation to generation, some with little explanation, but followed just the same. She took what she thought would be an easy way out. "We live by the *Ordnung*, which is our order of conduct, and owning instruments is not allowed."

A brief silence followed.

She felt Kade's eyes on her. "I still don't get it." When she didn't respond, he went on. "This arrangement of Shostakovich's is amazing. He is one of my favorite composers." Kade moved his thumb on the steering wheel, and the music grew louder. "Too loud?"

Sadie shook her head. She could feel the vibration from the sounds pulsating against her chest, growing bolder and more intense.

"Well, if anyone is going to bring forth emotion—it's Shostakovich."

Sadie couldn't agree more. She wished he'd be quiet so she could listen.

"Shostakovich ranks right up there, in my opinion, with some of the greatest composers—Bach, Beethoven, Brahms, and Mozart."

Sadie had no clue who he was talking about. But the passion in his voice made her want to hear more. "I think this music is very . . . sweet." She paused, tilted her head to one side. "But sad."

"You have a good ear." He turned to face her, and in the dark she could make out a smile. "Dmitri Shostakovich is known for his ability to invoke extreme emotions, often beautifully sad and sweet at the same time."

"Do you write musical notes or play an instrument?"

"No. I wish. I just enjoy listening to music, all kinds of music." He paused. "Besides, composers are strange people." He chuckled and spoke with an ease Sadie hadn't heard before. "Alexander Robert Schumann lived in the 1800s. He attempted suicide by throwing himself into a river. He was committed to a mental asylum and died not too long afterwards. People speculate that Tchaikovsky committed suicide too."

He seemed to be waiting for a response. *How does one respond to this?* "I expect it's *gut* that you are not one of these strange people, no?"

For the second time, he laughed. "Oh, I never said I wasn't strange. But I'd like to think I wouldn't kill myself." He shrugged. "Guess it depends on what day it is."

Surely he wasn't serious. "Taking your own life is a sin."

"That's what I hear."

They pulled into the driveway. And not soon enough.

Kade prepared a cup of hot tea, shuffled in his socks to the front window of the cottage, and gazed across the snow-covered space that separated the cottage from the main house. For the first time in weeks, he wouldn't mind some company. But the farmhouse was dark. He supposed Sadie wouldn't join him for a cup of late-night tea anyway. As a matter of fact, she'd probably be appalled by the idea.

He couldn't fathom what her life must be like. It looked like all work and no play to him, and without the modern conveniences. But the woman sure enjoyed music. There was a time when a great melody would quiet Kade's loneliness, take him away from all that plagued him, even invoke a sense of spiritual well-being. But not anymore. He still enjoyed a good tune, but any sense of spiritual calm eluded him. God had dealt him a rough blow three years ago. And his life continued to be a mess.

After Monica left, Kade had struggled to move forward without her in his life. Three years of marriage, and she'd split. No divorce. Only separation. Divorce wasn't a concept he'd ever been comfortable with. If two people vowed to love each other forever, then that's what it should be—forever. He'd loved Monica. Despite their problems, Kade would have never considered leaving, especially after the baby came. But three years had passed, and he'd lost hope that they would ever go back to being a family.

Monica, who was ten years Kade's junior, hadn't wanted children. Tyler was a surprise in so many ways. And Kade knew the only reason his wife fought so hard for custody of Tyler was for the money. When Kade thought a relationship might develop with Alicia, he'd called his attorney to draw up divorce papers, knowing that he should be legally divorced before he started dating anyone. But Alicia carted her gifts away before anything serious evolved. He halted the divorce proceedings. He didn't have the energy right now to follow through. There were no other prospects on the horizon, and divorce represented failure in his eyes.

Why hunt him down all the way in Lancaster County?

During the separation, she'd played as mean as any person Kade had ever known. He still loved Monica in his own way, but over time she'd stripped him of the love he once felt for her. During their phone calls, her voice was always laced with anger and resentment, despite the hefty check that she received every month.

Kade could still recall her pulling out of the driveway, Tyler strapped in his car seat, only two years old. It was the only time Kade could remember crying as an adult.

He'd thought about fighting for custody, or at least joint custody. But in the end, he didn't. He convinced himself that his choice to forgo a split arrangement was because a boy needs his mother. That thought was more comforting than the truth.

Kade knew that raising Tyler full-time, or even half of the time, was more than he could handle, and the job took a toll on Monica. Sometimes, she'd call him in the middle of the night, hysterical, complaining about what a bad hand she'd been dealt. But she was the one who left with their son, moved to North Carolina, and often refused to work with his schedule for planned visits. The first year she was gone, Kade traveled to North Carolina several times for his monthly weekend with Tyler, only to show up at an empty house. Monica later said that Kade's refusal to take Tyler overnight didn't provide her with any reprieve, so she didn't feel the need to accommodate him. She was breaking the law by denying Kade access to his son, and he could have pushed the issue. But again, he didn't.

In the rare times he did see Tyler, they spent a few hours at the park before Kade returned him to his mother. He just didn't know what to do with the boy. Tyler was hard to entertain. He wasn't like other kids.

Kade was eaten up with guilt that he hadn't tried harder to spend more time with his son. But there was work. Then there was Alicia, for a while. Somehow, forcing the issue of seeing Tyler kept taking a backseat. Somehow, six months had passed since his last visit. Now Tyler was five years old, and Kade didn't really know his own son. And the part that shredded his insides the most was that he was afraid to know him.

When Tuesday arrived, Sadie had something to look forward to. Today Milo would call, and she couldn't wait to hear the sound of his voice. It had been a long week. She hadn't done more than wave from afar to Kade since the night they went looking for Jonas, but today was the day she'd restock his refrigerator.

At least it wasn't snowing, and the temperature was up into the forties. The sun was shining, and slowly things were thawing out. So far this winter, Lancaster County had gotten more snow than usual. And she just read in the paper that another storm was coming in a week or so.

Sadie pulled on her boots, but decided to forgo her heavy jacket to wear her cape and bonnet instead. It might be a bit chilly with the wind, but she'd been bundled in the coat for days. She welcomed a trip to the market. Just not looking forward to the challenge of finding replacement items for Kade's groceries.

She was grateful that Kade continued to stack firewood on the porch, replenishing as needed. And Sadie continued to make fresh batches of tapioca pudding when the empty container showed up on the woodpile. But he stayed to himself, and that was fine by her.

She'd started this day the way she did every day, beginning with prayer, followed by a bowl of oatmeal. No sense making a big breakfast just for her. After she ate, she'd always do whatever cleaning was on her list for the day. Today, she dusted all the furniture downstairs. Some days it seemed a waste to keep things so tidy when she was usually the only one who ever saw the inside of the farmhouse. But she needed to keep up the practice for when she and Milo started a life together. Plus, she couldn't let Lillian or any of the other women catch her house in a mess.

Next was tending to the few animals she had left—two horses, an old milk cow that no longer produced, and two pigs. It was enough to handle—feeding them all, brushing the horses, and cleaning the stalls. On Mondays, she fired up the gasoline motor for the wringer and washed the clothes, then hung them to dry outside. The clothes would often freeze this time of year, but when that happened, she'd cart them in and drape them across the furniture near the fireplace. There was always something to do, even if it was a simple chore like mending a dress hem. She baked daily for herself, and also for others, like Lizzie. And lately, she'd been baking for her renter as well.

Her schedule varied when it was her day to tend the shop. Lillian's sisters-in-law, Rebecca and Mary Ellen, were taking their turn today, so it worked out that Sadie could go to market. She was getting ready to step into the buggy when she heard Kade call her name.

She turned around to see him walking toward her.

"I'm on my way to market, Mr. Saunders. I'll be back shortly to restock your refrigerator." She pulled her cape tighter around her and wondered if she'd made a mistake by not wearing her heavy coat.

"What happened to calling me Kade?" He didn't wait for a response. Instead, he swooshed his hand the way he does. "Anyway—"

And that was all it took.

"Why do you do that?" She put her hands on her hips and glared at him.

"Do what?"

"That shushing thing you do with your hand. It's most rude." Right away, she wished she hadn't said anything. His face drew a blank. "I'm sorry. I didn't mean to—"

"No. It's okay. I've heard that before, and it's a terrible habit."

He held his hands up as if Sadie had a gun pointed in his direction. "I won't do it again. I promise."

"Is there something you need?"

"Yes. A ride."

"What?" *Impossible.* What was he thinking? She couldn't be seen driving the *Englischer* to town. Besides, he had a car. "I'm sorry. I don't have time today. I have many errands to run. You understand, no?"

He walked around to the other side of the buggy and opened the door. "I must have run over something the other night. I've got two flat tires and only one spare. So, I'm grounded here with no wheels unless you can take me to get a couple of tires. I won't slow you down on your errands."

Rebecca and Mary Ellen would see them leaving, and no telling who might see them at the market. *No, no.* But she was at a loss as to what to say.

Kade sat down on the double seat beside her and closed the door.

She turned to face him. "Mr. Saunders—I mean, Kade—you can't come with me."

"Why?"

"Well, because . . ." She heard her last word squeak out in frustration. "It wouldn't be appropriate." She held her chin high.

"What exactly would be inappropriate about it?" He shifted sideways in the seat and faced her. His leg brushed against her knee. She jumped and scooted away from him.

"Ohhh," he said as he drew out the word. "I think I see." He rubbed his chin and kept his eyes fixed on her. It was most uncomfortable, and she could feel a blush rising from her neck.

"It would be improper for you to be seen with me," he continued, more as a question than a statement.

"*Ya.*" She drew her eyes from his and looked down.

"So, let me get this straight." He paused, but held his position next to her. "It's okay for us to ride together in a car when *you* need something. But now that I need something, it's not all right to be seen together?"

There was humor in his tone, but Sadie found her circumstances anything but amusing. This was serious. And he had a point. How was she supposed to argue? She opened her mouth to speak, but nothing came out.

"Never mind." He opened the door and stepped down. "I'll call someone to come out here and take care of it." He shook his head.

"*Danki,* Kade." She tried to sound chipper and waited for him to respond.

But he just stood there, staring at her. She wanted to look away, but his eyes seemed to lock with hers.

"Well, okay, then," he finally said.

Kade closed the door and turned away without looking back. He began walking toward the cottage.

Sadie felt badly about his predicament, but it didn't outweigh the relief she felt at not having to spend the morning with him or risk being seen. What if Bishop Ebersol or one of the elders saw them together? Sadie knew she was already pushing the limits by housing a single man in the cottage. It had only been allowed because those in charge knew it was difficult to lease the cottage this time of year and that Sadie needed the income. Carting him around town would be looked down upon.

She motioned the horse into action with a gentle flick of the reins.

Monica was about two hours from Lancaster County. After three days of driving, potty stops, food breaks, and unfamiliar hotels, she was exhausted. It would have been a ten-hour drive if she had been traveling alone, but with Tyler, that was impossible. Her restless five-year-old was only good for about two hours in the car, and even that was a struggle. She was hoping they could make it to the place she knew Kade was staying without another delay.

In her wildest dreams, she couldn't imagine what would bring Kade all the way to the heart of Amish Dutch country in the winter. Kade hated the cold.

She glanced over her shoulder at Tyler, who had dozed off, and noticed how much he looked like his father.

Monica knew she'd made a mistake by not agreeing to joint custody of Tyler. Turns out, it had backfired on her. She never realized how much work it would be raising Tyler, and it had gotten harder and harder each year. How nice it would have been for Kade to actually keep Tyler for days or weeks at a time in Los Angeles. Instead, Kade barely saw his son and wouldn't even keep him overnight when he did visit. Now, Kade had managed to go six months without seeing him.

But if she hadn't fought hard to keep Tyler, the money wouldn't have been enough to sustain her way of life—a life that Kade had introduced her to. Until now. Her new fiancé had enough money for both of them, and it was Kade's turn to be a parent. She was tired and deserved this opportunity. Her fiancé was kind, handsome, wealthy, and all the things she had thought Kade was when she married him.

Leaving Tyler with Kade would be a high price to pay for her happiness. She loved her son. But she was only twenty-seven years old. She had her whole life to live, and she planned to follow her own dreams—dreams Kade never encouraged. Plus, there would be theater, shopping, nights on the town—all the things she'd missed since Tyler was born.

Monica needed this time to pursue her interest in interior design. Kade had wanted her to stay at home and take care of Tyler, forgoing her own dreams while he pursued his. Well, now it was her turn. Her opportunity. And she was going to take it.

It would be hard on Tyler to leave his school, but Kade would be able to enroll him in another school. Probably even a better school. And Kade would be able to provide Tyler with opportunities Monica couldn't, even with the money Kade gave her.

She twisted her head over her shoulder again. "I love you, Tyler," she whispered, suddenly wondering if she could go through with it.

Kade paid the guy for replacing his tires and huffed out a "Thanks."

The man did a good job and was careful with Kade's car. It wasn't *him* causing Kade's exasperation. Kade was frustrated with the backward ways of the Amish, one redhead in particular. Not that he'd been looking forward to changing his tires in the snow—which would have probably taken him three times as long

as the tire guy—he was mostly hoping for a little company following his few days of solitude. He thought the ride in the
country might do him good. *Wait till next time* she *needs a ride.*

Who was he kidding? Kade knew he'd help the Amish woman
with anything she needed. There was something about her that
portrayed both vulnerability and strength. And he wasn't sure
which characteristic was more prominent. He smiled, remembering the way she shoved him after she hit her head, deciding
strength prevailed. Strange folks, the Amish. You'd have thought
Kade was making a pass at her the way she acted.

Kade decided to take advantage of the somewhat warmer
weather. Not *that* much warmer, but bearable. He zipped up his
jacket and took a seat in one of the rockers on the front porch.
Later, he would venture out to keep from getting cabin fever. He
knew the towns of Bird-in-Hand and Intercourse were nearby.
Maybe he'd do a little sightseeing.

Perhaps Val had been right about coming here. The place had
a peacefulness about it that he certainly didn't have in L.A. or
any of his other frequented retreats. Almost spiritual.

But Kade resisted the idea. He'd stopped reaching out to God
three years ago. He had prayed that all the doctors were wrong
about his son, but they weren't. Then Monica had left with Tyler,
and Kade slowly shut himself off from communication with God.
His parents had raised him in a nondenominational Christian
church, and for most of his growing-up years, the Lord was an
important part of Kade's life. But it was hard to trust this God he
didn't know anymore, or understand.

And Tyler. His only son.

Why? Why would God allow a child to be born into this world who has zero hope for a productive life?

And why was Monica coming here? *If that's even true.*

He'd no sooner had the thought when a car turned into the driveway.

5

THE BLACK CAR DOOR SWUNG OPEN, AND A MATCHING black, spike-heeled boot emerged and landed hard on the packed snow. Kade watched Monica twist toward the backseat, her head topped with short, blonde locks, like he remembered. He watched her lips moving, and his heart raced with long pent-up emotions bubbling to the surface. Anger. Resentment. Regret. Kade knew these sentiments stemmed from his own behavior, as well as Monica's.

Kade saw a crown of light-brown hair bobbing in the back-seat. *Tyler.*

He wanted to run to his son, embrace him, and beg the boy to forgive him for his absence. But he was immobilized with fear of the unknown. How much had Tyler changed in the last six months? Kade knew from his past visits with Tyler that his son's ability to reason and understand was one-dimensional at best. Had things gotten worse? *Maybe better.*

He knew he should move. Walk toward the car. Anything.

Monica pulled herself to a standing position and rested her elbows on the car door. "Hello, Kade."

She was as lovely as ever, but his heart didn't skip any beats.

All that they'd had—gone. Too many bitter arguments, too much time gone by. What could she possibly be doing here, so far from home? Kade could think of only one thing. She's finally come for a divorce.

"Don't you want to come see your son?" She closed the door and folded her arms across her chest.

Monica was already opening the back door by the time Kade hit the second porch step. He headed across the snow, his heart filled with trepidation, his head swirling with questions. He stared at the back of her black leather jacket while she unbuckled Tyler's seat belt.

Kade swallowed hard. Then inhaled the crisp, cool air, blew it out slowly, and watched it cloud the space in front of him. He recalled the photo of Tyler that he kept in his wallet and wondered again how much his son might have changed. In the picture, it was as if Tyler was looking intently at something, but yet at nothing. A blank stare.

Kade warmed his hands in his pockets. And waited. His heart continued to thump at an unhealthy rate.

Monica lifted Tyler from the seat and placed him on the snow in front of her. He was dressed in blue jeans and a red coat, and he was toting a metal lunch box with Spider-Man etched on the front.

Tyler smiled, and a warmth filled Kade's insides. He remembered the first time Tyler smiled when he was a baby and when his son had taken his first step.

"Hello." Kade leaned down and put his hands on his knees.

Tyler didn't answer. He was taking in his surroundings.

"Can we please go in?" Monica's tone was familiar, laced with attitude. "I've had to go to the bathroom for the last twenty miles, and it's cold out here."

"Monica, what are you doing here?" Kade couldn't take his gaze off of Tyler, whose eyes were all over the place—glancing toward the barn, then the main farmhouse, and back to Kade. Then he'd start all over again.

"Can we talk about it inside?" Monica reached for Tyler's hand. "Tyler, inside."

"Tyler, inside," Tyler repeated.

Kade loved the innocent sound of Tyler's voice, even though Tyler didn't talk much. The testing began six months prior to his second birthday. Six months after Tyler's second birthday, Monica had left. His family gone.

"Sure," Kade said. He motioned them toward the cottage. "I can't imagine what brought you all the way to Lancaster County." He shook his head and followed behind them.

Monica didn't turn around. "Well, I can't imagine what brought you all the way out here either. You hate the cold."

He decided not to bother with an answer. "The bathroom is that way." Kade pointed to his right.

"Tyler, I'll be right back. You sit here and play." Monica eased Tyler to a spot in front of the fireplace. Tyler opened his lunch box and dumped colorful plastic letters all over the tan carpet— the same kind of letters Kade remembered having as a child.

"Whatcha got there?" Kade squatted down on the floor beside Tyler.

Tyler looked at him. Well, not *at* him. At Kade's shirt. Kade glanced down at the word *Nike* printed across the front of his sweatshirt. Tyler was homed in on the word and seemed mesmerized by it. "Nike," Kade said softly.

"Nike," Tyler repeated. Then Tyler turned his attention back to his letters and located an *N*, then an *I*, *K*, and finally an *E*. He placed them in order, and without looking at Kade, said the word again.

Monica entered the room. Kade stood up and turned to face her, excitement in his tone. "He can spell. When did he learn to spell?"

She started to say something on impulse, Kade could tell. But she stopped herself. "During the last six months."

Kade chose to ignore the dig and turned back toward Tyler. "Can he read too?"

"Yes." She sighed. "But Kade, he doesn't know what he's spelling or reading. I mean, he can't comprehend it."

She walked toward the couch, sat down, and crossed her legs. Monica had great legs, but her tight blue jeans didn't have any effect on him.

Kade followed her to the couch, but he didn't sit down. She still hadn't explained the reason for the visit.

"But he *does* read?" Kade knew his tone was filled with hopefulness. Maybe the doctors had been wrong on some level.

Monica rolled her green eyes. "Yes. He reads. He picks up books all the time, and sometimes he reads aloud. But he has no idea what any of it means."

"Are you sure?" Kade felt his hope slipping.

Monica nodded, then said, "Guess you're wondering why we're here?"

Kade arched his brows and waited. It seemed like a rhetorical question.

"Well," she went on, "I'm going to get married, Kade." She paused, as if waiting for a response.

Maybe it should have stung. But Kade didn't feel much of anything.

"But first I need you to sign on the dotted line. I'm sure this doesn't come as a shock to you."

She reached into a big, black bag and pulled out a hefty stack of legal papers bound by a clasp at the top. "Feel free to read through them, but it's a replica of the papers you drew up a while back. A copy had already landed on my attorney's desk when you decided not to follow through with the divorce." She crinkled her forehead. "I never understood why you didn't go through with it. Anyway, the sooner you sign them and get them in the mail, the sooner I can get married, settled, and come back for Tyler."

What? Panic engulfed Kade. *Surely not.*

"I couldn't wait three months for you to get home to Los Angeles, so I packed up as much as I could for Tyler and brought it with me. It's time for you to be a father." Her scalding eyes challenged him to a duel. Well, it was about to be on.

"What?" It was all Kade could muster up.

"Don't look at me like that. I gave up my life to take care of Tyler while you were off building skyscrapers. It's your turn for a while."

Kade narrowed his eyes and inched toward her, towering over her on the couch. "Those skyscrapers provided you with a very nice lifestyle." He glanced over his shoulder at Tyler and lowered his voice to a whisper. "I don't know what you're thinking. You can't leave him here. I mean, I love my son, but—"

"Love him? You don't even know him!" Monica didn't bother

to keep her voice down. The familiarity of her sharp, shrill tone sent a chill up his spine. "I'm going, Kade. And that's all there is to it." She bolted from the couch and headed toward the front door. She turned around as she reached for the knob. "So, you can either help me with his things, or I'll get it all myself."

Kade laughed, despite himself. This couldn't be happening. *Mothers don't do this sort of thing.* "This is ridiculous," he said. He followed her to the door. "If you needed a vacation, or some time to get married, or whatever . . . you could have called me so I could make arrangements."

She stepped outside the door and waited for Kade to join her on the front porch. "Arrangements?" She was yelling now. "I tried plenty of times to make arrangements with you in the past, and it never fit into your schedule, and . . ."

Kade waved his hand in front of her, trying to shush her, and was suddenly reminded of Sadie. He dropped his hand to his side. "That's bull. And you know it. You never wanted to work with my schedule. You intentionally made it difficult for me to spend time with Tyler. You went all the way to North Carolina to ensure it." Kade didn't shut the front door all the way, and he glanced into the den. "Is he okay in there by himself?"

"He's fine."

Kade left the door ajar anyway.

Monica marched to the black Lexus and popped the trunk. Kade followed.

"My family is in North Carolina," she said. "And I wanted to be near them. You had plenty of opportunities to spend more time with Tyler, and you chose not to."

"Don't even bother taking out any of those things." He pointed to the suitcases piled in the back. "I'll get you a hotel room, and we'll figure out what to do in the morning." Kade chuckled in disbelief. "But there is no way you can just show up here and drop off Tyler like this."

One by one, she pulled suitcases out of the trunk and set them on the ground. "I suggest you get these into the house before the snow gets everything all wet."

Monica had that look in her eyes. The look she had the day she took Tyler and left. There was no talking her out of it. But he was darn sure going to try. "Monica, what kind of mother abandons her child like this? Maybe you're just having a rough time right now. And with a little notice, I'd be glad to help out with Tyler."

She practically threw the last suitcase at him, a small, red one. Then slammed the trunk. "Abandoning? Do you want to talk to me about abandoning? You are the one who abandoned your son, and now you can make things right!"

"You left *me*, Monica! I did not leave you. When I said I'd love and cherish you forever, I meant it."

"You are not going to make me feel guilty about this. You are not!" She stormed up to the cottage. Kade was on her heels.

"You've done some crazy things, Monica. But you can't leave Tyler here. I don't know the first thing about taking care of him."

She twisted her head around as she walked up the porch steps. "Well, I guess you're going to learn."

Without missing a beat, she went to the couch and retrieved the big, black bag she had carried in on her shoulder. She reached inside and pulled out a thick, black binder and dropped it on the couch beside the divorce papers.

"That is your Bible, Kade. Read it. It will tell you everything you need to know about Tyler, about his schedule, and everything I have learned about having an autistic child. Tyler is considered high-functioning, compared to some of the children in his class who don't speak at all and who can't do simple things, like feed themselves or go to the bathroom on their own."

Kade ran his hands through his hair, exhaled loudly, and said, "I'm sorry, Monica. You can't leave him here. I want to be a part of his life. I always have. But you can't just show up here and do this."

She squatted down beside Tyler, who seemed oblivious to the commotion around him. Cupping his cheeks in her hands, she was crying. "Mommy loves Tyler."

He smiled. "Mommy loves Tyler."

Kade watched in horror. How she could leave a child that she had raised since birth? He knew it was hypocritical, but the thought still surfaced. Second, if she really did walk out that door, what in the world was he going to do?

Monica threw her arms around Tyler. "Mommy loves Tyler soooo much."

"Mommy loves Tyler soooo much."

And with that, she ran out of the cottage. Kade was right behind her and grabbed her arm before she reached her car.

"Let go of me!" There was the hysteria he had heard so many times on the phone. "I have to go! I have to, Kade! Don't make this any harder on me! Do you understand me? I have to go!" She wriggled out of his grasp, and tears streamed down her cheeks. "Read the book. Keep him on schedule."

"Monica," Kade breathed in desperation. He glanced back and forth between her and the cottage. "You can't be serious!"

She slid into the front seat and rolled down the window. "I'll be back for Tyler when we get settled."

"You can't drop him off like this, Monica, with no warning. You have no idea what my schedule is!"

"Oh, I know exactly what your schedule is! You're taking some sort of hiatus from life. You should fire your secretary. All I had to do is get a girlfriend to call your office, and the woman pretty much spilled your entire life story to my friend." Her face twisted with rage. "So you know what, Kade? You can enjoy your little vacation and get to know your son! I need this time for *me*! Do you understand me? So, don't make me feel guilty! Don't you know—"

Kade wasn't hearing her. There was something about her hysterical tone . . .

He began to plead with her again not to do this.

She was still yelling when she rolled up the window.

As she turned the car around and headed toward Black Horse Road, Kade thought about her words. *I'll be back when we get settled.*

Kade wondered if she would come back.

Sadie pulled into her driveway, relieved that she'd be able to get out of the cold. She should have worn her heavy coat. The sunshine and rise in temperature had been misleading. Once on the road to market, her black cape had been no defense against the biting wind.

"Whoa," she instructed Buck, glad the horse no longer lived up to his name.

She made several trips to the kitchen, unloading her bags.

Now she would sort out Kade's groceries and prepare herself for a trip to the cottage. Perhaps he had ventured out to repair his tires now that the weather had improved. But no. His car was in the barn.

She separated Kade's items and began to put her groceries in their proper place, then realized she forgot to check the mail. Without stopping to wrap up, she walked out of the kitchen door and hurried to the mailbox at the end of the driveway.

Nothing. Disappointment tugged at her heart, but she reminded herself that today was Tuesday. Tonight Milo would call, just as he had since they'd set up the weekly phone schedule two years ago, shortly after they began writing letters. The thought lifted her spirit as she headed back into the house.

She redressed in her bonnet, cape, and boots, which not only protected her from the weather, but also from Kade's curious eyes. More than once, she'd caught him staring at her, which made her uncomfortable.

Perhaps Jonas and the elders had been right. How much did she really know about the fancy *Englischer*? Was she really safe out here alone with him? But then she recalled the way he handled Jonas. Sadie didn't think he was dangerous or bad.

Kade's groceries fit in three small plastic bags that she draped over one arm. She pulled the full container of tapioca pudding from the refrigerator and balanced it against her chest. She planned to unpack his things quickly, then scurry back home.

But she'd only taken two or three steps toward the cottage when she heard screams. Continuous shrill hollering, like she'd never heard the likes of before. She stopped walking, stared at the cottage, and listened. Sounded like a child. She turned toward the barn where she could use the phone. In her community, they tried to keep the *Englisch* police out of their lives if possible, but something bad was going on inside that cottage.

She quickly shuffled across the snow with the grocery bags and pudding. Then she stopped and looked toward her shop up near the road. Mary Ellen and Rebecca's buggies were parked outside. Couldn't they hear this child crying for help? She decided they couldn't, and she continued on her trek. But then the shrieks grew louder and louder.

There's no time. She set the food down in the snow and ran toward the cottage instead. With courage she didn't know she possessed, she sprinted up the porch steps and flung the door open. She stood in the entryway, her heart racing. Kade was squatting down beside a small boy in front of the fireplace, begging him to please stop hitting his head on the floor. He looked up at Sadie with fearful, desperate eyes.

"Please help me." He attempted to wrap his arms around the boy, who pulled away and continued bumping his head against the carpeted floor.

Sadie grabbed a throw pillow from the couch and ran to their side. She squatted down beside Kade and placed the pillow underneath the child's forehead. At least the pillow would soften the blows to the boy's head.

"I've tried picking him up, but he bit me," Kade said. He held up his left arm, pushed back his sweatshirt, and revealed a prominent set of teeth marks on his forearm. "I don't know what to do. He's never done anything like this. He's hurting himself, and I don't know how to make him stop, and . . ."

Kade's voice trailed, and his eyes begged her for an answer she didn't have.

"Who is he?" she asked.

"My son." He reached out to touch the boy's head, only to have the child scream even louder.

"Your son?" She narrowed her brows at him. "Have you done something to this child, to make him act this way? Have you hurt him?"

She wished she'd never said it. Kade sat there staring at her in disbelief, his face registering torment, and his eyes glassy and wide.

Sadie didn't wait for him to answer. She had her answer.

"Hello," she said to the boy, in a voice loud enough to rise above his cries. She leaned closer. "My name is Sadie. What's your name?"

No response. She looked up at Kade. "What's his name?"

"Tyler." Kade tried again to reach out to the boy, who began flailing his arms wildly and continued to bang his head on the pillow in front of him.

"Tyler, do you like pudding? I brought your *daed* some pudding." The child stopped screaming, but he continued to bang his head. Sadie looked at Kade, who nodded at her progress, and then she turned her attention back to Tyler. "It is yummy pudding, and I sure would like for you to try some."

Tyler didn't look at her, but his destructive behavior began to subside. "Tyler likes pudding," he mumbled.

She glanced at Kade, who ran his hand through his hair, sighed deeply, and said, "Did you really bring some? Because I'm out of pudding."

The boy didn't seem to hear Kade and repeated, "Tyler likes pudding." He sat straight up, and his eyes began to jet around the room, as if he was searching for something.

"*Ya*. I made you more pudding," she told Kade. "It's outside." Sadie turned back to Tyler. "Why don't I go get you some pudding?" She slowly stood up.

"I'll go get it," Kade said. He jumped to his feet and moved toward the door. "Where is it?"

Sadie kept her eyes on the boy, who had begun playing with plastic letters on the floor next to him, as if nothing had ever happened. "Near the barn, along with your groceries."

Kade was out the door before Sadie could say anything else. *His son?*

She reached over to touch Tyler's arm. He didn't look at her, but jerked away and flinched.

"I'm sorry," she whispered.

Kade returned, dropped the groceries inside the door, and headed toward the small kitchen with the container of pudding. "I'll put some pudding in a bowl for you, Tyler," he said.

Tyler lined his letters up in no particular order. He was calm. Sadie saw Kade searching for a spoon, pulling drawers open. She allowed herself a look around the cottage. It was a mess. Dishes were piled in the sink and clothes strewn across the back of the couch. He really should have opted for the housecleaning service she offered with the rental, although she was glad he hadn't.

"I should go." She stood up and smoothed the wrinkles in her black apron.

"No. Wait." Kade slid a spoon into the bowl of pudding and walked toward her and Tyler. He offered Tyler the bowl of pudding, which the boy accepted. A smile swept across Tyler's face.

"Tyler will be all right, no?" Sadie took a step backward and put some space between her and Kade.

"His mother dropped him off here, so she could run off and get married." Kade put his hand on her elbow and gently coaxed her away from Tyler and toward the far side of the den. "Tyler's autistic."

Sadie didn't know what that meant, but she edged out of Kade's grip and turned to face him. "But you said he was your son. How—"

"His mother and I have been separated for three years, and now she wants me to sign the divorce papers so she can remarry." He pointed to the bound papers on the couch. "She left him here without any warning, and she expects me to keep him until she gets *settled*." Kade shook his head, then looked up at her. "I haven't seen him in six months." Then, as if trying to hide shame, he added, "But I used to see him once a month . . . when his mother would let me."

And this is acceptable parenting in the Englisch *world?* She wanted to ask him why he rarely saw his son, but it was none of her business. "I must go." She turned and headed toward the door.

"Wait." He was following her, so Sadie paused at the door. "Tyler lives a long way from me. That's why I don't see him much."

Sadie nodded.

"Thank you for your help," he said. "Do you want a cup of coffee, or some tea?" His tone was desperate, and Sadie knew he was afraid to be alone with the boy.

"No. *Danki.*" She reached the door and pulled it open. Then she turned to face him again. "Do you need anything? For the boy?"

"I don't know." Kade rubbed his hand against the stubble on his chin. He turned toward Tyler, who was content with his pudding and sighed. "I don't even know my own son."

Sadie couldn't take her eyes from him. Maybe it was the sadness in his voice, but she had a sudden urge to offer him a hug, a thought she quickly squelched, feeling ridiculous. She had no business here. "I'm sorry for the intrusion. I shouldn't have burst through the door like I did, but—"

"No. Thank goodness you did." He smiled. "Turns out the kid likes your tapioca pudding as much as I do."

Sadie looked down at her shoes and hoped he wouldn't notice the flush in her cheeks. "I have to go." She turned around, then walked across the threshold and down the steps, with Kade following her. Thankfully, he stopped at the bottom porch step. Sadie hurried across the snow and didn't look back.

"Thank you again," she heard him say.

But she kept focused on the farmhouse ahead of her, mentally calculating how many days Kade had already been here, and how many days until he'd be gone.

Kade knew he needed to feed Tyler more than just tapioca pudding. He indulged the boy with two more bowls and used the opportunity to begin scanning through the black binder Monica had left him, fighting the wave of panic that overtook him with each page. Kade had never been around Tyler for more than a few hours at a time. How would he ever maintain Tyler's schedule? Up at seven. Breakfast at seven thirty. Brush teeth and get dressed at eight o'clock. Then a gap—go to school at eight thirty and return at three thirty.

He glanced at Tyler when he heard the spoon clink against the empty bowl. But Tyler set the bowl aside and began playing with his plastic letters. Kade kept scanning the pages. Four o'clock, reading time. Four thirty, outside playtime. Five o'clock, sing songs. Six o'clock, more reading. Dinnertime was at seven, followed by brushing teeth and a bath. Bedtime, eight. *Leave the light on* was highlighted in yellow marker.

Kade turned the page to find a list of likes and dislikes. The list of dislikes was far longer than the likes.

Likes to read, sing, play with plastic letters, take his shoes off and on, listen to running water from the tap/tub, carry his Spider-Man lunch box from room to room, and his favorite self-stimulatory behavior is to clap his hands.

Kade took a deep breath and read the column of dislikes.

Does not like to be touched casually—e.g., patted on the head, brushed against, have a haircut, etc. But does like to be hugged tightly and will say the word *hug*.

Does not socialize well with other children, often becoming agitated. Is afraid of the dark. Doesn't like to get off schedule, will scream.

Kade was afraid to move, to breathe, to do anything that might draw attention to himself and distract Tyler's calm mood. He turned the page, still with visions of Tyler's earlier head banging fresh on his mind. During their few visits to the park, Tyler had never behaved in such a way. Tyler had thrown fits before, but nothing like today. More dislikes on the following page.

Doesn't like the television on. *Not much to watch anyway.*

Dislikes any green food—peas, green beans, celery, lettuce . . .

Footsteps moving his way sent a rush of adrenaline through Kade. He closed the binder and looked up to find Tyler facing him. Neither said a word, and Kade feared another explosion. Tyler surely wasn't on his schedule. Kade glanced at his watch. Three o'clock. Tyler would normally be in school. *Please don't scream.*

Kade took in the boy's features, remembering him as a toddler. His blue eyes were still filled with wonder yet seemed to look right through Kade. To Kade's surprise, Tyler smiled, his face lighting up, and Kade returned the smile. "Hi," he said with caution.

"Hi." Tyler kept smiling. Then with his arms at his side, Tyler said simply, "Hug."

"You want a hug?" Kade recalled the bite he received when he'd tried to touch Tyler earlier, but that was before he'd read Monica's notes.

"Hug," Tyler repeated.

Kade pulled the boy to him, slowly at first. But Tyler seemed comfortable, and Kade brought him closer and wrapped his arms tightly around his son's tiny frame. Kade buried his head on Tyler's small shoulder, and for the first time since Monica left with his son, Kade cried.

Sadie wrapped her arms around her knees as she sat on the small stool in the barn, shivering and waiting for Milo's phone call. She knew it was well past eight o'clock, and she was tired, cold, and growing irritated. Milo knew she had to sit out in the cold barn, and for him to be late calling was disrespectful.

She couldn't help but wonder how things were going with Kade and Tyler. She assumed Kade's son must be mentally slow. She recalled Martha and Jacob's boy, Amos, who was born a few years back, his mind and behavior different from other children's. A special child of God.

She squeezed her arms around her knees even tighter, the bitter cold a harsh contrast from the more pleasant temperatures earlier in the day. Maybe something had happened to Milo, a situation that prevented him from calling. Worry replaced her irritation as her mind speculated about what could be keeping him from phoning. He never missed a Tuesday call.

Wild dogs howled in the distance, interrupting the eerie quiet that surrounded her. Again, her thoughts turned to her renter and his son. Kade had looked so lost, so unprepared to care for the boy. Divorce. Such a tragedy, a circumstance unheard-of in her community, where marriage was a sacrament, never to be severed. She wondered what could have happened between the two of them. Sadie remembered what a hard time Martha and Jacob had when Amos was born, the difficulties with a special child. All the more reason for young Tyler to have two parents. Perhaps Kade and his wife would not go through with the divorce.

None of her business, Sadie reminded herself. She lifted herself off the stool and picked up the lantern from the small table where the phone rested. She walked toward Kade's sleek, black car and peeked inside, recalling their trip in search of Jonas. Why did anyone need all those gadgets? She shook her head and walked slowly out of the barn, taking careful steps into the snowy yard now icing over as the night temperatures dropped.

The familiar loneliness was her only company. She fought the knot in her throat and picked up her pace, wanting to get inside—secure in her bed, where she could have a proper cry while tucked beneath the thick counterpanes. Milo's Tuesday calls sustained her from week to week.

She heard the cottage door open and briefly spun around to see Kade loading a piece of firewood into his arms, but then quickly turned back toward the farmhouse.

"Hey!"

She wasn't in the mood to make polite conversation, but she stopped and turned around. "*Ya?*"

"Are you all right?" The door to the cottage was wide-open, and Kade had taken a couple of steps further onto the porch, still toting the firewood.

"*Ya.* I'm *gut. Danki.*" She waved, turned around, and quickened her steps. She'd almost made it safely to the farmhouse when she heard him call her name. She sighed, turned around. "*Ya?*"

"Do you want to come have a cup of coffee with me?"

"No. *Danki.*" She turned and walked faster, nearly slipping on the icy snow.

"Please?"

Sadie stopped but didn't turn around. Maybe it was the pleading tone in his voice. Maybe it was her own desperate loneliness, her need to be in the presence of another human being. But suddenly, she found herself considering Kade's offer.

6

SADIE OPENED HER EYES THE NEXT MORNING AT DAY-
break, eyes swollen from crying herself to sleep the night before.
She'd overslept, but who would notice anyway? She rolled onto
her side, tucked the quilt around her chin, and warmed herself
against the chill in the room. Loneliness tore at her heart as she
reached over and draped an arm across Ben's side of the bed. She
closed her eyes and pretended he was lying beside her.

Spending time with the *Englischer* would have been unsuitable
at best, no matter how much she longed for companionship.
Thankfully she'd had the strength to give him a big hearty no
before bolting up the stairs and into the farmhouse. She'd barely
made it into the den when the tears began to spill. *God, please don't
let me be alone the rest of my life,* she prayed.

Today was her day to work at the shop with Lillian, so she
reluctantly pushed back the covers and stepped out of bed. She was
usually a woman of vigor, but now, the hole in her heart seemed to
be dragging her to a place she didn't want to be.

She said her regular morning devotions, praying hard that
God would send Milo to her, that they would fall in love and live
the rest of their lives the way He intended for them, and that they
might be blessed with lots of little ones to fill their hearts with

joy. She knew that to ask for such things was not in line with her upbringing. It would have been better to ask for God's guidance and accept that His will would be done.

Sadie bundled up and headed toward the shop after a few bites of toast with apple butter. She'd already heard Lillian pull up in her buggy twenty minutes earlier. She glanced across the yard at the cottage. All was quiet. She wondered how the boy was doing and how Kade was faring.

When Sadie walked in, the heaters were already lit, and Lillian was opening the blinds. "Sleeping in this morning?" Lillian winked.

"*Ya*. I reckon so." Sadie opened the last blind, flooding the room with sunlight.

"We better enjoy all this sun while we can," Lillian said. She wrapped the cord from the blind around a nail on the wall. "Friday we're in for another hard freeze, and the newspaper said blizzard conditions."

"*Ya*, I heard." Sadie tied off her cord and headed toward the sales counter on the right side of the room.

Lillian marched over to the counter and gazed up at Sadie. "Have you been crying?"

Sadie took a deep breath. "Milo didn't call last night."

"Hmm. Maybe something came up. I'm sure it's nothing to worry about."

"He's never missed a Tuesday call." Sadie began to total up receipts from yesterday's sales.

"Maybe he will call tonight, no?"

Sadie shrugged. "Maybe. But he'll have to leave a message. It's a mite too cold for me to sit in the barn and wait for him to call."

Lillian didn't say anything for a few minutes, but fumbled nervously with papers on the counter. "Mary Ellen said that she and Rebecca saw you go running into the cottage yesterday. She said that you dropped the *Englisher's* groceries on the ground and burst in the front door."

"Were they spying on me?" Sadie didn't look up at Lillian, but kept pushing numbers on the small calculator.

"They said they thought they heard screams coming from the cottage. When they looked out the window, you were running inside. Mary Ellen said they were worried about you, so they watched out the window until they saw you heading back to the farmhouse. They weren't sure how involved they should get."

"As it turns out, Mr. Saunders has a son." She glanced up to see Lillian waiting for more. "He has a wife who he's been apart from for three years. She wants to remarry, so she brought him some divorce papers to sign and dropped the boy off with him. And . . ."

"What?" Lillian's eyes were wide.

"He hasn't seen the boy, Tyler, in six months, and Tyler's mother wouldn't let him see Tyler much before that. Tyler is like Martha and Jacob's boy, I think, screaming and banging his head on the floor when I walked in. I can't help but worry about . . ." She caught herself, looked down, and returned to totaling receipts.

"Worry is a sin," Lillian said. Then she patted Sadie's hand. "God will guide their way. I will pray for them."

Sadie merely nodded. She had included Kade and Tyler in her prayers last night, thinking she'd never seen such a lost man as Kade. *Hopefully*, she thought, *Kade has a good relationship with the Lord.*

Lillian began to sweep the wooden floor, and Sadie silently questioned her own relationship with God. Thoughts had been surfacing that she would never share with anyone, notions that continued to creep into her head, as if put there by the devil himself.

She gave her head a few quick shakes from side to side, as if that would clear the sinful thoughts from her mind. There was no questioning God's will. To do so went against everything Sadie believed in. But she couldn't understand His will for her these days, as her loneliness burrowed deep inside her. Perhaps she just needed to be patient, until the spring, when Milo would be here.

"How's Jonas?" she asked Lillian in an attempt to stem the confusion in her head.

Lillian stopped sweeping. "*Mamm* said it depends on the day. Some days he is perfectly fine. Other days are *baremlich*. He gets confused, wanders off, and tries to take the buggy if it's left hitched up, without letting *Mamm* know where he's going. Things like that. I know it's hard for *Mamm* sometimes, taking care of him on her own. She worries about him a lot."

"Jonas has no business doing such things. Just like the other night—"

"Sadie, I'm sorry I asked you to go into that place to get Grandpa. I should have gone. After all, I've been in those type places before. Before I was Amish."

"You shouldn't be in a place like that while you're pregnant." Sadie recalled the smoke-filled room, the patrons' questioning eyes, and the way Kade had handled Jonas. "You know, it was Kade who convinced Jonas to come with us." She paused. "He seemed to know exactly how to handle him."

"Hmm," Lillian said. "Well, it's a *gut* thing he did." She pointed toward the window. "There's Carley and Jenna."

The bell on the door chimed when Jenna burst into the room. "Hi!" She ran into her Aunt Lillian's arms.

"*Guder mariye, Jenna.*"

"Good morning to you too," the six-year-old answered.

Carley closed the door behind her. "She does pretty well with her Pennsylvania *Deitsch*, huh? With so many relatives speaking the language, Noah has taught her quite a bit. He still remembers much of what he learned before he left."

"*Ya*, she is doing *wunderbaar gut*," Lillian said. She eased out of the hug. "Do you want to go organize the dolls for me, Jenna?"

Jenna nodded and skipped across the store, her blonde ringlets bouncing down the middle of her back.

Carley reached into her purse and pulled out a piece of paper. "Can you look at this and see if I'm missing anything?" She handed the note to Lillian. "Noah and I have a couple coming in from Florida this afternoon. It's a man Noah went to medical school with, and they'll be staying with us for a few days. Of course, they are intrigued by the Amish, so I told them I would cook them an Amish meal."

Lillian scanned the note. "Wow. This is quite an undertaking. Usually turkey roast is reserved for weddings, but they should love it." Lillian ran her finger down the piece of paper. "Barbecued string beans, mashed potatoes, homemade bread, and shoofly pie." She handed the piece of paper back to Carley. "Do you have chowchow, applesauce, and some jams and jellies to serve prior to the main meal?"

Carley grinned. "No. I was hoping maybe my Amish sister-in-law could help me with that."

"Come by the house later, and I'll supply you with everything you need," Lillian said with a smile.

"Or—" Sadie cut in, "I could prepare the meal at my house for your friends."

Carley's eyes lit up. "Really? I know they would love to see the inside of an Amish home." She paused as her face grew serious. "But that's way too much work. I could never ask you to do that."

Sadie glanced at the ground, then sheepishly back at Carley. "I'd truly enjoy the company."

"But what about Noah? I mean, since he's been shunned and all. I wouldn't want to get you in trouble with the bishop."

"I'd be glad to cook for your friends, and I'm not worried about Bishop Ebersol. You know he mostly looks the other way when it comes to Noah." Sadie took the piece of paper from Carley. "What time?"

"Sadie, you're the best!" Carley gave her a quick hug. "You tell me what time is best for you. I'll go to the grocery store right now, buy everything, and bring it here. This is so sweet of you. Noah's friends will be so excited."

"I'm happy to do it." Sadie couldn't tell her how much she needed to have visitors in the house, someone to cook for and serve at her own table. Then she had a thought. "Carley, would you mind if I invited the *Englischer* and his son? The ones who are renting the cottage."

Lillian gave her a strange look, but Carley answered right away. "Of course not! The more the merrier."

Sadie glanced toward Lillian, and then back at Carley. "The young boy is special. I think he might be slow—mentally challenged I believe is the right way to say it." She shook her head. "*Ach*, never mind. I think it might be best not to. I don't know how the child will act, and it might be uncomfortable for your friends. The only reason I thought about it is that the child's mother just dropped him off with Kade, my renter, and the man hasn't been involved much in the child's life. He's clueless what to do with him. And since Noah is a doctor—"

"Say no more," Carley interrupted. "His friend, James, is a doctor too. There will be two doctors, and maybe they can help your friend with his son."

"He's not my *friend*. He's renting the cottage." She let out a long, audible breath. "But he seems rather lost."

"What time do you want to have supper?" Carley asked. "At the usual supper hour, four o'clock?"

"In the past when I've hosted *Englischers* for suppers, I have pushed back supper until seven. How would that be?"

"Perfect." Carley turned toward her daughter. "Jenna, let's go, sweetie."

"Lillian, my table hasn't been full in a long time. Do you, Samuel, David, and Anna want to join us, if it's all right with Carley?" Sadie glanced back and forth between the women.

"That would be great," Carley said as she reached for Jenna's hand.

Lillian rested her hands across her protruding belly. "*Ya*, that would be nice. But Anna has a *baremlich* cold. David is watching her for me today. I didn't want to bring her here like I usually do, for fear she'd get worse being carted outdoors. I think it best to keep her inside. Besides, I promised Lizzie I would bake her some bread. I appreciate the invitation, though."

"Lizzie sure eats a lot," Sadie said. "I told her I'd bake her some bread too. And last week, I took her a meat loaf, and she sent the empty dish back the very next day, by way of Mary Ellen, who'd stopped by to see her."

"She's a dear woman," Lillian said. "Frail little thing. But I agree with you. She eats like a horse. It's a shame she doesn't have children of her own. She does have several nieces and nephews who check on her, but they travel almost an hour to do so, by car from the Beachy Amish community." Lillian frowned. "I don't think they check on her enough."

"She has us to tend to her. Lizzie is easy to love," Sadie said. "I know she gets lonely."

Sometimes Sadie would offer to stay and keep her company, but Lizzie always declined the offer. Maybe Lizzie would accept Sadie's invitation to sit with her if she knew how much Sadie herself wanted the company. One thing Sadie knew about— loneliness. However, she wouldn't be lonely tonight. That is, not until she climbed into bed after her supper guests were gone.

"I'll be back with the groceries." Carley waved, and she and Jenna left.

Sadie began to wonder how she was going to approach Kade about joining them for supper. It seemed a bit forward. *But it's in Tyler's best interest*, she reminded herself.

⸺⸱⸺

Kade shifted his position on the couch and blinked his eyes into focus. Tyler was standing beside him, clad in blue-and-white pajamas, a yellow toothbrush dangling from one hand. Kade sat up, placed his feet on the floor, and tried to make eye contact with his son. But Tyler looked past him, although with a hint of happiness on his small face.

"Good morning," Kade said. He glanced at the clock on the fireplace mantel. Seven thirty. Kade reached for the black binder. They were already starting the day late. "Up at seven," he mumbled to himself. "Breakfast at seven thirty. Brush teeth and get dressed at eight o'clock." Then came the huge gap in time from eight thirty to three thirty when Tyler would have been in school.

How could Monica have done this? Kade could have prepared for this, with some warning. And he would have been at his own home in Los Angeles, not in a tiny, one-bedroom cottage in Pennsylvania Dutch country.

He thought about yesterday. There hadn't been any more fits or head banging, and Tyler went to bed right at eight o'clock in the bedroom. Kade left the light on as Monica's instructions suggested. Expecting problems, Kade was up until about one o'clock in the morning, fearful Tyler would get up during the night. But no incidents. And after Kade read every page in the black binder, sleep finally won out.

"Are you hungry?" Kade put the black binder back on the coffee table. Tyler didn't say anything, but he gently touched Kade's knee. Kade wanted to scoop Tyler into his arms, cuddle him, and somehow make up for the kind of man he knew himself to be—the kind of man who would've hired a nanny to do all this if he was home in Los Angeles. For a split second, he considered taking Tyler and going home. Then Tyler smiled. The familiar warmth Kade felt when Tyler arrived yesterday took the fear from his heart, even if only momentarily.

"Let's get some breakfast." Kade stood up and walked toward

the kitchen. He glanced back at Tyler to see him following, still toting the toothbrush.

"Cereal," Tyler said.

"Okay." Kade smiled, glad that Tyler was able to communicate what he wanted. He opened the cabinet where he stored the groceries Sadie brought the day before. Kade's preferred cereal had nuts and raisins, and he wondered if Tyler was going to eat it or not. He pulled a bowl from the shelf and filled it halfway.

Tyler walked over to the small, round table in the corner of the kitchen while Kade poured milk into the bowl. He took a seat at one of the four chairs and kicked his feet back and forth. Kade watched him out of the corner of his eye and allowed himself to fantasize that Tyler was perfect, a normal child.

Kade placed the bowl in front of Tyler and offered him a spoon. "Here's your cereal, Tyler."

"Cereal."

But Tyler didn't take the spoon. Instead, Tyler began tapping his toothbrush on the table, softly at first, then louder.

Kade tried to remember what Monica's notes said concerning ways to handle Tyler's unpredictable behavior, but with all the banging he couldn't think straight. "Tyler, let's don't do that." He reached for the toothbrush and attempted to pull it from Tyler's hand.

Tyler rolled his body from the chair, hit the floor hard, and rocked back and forth on his side, moaning loudly.

"Tyler, are you hurt?" Kade extended his arm downward, remembered the bite, and pulled back. Tyler's groans took on a high-pitched tone, and Kade squatted down beside him, unsure what his next move should be. "Think," he said aloud as he tried to recall the information he'd read the night before. *During a fit, ignore it, and refocus on something else.*

Kade walked to the middle of the floor in the den, scooped the plastic letters into the lunch box, and headed back to Tyler, who hadn't let up. He placed the lunch box beside his son, opened it, and began to randomly line up letters in no particular order. The wailing stopped.

Tyler sat up, as if he was cured of whatever ailed him. He began to sort through the letters, lining them up in what appeared to be a precalculated order, but there were no word formations that Kade could see.

Kade sat down on the floor beside his son and ran his hand through his tousled hair. How was he ever going to do this?

Sadie and Lillian had just finished a cup of chicken noodle soup when Sadie decided she would walk to the cottage to invite Kade and Tyler for supper.

"Go ahead." Lillian reached into a plastic bag beside her chair on the floor. "I need to hem these pants for Samuel anyway."

Sadie pulled her cape and bonnet from the rack. "Maybe it's not a *gut* idea to invite them for supper, but perhaps Noah and his doctor friend can help Kade with the boy."

Lillian glanced up at Sadie, then focused on the needle she was attempting to thread. "He is handsome, the *Englischer.*"

"He is odd," Sadie said in a firm tone. "A rich man who needs many gadgets."

"Being rich doesn't necessarily make him odd." Lillian looked up at her and waited for a response.

Sadie moved toward Lillian as she tied the strings on her cape. "It is not normal to be separated from your spouse for three years or to not have a relationship with your child. It's also not *gut* to need so many material possessions, and—"

"But he's *Englisch*," Lillian interrupted. "The *Englisch* collect possessions."

"So many of them? I reckon his home is filled with unnecessary items, like his automobile." Sadie raised her eyebrows. "I've never seen such a car. Lights, knobs, and switches everywhere."

"Sadie . . ." Lillian took a deep breath.

"*Ya?*"

"Only God can pass judgment. Sounds to me like you're judging this man before you really know him."

"Why would I want to know him? I'm just trying to help the boy, maybe get some doctors' advice about how that man should tend to the child. That's all." Sadie tied her bonnet and pondered Lillian's words. "You're right," she mumbled. "It is not my place to judge."

Sadie moved toward the door. "I'll be back."

Once outside, Sadie rigidly held her thoughts in check. She didn't understand why she was picking up unbecoming traits. She'd never been a judgmental person before. It was as wrong as anything she'd been taught. Judging, questioning God's plan for her life—all wrong. She'd need to pray for strength to keep her thoughts pure and righteous. Maybe even speak with Bishop Ebersol about the matters.

She neared the cottage, and a vision of Kade wearing only his pajama bottoms flashed before her. *Surely not.* The man would have all his clothes on this time of day. But she slowed her pace anyway. She leaned an ear inward as she walked. Nothing.

The curtains were closed. She looked toward the barn, and the fancy car was still parked inside.

The porch steps creaked beneath her feet, and she considered turning around. But she knocked, not wanting to get caught loitering on the porch again.

Kade opened the door. Thankfully, he was fully clothed in jeans and a pullover blue sweater. Sadie could see past him to Tyler, who was sitting on the couch, reading a book. *Interesting.*

"The boy can read, no?" Sadie asked. She stretched her neck to peer past Kade.

Kade looked over his shoulder and then turned back to face her. "Yes, but according to my ex, he can't understand anything he reads. In her notes, she says he has hyperlexia. It's a syndrome observed in children who are autistic."

Sadie knew the confusion registered on her face, but she just nodded.

"It's a precocious ability to read words far above what would be expected of a five-year-old." He glanced at Tyler again. "There's a whole bag of books in his suitcase, but he seems fond of the book you had on your coffee table."

"The only book in here is—"

"Come in out of the cold." Kade swung the door wide and waited for her to enter.

"No, I just came to invite you to supper. You and Tyler."

Kade smiled his crooked smile in a way that made Sadie immediately wish she hadn't asked him. "We'd love to," he said in a tone that furthered her regret. She'd need to clarify her invitation.

"*Mei Englisch* friend, Carley, and her husband are bringing guests for supper. They are doctors, and I thought they might be able to help you with your son. I don't know what this 'autistic' is you speak of, but you seem . . ." She paused. His smile had faded, but his eyes were fused with hers, and he was listening intently. "You seem like maybe you need some help with the boy."

"Come in." He gently touched her arm and coaxed her inside. "You're letting in cold air."

She inched inside. The door closed hard behind her, and Tyler looked in her direction.

"Hello, Tyler." She walked to where he was sitting on the couch. "You are reading the Bible, I see."

Tyler didn't say anything, but refocused on the Good Book. Sadie turned around to see Kade standing uncomfortably close to her. She backed up a step. "It will not be a fancy meal, Mr. Saunders. Just a simple—"

"Kade," he interrupted.

"It will not be a fancy meal, *Kade*. Carley and Noah's guests would like to learn more of the Amish ways, and I'm happy to cook for all of them. And you and Tyler, if you wish. Sometimes I host *Englisch* families in my home for supper." She raised her chin and shrugged dismissively. "So this is ordinary, quite common, actually."

Kade folded his arms across his chest. One corner of his mouth pulled into a slight smile. "Sure. Sounds great."

"Am I amusing you, *Kade*?" *This was a bad idea.*

"Yes, Sadie Fisher, you amuse me." His grin broadened. "I get the point—that you're not asking me to supper, not as a date or anything. This is something you do for guests."

In all her years, Sadie was certain she'd never been as embarrassed as she was at this moment. Except perhaps when she awoke on the couch with Kade leaning over her.

"What time?" Kade turned and headed toward the kitchen, but glanced at her over his shoulder. "I was going to make myself a cup of hot tea. Would you like some?"

"No. I must go. Supper is at seven o'clock." She turned to leave.

"Wait," he said as he walked back into the den. He stopped in front of her and put his hands in the pockets of his denim breeches. His forehead creased with worry, and then he sighed. "Maybe it's not such a good idea for us to come."

"Why not?" Sadie's response shone with disappointment, which caught her completely off guard.

Kade leaned toward her and whispered. "Tyler might not be ready for a social environment. I don't know how he'll do." His brows drew downward in a frown. "I don't know how *I* will do."

Sadie looked over at Tyler, who was still reading. Then she smiled at Kade. "Tyler is special. A blessed gift from God. You have to learn his ways. Although he seems happy and *gut* at the moment."

"Right now he is." Kade ran his hand through his wavy, brown hair. "Breakfast was another story."

"Cereal for breakfast," Tyler said.

Kade turned briefly toward Tyler. "Yes, cereal," he said. He shifted his eyes back to Sadie, his expression warm. "He didn't really like the cereal, but we did okay."

"You will be fine, Kade. You will learn Tyler's ways and he will learn yours while he's here."

Sadie continued toward the door and was almost there when someone knocked. *Lillian, perhaps?*

Sadie turned the knob and pulled the door open.

Her eyes grew wide, her jaw dropped, and she fumbled for words that weren't coming. *Definitely not Lillian.*

7

BISHOP EBERSOL TIPPED THE RIM OF HIS STRAW HAT back, drew his brows inward, and stared Sadie down the same way her father had when she misbehaved as a child.

"Bishop Ebersol." Her voice rose in surprise. "How *gut* to see you."

The bishop shifted his eyes and glanced over her shoulder. Sadie could hear footsteps approaching from behind. She stood, waited, and feared what Kade might say.

"Can we help you?" Kade asked. He was so close behind Sadie that she could feel his breath against her neck. *We?* There's no *we*, Sadie thought, hoping he'd hush.

She stepped forward onto the porch, forcing Bishop Ebersol to take a step backward. She twisted slightly to face Kade. "Good-bye, Mr. Saunders. I'm glad to see that your son is doing well." She smiled, then faced the bishop. "What brings you here, Bishop Ebersol?" She headed down the porch steps with hopes that the bishop would follow. He did.

Sadie took two steps into the packed snow and turned to see Kade still standing in the threshold. *Go in the house!*

Bishop Ebersol held firmly to the handrail and made his way down the steps. A man in his seventies, he wore a gray beard that stretched to the end of his chest. But he stood tall in his black overcoat and took each step slow and steady.

"Well, okay . . ." she heard Kade say. "Thanks for coming over. I'll see you at supper tonight."

Sadie cringed and knew she was about to get a good talking-to. She waited for the bishop to catch up with her and wondered if Kade was ever going to go back in the cottage.

"I think it would be *gut* for us to have *kaffi*, Sadie," Bishop Ebersol said in a tone that challenged her to argue. He pulled his coat tight around his neck, blocking a blast of cool air that seemed to come out of nowhere. The sun was shining, but it was a reminder of what was to come. By tomorrow, temperatures would be consistently below freezing. By Friday they predicted terrible conditions.

She'd give thought to the weather later. Right now, she suspected Bishop Ebersol had a few things on his mind pertaining to her renter. She got in step with the bishop and took slow strides toward the farmhouse, and then spun her neck around to see Kade wave. She raised her hand briefly in his direction, turned back around, and prepared herself for the harsh words to come.

They were almost to the house when she saw the mailman pull up to her mailbox, open the flap, and push an envelope inside.

She hoped the bishop wouldn't take too long.

Lillian watched out of the window of the shop as Sadie walked alongside Bishop Ebersol toward the farmhouse, a gloomy expression on her face. Lillian hadn't known what to say when the bishop questioned Sadie's whereabouts, so she had stumbled around saying Sadie was tending to errands around the property. It was the truth, however slightly stretched it might have been. But Lillian saw Sadie walk inside the cottage, and she knew the bishop was already uncomfortable about a single man as her renter.

Lillian shook her head. Sadie should have stayed outside on the porch.

She'd barely sat back down to finish hemming Samuel's pants when she heard the *clip-clop* of hooves. She set the project aside and walked to the front window. *Oh no.*

Lillian walked outside and met her grandfather at the buggy. Before he had time to step down, she said, "Grandpa, does *Mamm* know where you are?"

Jonas Miller scrunched his face in irritation. "Lilly, I am a grown man. I do what I want, when I want." He climbed out of the buggy, opened his black coat, and slipped his thumbs beneath his suspenders. "And *ya*, Sarah Jane knows where I'm at."

"*Gut*, Grandpa." She patted his arm tenderly. "We worry and love you, that's all."

"I know you all think I'm *ab im kopp*, but I reckon I just get confused sometimes." He started walking toward the shop.

Lillian put her arm through his and walked beside him. "No one thinks you are off in the head, Grandpa."

"*Gut, gut.*" He looked her way and smiled. "I was testing your Pennsylvania *Deitsch*, to see if you have kept up with your studies since marrying Samuel."

"*Ya*, I have." She opened the door and motioned her grandpa in. "Are you here just for a visit?" Lillian was still skeptical that her mother knew he was here.

"I reckon I can come just to visit *mei kinskind*, no?"

Lillian closed the door behind them. "You can visit me any-time."

"I see that Bishop Ebersol is here. Sadie get in some trouble for housing that single *Englisch* fella?"

"I don't know. Sadie was a little concerned about that, but Bishop Ebersol said it would be all right for her to rent the cottage. There weren't any specific rules about *who* to rent to, but—"

"Then what's he doing here?" Grandpa placed his hat on the counter.

"I think he's just checking on her, and . . . uh, then she happened to be inside the cottage when he came, and I really don't know what's going on." Lillian shrugged and took a seat on the stool behind the counter.

"I'll tell you what's going on. Trouble. I saw the way the *Englischer* was looking at your friend. You look out for her, Lilly. He don't strike me as the converting type, and he'll steal our Sadie away to the *Englisch* world."

"Grandpa! That is the most ridiculous thing I have ever heard. They barely know each other!" Lillian slapped him play-fully on the hand and grinned.

"You didn't know Samuel either."

"That was different."

"I don't know about that, and—"

The bell on the door chimed, hushing Grandpa.

"Is everything all right?" Lillian asked when Sadie walked in.

"*Ya*. Bishop Ebersol asked me a lot of questions, but when I explained about Mr. Saunders's son, he seemed to understand my concern for the boy." Sadie focused on Lillian's grandpa. "Hello, Jonas. What brings you here? Does Sarah Jane know you're here?"

Lillian sighed. She knew what was coming.

"I don't have to tell my daughter my every move. I am a grown man, and I can do what I see fit." Grandpa stood up, put his hat on, and tipped it in their direction. "As a matter of fact, I think I will go for a ride through the country."

"Jonas, I'm sorry if—" Sadie moved toward him.

"No, no. Nothin' to be sorry about." He started toward the door but turned around. "You girls take care of each other."

Kade put Tyler in the bathtub and placed the floating ducks all around him, like Monica had instructed in the black binder. Six little yellow chicks bobbed aimlessly around Tyler, who began to giggle.

Kade smiled. His son was as cute a kid as he'd ever seen. And at times like this, he forgot about Tyler's special needs. But it had been a hard day inclusive of another headbanging incident, and Kade worried how supper with Sadie and her guests would go. He was willing to chance it. He'd been alone and felt sorry for himself long enough. Maybe being around some other adults would do him good. And something about being around Sadie seemed to calm him. Perhaps it was the way she was with Tyler, or maybe because she was pleasant on the eyes. Either way, he found himself looking forward to the meal.

Tyler kept laughing, and Kade was mesmerized by the innocence of it all. He sat down on the tile floor beside the bathtub and watched his son, feeling like he could sit there forever. How had his life spiraled so completely out of control? He had more money than most would ever have, but barely an ounce of happiness. Yet, a bathtub full of yellow chicks was enough for Tyler. Something was amiss in Kade's life, and he'd never felt it more than right now.

He looked up at the ceiling. *What the heck?* he thought. He leaned against the wall and veered his eyes upward. "God, can You hear me?" It had been a long time, and he felt silly. But he pressed on. "Because I'm a mess. I need some help." He shook his head and fought his feelings of unworthiness. He knew from his upbringing that God welcomes those who have strayed, but Kade was struggling to reconnect. Carrying the burdens of his past would only hinder this effort. He knew this. But his regrets pressed down on him like a heavy weight on his chest, testing how much pressure his heart could take.

Tyler was still giggling and pushing the ducks around the tub. Kade was feeling something he hadn't felt before—confusing waves of emotion and an inner voice that seemed to beg him to take a good, hard look at his life, to reevaluate his place in the world.

He'd been crushed when Monica left. Highly perturbed when he lost almost two hundred thousand dollars in a business deal recently. And extremely disappointed when Alicia pulled out of their friendship. He also had a son whom he barely knew, which pained him now more than ever. But worst of all had been finding his father dead near his parents' Malibu home. He recalled his father's lifeless body, his eyes and mouth gaping open. A chill ran up Kade's spine, and he squelched the thought.

Kade's life had had its ups and downs for sure. But these feelings he was having . . . They were different.

Kade pushed one of the yellow ducks back in Tyler's direction.

"My duck," Tyler said as he continued to be entertained by the floating toys.

"Yes, your duck." Kade forced a smile, but he was anything but happy. And he should be—happy. *Shouldn't I?*

Despite the downs in his life, there had certainly been ups. He was wealthy. He'd traveled the world and experienced things most people never would. His doctor had recently told him that he was in perfect health. He had it all, really.

Then why was something pecking away at his insides, like a chisel chipping away at all that he'd ever known, and hinting that there was something else on the horizon?

Contentment? Is this what I'm lacking?

Kade gazed at his son and thought about the life he'd lived thus far. Right now, at this moment, he felt . . . *What do I feel?* He thought about it some more and summarized his emotions.

Fear, regret, hope, and love for my son.

His stomach knotted, and he fought the pangs of shame in his heart. *I want to be a better man.*

Kade looked up again, and this time he didn't feel ridiculous. "Show me the way, Lord. Show me the way."

Kade glanced at Tyler, who for the very first time stared straight into Kade's eyes. Kade didn't even want to blink or move—afraid he'd lose the moment. "Hey buddy," he said softly, wishing, praying Tyler could communicate with him.

The kid got the strangest look on his face. Kade didn't care. He was thrilled that he seemed to be holding his attention. "Tyler?"

Tyler smiled, which instantly invoked a smile from Kade. It was a rare moment, Tyler's eyes fused with Kade's, as if he were looking into Kade's thoughts, his soul.

"Tyler?" His son's eyes were still locked with his.

Tyler opened his mouth to speak, and Kade waited.

Tyler spoke softly, with perfect pronunciation, and with a gleam in his eyes. "The Lord is our King; He will save us."

Then Tyler returned to splashing around in the tub with his ducks, as if something incredibly profound hadn't happened, something that would change the core of who Kade was as a person, a man . . . a father.

Sadie pulled the turkey roast from the oven. She placed it on top of the gas range next to a casserole dish filled with barbecued string beans. The potatoes were cooked and cubed, and she had already added butter, milk, salt, pepper, and cream cheese. She'd mash them right before her guests arrived. Her table was filled with homemade bread, applesauce, and an assortment of jams and jellies, and she'd prepared a traditional shoofly pie for dessert. If the supper went as smoothly as the meal preparation, all would be well.

She stepped back to inspect her place settings for seven. Sadie couldn't remember the last time she used the plain white china, a wedding gift from Ben's parents. The long wooden table stretched almost the length of her kitchen, backless benches on either side. She recalled the hours Ben spent making the table, for the large family they would never have.

Sadie closed her eyes for a moment and bit back tears. She refused to allow her shattered dreams to put a damper on this evening. Company was coming, and she felt good about sharing her home and a meal with friends. Carley and Noah were as fine a couple as she'd ever known, and she felt sure their friends would be a pleasure as well.

Kade and the boy. She felt a nervous anticipation about them being at supper. Kade made her incredibly uncomfortable, but she worried for the boy's well-being. Hopefully, Dr. Noah and his *Englisch* friend would be able to guide Kade on how to tend to Tyler.

She adjusted the tall, propane floor lights, one on either side of the roomy kitchen. Then she lit the two white candles in clear glass votives that she'd placed on the table. Everything was ready. She had just enough time to reread Milo's letter that had arrived earlier. But no matter how many times she read it, she couldn't shake her recent doubt that he would ever actually show up. She wanted to believe him. She needed to believe him. Her faith in Milo had been slipping, and along with it, her faith in God's will for her—a sin far greater than her heart could bear. She would need to pray harder that she not be tempted to doubt His plan for her. *God is great, and all things are of Your will*, she silently prayed.

She pulled Milo's letter from the kitchen drawer where she placed it earlier and unfolded the single piece of paper.

My Dear Sadie,

I hope that you are doing gut and that you are staying warm during the kalt wedder. Soon I will be traveling to see you and will finally be able to hold you in my arms. The spring will not arrive fast enough for me. I spend my afternoons working to ready my farm for a visit from you someday, but lately it has made wet on many days in the week.

God continues to bless my new business with more and more customers. Each morning, after tending to the animals, I am able to work in the barn on furniture the Englisch have ordered. It pleases me to work with my hands and be able to make a necessary living. I finished the cedar chest I have been working on for John, the one I wrote to you about. He is most anxious to surprise his wife with it.

Church service will be at my home this Sunday. Mei sisters, Mary and Rachel, will prepare the meal for afterwards, along with mei mamm.

I must go for now, but I will write to you again very soon. You are in my thoughts and prayers.

Em Gott Sei Friede,
Milo

"And God's peace to you as well," Sadie said aloud. She tapped the envelope against her hand a few times, then folded it and put it back in the envelope. *Hmm.* His letters were growing shorter and less enthusiastic, which matched her attitude. Maybe Milo was tiring of their correspondence.

She sighed, and then began to mash the potatoes. Moments later, there was a knock at the door.

———————

Lillian parked her buggy and walked up the dirt driveway to Lizzie's small farmhouse. It was set so far back in the woods you wouldn't know a house was even back there. She'd offered to drop off the bread Sadie had baked for Lizzie this morning because it was on her way home from Sadie's shop.

Surely Lizzie won't need more bread for a few days. As much as she enjoyed the days she worked at Treasures of the Heart, she was always behind on her household chores for that day. Plus she'd stayed late at the shop today to finish reorganizing the quilts by price, a project she shouldn't have started so late in the afternoon. There would be plenty to do when she got home, especially since the baby was sick as well. She'd been up with Anna the past two nights. She was glad Sadie had baked bread for Lizzie and that she didn't have to tackle that chore when she got home.

She knocked on Lizzie's door and heard movement from within the house. Lizzie had to be home. When there was no answer, she knocked again and waited. It was already dark, and the temperature was dipping into the twenties. *Hurry, Lizzie. I'm freezing out here.*

Lizzie hadn't owned a horse and buggy in years and relied on her friends to cart her to town when she was feeling up to it, which wasn't often these days. She mainly stayed to herself. They all felt sorry for Lizzie. Lillian couldn't imagine how lonely she must get.

Definitely movement inside. Lillian pounded hard on the door, and then paced the porch while rubbing her hands together, thankful for her thick, black gloves. From the west end of the porch, she could see a light coming from her grandparents' farmhouse across the pasture. Mom was probably already preparing Grandpa's supper, something fabulous, no doubt. Lillian wished she could head over there, sit down, and eat a hot meal with her mother and grandpa. But too much to do at home.

She'd left a prepared pot of stew in the refrigerator for Samuel and David. She always left something easy for them to heat up on the days she went to the shop. Samuel was a stickler about eating at four thirty.

Her stomach growled. She raised her hand to pound on the

door again, but stopped when she heard footsteps in the kitchen. *Thank goodness.*

"I'm coming, dear," she heard Lizzie call out. "I've been waiting for you!"

Huh?

The wooden door swung open, and Lizzie was grinning from ear to ear. A silly little grin that vanished the moment she saw Lillian.

"What are you doing here, Lillian?" Lizzie didn't open the screen door or invite her in from the cold.

"I brought Sadie's bread for you." Lillian lifted up the plastic bag she had hung across her forearm, with two loaves of bread inside.

Lizzie pushed the screen door open and almost ripped the bag as she pulled it off of Lillian's arm. "*Danki,* Lillian. So kind of you to drop it off." Then she let the screen door slam, smiled briefly, and started to push the wooden door closed.

"Wait!" Lillian said.

"*Ya?* What is it, dear?" Lizzie peeked around the wooden door. Her gray hair was tightly tucked beneath her *kapp,* and she was dressed plain, as she always was. But something was different. Her eyes seemed brighter, her face less wrinkled.

"Is everything all right, Lizzie?"

"*Ya, ya. Wunderbaar gut.*" And she slammed the door closed.

Lillian just stood there. Many times, Lizzie had declined offers of company, but Lillian had just assumed she wasn't feeling well. Quite clearly, Lizzie was feeling mighty fine today. That was the most zest she'd seen in Lizzie's demeanor since she'd known the woman. *Well, that's good,* she thought, as she finally turned to walk down the porch steps. Surprising, but good.

Her feet had just hit the snow when she heard whistling coming from the side of the house. A body rounded the corner, but it was too dark to see. She strained to focus on the approaching mass.

"Lizzie girl, I'm here!" a loud voice bellowed.

Lillian's jaw dropped as the male figure came into view. At about the same time, the man dropped a handful of flowers to the ground.

Lillian closed her mouth, but her eyes were wide.

"Lilly, what in the world are you doin' here?"

Lillian folded her arms across her chest. "I might ask you the same thing, Grandpa!"

8

AFTER INTRODUCTIONS HAD BEEN MADE, SADIE PLACED the turkey roast, mashed potatoes, and green beans on the table while Carley poured everyone a glass of tea.

"This looks wonderful, Sadie," Noah's friend Evan said. The balding man had soft, gray eyes beneath gold-rimmed glasses, and a kind expression.

"Danki," Sadie said. She smiled and took a seat at the head of the table, with Carley and Noah on each side of her.

"And this tea is delicious," Evan added after he took a drink from his glass. "Very sweet, and I like that. The sweeter the better." He smiled.

"We call it meadow tea," Sadie explained. "It grows wild in meadows along the creek."

Evan nodded his approval. Tyler and Kade sat on Carley's bench, and Noah's friends sat beside Noah on the opposite side. Sadie explained that the Amish pray silently before meals and asked if everyone would bow their heads in a prayer of thanksgiving for the food before them.

When they all raised their heads, Evan's wife, Shelly, was the first one to speak. "And it smells fabulous as well," she said.

Noah loaded his plate with mashed potatoes, and everyone

followed by serving themselves whatever was nearby, and then passed each dish to the right.

Kade spooned food onto Tyler's plate, and then his own, each time an item was handed to him. He kept a fearful eye on Tyler.

Amid the small talk, Tyler's hands were all over the place—picking up utensils and then putting them down, sticking a finger in his mashed potatoes, tapping his piece of bread on the table, and then spilling his tea—mostly in Kade's lap.

As the liquid rolled across the table, Tyler began to scream. Kade sat with his mouth open for a moment and stared down at a lap full of tea. Then he shook his head. "I knew this was a bad idea. I apologize to everyone, and . . ." He attempted to calm his son, but Tyler flung himself onto the floor and continued to cry.

Shelly, a tiny little woman with short brown hair, jumped up first and ran around the table to Tyler. Kade had turned around on the bench and was staring hopelessly at his son. Sadie watched Kade's face redden with embarrassment.

Shelly squatted down and reached her hand out toward Tyler, but she pulled back quickly when Kade practically yelled, "Watch out! He bites."

Sadie narrowed her eyes in Kade's direction and fought the urge to tell him that Tyler is not a dog. Then she got up and walked to where Shelly was squatting and joined her. "Tyler likes tapioca pudding. And if Tyler is a *gut* boy, I have some saved just for him."

"Is he . . ." Shelly glanced up at Kade, who was still sitting on the bench, facing them.

"Autistic," Kade answered. "Again, I apologize. We should probably go and . . ."

Tyler stopped crying, and then sat up and looked at Sadie. Sort of. His eyes darted around the room. "Hug, hug, hug."

Instinctively, Sadie started to wrap her arms around him, but she stopped when she recalled how he'd pulled away from her when she was with him at the cottage.

"He actually wants a hug," Kade said. He leaned down toward the boy, but Sadie beat him to it and pulled Tyler into a hug.

Kade dabbed at his soaked blue jeans, and then put the wet napkin on his plate. "I think we'd best go. I apologize for—"

"Nonsense!" Shelly said. "We have three children close to his age at home with my mother-in-law. Rest assured, we've seen bigger messes than this." She smiled in Kade's direction. "You absolutely must stay."

What a lovely person, Sadie thought, as she continued to hug Tyler.

"Heck, I've had a whole plate of food dumped in my lap before," Evan added with a chuckle. "Did she mention that two of our angels are twins? Double trouble on some days." He laughed again.

Kade still looked extremely embarrassed by the whole display, but he managed a smile.

Tyler continued to snuggle against Sadie, and she whispered in his ear. "Tyler, you're a *gut* boy."

He eased out of her arms and smiled. "Pudding."

"*Ya*, pudding for Tyler after he eats his supper. Can you do that?" His big, blue eyes looked through her, but his smile seemed to say yes. He stood up and climbed back into his spot on the bench beside Kade.

"He's adorable," Shelly said. Then she grinned at Kade. "But you're soaked, huh? I've been there."

"I have some clothes in the bedroom that might fit you," Sadie said to Kade. He arched questioning brows. "They were my husband's," she added. Then she couldn't help but grin. "I'll go see about some dry pants for you."

"No, Sadie. Let's all eat," Kade said. "Really, I'm fine for now." He spoke in a way that seemed intimate to Sadie, for some reason, as if they were more than just the acquaintances they were. She knew she was blushing, and she was glad when Noah spoke up.

"Did you say Tyler is autistic?" Noah asked Kade once they were all settled and eating again.

Kade swallowed, and then said, "Yes. He is."

"There's a boy about Tyler's age in the Amish community who is autistic," Noah said before turning to Sadie. "Jacob and Martha, those are the parents' names, right?"

"*Ya.*" Sadie waited for Noah to say more. This is what she'd hoped for.

"The boy's name is Amos," Carley added. "Martha has brought him to the clinic a few times for a recurring cold." She paused. "I've gotten to know a lot of the Amish since I work as a receptionist at the clinic."

Noah finished off a bite of turkey roast. "But unlike Tyler, Amos is nonverbal. He doesn't speak at all. Tyler seems to communicate quite well. Is Tyler enrolled in a school that specializes in behavioral therapy?"

"He has been going to a special school." Kade glanced at his son. "I'm afraid I haven't been around Tyler much. I live in Los Angeles, and Tyler lives with his mother in North Carolina." He paused. "Actually, I haven't seen Tyler in six months. I'm not sure exactly how much he understands at this point."

There was an awkward silence as everyone seemed to be wondering about Kade's statement, but Kade must have decided to make the most of having two doctors present. "In my notes from my soon-to-be ex-wife, she says that Tyler has hyperlexia. Can you explain a little about that?"

"Usually autistic children who present with hyperlexia listen selectively. You'd almost think they were deaf if you didn't know otherwise," Noah said. "I noticed that with Amos in my office. But Tyler seems tuned in to what you're saying."

Kade hung on Noah's words. "What about reading? Tyler reads."

"But does he understand what he reads?" Evan asked. "Although I haven't treated any autistic children, it's my understanding that children with hyperlexia show an intense fascination with numbers or letters, but that doesn't mean they can count or read. Or even if they can, it doesn't mean they can comprehend."

Kade paused, rubbed his chin, and seemed to be weighing Evan's comments. "So, he repeats what he reads with no understanding?" Noah had a mouthful and nodded. Kade went on. "That's what it says in my notes from Monica, my ex, but this afternoon, something . . . something happened, and it was—it was odd."

They all waited. But Kade didn't elaborate.

"Tyler's reading skills can help him to develop language, but it's getting him to understand what he's saying that is the hard part," Noah said.

"He certainly understands tapioca pudding," Sadie said affectionately.

"Tyler likes tapioca pudding," Tyler said. Then he smiled in a way that touched Sadie. *How blessed his mother is*, she thought. And Kade too.

"Maybe he understands more than you think," Evan said.

Kade got the strangest look on his face. "Maybe."

An hour later, everyone was still gathered around the table. Tyler was into his third helping of pudding while the others ate shoofly pie and drank coffee. The conversation had drifted from autism to music, and Kade found someone who shared his passion for the subject—Evan. They talked a lot about things to do with music that Sadie didn't know anything about. But watching Kade have such an animated conversation with Evan, often talking with his hands and laughing, made him seem more *real* to Sadie.

Everyone's mood was light, the conversation good, and they all seemed to be having a good time. A successful supper, despite the rocky beginning. Shelly asked lots of questions about the Amish, all of which Sadie gladly answered. She loved to talk about the beliefs of the Amish, their strong faith and plain ways. However, more than once she felt as though she was ministering to herself about the importance of believing all things to be of God's will.

Twice while she was talking, she had looked at Kade and found him staring at her in a way that she found most inappropriate. She had blushed and felt almost . . . flattered. Tonight, she'd pray to cleanse herself of such thoughts.

"*Ach*," she said to Kade when she was clearing the dishes. "I forgot to round you up some clean breeches. You don't want to walk to the cottage like that. You'll freeze for sure."

He waved his hand to shush her, but then quickly jerked the action to a stop. "Sorry," he said. "It's okay, really. I haven't even noticed it. I should probably take Tyler and be on my way."

"Look." Sadie pointed to the couch in her den, where Tyler had been playing with his plastic letters. "He fell asleep."

"You said earlier that your company builds high-rises," Evan said. "If Sadie's not in too big a hurry to get rid of us, I'd like to hear more about that."

Kade turned to Sadie.

"No rush at all," she said much too quickly. "I'll go get you some pants." She hurriedly left the room and retrieved a lit lantern on a table in the den. She headed down the hall to her bedroom and wondered why she felt elated that everyone—particularly Kade—wanted to extend their visit.

Kade stood up from the table. This had turned out to be the best night he'd had in ages. He was looking forward to spending more time with all of them—especially Sadie. Something about that woman seemed to have a soothing effect on him. He hung on her every word when she talked about her strong beliefs, about God's will, and the ways of the Amish. Several times, he recalled what Tyler had said during bath time. It sent a rush of possibilities through his mind. Could turning his life back over to God quiet the unrest in his soul and lead Kade to the calm existence he longed for? Was God trying to communicate to him through Tyler? *Is God the answer?*

He wasn't sure about any of it, but for the first time in a long time, he felt a sense of hope that seemed to center around the prospect of a relationship with God.

Sadie's wooden table with modest china hardly compared to the tables he'd dined at over the years. Senators, heads of state, religious leaders, and those comparable in power only to others in Kade's elite circle. And yet, it was the best dinner party he could remember attending.

He thought back to dinner in his household when he was growing up. Formality was something that had been handed down from generation to generation. Dressing nicely for the meal was a requirement, and if a child made an outburst at a dinner party, like Tyler's this evening, a nanny would have rushed him away. Kade was twelve before he realized that everyone didn't have live-in housekeepers and nannies.

Tonight the warmth and kindness he felt were real and heartfelt, the conversation was appealing, and the people held no pretenses. He smiled.

"Excuse me, please," he said to everyone.

The hallway was dark as he walked to where he thought the bathroom was. He paused at the first closed door on his right, and then gently pushed it open. Darkness. He remembered Sadie telling Shelly that a lantern was lit in the bathroom. He quietly pulled the door shut and took a few more steps down the hallway to the next door on his right. It was slightly open, and he could see light inside.

He pushed the door wide and walked right into Sadie holding a lantern in one hand, a pair of slacks in the other. They barely bumped, and she stepped back and lifted the lantern to see his face.

Kade could certainly see her face in the dim light—soft shades of ivory skin and blue eyes sparked with indefinable emotion. A strand of wavy red hair had lost its place beneath her prayer covering and draped across her face. She didn't move, didn't breathe, when Kade gently brushed the strand from her cheek. For what seemed like an eternity, they stood in the threshold of what evidently was not the bathroom and gazed into each other's eyes.

"Here," she finally said. She pushed the pants toward him and slowly eased her way around him and was gone.

What just happened?

———

Sadie rushed down the hall to rejoin her guests.

What was that?

Everyone was laughing and carrying on about their high school years. It was a conversation Sadie couldn't add to, since Amish schooling only ran through the eighth grade.

"Sadie, this is way past your bedtime, I'm sure," Carley said when Sadie took a seat at the head of the table. Only coffee cups and empty pie plates lined the table now, and she fought the urge to yawn.

"It's fine," she said. "I enjoy you all being here."

"Well, it was a wonderful meal," Noah said.

The others all commented about the food, the company, and what a nice night it was. But Sadie barely heard them as her eyes met Kade's when he reentered the room. Then she couldn't help but grin. Ben had been a tall man, almost six foot, five inches. Kade was tall, too, but lacked about three inches of Ben's height, and the black pants dragged the floor.

Kade smiled back at her. "At least they're dry," he said as he glanced down at the floor.

"Tell us a little about your business, Kade, and then we're going to let Sadie get some rest," Evan said. "From what she said earlier, her day starts very early, and I know we're keeping her up too late."

Sadie shook her head and repeated, "It's fine."

Kade glanced at Tyler, who was still sleeping soundly, and then he sat down at the table, but not before giving Sadie a look that seemed to confirm that something had happened in the hallway.

Ridiculous. She pulled her eyes from his.

"Not much to tell," Kade said modestly. "We build high-rise office buildings. We're currently working on two projects, one in Dallas and one in Chicago."

Evan rubbed his chin. "What did you say your last name was?"

"Saunders," Kade said.

Evan's eyes grew wide and assessing. "As in Saunders Real Estate and Development?"

"Yes," Kade answered, as if it was no big matter.

Evan sat up a little taller and looked at Noah. "Do you realize who we're dining with?"

Kade lowered his head, and Sadie could tell he wasn't comfortable with the direction the conversation was going.

Noah smiled. "I do now." He turned to Kade. "I recognize

you now from a recent issue of *Forbes* magazine. You were on the cover."

Kade forced a smile and nodded.

"Uh, no," Evan said. He shook his head. "I didn't see that. I saw Kade on a cover of *Newsweek* a while back."

Shelly's thick lashes opened and closed, her green eyes wide with astonishment. "Good grief," she said softly. "I read an article about you too. And there was a picture of you and the president."

"Of the United States?" Sadie brought her hand to her chest. *Who is this man?*

They all smiled at Sadie's outburst—all but Kade, who shrugged, as if having your picture taken with the president was nothing impressive.

Sadie glanced around her plain kitchen, void of electricity, modern conveniences, and all the things she was sure Kade was used to—things far fancier than Sadie had ever even seen.

Then, as if Carley was reading Sadie's mind, Carley asked, "Kade, what in the world brought you to Lancaster County for three months? This has to be incredibly different from what you are, um . . . used to."

Kade folded his hands on the table and slowly looked around at each of them. He laughed in such a way that it didn't seem genuine, and he shook his head. Then he focused on Sadie and spoke the one word Sadie couldn't have guessed if she had bet all the peas in a summer garden.

"God," Kade said softly. He shifted his gaze to Tyler for a long moment. Then glanced around at each of them again and smiled.

"Seriously?" Shelly asked after a few awkward moments of silence.

Evan twisted his mouth to one side and seemed equally curious about Kade's response. Noah and Carley looked at each other and smiled. They were so in love, the type of love blessed by God. How Sadie's heart ached for such a love as theirs.

Sadie locked eyes with Kade, and as it was in the hallway, she had trouble looking away. So she didn't. Their eyes were still fused when Kade answered Shelly. "Yes, seriously," he said. Then he paused to glance at Tyler again. "And I don't think I realized it until today."

"I think that's as good a reason as any." Noah smiled, dabbed his mouth with his napkin, and then stood up. "I think we need to let Sadie get some sleep."

Carley, Evan, and Shelly all stood up. The two couples hugged Sadie and thanked her repeatedly for a wonderful supper. Kade rose and shook each of their hands, but oddly he made no attempt to arouse Tyler and be on his way home.

"Don't forget Tyler," Sadie teased. She pointed toward the small, tan couch in her den.

"Not likely." Kade stood beside Sadie and waved to everyone as they walked out the door.

She waved good-bye to her guests and attempted to smile, in between darting her eyes at Kade. *He can't stay.*

Then Kade closed the door, as if he owned the place.

Stunned, Sadie turned to face him, but backed up a step when his eyes met hers in a way that was becoming more and more unsettling. She was terribly embarrassed that her guests, especially Carley and Noah, saw that Kade did not leave.

"I'll help you with Tyler." Sadie backed up another step, drew her eyes from his, and headed toward the couch.

"Sadie, wait," Kade whispered.

"*Ya?*"

"I was hoping maybe you and I could talk for a little while." He looked quite silly in Ben's pants. "I promise not to keep you up much longer," he added when she shook her head.

"No. It's not proper for you to be here. You have to go." She edged toward Tyler.

"Wait," he said again. "Who's going to know?"

"I will know," she said in a loud whisper. "And God."

"That's what I want to talk to you about." He moved closer. Much too close.

Sadie folded her arms across her chest. "You want to talk to me about God?"

"Yes. Something happened today, and I need to talk to someone about it, and . . ." Sadie could hear his shirt pocket vibrating, and Kade pulled out the tiniest portable phone she'd ever seen. "Excuse me a minute. It's a friend of mine from L.A."

Kade walked toward the kitchen, and Sadie waited in the den.

"What's up, Val?" Kade asked from around the corner.

Sadie continued to wait. It was quiet for a bit. She squatted down beside the couch and gently touched Tyler's back. So sweet. She wondered how the boy had managed to sleep through all the talking in the next room. The fire was dwindling. She'd need to put another log on before she went to bed. She sighed and wondered how soon that would be. *It is completely inappropriate for him to be here.*

Kade rounded the corner and stopped in the middle of the room. His expression caused Sadie to stand up and take a step toward him. "Kade?"

He put his hand over his mouth and looked down, and then blinked hard.

"Kade, what is it?" She took another step toward him.

His head slowly lifted. "I have to go."

Sadie would have thought, *Thank goodness*, but something was wrong. Terribly wrong. "I'll help you get Tyler," she said, although she didn't move.

"No." He ran a hand through his hair. "I mean, I have to go. I have to leave Lancaster County. I have a flight out Friday morning. Me and Tyler have to go."

He walked to the couch and gently lifted Tyler into his arms, and then buried his face in the sleeping boy's shoulder and stood there holding his son.

Sadie didn't know what to say, what to do. She waited.

Kade lifted his head, and even in the dimly lit room, Sadie could see his eyes glassed over with unspoken pain.

"Kade?" She was now right in front of him, staring into tear-filled eyes that threatened to spill at any moment. She touched his arm, a gesture she wouldn't have considered just five minutes earlier.

"It's Monica," he said softly.

"Monica?"

"Tyler's mother." He stared into Sadie's eyes. "She's dead."

9

SADIE BUNDLED UP FOR THE BELOW-FREEZING TEM-
perature and walked onto the porch. Ominous clouds hung low
as night gave way to day, and Sadie knew that this morning's
weather was the best it would be for several days. The temperature would drop throughout the day and overnight before several
feet of snow fell.

Last night, Kade had left immediately after telling her the
news about Tyler's mother. He'd clung tightly to Tyler and, with
tears in his eyes, mumbled something about a car accident. When
the front door closed, Sadie had wept, and then prayed for both
of them. They'd be leaving tomorrow morning, and Sadie couldn't
help but wonder if she'd ever see them again.

Sadie imagined Kade had scores of people to help him with
Tyler when he returned home to Los Angeles. A man of his
wealth would surely enroll Tyler in a fine school. But would he
ever really get to know that precious child? She was busy speculating about the two of them when she stepped onto the snow
and headed toward the shop. The women had decided to meet
and devise a plan to check on each other over the next several
days. Sadie couldn't remember a storm of such proportion being
forecast in Lancaster County. If the weather predictions held
true, blizzard conditions were on the way.

She was the first one to arrive at the shop, so she pulled the blinds and started to light the heaters. Lillian and Sarah Jane walked in, and Sadie walked toward them.

"Sadie, have you been crying again?" Lillian asked. "Still no word from Milo?"

"No, I did hear from Milo. It was a short letter, but a letter." She shrugged and then sighed. "But I did shed a few tears last night."

Sadie proceeded to tell Lillian and Sarah Jane the events of the prior evening.

"That's *baremlich*," Lillian said. "That poor child. I guess Mr. Saunders will be getting to know his son on a permanent basis." She shook her head.

"I reckon," Sadie said. She wondered if Tyler would understand the loss or not.

"Well, I have a story that might cheer you up." Lillian smiled at her mother, and then looked back at Sadie. "It's about Grandpa."

Sarah Jane shook her head. "Silly old goose," she said fondly.

Sadie listened with amusement as Lillian told her about finding Jonas at Lizzie's house. "But you think it is *gut*, no?" she asked when Lillian had finished. "Lizzie is a dear woman, and of course, I love Jonas."

"I think it's *wunderbaar gut* that Grandpa has someone to spend time with and play chess," Lillian said. "I was just . . . shocked."

"That must be where Pop sneaks off to sometimes, those times when he is on foot." Sarah Jane hung her black cape on the rack and untied her bonnet. "Because he can walk across the pasture to get to Lizzie's house."

"Does it bother you about—I mean, do you care since . . ." Sadie tried to reword what she was trying to say. "Your pop was married to Irma Rose, to your *mamm*, for a long time."

"No, no, no," Sarah Jane said. "I'm happy for him to have someone to spend time with. The only thing that upsets me is when he takes the buggy or takes off on foot without telling me where he's going." She chuckled. "I guess he's mostly at Lizzie's."

Sadie and Lillian locked eyes, both knowing that Lizzie's house wasn't always the place Jonas went.

Lizzie had been watching the clock for nearly forty minutes. Jonas said eight o'clock. She reached for the battery-operated contraption he'd given her yesterday, before he'd been caught sneaking to her place later that afternoon.

She chuckled. Jonas seemed to enjoy the sneaking around more than the games of chess they played, always trying to keep his daughter and granddaughter on their toes. She'd told him repeatedly not to be worrying them in such a way. Lizzie was glad Sarah Jane and Lillian knew about their friendship now. Maybe she'd get to see more of Jonas. How she loved that feisty old man. It had been forty years since she'd loved that way. The good Lord took her Johnny much too soon. But after all this time, Lizzie had Jonas.

She tried not to pay it too much mind when Jonas called her Irma Rose every now and then, or when he seemed to think she *was* Irma Rose and would recall times they'd spent together. He'd certainly loved his Irma Rose. She turned up the volume, twisting the dial on the walkie-talkie just the way Jonas had showed her. She laughed when she heard his voice.

"Breaker, breaker. You there, Lizzie?"

She laughed harder. "Oh, my!" she said aloud to herself as she fumbled to push her own talk button. "Jonas, is that you?" And, as he'd instructed, she released her hold on the button.

It was quiet for a few moments. "Who else would it be, Lizzie?"

She pictured Jonas at home, with his big, bushy, gray brows edged upward. And she was thrilled that he called her by her name. Lizzie put her hand to her chest and smiled, feeling more alive than she'd felt in a long time. They'd only been spending time together for two months, but during that time, her arthritis had been better, her appetite had improved, and she had a kick in her step that she didn't have before she fell in love with Jonas Miller. Lizzie hadn't shared her feelings, but surely he knew.

"I reckon the weather's gonna be frightful the next few days." Lizzie released the button. She dreaded being cooped up at home with no visitors, no way to leave—and no Jonas to keep her company.

"Gonna miss me, now, aren'tcha?" She heard him chuckle.

Yes, I am. "I'll miss beating you at chess."

"Has that ever happened?" Lizzie heard him snort out a laugh.

"I reckon it's happened several times, Jonas Miller!" She threw her head back and laughed. She felt like a schoolgirl who had a crush on the most wonderful boy.

"You didn't forget our promise we made to each other, did you, now?"

Lizzie pressed her lips together, knowing the serious nature of the promise she and Jonas had made to each other a while back.

They didn't speak of if often, but with each passing day, it seemed more and more important. "No, Jonas, I did not forget."

She could only hope that *he* wouldn't forget either.

Kade watched with fascination as Tyler read the Bible. And he waited with nervous anticipation for Tyler to reveal some sort of message for Kade. But then Kade shook his head and wondered if he'd made too big a deal about the verses Tyler had spoken before. Probably a coincidence, repeating what he'd read.

If that was his line of thinking, why did he continue to encourage Tyler to read the Scriptures? Tyler was content reading, but his son didn't say a word. Kade was jarred from his musings by his cell phone.

"Hey, partner. Monica's parents have made the arrangements," Val said. "Friday at two o'clock in her hometown. You're going to be pushing it to get there from the airport in time. I had Tina at your office arrange for a car to pick you up. Which reminds me, should we go ahead and have someone fly to Pennsylvania to drive your car back? I'm sure you have no intentions of returning there."

Kade still couldn't believe Monica was gone. He had loved her so much at one time, but his heart ached more from those memories than from missing her now. "I haven't really thought about it."

"Is Tyler going to do all right on a plane?"

"I hadn't really thought about that either." Kade knew that was something he'd better think about now. "I didn't see anything in Monica's notes about Tyler *not* flying."

"Listen, I went ahead and took it upon myself to call Penelope and told her to go ahead and start interviewing nannies. And what about a school for Tyler? Do you want him to live at home and attend a special school, or do you want to send him to a school with in-house boarding?"

"What?" This was all happening way too fast. "I mean, I don't know, Val. I haven't had time to think about all these things." His housekeeper, Penelope, had been with him for years, but she wasn't qualified or energetic enough at her age to take care of Tyler. "I don't want him living away at a school, though. I want him with me."

"You still want a nanny, though. Right?"

Kade took a deep breath. "We can talk about all that later." He glanced around the simply furnished cottage, the cozy fire, and Tyler sitting quietly and reading on the floor. And he could see through the window that it was starting to snow. It was like something out of a Thomas Kinkade painting. He wasn't ready to leave.

"Does Tyler seem to understand what happened?" Val asked.

"No. I tried to explain it to him, but he didn't seem to comprehend what I was saying." And that truly saddened Kade. Monica was his mother, and he wished for her sake that Tyler had some sort of feelings about her death, even if only mild ones, to honor the woman Monica had tried to be. On the other hand, he felt relief that Tyler wasn't grieving from the loss.

"So, what do you think about having someone fly there and drive your car back?" Val asked again. "That way you wouldn't have to go back there."

Something about that idea bothered Kade. He couldn't put his finger on it, but Sadie's face flashed before him. He recalled the way they had looked at each other in the hallway, and again in the kitchen. Something about her stirred things inside him. Not manly things, as he would have expected, but more of a spiritual whirlwind. It was confusing, and not something he was sure he was ready to walk away from for good.

He remembered the way Sadie had talked about her relationship with God during dinner. She talked about Him as if He were a close friend of hers, someone she chatted with regularly.

"No, I'll come back to get the car."

"I'm so sorry about all this, Kade."

Kade was sure he heard Val's voice crack, and it touched him that his friend truly felt for his situation.

Val filled him in on a few more details, and they said their good-byes.

Sadie and Lillian closed all the shutters outside the shop in preparation for the storm. Lillian and Sarah Jane said they would check on Lizzie on their way home. Sadie imagined they were curious about Lizzie's friendship with Jonas and wanted to take the opportunity to talk with her. She smiled when she recalled the story about Lillian catching Jonas coming to Lizzie's. How sweet if they were courting at that age, she thought.

Milo's letter was on the kitchen table when she walked into the house through the kitchen door. She didn't have an urge to read it. Instead, she pulled open her kitchen drawer and tossed it inside. It landed on top of some other household papers. It didn't seem to warrant a place upstairs with her other letters, which she had treasured for so long. *Too long.*

Sadie poured herself a glass of meadow tea. She'd just sat down at the table when a loud pounding on the front door caused her to jump up.

She hurried around the corner of the kitchen and flung the door open. Snowflakes dotted a heavy, brown quilt in Kade's arms. "Kade, get that child in here," she said. "What are you doing out in this weather?"

He pulled the quilt back from Tyler's face. The boy was smiling from ear to ear. "Fun!"

Sadie laughed. "Your *daed* bringing you all bundled up out into the snow is fun, no?" She leaned down closer to Tyler.

"The faster I clomped across the snow, the more he bounced, and the louder I could hear him giggling." He set Tyler on the floor, and the boy immediately wrapped his arms around Sadie's legs.

"Hug," he said.

Sadie squatted down and embraced Tyler. "I *lieb* hugging you," she said, nuzzling him closer.

After a few moments, Kade eased onto the couch. Sadie pulled away from Tyler and walked to a rocker on the other side of the room. Tyler followed, and she was surprised when Tyler crawled into her lap.

"Tyler really seems to like you," Kade said, and then frowned. "More than he likes me."

"He's used to having a mother, and . . ." She stopped. "I'm so sorry for your loss, Kade. And for Tyler."

Kade leaned back against the couch. "I loved her very much at one time." He paused and looked hard at Sadie. "But now all I have are memories of that love. I haven't loved her—in that way—for a very long time." He shook his head. "But it's still painful to think of this happening to her." His eyes shifted to Tyler's tiny face, burrowed against Sadie's chest. "I don't think Tyler understands."

Sadie could see the despair etched across his face. "What brings you out in this weather?" she asked when Kade seemed permanently lost in thought. She thought briefly about being alone with him, or at least without the company of other adults, but she suspected these were special circumstances.

"I think Tyler is missing one of his plastic letters," Kade said. He rubbed his stubbly chin.

"I don't know how he knows this, but every time he dumps them from the lunch box, he starts to cry. He keeps holding up the *E* letter, and when I took inventory, it appears that there are four of every letter, but only three *E*s."

Dark circles under Kade's eyes indicated he might not have slept much last night. "Maybe it's in between the cushions on the couch," she said.

Kade began to search the couch, lifting the cushions slightly as he went.

Sadie glanced out the window. Heavy blankets of snow were falling. "Kade, you are going to have a *baremlich* time traveling. It will be much worse by morning. You might not be able to get out."

"I was thinking about that. Maybe I should leave for the airport this afternoon and get a room near there."

Tyler laid his head on Sadie's shoulder, and she gave him a squeeze. "He is such a precious gift from God. You're so very blessed, Kade."

Kade continued to search for the missing letter, running his hand along the part of the couch where the back met with the seat. "Why don't you have any children, Sadie? You're so good with Tyler and all, and I was just wondering. I mean, I know your husband passed, but . . ." He paused and looked up at her. "Sorry. It's none of my business."

"Ben and I wanted children very much. God didn't see fit to bless us with any before Ben died." This was a conversation she didn't want to have, especially with Kade.

"Well, you would have been a great mom." Kade smiled. "Maybe you still will someday. I understand you have a suitor."

"What?" Who had he been talking to?

"Your elderly friend, Jonas. He told me about a man from Texas who is coming to see you soon."

"Ah, yes," Sadie said. She didn't feel the need to elaborate and looked away from his questioning eyes.

"I hope it works out for you."

Maybe it was the way he said it, but somehow Sadie felt the comment was not genuine. "*Danki*," she answered anyway, and then stood up. She attempted to put Tyler down, but he clung to her neck, so she balanced him on her hip.

Kade stood up, holding the missing *E*. He edged closer to her and gazed into her eyes in a way that he surely shouldn't. Her mouth went dry, and she could feel the flush in her neck traveling upward to her cheeks. When he gently grabbed her forearms, she couldn't have moved if she wanted to. But just when she was sure the unthinkable was about to happen, Kade's eyes drifted from hers. He leaned down and kissed his son on the head.

"Here's your letter, Tyler," he said, still holding one of Sadie's arms. He offered Tyler the letter with his other hand. Then he leaned around his son and kissed her on the cheek. His lips lingered against her skin, and Sadie's heart pounded and pulsed as a wave of panic overtook her. Even with Tyler safely between them, she abruptly pulled away. The feel of a man so close to her, his tenderness, his lips . . .

Oh no. Sadie took an abrupt step backward, and he was forced to drop his hand from her arm. She knew her eyes were reflective of the sinful thoughts racing through her mind. "Please leave," she said softly, refusing to look him in the eye.

"Sadie," he whispered. He took a step closer, but she stepped back further. "I guess, in my world, it's acceptable to make such a gesture of friendship. I'm sorry if I offended you in any way."

Sadie knew that it was not so much his gesture that was inappropriate, as much as her reaction to the feel of his lips on her cheek.

"I won't let it happen again." He stepped back and held his palms up.

She nodded, but wondered if he could keep his word. Or if she wanted him to.

And that thought terrified her.

It was an hour later when Kade loaded the suitcase in his car. He buckled Tyler in the backseat and couldn't stop thinking about Sadie. Evidently, his mild gesture of affection rattled her quite a bit. If she'd only known how badly he'd wanted to kiss her on the lips, she would have appreciated the restraint he used.

He pulled the car out of the barn, edged his way backward in the snow, and then turned the Mercedes around. Maybe he should have left earlier. Much earlier. Large snowflakes froze against the windshield and made it almost impossible to see. He turned up the heat and defrost in the car and headed down the driveway. When he turned onto Black Horse Road, he began to worry that this was a mistake. The snow was much worse today than it was the night they'd looked for Jonas.

He could feel his back tires spinning, and the trees on either side of the road blew wickedly in the wind.

And it's supposed to be worse tomorrow? He couldn't imagine. If he could make it to Lincoln Highway, the snow plows would be in force, and it shouldn't be too terribly bad on the way to the airport. He hoped.

Kade pushed on the gas in an effort to free his spinning tires. But he wasn't moving. "Oh, great!"

"Oh, great!" Tyler echoed from the backseat.

Kade didn't know anything about driving in this slush, but as he revved the engine a final time, one thing was clear. He wasn't going anywhere.

10

SADIE STEPPED ONTO THE PORCH TO RETRIEVE A LOG for the fire.

"*Ach!*" The biting wind nipped at her exposed cheeks and whipped through her cape as she heaved a log into her arms. She was grateful that Kade had replenished the wood stack on the porch before he left. He'd exited so abruptly with Tyler that she didn't have a chance to thank him.

After their encounter, Kade had told her he would be back to get his car and other personal items, but he wasn't sure when. Then he quickly left. But his tender kiss on her cheek replayed again and again in her mind, stirring things inside Sadie that brought on a wave of confusion.

A flurry of snow blew underneath the porch rafters and dusted her dark clothing with sprinkles of white powder. But it was nothing compared to the swirl of activity beyond the porch—whirlpools of wind and snow twirling beneath graying skies, as if churning out one last dance before the lights went out. She flung the door open to go back inside.

"Sadie!"

It was faint, but she heard it—a man's voice. She stopped before crossing the threshold, twisted her head around, and peered into the wintry mix, scanning the snow-covered land. Her eyes tried to focus on . . . *Kade?*

Adrenaline pumped through her and rendered her oblivious to the frigid air as Kade came into view amid the thickening snowfall, carrying Tyler. She dropped the log next to the pile. Inside, she fumbled as she pulled on her boots, gloves, and heavy coat, then bolted out the door and down the porch steps to meet Kade and Tyler.

"What happened?" He was white as the snow and looked like he might keel over any second from exhaustion. She couldn't even see Tyler all bundled up within the same brown blanket as before.

Sadie coaxed them inside, then led them to the fireplace. Kade gently pulled the blanket from around Tyler, who looked around. "Warm yourselves," she said.

Kade's teeth were chattering as he held his hands in front of the fireplace. Tyler began to pace the living room.

"The storm is already too bad. My car got stuck," Kade said. He shook his head. "No one is going anywhere in this. I waited too long to leave."

"I'll go make *kaffi* for us and cocoa for Tyler." Sadie unbuttoned her coat on the way to the kitchen and hung it on the rack. The storm had turned the sky prematurely dark, so she lit a lantern and placed it on the counter.

When she returned with their warm drinks, Kade was putting his gloves back on. "I need to go back to the car and get the suitcase. Tyler won't be happy for long without his letters, plus the black binder is in there, and everything else." He sighed with dread. "Can you keep an eye on Tyler?"

"Of course."

Tyler continued to shuffle aimlessly around the den, clapping his hands.

"It says in my notes clapping his hands is self-stimulatory behavior," Kade said.

Sadie wasn't familiar with Kade's *Englisch* words, but she nodded. The clapping seemed to be entertaining the boy.

"He is going to realize something is missing soon," Kade said. "I'll hurry back."

Sadie peered out the window. "It's almost completely dark outside, and yet still early."

Kade didn't respond, but seemed to be mentally preparing himself to venture back out into the storm. He rubbed his gloved hands together, took a deep breath, and pushed the door from the den open.

Sadie silently prayed that God would keep him safe. Then she brightened the room by placing two more lanterns on opposite sides of the den.

Kade was only gone for a few minutes when she noticed Tyler becoming agitated. The boy's lips curved downward, and he began to run his hands through his hair, causing the light-brown locks to stand straight up.

"Tyler, do you want to read for a bit?" Sadie sat down on the couch and hoped that Tyler would do the same. After a few minutes, he did. Sadie brought the lantern closer and handed him the Bible she kept on the table. She watched him slowly turn the pages, almost as if he was searching for something.

With the boy quiet and occupied, Sadie's thoughts turned to Kade and how different Kade's life would be now, raising his son full-time. She tried to envision Kade's home, most likely filled with expensive furniture and trinkets. Such a handsome man, too, probably with many *Englisch* women pursuing him in his home city.

She touched her cheek and recalled the gentle way he'd kissed her, and then forced herself to think about Milo. *I'm tired of being alone, Lord.* Spring wasn't long to come. Surely Milo would be here.

But Sadie knew that it was more than just lack of a man in her life. Questioning God's will was causing her to feel an emptiness that went beyond loneliness. Almost as if she were slowly losing a treasured friend, or not nurturing a relationship that was vital to her well-being.

Tyler was still flipping pages, and Sadie watched him begin to turn them slower as he reached the book of Job, and then the book of Psalms. He ran a finger along each line of tiny print, and Sadie felt sad that Tyler probably had no understanding of what he was reading, these words to live by. But she also knew that God had a special place in His kingdom for children like Tyler, a reserved seat for His precious little ones who perhaps didn't have the privilege of understanding His love for them.

Sadie leaned her head back against the couch and sighed. She felt guilty that she *was* able to understand God's love for her, but yet she was seeing fit to question His will. Her heart was heavy, and she feared she'd never find true happiness again. Hope seemed to be slipping away, little by little. *I want to believe, Lord, that happiness is coming for me. Please give me the courage and strength to always know that Your will shall be done.*

Tyler shifted his weight on the couch, and Sadie turned her

head in his direction. He stopped scanning the pages, his small finger parked near the upper-left corner of page 349 of the Old Testament. "Be of good courage," Tyler said slowly. "And he shall strengthen your heart, all ye that hope in the Lord."

Sadie eyed the young boy with wondrous speculation as chill bumps rose on both her arms. "What?" she whispered, unsure if she'd heard him correctly. But Tyler's head was reburied in the pages of the Good Book.

She was still thinking about Tyler's statement when Kade returned. He heaved through the door, slinging snow everywhere, then dropped the suitcase and moved quickly toward the fireplace. "It is unbelievable outside," he said through chattering teeth. He pulled his gloves off and held his palms to the fire.

Sadie couldn't speak as her thoughts spun into a thick mass of bafflement. Speculations about Tyler's words swirled in her head, visions of Kade's kiss lingered in her mind, and she fought to ward off the worry in her heart.

Kade pulled off his coat and sat down on the couch beside Tyler. "Did everything go okay?" He steered his eyes in Sadie's direction.

"*Ya.*" Sadie eased into one of the rockers, gave it a gentle push with her foot, and tried to clear her head.

Tyler sat up a little bit taller and glanced toward his father. "Hey, partner," Tyler said boldly.

Sadie giggled, glad for a distraction from her own thoughts. "That's cute, his words."

Kade gazed at his son with eyes longing for more than Tyler was able to give him, but yet tender and kind. Loving. "Yeah, I have a friend who says that all the time too," Kade said. He looked up at Sadie. "My friend Val seems to start every conversation with 'Hey, partner.'"

"Reckon it must be where Tyler heard it."

"No." Kade shook his head. "Val hasn't seen Tyler since Monica took him and left Los Angeles. So, not for about three years."

Tyler began to flip through the pages of the Bible, and Sadie reflected on what Tyler had said before Kade arrived, toying with the idea of mentioning it to Kade.

"Cool beans," Tyler whispered without looking up.

Sadie giggled again at the strange comment, but she thought she saw a troubled expression sweep across Kade's face.

Unease threatened to suffocate Kade as he realized that one of the few things he still held sacred—his friendship with Val—suddenly felt at risk.

"My friend Val says that too." Kade eyed Tyler suspiciously. "Tyler, do you know Val?"

"Val loves Mommy," Tyler said softly. His son didn't look up to see the stunned expression on his dad's face.

But Kade could feel Sadie's eyes on him, and for the moment, he chose not to look at her, fearful she'd see right through him at the rage in his mind—wicked thoughts directed at his dear friend Val. Had the only person he trusted betrayed him?

Kade recalled the conversation when Val told him that Monica was bringing Tyler to him. Val had sounded odd on the phone, but Kade hadn't thought too much about it. Then there was the call from Val about Monica's death. Val seemed shook-up, but

Kade wrote it off as concern about Kade's own situation, not feelings of loss that Val might be having of his own.

It was all clicking—Val's trips, his withdrawal from discussions outside of the business arena, and overall detachment from the friendship. Val wasn't mending his soul. He was planning to marry Kade's wife and raise Kade's son! *When was he going to tell me?*

Val's real estate development company was successful, yet considerably smaller than Kade's corporation. They'd often combined resources to score ahead of the competition, with Kade always pulling most of the load. And he'd never minded. Val was his friend. *Was.*

If Val had come to him, told him that he was in love with Monica—that would be one thing. At least he'd have known that Tyler would be raised by a good man. But to lie and sneak around like this . . .

"Hey, partner," Tyler repeated again with a giggle.

Kade rose abruptly, put his hands on hips, and began to pace. His heart pounded, his stomach churned, and he resisted the urge to verbalize the thoughts in his head.

"Your face is red," Sadie said cautiously.

"That happens when I'm mad, and I am madder than—" He caught himself as Sadie warned him with her eyes to choose his words carefully.

She rose from the rocker, sighed, and said, "'T'will be completely dark soon. Might be best to get Tyler to the cottage before nightfall."

Kade nodded, even though heading back to the cottage was the last thing he wanted to do. The weather was crummy. His mood was worse. Last thing he wanted to do was be alone with Tyler at the cottage. He started the bundling process. First, Tyler's coat and mittens, then his boots. Working slowly, he glanced at Sadie and decided, for once, to say what was really on his mind.

"Sadie." He watched her expression take on a hint of wariness, but Kade pressed on. "I'm having a really bad day." He quit struggling to push Tyler's wriggling foot into the boot, sighed in frustration, and sat on the couch. Tyler stood with one boot on but didn't seem bothered. Sadie waited for him to go on, but she clearly wasn't going to make any offers to console him. He took a deep breath. "Can we stay for a while?"

"I—I don't know if—"

"If it's appropriate," he finished.

"*Ya.*" She pulled her eyes from his—her big, blue eyes that, for an instant, seemed to defy her words. And it was enough to give Kade hope.

"We wouldn't stay long. I thought maybe we could have a cup of coffee and talk. We're both alone out here and could be for days evidently."

Her eyes locked with his in a way that confirmed Kade's initial thoughts. *She wants us to stay.* But Kade also knew that if he didn't work fast, she'd boot them out anyway. He grinned in a playful way. "It's cold outside."

She smiled back. "*Ya*, it is."

"Sadie, no one will ever know that we're unsupervised under the same roof together, I promise. No one is going to be out in this weather, and I won't tell a soul. I would really enjoy talking with you. My life is a mess." He shook his head. "But you seem to have a clearer picture of how to have a more peaceful existence. I'd be interested to hear about that."

"We live in very different worlds, Kade." Something in her tone sealed the deal, and Kade knew they would be staying.

Sadie lit more lanterns than were probably necessary in her kitchen. It was light and bright—nothing like the weather outside, Kade's mood, or the fear she felt at him being here. If Bishop Ebersol knew about this . . . But she knew her fear ran much deeper than getting caught by the bishop.

She tried not to think about it and pulled a container of beef stew from the freezer. As she ran it under the hot water from the sink, she wondered what Lillian would say about this. Of all her friends, Lillian was the most lenient when it came to the Old Order ways, but mostly because she hadn't grown up Amish. Sadie knew that Lillian still struggled with the rules from time to time, but never with her faith—an area Sadie seemed to be having trouble with these days.

Sadie remembered how vibrant she used to feel, how her spirited characteristics had brought her and Lillian together as friends in the first place. Lillian had the same zest for life that Sadie had. Until recently. Sadie's lighthearted spirit had darkened, and it scared her.

She bowed her head but cut her prayer short when she heard Kade returning from the bathroom with Tyler.

"Here is coffee for you, and some milk for Tyler," she said when Tyler and Kade walked into the room. She carried the semithawed stew to a pot on the stove and dumped it in. "Tyler, I think I might have some tapioca pudding in my refrigerator just for you." She turned her head to face him. "Would you like that?"

Tyler didn't respond and seemed more interested in the streams of light shining brightly throughout the kitchen.

"Wow. It's bright in here." Kade walked to the lantern Sadie had placed on her china hutch across the room. "Do you mind if I turn this one off?"

Her eyes grew wide. "*Ya!* I mean, no! Don't turn it off." She turned around in time to see that side of the room grow dark and Kade's brows rise in surprise. "It's all right, I reckon," she added, and then spun quickly around so Kade wouldn't see the pink in her cheeks.

"I can turn it back on, if you'd like," he said cautiously.

Sadie vigorously stirred the stew. "No. It's okay."

She glanced around the room. Darker than she would prefer. A tad too intimate.

Supper was uneventful, except that Tyler burst into laughter for no apparent reason on several occasions, which kept the mood light. And his outbursts had been contagious. Sadie and Kade both laughed along with the boy, and Sadie realized what a long time it had been since she'd had a good, hearty chuckle, the kind of sidesplitting laughter that Tyler's bubbly giggles brought out in her. *Such a sweet sound—a child's merriment*, she thought as she began to clear the dishes.

"Let me help you." Kade stood from the wooden bench.

"No, it's fine," Sadie said. Besides, she doubted Kade had cleared too many tables in his life. For that matter, neither had Ben. In her community, men didn't help with cooking or cleanup. It was work for the womenfolk. But Kade walked toward her with his and Tyler's plates and placed them in the sink.

"I don't remember the last time I've laughed like that," Kade said. He turned around, leaned against the counter, and watched Tyler playing with his lunch box full of letters at the kitchen table.

"Nor do I." Sadie added dishwasher soap to the running warm water. She turned briefly toward Kade, but Kade was still gazing at his son. "He is such a joy, Kade."

"He's so handsome to be so . . ." Kade sighed.

"Special? Is that the word you are searching for?" Sadie placed the first clean dish in the drainer. Kade didn't answer, but instead picked up the plate and began drying it with the dish towel nearby. "No, please. I'll do that," she said. Not only was it not a man's place to take on the chore; it wasn't *Kade's* place to act in such a familiar way.

But Kade finished drying the plate. "Where does it go?"

"Top shelf of the cupboard." Sadie pointed upward to the cabinet on the wall in between them. He edged closer to her, pulled the door open, and put the plate away. He smelled good. Like cologne she smelled on the *Englisch* men in town. Unease settled over her again.

Tyler ate most of his beef stew. Sadie was hoping both Tyler and Kade had forgotten about the tapioca pudding and that they would be on their way soon.

"Thanks for having us for dinner, Sadie. When I asked if we could stay, I didn't necessarily mean you had to cook for us." He smiled his crooked smile, the one that always showed a kinder side of him. "But that stew was fabulous."

"*Danki.*" Sadie glanced at Tyler in hopes that Kade would go join the boy at the kitchen table and not stand so close to her.

"My mom didn't cook a lot when I was growing up. But every

once in a while she'd take over the kitchen from Nelda, and when she did, she'd always cook a roast or stew." Sadie turned to face him as she dried her hands. He was far away, his eyes reflective of times past. "Your stew reminded me of those times when my mother cooked." He paused and looked toward Tyler. "They were good times."

"Was Nelda your servant?" Sadie couldn't imagine such a life.

Kade grinned. "*Servant* might be a strong word. She was our cook, and she also handled parties that my parents hosted, things like that. And she oversaw the other staff—my nanny, the house-keeper, and the yard guy."

Sadie didn't understand. "Then what did your mother do?" Right away, she realized the shock in her voice. "I mean . . . I, uh, didn't mean to be disrespectful. I just—"

Kade chuckled. "It's all right. I know what you meant. And, believe it or not, she stayed really busy. She was involved in a lot of charity events, played tennis twice a week, hosted a literary club once a month, and spent a lot of time traveling with my father."

"Oh," Sadie said.

"It must sound like a shallow way to live to you." Kade cringed a bit.

"*Ach*, no. I would never judge." She recalled Lillian's comments about that very thing, and then added, "I'm sure your *mamm* is a *gut* woman." But how fulfilling could a life like that be? Sadie wondered. Some of her most gratifying moments had been serving Ben his meals, taking care of their home, and growing her own vegetables. And she continued to dream of the day she could mother children of her own.

"Maybe we could have our tapioca pudding in the den

where it's warmer? I noticed you trembling." Kade walked to the kitchen table.

Sadie didn't move for a moment. She knew that her trembling had nothing to do with being cold.

"Tyler, let's put your letters in the lunch box and take them into the den," Kade said. Tyler looked like a fit might be coming, but he allowed Kade to move him into the den.

"I'll be in with the pudding shortly." She pulled the container from the refrigerator and filled three bowls.

"Do you have all these people in your home in the city?" she asked when she handed Kade and Tyler each a bowl of pudding.

"What?"

"These nannies, cooks, and other servants." She didn't wait for an answer, but went to go retrieve her own bowl. Then she took a seat in the rocker across from the couch where Kade and Tyler sat.

"I do have people who live in my home and help with things. I work a lot," Kade said.

"Will these people take care of Tyler when you return home?"

"I suppose so," Kade said after he finished a spoonful of pudding. Then he shook his head, as if something had suddenly angered him. "My so-called friend Val is supposedly checking into someone to care for Tyler."

"This man is no longer your friend, no?"

"No," Kade huffed. "But let's not talk about that. Tell me about you. Parents? Brothers and sisters?"

"*Mei* parents have both passed. *Mei mamm* when I was young, and *mei daed* died a few years back. I have one sister who lives in Ohio."

"My father died when I was nineteen."

Sadie waited for him to mention his mother and whether or not he had brothers and sisters, but he took another bite of pudding. Tyler was starting to get restless, Sadie noticed. He handed Kade his empty bowl and began to bang his head against the back of the couch.

"I guess he's getting tired," Kade said.

Sadie stood from the rocker. "I'll take those." She reached for Kade's bowl as he took the last bite, and then she grabbed Tyler's empty bowl from the coffee table.

They'll be leaving now, she thought as she headed to the kitchen. She washed the bowls and put them in the rack to dry.

She rounded the corner back to the den, prepared to help Kade bundle Tyler up so that they could be on their way, although it didn't appear they were going anywhere. Tyler's head was in his father's lap.

"He must be really tired," Kade said. "Usually he makes it until eight o'clock." He glanced at his watch. "It's only seven."

Sadie slowly backed her way into the rocker.

Tyler's eyes closed, and Kade leaned back against the couch, giving Sadie the strangest look. "You're nervous to be around me, aren't you?"

"What?" She fought the tremble in her voice.

"I mean, I know you're worried that someone will find out that we spent time together, but I also think I make you nervous in general." He paused and tilted his head to one side. "Why is that?"

Sadie sat up straighter. "I assure you, Kade, I am not nervous." He was arrogant, but intuitive as well.

He eased Tyler's head off of his lap, and then he leaned

forward with his elbows on his knees and folded his hands together. "Sadie, I appreciate you letting us stay."

Yes, well . . . now it is time to go.

"And I think I know why you're nervous," he went on.

"I'm not nervous, Kade," she said again with a shrug.

"Sadie, I just want to talk to you. Actually, there is something specific I want to talk to you about." He paused and took a deep breath. "I'm not here to come on to you or anything like that. I'm not going to try to kiss you or—"

She jumped up. "You need to leave, Kade."

"Whoa." He held his palms toward her. "I'm sorry. I just thought you'd like to know that I have no interest in anything but friendship."

"Of course I know that," she snapped in a whisper. "But we don't talk of such things."

He grinned. "Okay, I won't say the word *kiss*." He emphasized the last word.

Sadie put her hands on her hips. "Are you making fun of me?"

His face grew somber. "No. I would never do that. I respect you more than probably any woman I've ever met. Really. You're not like the women I know. And I apologize again. Can we please sit here and talk for a while? I'll put another log on the fire, and maybe we can have a cup of coffee and talk. There really is something I'd like to talk to you about—something Tyler said to me."

Sadie sat back down. She needed to sit down. The conversation had taken a turn that was not fit, but even more bothersome was that Kade said he had no interest in her outside of friendship. Suddenly she wanted to ask him, "Why not?" It was a fleeting thought, but it had popped into her head for reasons she didn't understand. She opened her mouth to tell him that he must leave.

Kade spoke first, though. "Do you believe that God can talk to us through other people? Tyler quoted a Bible verse to me yesterday, and it gave me chills." He shook his head. "It was so perfect for what I was feeling at the time, that I can't stop thinking about what he said, and—"

Sadie had unconsciously put her hand over her mouth.

"Are you okay?" Kade asked.

She dropped her hand to her lap and nodded. "Go on," she said as she thought about whether or not she would tell Kade that Tyler had also quoted a scripture to her earlier, at a most appropriate time.

"The funny thing is," Kade said, "I haven't been on very friendly terms with God lately. I've been distant from any kind of relationship with Him for several years. My faith, or lack thereof, was one of the reasons I came here. Sort of." He shrugged. "Anyway, does that make sense? Have you ever heard of anything like this happening?"

Sadie smiled. "As a matter of fact, I have."

And for the first time since she'd met Kade Saunders, Sadie didn't feel nervous. She stood from the rocker. "Why don't I go make us some coffee?"

11

KADE ADDED ANOTHER LOG TO THE FIRE WHILE SADIE prepared coffee in the kitchen. The fresh-brewed aroma permeated the house, complementing the comfort of Sadie's home. He felt surprisingly at ease here, despite the austere decor and lack of electricity.

Tyler slept soundly on the couch, only his eyes and nose visible under the quilt Sadie had spread over him. Kade was glad he wasn't spending the evening alone at the cottage while Tyler slept. He was anxious to know more about Sadie. Her simplistic life intrigued him, but so did the woman herself. Kade suspected that, despite her nervousness around him, Sadie was more complex than she appeared.

He was tempted to excuse himself, go out on the porch, and make an overdue phone call to Val, but that would only solidify what he already knew to be true. Plus it was too cold to venture outside for anything more than another log for the fire.

"Here you go," Sadie said when she walked into the den, holding two cups of coffee.

"Thanks." Kade accepted the coffee and took a seat in one of the two rockers across from the couch. Sadie sat down in the other chair, and then sipped from her cup. For a few moments, he couldn't pull his gaze from her.

Sadie's blue eyes twinkled in the dim light, but Kade recognized the hints of sadness beneath her radiant glow. He'd seen those eyes in the mirror—the look of loneliness. Her ivory skin, void of any makeup, was flawless, and her lips had retained their youthful color. Loose strands of wavy, red hair wisped against her cheeks from underneath the cap on her head.

The women Kade knew spent a fortune in professional services to render a look that came naturally to Sadie. And she wasn't even trying to be beautiful. He'd never wanted more to tell a woman how lovely she was than at this moment, but she looked up, and her eyes met Kade's. He knew he would alienate her if he voiced his thoughts, probably even win an escort to the door.

"So, about my question," he began instead. "Has anything like what I described, the thing with Tyler, ever happened to you? It left me feeling . . . strange."

Sadie took another sip of her coffee. She seemed more relaxed, he thought. "*Ya*, today."

Then she smiled, broadly. So much so that Kade wanted to smile back at her, but he had questions, so many questions. "What do you mean, *today*?"

She crossed her legs beneath a dark-blue dress and black apron. Only black leather shoes and socks of the same color were visible. "I had the same thing happen to me today." She pushed the rocker into motion with her foot and seemed to be challenging him to question her further.

"Today?" Kade twisted his mouth to one side and narrowed his eyes. "*Today* someone quoted a scripture to you?"

"*Ya.*" She pushed back a strand of hair. "And, like you, it happened at a time when I most needed to be reminded of God's love for us."

"Really? So, this scripture that someone read—"

"It wasn't *someone*, Kade," she interrupted. Her eyes met his in a way that made Kade anxious. Something big was coming. "It was *Tyler.*"

It had been a long time since Kade had felt a jolt like the one Sadie had just given him. "What?"

"I think you heard me." Her tone was strong, but her eyes soft. "I had just said a prayer about . . . about something important to me. Tyler read a scripture that seemed to be speaking directly to me."

Kade could feel the wrinkles on his forehead deepening as he narrowed his eyes in her direction. "Well, these have to be coincidences, right?"

"What do you think?" She raised her brows, challenging him to give this some extra thought.

"I told you, I've rather strayed from my faith for the last few years. It's hard for me to imagine it as anything more than a coincidence." He paused, shrugged. "But if the same thing happened to you, maybe it's plausible." Then he paused again. "No. No, I don't believe that's how God works. Tyler read something and simply repeated it."

"Then why are you so bothered by it?"

He shook his head in defeat. "I don't know."

"Who are we to judge how God works His miracles?" Sadie's glow dimmed. "And who are we to question His will?"

"I guess I question it sometimes."

She took a deep breath. "In my community, we believe that all things are of God's will and are not to be questioned."

"Well, that's impossible." He took a sip of his coffee. "When your husband died at such a young age, was that God's will?"

Crud. Why did he have to go and blurt that out? Her eyes glazed over almost instantly. "Oh, Sadie. I'm sorry. I should have never—"

"It's all right." She rapidly blinked away any sign of tears. "At a time of mourning, I think it's only human to question God's will for a short time. I grieved for my husband, and it was harder for me to see God's goodness during those first few hours."

"*Hours?* What about *months? Years?* I haven't been able to see His goodness for three years, since we found out that Tyler . . . that Tyler was autistic."

"He is a perfect little boy, Kade," she said with such conviction that Kade wanted to believe her.

He kicked his rocker into sync with her rocker and stared at the fire, filled with recollections of Tyler's birth, how proud he'd been, and how he believed Tyler to be the perfect boy. And then, all his hopes and dreams were ripped from him two years later. "He'll never, you know, *be* anything." He turned and looked hard at Sadie. "Please, Sadie, don't get me wrong. I love my son, and I always will. But for me to accept his autism as God's will—well, I can't do that. He'll never play baseball or any other sports. And that's okay. I'm not a huge sports fan anyway. But he'll never do any of the things other kids can do—like ride a bicycle, for example, or climb a tree, or—"

"How do you know these things?"

"He can barely stay focused on anything for more than a few minutes, and he's uncoordinated." He adjusted his sharp tone. "He'll never know what it's like to be in love, or how much I love him, for that matter."

"How do you know?"

Kade shook his head. The woman was beginning to frustrate him. "Because I just know."

Sadie could see the pain in his expression. She thought for a moment about how to help Kade to see things in a different perspective.

"Kade, he'll also never know about murder and crime, or other *baremlich* things that plague the world. And Tyler will always be pleased by the simplest of things in life, like a bowl of tapioca pudding. He'll never suffer grief as we know it, mourn a dear pet's departure, or question a friend's betrayal. Tyler will rejoice in the *gut* moments that he can understand, but not lose himself in the bad moments, like so many of us do."

When Kade continued to stare at her but didn't say anything, she went on. "Kade, if you can believe that all things are of His will, a calm will sweep over you and bring a peacefulness that only comes from God's love."

Sadie felt the sting of her own words, knowing she hadn't been living by what she told Kade. She pulled her eyes from his gaze and sighed.

"Do you really believe that?" He sounded so skeptical. How was she going to make Kade understand when her own ugly doubts were flailing about?

But she sat up taller and confidently said, "*Ya*, I really do believe that." *And I will stop having doubts.*

"I have to admit," Kade began cautiously, "when Tyler quoted that passage from the Bible to me, at that moment I felt the presence of God, and I think I might have had a glimpse of the peacefulness you're talking about." He paused and rubbed his chin. "And for you to have had a similar experience with Tyler—I don't know. It puts a whole new spin on this."

They both sat quietly for a few minutes and stared at the crackling fire as orange embers drifted upward and out of sight. Sadie could hear the thrashing wind beating against the house, and she could feel the cold air sneaking in around the windowpane behind her.

She was glad the conversation had quieted. Kade and she were unequally yoked, and it wasn't her job to minister to him. But no sooner had the thought registered when she realized that by ministering to Kade, she'd been ministering to herself as well.

"It's something to think about," Kade finally said. Then he cocked his head slightly. "How do you do it? Live here?" His voice was tender as he motioned his hand around the room. "Like this?"

"It's the only life I've ever known. I don't need all the material things and conveniences you have in your world."

"But aren't you curious about what you might be missing?" Kade asked. "For example, I know you enjoy listening to music, but yet you don't own a radio. Wouldn't you like to experience the things in our world?"

This was exactly what her parents had warned her about. She could recall her father's words. "To be unequally yoked with nonbelievers will tempt you to stray from our ways and our beliefs," he'd said when she was young.

"I have experienced as much as I need to in your world," she said firmly. "When an Amish teenager turns sixteen, we begin our *rumschpringe*—a running-around period which lasts until we choose to be baptized into the faith or leave the Old Order. During this time, we do many of the things *Englisch* teenagers do. Go to the movies, ride around in cars, visit the shopping malls. Things like that."

"And, obviously, you chose to stay. Have you ever regretted it?"

"Never. Not one day of my life." Her faith might be slipping a tad, but she'd never wanted to live in the *Englisch* world. "We live a simple, mostly uncomplicated life. Can you say the same thing?"

Kade rolled his eyes. "No, I can't. My life has been complicated for as long as I can remember. I wish it was different." He shook his head.

"Then change things."

"I guess in my own way I'm trying, little by little. Coming here was supposed to be a start in that direction, time to get away from everything and everyone, get some perspective. But you see how well that went. My life followed me. First Monica showed up . . ." He looked toward the ground. "Then her death, and then this afternoon I find out that my closest friend has been spending time with Monica, making plans behind my back."

"Do you know this for sure?"

"Yeah, I guess I do. I haven't confirmed it, but some things are starting to make sense now."

Sadie was quiet for a moment, then said cautiously, "If this is true, I bet your friend is hurting."

Kade didn't answer.

"Sometimes when we see past our own pain and into the heart of another, our own self-healing begins."

Kade looked up and turned toward her. "Can you see into my heart, Sadie?"

"I . . . I'm sorry if I offended you. I just—"

"You did not offend me at all, Sadie. I'm serious. Can you see into my heart? What do you see? I'd like to know."

Sadie wasn't comfortable talking to him about such things, but she should have thought about that long before the conversation became so intense. She recalled her own words—and wondered if she could see past her own pain and into Kade's heart. She decided to try.

"I see a man who has been blessed with great wealth, but who is as unhappy a man as I've ever seen." She paused to see him hanging on her every word. "But every now and then, I glimpse a different man, the man you long to be."

Kade stared at her, as if in awe. He let out a heavy sigh. "You are exactly right." Then he surprised her. "What about you, Sadie? I think you, too, have been blessed with great wealth, maybe not monetarily—but a wealth of spirit and faith. But you don't fool me either. I see the sadness in your eyes as well. You do a much better job of masking it than I do, but it's there."

Sadie turned away from him, afraid he'd see her blinking back the tears. "You are exactly right," she echoed. She turned to face him, and they sat staring into each other's eyes.

Then Kade smiled. "If you could do anything in the world, what would it be?"

"What?" She couldn't help but feel lighter suddenly.

"If you could do anything in the world, go anywhere, have anything, Amish or otherwise, what would it be?" Kade rested his elbow on the arm of the rocker and cupped his chin. "Anything."

"You are serious, no?" What a wonderful question, she thought, and an easy one to answer.

Kade nodded. "And if money were of no concern."

She smiled. "I would have a spouse to love and children to care for."

"So, the old adage that money can't buy happiness rings true for you?" His voice was kind, tender. "Of all the things in the world, you'd choose the love of family."

"*Ya.*" She twisted in her chair to face him. "What would you choose?"

And much to her surprise, he said, "The exact same thing."

"You are halfway there." She nodded toward the precious child sleeping on the couch.

Kade rubbed his chin for a moment and stared at Tyler. "Yes," he finally said. "You're right." Then he smiled. "I've never known anyone like you, Sadie."

"Nor have I known anyone like you, Kade." She returned the smile, and they sat silently again, but there was no mistaking the looks passing between them, and it sounded alarms for Sadie. "It's getting late," she said.

"You're right. I'm sorry. I didn't mean for us to stay this long."
He stood up and moved toward Tyler.

"Let the boy sleep," Sadie said. "It's too cold to take him
outside, and it would be a shame to wake him up. I reckon you
can come for him in the morning."

"That would be great." Kade peeked behind the closed blind
toward the cottage. Gusty wind continued to mound snow up
against the house. "I guess I'm going to miss Monica's funeral."

"I'm sorry. The worst of the weather will be here tomorrow
and not start clearing until Saturday or Sunday, and I suspect we
might not be able to travel for a day or two after that. My friends
and I decided to close my shop until Wednesday."

Kade continued to look out the window. "Wow. I've never
seen anything like this. Look at the snow piling against the
house." He stepped aside, and Sadie took a brief look but
quickly backed away. Kade let the blind go and turned to face
her. "What time should I come for Tyler in the morning? I
mean, I'll come early. I don't want you to have to feed him
breakfast." Kade grimaced. "Breakfast can be an ordeal with
Tyler some mornings."

Sadie couldn't remember the last time she'd cooked a big meal
for breakfast, with eggs, bacon, homemade biscuits, jams, and jellies. An excitement she hadn't felt in a while rose to the surface.
"Breakfast will be at seven o'clock. I will cook for you and Tyler."

"Really?" Kade smiled. "I think that would be great."

But then Sadie began to worry. "Although I . . . I don't cook
fancy, Kade. Like those items you have for breakfast. I can make
eggs, bacon, biscuits, and—"

"Perfect!"

"Do you like such foods?" She questioned him with her eyes and wondered if he was just saying so.

He chuckled. "I honestly don't remember the last time I had a traditional breakfast. I don't cook, so those breakfast cereals are about all I can handle in the morning. I would absolutely love what you mentioned. It would be a treat."

"All right. *Gut.*" She began to wonder what types of jams and jellies she had, whether she would prepare scrambled eggs and bacon or make omelets. This gave her something to look forward to in the morning. Company for the breakfast meal.

Kade pulled on his coat and gloves. "Then I guess I will see you in the morning," he said.

It was an awkward moment. Even Sadie felt like a hug was in order, but neither moved forward. Instead, Kade turned to open the door. "Bye," he said.

Sadie watched him trudge out into the storm, fighting the wind as his boots sank calf-deep in the snow. She didn't remember ever seeing the weather this bad. Hard to believe that it would be even worse by morning.

Kade couldn't get into the cottage fast enough. He could barely feel his numbed cheeks. Plus, Val had a phone call coming. He flipped the switch on the thermostat in the kitchen, glad to have central heat in the cottage. Sadie's home had been warm enough with the roaring fire and portable gas heaters, but Kade had let the fire die out since he was leaving town—or thought he was— and it was more than a little chilly.

He peeled off the heavy coat he'd borrowed the other night

and hung it on the back of a kitchen chair. What a storm. He'd never seen anything like this, even in all his travels. Kade eased onto the couch and untied his tennis shoes, thankful the black boots had kept them dry. He propped his feet up on the coffee table and looked around the room. It was eerily quiet, but the wind howled with a vengeance outside. In the dark, he could hear icy branches snapping, and it sounded like something flew against the barn. How nice it would have been to curl up on the couch with Tyler in the coziness of the farmhouse. But mention of that would have certainly scared poor Sadie to death.

It was hard to believe that there were women like her around. Honest, decent, and with a goodness he didn't remember seeing in a woman. Sadie was dedicated to living the life she spoke about, driven by her beliefs and a real understanding about a relationship with God. Strong in her faith—and beautiful. He shook his head. Why couldn't he have found a woman like that, instead of the Monicas and Alicias of the world, who were only after his money? But he had to admit, his heart ached over Monica's death. So young. And Tyler's mother. If Kade was honest with himself, he'd have to admit that having Tyler full-time scared him. As much as he wanted to know his son, he also knew it would truly be a labor of love. And what if he failed at it? How would he know if he was a good father?

He pulled out his cell phone, prepared to tear into Val, but Sadie's words kept sounding in his head: "Sometimes when we see past our own pain and into the heart of another, our own self-healing begins."

Kade stared at the phone.

12

LIZZIE AWOKE IN THE WEE HOURS OF FRIDAY MORNING to the sound of Jonas's voice.

"Lizzie, you all right?"

She rolled over in bed and fumbled for her glasses on the table next to her. Then she put on gold-rimmed spectacles and blinked her eyes until the bedside clock came into focus. *Three fifteen. What in the world?* Her hip popped as she felt around the table for her flashlight—amid the bottles of pills, tissues, and a glass of water. When her hand landed around the base of her flashlight, she turned it on and found the walkie-talkie.

"I'm here, Jonas," she said wearily. "Are you and Sarah Jane all right?"

It took a few moments before Jonas answered. "*Ya.* But I woke up worried. You oughta not be there by yourself, Irma Rose."

Lizzie hung her head and sighed. Then pushed the Talk button. "It's Lizzie, Jonas."

"I know. And it be *baremlich* outside. Don'tcha be goin' out there."

She grinned. *Why would I be going outside in a blizzard at three in the morning?* "I won't, Jonas."

"*Gut.* Huggy bear don't wanna find you all froze up and buried in the snow."

Lizzie laughed out loud, now wide-awake. She loved when Jonas referred to himself as huggy bear, a pet name he'd chosen for himself. "All right, *huggy bear.* I promise not to go outdoors."

"I'll be seeing ya, Lizzie."

She smiled. *All right, my love.* Her finger was on the Talk button, but Jonas spoke again before she had a chance to push it. "Lizzie?"

"*Ya?*"

She waited for a while, but no response. "Jonas? You all right?" she finally asked.

"I sure am missin' you."

Lizzie touched her palm to her chest and closed her eyes. *Oh my.* "I miss you, too, Jonas."

"Good night, Lizzie."

"Good night."

She set the walkie-talkie back on the table but didn't lie back down. She was fully awake now, and thoughts of Jonas swirled in her head. Lizzie fluffed her pillows behind her and sat up a little straighter. Her hip was aching a bit, and her bedroom was a mite cold, but inside she was warm and fuzzy. She dreamed of Jonas asking her to marry him someday. So many times, Lizzie had fought the urge to tell him how much she loved him, but Jonas was the type of man who needed to do things in his own time. And he'd loved Irma Rose so much. Lizzie knew it was hard for him to give his heart to another.

But tonight he said he misses me. She knew that was a big step for Jonas. He teased her a lot and referred to himself as huggy bear more than she actually called him by the name, but he'd never said he missed her or anything to hint that he might be feeling what Lizzie was feeling.

———

Sadie flipped the bacon in the skillet, checked on the biscuits in the oven, and then stirred the eggs. Tyler was eating a bowl of tapioca pudding at the kitchen table. She hoped Kade wouldn't mind, but when Tyler woke up on the couch, he had been confused, and the tapioca pudding calmed him down. Sadie was up and cooking before Tyler awoke, but when he stumbled into the kitchen, Sadie could tell by the look on his face that he was not a happy little boy. And one thing Sadie knew to be true—tapioca pudding made Tyler happy.

She glanced over her shoulder at Kade's son. A handsome fellow for sure. Sadie had placed several jars of jam on the table, and Tyler was busy arranging them in a circle between bites of pudding. She smiled. No harm done. She'd been careful to keep knives off the table, or anything else Tyler might be tempted to play with, since Sadie still wasn't sure of his habits.

Sadie prepared some oatmeal, after deciding against scrapple. The mushy mix of cornmeal and flour wasn't for everyone. She recalled when Lillian first arrived in Lancaster County, before she converted. When Lillian found out the traditional dish also contained leftover pieces of pig, she wouldn't touch it—and *still* wouldn't, to this day. "I'm not eating pig guts, toes, and ears," Lillian had said firmly.

Sadie rather liked it. But then, she'd grown up eating it, like most of the people in her community.

"How is your pudding, Tyler? Is *gut*, no?" She wiped her hands on her apron and walked toward him, but he didn't acknowledge the question. He continued to rearrange the jars of jam; then he'd take a bite of pudding, and then start all over again. But all the while, he was smiling. And Sadie was too. The smell of breakfast cooking, a guest for breakfast, a child in the house—it all felt so nice. She even found herself humming.

She walked to the kitchen window and looked outside. The only thing that threatened to put a damper on her spirit was the weather. It was frightful outside, and as the newspaper had predicted, much worse this morning. During the night, she heard branches snapping and loud noises that sounded like small items being tossed around or slammed against the barn or house. She'd tried to secure everything in the barn before the storm, but maybe she'd missed some things.

Blustery winds continued to swirl the heavy snow, burying everything in a blanket of white. Thankfully, no trees grew near her house. In the distance, she could see toppled branches covered in thick ice, the limbs quickly being buried by a mix of ice and snow. Sadie had never seen the weather like this. She began to wonder if Kade would be able to make it the short distance from the cottage to the farmhouse.

She heard a knock, and the kitchen door opened.

"This is unbelievable!" he said when he came in. "I wasn't sure I was going to get here before I froze to death. I can't feel my cheeks."

Sadie put her hands on her hips. "Kade, there is a face covering inside your hood. Why didn't you pull it around your face?" *He really doesn't know anything about cold weather.*

He shrugged, then smiled. "I don't know."

Sadie swiveled toward the oven. "I need to stir the eggs." She could hear his footsteps behind her.

"Hey, Tyler." Kade took a seat on the bench across from Tyler. "What are you doing?"

Sadie pulled the spoon from the skillet and placed it on the counter, then turned to face Kade and Tyler. "He's been having a *gut* time rearranging the jams and jellies," she said. Kade turned toward her and smiled.

Why did her heart have to flutter so when he was near?

After breakfast, Kade helped Sadie clear the table—again—as if it was the most common task in the world. She'd asked him not to, but he'd insisted—again. Kade had carried on all through breakfast about how delicious the meal was, and Sadie knew she'd blushed more than once.

She didn't have much to do this time of year, even more so with the weather this way, but Kade didn't appear in much of a hurry to leave either. Once the kitchen was clean, he sat down on the rug in the den with his son and made words with Tyler's plastic letters. Sadie excused herself for a moment.

She was returning from the bathroom, and as she neared the den, she heard Kade's voice.

"Tyler, I'm going to make a good life for you," he said. "I'm going to be a good father."

His words touched Sadie, and she knew she would continue to pray for both of them, even when they were gone.

Kade glanced up at her when she walked into the den. "We're making words. Do you want to join us?"

This is not the same man who showed up a few weeks ago, Sadie thought, as she sat down on the rug across from Kade.

"My mother loved to play Scrabble when I was a kid," Kade said. "I know this is a far cry from Scrabble, but playing with Tyler like this reminds me of those times. It was one of the few things we did together, usually on a rainy afternoon when I got home from school and couldn't go outside to play, and she couldn't play tennis and didn't have any other commitments."

"Is your *mamm* . . . ?"

"Alive?" Kade pulled his eyes from hers. "No, she died right before Tyler was born. Breast cancer."

"I'm sorry." Sadie could see that it was a tender subject for Kade. "Do you have brothers and sisters?"

"No. I'm an only child." Kade leaned in toward Tyler. "Guess you will be, too, buddy."

They sat quietly for a few moments, and Sadie thought about Kade's comment. *Does he assume he will never remarry and have more children?* It was customary to remarry quickly in her community, after the death of a spouse, but perhaps the *Englisch* did things differently.

After a while, Kade opened up to her in a way that surprised Sadie. He told her how his father had developed Alzheimer's disease as a fairly young man. That it was similar to the confusion that Jonas was having, which explained how Kade had known how to handle Jonas at the pub. He said that, just like Jonas, his father would be lucid some of the time, but then would get disoriented, often while he was at work. When that happened, he would leave and later call Kade's mother from somewhere unfamiliar and tell her he didn't know how he got there.

He went on to tell her that when he came home from college one Friday night, his mother told him that his dad had been missing since the day before. Police, neighbors, employees—everyone was looking for Paul Saunders. Kade ended up being the one to find his father in a field behind a neighbor's estate the next day. He described what his father looked like after being dead almost two days in the hundred-degree heat. The police believed that he'd gotten lost, couldn't find his way back, and ended up having heatstroke. It was a heartbreaking story, and Sadie couldn't imagine what it must have been like for Kade.

"Do you know I never told Monica about that?" He shook his head. "I mean, she knew a little bit about what happened, but I never felt comfortable enough to talk about it."

Sadie was touched by the comment and realized that she felt unusually comfortable talking with Kade as well. An *Englischer* with whom she had nothing in common. She shared her story about her father's death, although thankfully, it wasn't as dramatic—a heart attack. Not long after that, she told him about Ben. Kade listened with compassion and sympathy. By lunchtime, she and Kade were clearly in a new place. It was bewildering, yet wonderful. She hadn't talked to anyone like this since Ben. And, if she was honest with herself, she and Ben seldom had such deep conversations. Their relationship had brought her comfort and reassurance, knowing she was loved unconditionally, but they rarely spoke about emotional matters. Perhaps they'd never needed to.

Kade had suggested that maybe Tyler would like to draw, and Sadie had rounded up a pad of paper and some pens. Circles. Tyler liked drawing circles, and he occupied himself for a bit longer.

"I called my friend Val," he said as they sipped on a cup of hot cocoa. His face scrolled into a frown, and Sadie waited for him to go on. "But I didn't tell him I knew about him and Monica." He paused. "I'm not for sure, and I think I'd like to keep it that way.

Besides . . ." He took a deep breath. "I've known Val for a long time, and I could hear in his voice that he is suffering."

"That must have been very hard to do, no?" Sadie couldn't understand the life Kade led, but she was appreciating her life more and more. Guilt once again rose to the surface as she realized that, despite her own suffering, she'd been blessed in so many ways.

"It wasn't as difficult as I thought it would be. At first, I wanted to lash out at Val. And a few weeks ago, I would have." Kade stood up and grabbed a log from beside the fireplace and tossed it on the fire. "But something about being here, about spending time with Tyler, with you—" He twisted around to face her for a moment, and then returned to the fire, pushing the wood with the poker. "I'm questioning what my entire life has been about. And the kind of person I've been and who I might become." Then he chuckled. "Sounds nuts, huh?"

"No," Sadie said in a somber voice. "I don't think so. It's only natural sometimes to question one's place in this world."

He walked back over to where Sadie and Tyler were sitting on the floor, but he didn't sit down. Tyler toyed with Kade's shoestring, and Kade zoned in on Sadie, a serious expression on his face. "Do you have any idea how much money I have?"

What an odd question. "No, I do not."

Kade grinned. "And you don't care in the least, either, do you?"

Sadie wasn't sure if he was angry or grateful. But he was right. "No," she said simply. In his defense, and to be truthful, she added, "But money is measured in our community, just like in the *Englisch* world. Just not in the same way."

"What do you mean?" Kade sat back down in time for Tyler to hand him a picture of dozens of tiny circles. "This is great, Tyler." He reached out to touch the boy, but Tyler pulled away. Sadie thought about how Tyler had sat in her lap earlier. *Perhaps it's because I am a woman.* But she could see the hurt in Kade's eyes. She took a deep breath and thought out her response.

"There are those in our Old Order district who have more money than others. For example, Elam Lapp has a fine carpentry business. He makes a *gut* living. For Christmas, he gave his seventeen-year-old daughter a solid piece of oak furniture." Sadie paused when Tyler handed her a picture similar to the one he made for Kade. "*Danki*, Tyler." She smiled at Tyler, and then turned back to Kade. "But John King gave his daughter, Ellie, of the same age, an oak box to put on her bedside table, for keeping her personal items in. Not worth nearly as much money, but I bet Ellie found it equally as pleasing, because her *daed* made it for her." Sadie paused. "We do not value money the same way as the *Englisch*. It is necessary for survival, but one man's wealth is not weighed against another's."

"Maybe we're not as different as you think. I'm sure there are similar situations among *Englisch* families."

Sadie couldn't help but wonder what the extent of Kade's wealth was. "Is it rude to ask you how much money you do have?" She raised her brow.

Kade laughed. "I suppose you would think it silly if I said I didn't know?"

"*Ya,* I would." And she meant it. She knew how much money she had, or didn't have, at all times. "We might be plain, Kade, but we know that it takes money to survive. It used to be that our men worked the farms and made a *gut* living, but now only a few are able to do that. Womenfolk help out by working in bakeries and selling jams, jellies, quilts, and crafts. Our way of life is changing a bit, but we still adhere to the *Ordnung* and try to stay as disconnected from the *Englisch* world as we can."

"Why is that, anyway?"

"What?"

"Why do you have to stay disconnected from our world? How does that benefit your community?"

"To be unequally yoked is threatening to our people." This was a conversation he most likely wouldn't understand, but Sadie didn't understand much of what Kade said or believed either.

"How do I threaten you?" He leaned back on his elbows, crossed his ankles. Kade Saunders looked most comfortable in her home.

"I don't question my faith, Kade. Nor do I question the faith of those in my community. We *know* what we believe and practice it in our daily lives." Sadie felt a pang of conscience but pressed on. "That's not to say that someone in the *Englisch* world does not have the same faith that we do. We just don't know for sure. Here in our community, we know, with no doubts. There is no threat that someone will steer us from what we know to be true. It would be unheard-of."

Kade was still resting on his elbows. "So you don't want anyone from the *Englisch* world to tempt you to leave here?"

"No, that's not exactly it. We have an opportunity to leave during our *rumschpringe*. If we choose to leave prior to our baptism, we will not face a shunning. Once we are baptized, we have vowed to God a life dedicated to serving Him by following the *Ordnung*.

We don't feel temptation to leave, but if we are unequally yoked, nonbelievers can cause us to question our faith, and questioning of God's will is not something we believe in." Again, Sadie's guilt came to the forefront, fueled by her own lack of trust in God's will lately.

"So anything that happens, no matter how bad, is God's will?" Kade narrowed his brows and pressed his lips together for a moment. "I admire your ability to believe that."

"There is nothing admirable about it. To question God's will is not something we ever . . ." Sadie turned away from him. How could she continue to preach to him when she was repeatedly failing at this very thing?

She drew in a deep breath, gathered herself, and turned back toward him. "Perhaps I am not the person to tell you of these things."

Kade smiled, his eyes brimming with tenderness and compassion. "I think you are just the right person."

Sadie lifted herself from the floor and walked to the window, confused by how easily she had shared her most intimate feelings with Kade. *He might be* Englisch, Sadie thought, *but he is still a man.* She had been guilty of returning Kade's tender gazes. It had been hard not to, after all they had shared this morning. But she was wrong to encourage any thoughts that might hint at more than friendship.

She stared out the window and wondered if Kade was having any ideas about going back to the cottage. The storm didn't seem any worse, but it didn't seem any better either. Sadie looked over her shoulder at Kade. The man didn't look like he was going anywhere, stretched out across the rug beside his son. She turned back around and couldn't help but grin. If Bishop Ebersol knew about this . . .

But then she reminded herself of the seriousness of her actions. The bishop might not find out about this time spent with Kade, but Sadie knew she was crossing the line. *And God knows.*

She didn't have the heart to force Kade to bundle up Tyler and carry the child out into the storm. With the way the wind was swirling around, it would actually be quite dangerous. Hopefully, conditions would improve soon. She decided to lighten the conversation.

"Maybe when the storm clears, you and Tyler can build a snowman." She walked back over to the middle of the room and took a seat next to Tyler. "Do you think you would like that, Tyler?" Tyler didn't acknowledge the question. By now, he'd drawn mazes of circles on at least twenty different sheets of paper.

"I've never made a snowman," Kade said. He sat up and leaned toward Tyler. "Maybe when the weather gets better, we'll do that together, Tyler."

"You have never made a snowman? Not even as a child?" Sadie raised her brows, thinking how sad that was.

"I grew up in Los Angeles. We don't see much snow. By the time I saw *real* snow, I was too old to build a snowman."

"Nonsense," Sadie exclaimed. "You are never too old to build a snowman. Every year after the first *gut* snowfall, *mei daed* would get up early and surprise me with a snowman outside my bedroom window." She giggled at the recollection. "Each year, he would come up with a different theme for the snowman, or snowwoman, as it sometimes turned out to be." She put her finger to her chin.

"One year, I awoke to find a snowman that was built to look like he was standing on his head. Pop put two sticks up top for his feet, and he made the face upside down on the bottom ball of snow." She laughed. "It was funny. Pop called that snowman 'Sadie's silly friend.' One time, he made two people holding hands. He called them 'the happy couple.' Sometimes, he dressed them in clothes, or had them holding brooms or pots, or some other sort of prop. There was this one time—" She stopped and grinned. "This must be terribly boring for you."

Kade gazed at her with a glint of wonder in his eyes. "Sadie, I don't think there's anything you could say that would bore me."

She pulled her eyes from his and focused on Tyler. "Look at all the circles." She rummaged nervously through the loose papers scattered about. Maybe it was his tone of voice, perhaps the way he'd looked at her, but . . . the alarms were sounding again.

"Sadie?" He leaned back, resting on his palms behind him.

She didn't look up and tried to sound casual. "*Ya?*"

"Look at me," he whispered.

Sadie lifted her eyes to meet his.

"We're not doing anything wrong, Sadie. You do realize that, right?"

"I know that," she said with a shrug. She turned toward the fire. "We need another log, I reckon. I can get it this time." She started to get up.

"I'll get it." But Kade didn't move. "In a minute."

Sadie took a deep breath and waited for him to go on.

"Do you remember what I told you last night?" Kade asked. "I just want to be your friend. I enjoy your company. Everything is fine, Sadie."

"*Ya*, I know." She shrugged again, but Kade was clearly tuned in to her worries.

The last thing Kade wanted to do was rattle his new friend—this amazing, intriguing, beautiful woman. And she had the playfulness of a child at times, like when she talked about the snowmen, her face aglow with memories. *She is something.* But Kade knew he'd need to go easy with any comments or looks that might hint at what a wonderful person he thought she was. He was having trouble, though. This woman was stirring things in him that he didn't quite recognize. In his world, it would only be natural to act on such thoughts, or at least voice them. But this woman's goodness was so *real*, and Kade knew he would never disrespect her in any way.

"Are you hungry?" she asked Kade. "I can hear poor Tyler's tummy growling."

"Tyler's hungry," Tyler said, without looking up from his current project—more circles.

Kade glanced at his watch and couldn't believe it was nearing lunchtime. When he'd sensed that the conversation about the status of their friendship made Sadie uncomfortable, he had changed the subject. Her eyes shone with wonder when Kade told her about some of his travels around the world.

His expression stilled and grew serious. "You know, I'm worried that we might be wearing out our welcome." He sure hoped not, though.

Sadie nodded toward the window. "If you would rather go out into this weather instead of having peanut butter spread on homemade bread, that's fine with me." She grinned.

One minute, she seemed nervous as a cat. The next minute, she was playful and almost . . . flirty. Mixed signals for sure. "I think Tyler and I would much rather stay and have a sandwich with you, as opposed to going out into *that*." He pointed toward the window. "Besides, I don't think I've had a peanut-butter-and-jelly sandwich since I was a kid. And even then, it wasn't very often."

Sadie stood up, smoothed the wrinkles from her apron, and said, "Actually this peanut butter spread is different from the peanut butter in jars that the *Englisch* use. And we like to put cheese spread on our bread and then top it with the peanut spread, but if you'd like—"

"No, no." Kade stood up. "We'll have whatever you're having. Sounds great."

Kade followed her into the kitchen. "Can I help?"

"No, it's fine. You can play with Tyler while I get things ready." She walked toward the cabinet and pulled out a jar of peanut spread, then a jar of cheese spread. Kade plopped himself down on the bench in the kitchen.

"So, it's homemade bread, topped with cheese spread, and then topped with peanut butter spread?" he asked.

"*Ya*. We serve this after Sunday church service, but I eat it sometimes for lunch." She twisted the lid on the peanut spread and placed it on the counter, but the lid on the cheese spread wasn't budging. After banging the edge on the countertop, she tried again.

Kade was on his feet and standing next to her right away. "Here, let me," he offered. The lid unwound with ease, and Kade handed it back to her, but he was in no hurry to leave her side. She smelled so clean and fresh, not bathed in perfume, like most of the women he knew. He breathed in the smell of her one more time before he headed back to the bench.

"Tyler, are you ready to eat?" Sadie walked into the den to find Tyler still occupied with his drawings.

"Tyler hungry."

"You come right this way," she said. "I have a special lunch prepared for you."

Sadie returned with Tyler by her side. "Why don't you sit by your pop—I mean, your *daed*—and I'll get you some milk."

Tyler slid in beside Kade. "You sure have been a good boy, Tyler," Kade said. He was surprised at how self-entertaining his son had been.

"Tyler's a good boy," Tyler said as he reached for the salt in the middle of the table.

"Oh, I don't think we need any salt." Kade reached for the salt shaker in Tyler's hand. Mistake. Tyler began to scream at the top of his lungs.

"What's wrong?" Sadie was quickly by his side.

"He's trying to pour salt all over everything," Kade said, struggling to get the salt shaker from Tyler.

"Maybe you should let him have it," Sadie said.

"In Monica's notes, it said that he'll scream to get what he wants, but that if you give in, he'll always do that." Kade pulled the salt from Tyler's grip. "You can't have this, Tyler," he said in a firm voice. Tyler screamed even more and began to bang his head on the table in front of him.

"Oh, man." Kade ran his hand through his hair. "Tyler, please don't do that." *Think. Think.* "The itsy-bitsy spider walked up the waterspout . . ." Kade began, recalling that Monica had mentioned that he liked that particular song. Tyler stopped crying and wiped his eyes. It was working. "Down came the rain and washed the spider out . . ." Kade was surprised he remembered the song from his childhood. He even remembered the hand motions and began to dribble the rain with his fingers. Tyler started doing the same thing, with a big smile on his face.

Kade was ending the song when Sadie put a plate in front of Tyler. "Here you go, Tyler. My specialty." Then she looked at Kade. "See, you are learning Tyler's ways." Then she giggled.

"What?" He loved the way she laughed.

"It's funny, and nice, the way you sang to him." Her face lit up the playful way it did sometimes. Kade nodded, a little embarrassed.

Tyler dug in almost immediately. "Good," he said, his mouth full.

Sadie placed Kade's plate in front of him. It was the most interesting lunch he'd ever been served. In addition to the sandwich, there was something on the side that looked like applesauce, and something else he'd seen in his refrigerator at the cottage but hadn't tried.

"That's applesauce and chowchow," Sadie said when she saw him eyeing his plate. She sat down across from them at the table. "It's *gut*. Try it."

The applesauce was fine, but he didn't care too much for the chowchow—mixed vegetables in some sort of pickling sauce. He wasn't much of a pickle eater. "It's great," he lied. The peanut butter and cheese spreads on the bread were delicious, though. *Who would have thought?*

"*Danki*," she said.

After lunch, they resumed their places in the den. Sadie had found several things to entertain Tyler. Two decks of cards, a doll, which oddly didn't have a face, and a bag of building blocks she said she kept on hand for visitors' children. Tyler loved the blocks and stayed entertained for the next four hours, during which time Kade and Sadie swapped stories about their childhoods, their parents, Alicia, Ben, and a host of other topics.

"You are so easy to talk to," Kade said during a break. *I could stay here forever.* He was so detached from the life he knew, and he couldn't remember being happier.

"It's easy to talk to you too." Kade could tell it was hard for her to say, and her eyes avoided his. She glanced out the window. "This is supposed to be the worst of the blizzard," she said. "Tomorrow morning should be much better, but we might be snowed in for a few days."

Excellent, he thought. *Just me, Tyler, and Sadie.* The thought brought him a sense of comfort.

Sadie started to help Tyler build his fortress, and Kade sat watching the two of them. Every once in a while, both Sadie and Tyler would laugh out loud, like when the blocks came tumbling down around them. It was a vision, for sure.

Kade realized that Monica had been put to rest by now, and he'd missed it. His heart ached about missing the funeral and about Monica's death. He was feeling a little guilty that he hadn't thought more about it during the course of the day. To Kade's surprise, he hadn't thought about Alicia in several days either. He wasn't thinking about much of anything—except Sadie and Tyler.

Sadie was at her most beautiful when she laughed. He didn't think he'd ever tire of hearing her laughter. When she looked up unexpectedly and found Kade almost drooling over her, she stopped smiling and looked uncomfortable.

"I'm sorry," he blurted out, shook his head. "It's just . . ." He wanted to tell her that she was a beautiful person, inside and out. But he knew he couldn't. She'd fold up with embarrassment. "Nothing," he said instead. His thoughts were venturing into a forbidden zone, and he kept forcing himself not to look at her lips. Kade knew he needed to leave.

"Tyler, we've outstayed our welcome," he said in a regretful voice. "I should take him and go home. I mean to the cottage."

Sadie's mouth flew open. "The weather is awful outside." She nodded toward the window.

"I know. But at least it's daylight. And it might not get any better. Probably best to go now, before it gets dark." *And before I say or do something I shouldn't.*

"It won't be dark for a bit yet." Kade was more than a little glad that she didn't want them to leave, but just the same, he knew he needed to leave.

He bundled up Tyler, and Sadie retrieved an extra blanket for Kade to wrap around Tyler.

"I wish you didn't have to go out in this, especially with the boy," she said with concern.

"It wouldn't be fair to leave Tyler here with you again," he said. "And actually, I missed the little guy last night." Kade found this thought somewhat surprising, but true.

"I will miss him too." She smiled at Tyler.

"Tyler loves Sadie," Tyler said.

Sadie grabbed her chest, and her eyes lit up. "Tyler, I love you too!"

"Wow. He's never said that to me," Kade said, not hiding his disappointment.

"He will." Sadie smiled.

Before Kade put on his heavy coat, he pulled her into a hug and held her close, begging her with his embrace not to push him away.

And she didn't. Sadie clung to him as tightly as he was clinging to her. Something was happening. They both knew it.

"Thanks for everything," he whispered.

"You are welcome."

But neither of them pulled away. Not until Tyler began to stomp his feet, and Kade forced himself from her arms.

"Bye," he whispered. And Kade picked up Tyler and headed into the storm, protecting his son the best he could.

It wasn't until they were settled in for the night that Kade had a thought. An idea that brought a smile to his face.

Sadie Fisher is in for a big surprise.

13

SADIE SAT ON THE EDGE OF HER BED AND YAWNED. There had been no sleep in between the thrashing winds and her all-consuming replays of the hug she had shared with Kade—the feel of his body next to her, the way he clung to her, as if letting her go would sever whatever it was that was happening between them. And Sadie knew that something was happening, a thought that terrified her. But it had been so long—so long since she'd been held by a man.

She shook her head. A grown woman—an Amish woman, at that—should fend off such temptation, no matter the attraction. But Sadie couldn't deny her attraction to Kade, a man she at first thought to be shallow and arrogant, an *Englischer* she assumed had no regard for anything except his money. In reality, Kade was a lost man struggling to renew his faith and to find his place in this world, not so unlike Sadie in that regard. And now Kade would face those challenges while raising a special child who he didn't know very well. She reached down to tie her shoes and noticed that for the first time in two days, the wind wasn't howling outside.

Maybe the worst of the storm has passed, like the newspapers predicted. She walked to the window and pulled up the blind, and then brought both hands to her mouth and gasped. *I don't believe it.*

Her entire body shook as she laughed out loud at the funniest-looking snowman she'd ever seen in her life. Or snowwoman . . . or snow-*something*.

She peered outside for any sign of Kade. The snow had stopped, and the trees gently swayed against the dying winds. Delicate, orange rays pushed through clouds that seemed hesitant to give in to the sun's full force, revealing a wintry wonderland that glistened with tranquillity for as far as Sadie could see. A welcome sight, indeed. She glanced over her shoulder at her clock. Seven thirty. Granted, she had slept in following her restless night, but Kade must have gotten up early to create the . . . *thing* in front of her window. She bent over laughing, having never felt more flattered in her life.

Visions of her father came to mind. Sadie could almost see him perfecting a masterpiece, applying the finishing touches—a nose, a mouth, a scarf, a hat . . . Although when she looked at the masterpiece Kade had created, she pictured her father with his hands on his hips, head cocked sideways, saying, "What is this silly *Englischer* trying to do?"

It was the worst snowman Sadie had ever seen. Three lopsided balls gave the impression that this snowman had partaken in too much of the bubbly, swaying to one side as if being pushed over by the wind. The middle of the creation was larger and rounder than the top and bottom portion, and Sadie wasn't sure, but it looked like the thing had tiny arms molded out of snow, jetting straight out from each side.

She recognized a green, plastic kitchen glass at the end of one of the limbs. Must be what the snowman drank his bubbly from, she surmised, giggling aloud. Bright-yellow lemons were pushed into hand-molded eye sockets, and Kade had drawn big, black pupils in the middle of each one, giving his snowman a most frightening demeanor. Mr. Scary Snowman had a carrot for a nose—at least Kade had gotten that part right. And there must have been a hundred toothpicks in the shape of a wide grin, making Kade's handiwork the happiest scary snowman she'd ever laid eyes on.

A blue and red tie wound around Mr. Scary Snowman's neck and fell the length of the middle clump of snow, and a blue baseball cap finished off his attire. Sadie shook her head, and then hurried down the stairs two at a time with a childish enthusiasm she recalled having each time her pop surprised her with the first snowman of the season. And the fact that Kade had created this ridiculous structure outside her window touched her in a way she knew wasn't good, a way that made her want to run into his arms and thank him for making her laugh and feel so alive again.

She bundled herself in her heavy coat, gloves, and boots, and she was off. She glided across the icy, slick porch until she reached the steps. Grabbing the rails, she eased down each snow-covered step, and then plowed across the soft snow, periodically sinking to her shins. The wind and snow might have ceased, but it was so cold her teeth were chattering. She didn't care. She was anxious to have a closer look at what she would now call Scary Drunken Snowman.

Cameras were forbidden by the Old Order, but she'd never wished she had one more than at this moment. She stood face-to-face with it and noticed that several of the toothpicks had fallen out of the happy smile, leaving Scary Drunken Snowman with a rather toothless look. She was laughing when she heard the cottage door open. Kade held Tyler's hand as they made their way down the front steps.

"Well, what do you think?" Kade yelled across the snow-covered space between them. He heaved Tyler into his arms and picked up the pace.

Sadie knew she was grinning from ear to ear, and she pinched her lips together to try to stifle the laughter that threatened to erupt. "*Gut*," she said quickly. She pursed her lips together again. Kade was out of breath by the time he and Tyler joined her.

"The baseball cap was Tyler's idea," Kade said with pride, panting a bit. "But I think the tie is what topped him off, don't you?"

"*Ya, ya,*" Sadie said. She was still trying not to laugh since Kade seemed so proud of his work. Hard to believe, but she figured she'd better go along. "It's lovely," she said. Then she couldn't hold it anymore. She bent over, put her hands on her knees, and laughed in a way that she couldn't remember ever laughing. It was a gut-wrenching, snorting sort of laugh that she would have been embarrassed about if it didn't feel so good.

"Are you laughing at my snowman?" Kade asked. He lifted his chin and turned toward Tyler. "Do you think Miss Sadie is laughing at our snowman?"

Tyler started laughing so hard that Sadie only laughed harder. "Miss Sadie funny," Tyler said.

"I'm sorry," Sadie managed to say between snorts of laughter. "It's just that—" She started up again.

Then Kade started laughing, and it was as if the world stopped spinning for a few seconds, the three of them lost in a perfect moment. A child's laughter, a glistening snowfall, two grown-ups reveling in silliness. And Sadie planned to enjoy the rarity of such a moment for as long as she could. She gathered herself, leaned down, and rolled the white powder into a perfect round ball.

"I suggest you run!" she said.

Kade looked ridiculous, lifting his legs up to his waist in an effort to step through the snow removing him and Tyler away from her line of fire. "What's Miss Sadie doing?" Kade yelled. His eyes shone with playful tenderness as he looked at his son. And Tyler laughed so hard, Sadie was sure Kade was going to drop the boy.

She heaved the snowball, making sure to hit Kade in the leg, and not Tyler. Then Tyler wanted in on the game, and he squirmed his way out of Kade's arms. Tyler sank into the snow, picked himself up, and started rolling the snow into a ball.

"You're in trouble now!" Kade yelled. "Tyler seems to have easily picked up on this game." Kade leaned down and helped Tyler squeeze the snow into a tight ball. "You better run, pretty lady!"

Pretty lady? Sadie should have been colder than cold, but she felt warm. She hiked her dress up, her big, black boots sinking into the soft snow. It was not her most ladylike behavior, that was for sure, but she bolted across the snow anyway, laughing the entire time.

"Throw, Tyler!" Kade yelled.

And the boy heaved the snowball and smacked her in the middle of her back.

"Are you okay?" Kade seemed serious all of a sudden as he trudged toward her.

She was fine, though, and wasted no time scooping up her own handful of snow. "You better run, the both of you!"

"Run, Tyler!" Kade yelled. He reached for Tyler's hand, and the two of them ambled through the snow.

One thing Sadie knew how to do, and that was to make a fine snowball. She added snow, packed it tighter, and then took aim, thrusting her handmade weapon—right into the back of Kade's head. Over he went.

"Oh no!" she yelled. Kade was facedown in the snow. "Oh no! Oh no!" She fell to her knees and leaned over him. "Kade, are you all right?" Tyler stood at her side, as if he, too, were wondering if his father was going to get up.

Then, without warning, Kade rolled onto his back, grabbed Sadie, and pulled her down beside him, yelling and laughing the whole time. "Gotcha!"

She was completely rattled, yet she couldn't stop laughing as she lay beside Kade in the freezing snow. He reached for her hand, squeezed it, and didn't let go. Then the realization of what was happening hit her hard, and she tried to wriggle her hand from his grasp. He tightened his hold and looked over at her. "I don't remember when I've had this much fun. Please, let's don't analyze it."

But despite the merriment, Sadie pried her hand from his and forced herself to stand up. Kade stood up as well. She reckoned his teeth were knocking together about as much as hers, and Tyler looked frozen as well. "Coffee is what we need, and some hot cocoa for Tyler," she said.

"Yes. Coffee and cocoa," Kade said.

They cumbersomely made their way to the house. Kade carried Tyler. Once inside, Kade added logs to the fire, as if he lived there. And Sadie prepared coffee, cocoa, and breakfast—as if both Kade and Tyler lived there. It should have been awkward. It seemed anything but.

The day was spent much like the previous day, soaking up the heat from the fireplace, playing games with Tyler, and talking—lots of talking. Sadie knew, with every inch of her being, that she was in a dangerous place, but why would God give her a glimpse of something so magical if it were wrong? So she allowed herself to go with it.

In the evening, she said good-bye to both Kade and Tyler, and another hug followed, this one more tender and longer than the time before.

And that's how the threesome spent the next three days—sharing breakfast, lunch, supper, and games and conversation in between. And the now-customary hug ended the day, before darkness settled.

But on this Tuesday night, only a while before Milo was scheduled to call, Kade pulled from the hug and gazed into Sadie's eyes in a way that she knew he was going to kiss her. She'd never wanted anything more in her life, she was quite sure. But she gently nudged him back. He didn't push, and they stared at each other in a way that seemed not to need any words.

"Good night," he said softly.

"Good night." She leaned down. "And good night to you, Tyler."

"Tyler loves Sadie." Sadie pulled Tyler into a hug, and he fell into her arms.

"I love you, too, Tyler."

"He still hasn't said that to me," Kade said. He dipped his head slightly as his eyes darkened with emotion.

"He will." Sadie smiled up at Kade, Tyler still holding tight.

"Come on, Tyler," Kade said. "We better let Sadie get some rest."

Sadie waved to them from the porch as they made their way back to the cottage. She checked the clock on the wall. For the first time, she considered not going to the barn to wait for Milo's call at eight o'clock. He had already failed to call her the week before, and it was dreadfully cold. And if she was honest with herself, she'd admit her head was filled with thoughts of Kade and Tyler these days. She hadn't thought much about Milo, nor had she reread any of his letters. But Sadie watched the clock until time for him to call, and then she headed to the barn.

At ten after eight, she left the barn with a new emotion that Milo didn't call: relief.

The next morning, Sadie heard the snowplows on Black Horse Road. Life would resume to normal. She'd no longer be hidden away with Kade and Tyler. Today, she'd open the shop with Lillian, and yes, things would return to normal.

Then why did she feel that something inside her would never feel normal again? Something had changed. Her spirit had changed, her willingness and ability to feel happiness. She'd been happier than she had been since Ben died.

She recalled her many prayers for God to grant her happiness. And He had. But why this way? It was a reality she couldn't have, a happiness that had no place in her world. She was instantly back where she started, questioning God's will for her.

"I am so glad to be out of the *haus*," Lillian exclaimed when she met Sadie at the shop that morning. "You know how much I love my Samuel, David, and baby Anna, but they were about to make me bonkers." Lillian laughed. "I think we all got a touch of cabin fever." She cut her eyes in Sadie's direction. "Oh, Sadie. I can't imagine how it must have been for you, all these days alone out here. That must have been equally dreadful." Lillian shook her head, frowning.

"*Ya*," Sadie said. "Dreadful." She pulled her eyes from Lillian's, afraid Lillian would pick up on Sadie's variation of the truth.

But her friend went on to ready the shop for business. And without much traffic, since the weather was still uncomfortably cold, Lillian spent most of the morning telling Sadie about her confinement indoors with Samuel and David. "They are so used to being outdoors, it's hard to keep them entertained," she said.

Sadie listened and chose not to share her adventures with Lillian, even though Lillian was her best friend and the one person who would most understand how Sadie had allowed herself to slip into a situation that was unacceptable at best. She'd no sooner had the thought when the bell on the front door of the shop rang. And in walked Kade and Tyler.

"I thought it was time we checked out Treasures of the Heart," he said with a smile.

Sadie jumped up. "Kade, what are you doing here?" She knew her tone revealed the alarm she felt at being around Kade with Lillian in the room.

Kade smiled and seemed to pick up on Sadie's unease. He walked to where Lillian was sitting on a stool by the counter. "Nice to see you again, Lillian." He extended his hand to Lillian.

"Nice to see you as well," she said. "And who is this young fellow?" Lillian leaned down toward Tyler.

"This is Tyler," Sadie interjected. "Isn't he a handsome little man?" Sadie was beaming with the pride of a mother, she knew, but Tyler had stolen her heart, and it was hard to hide.

"Sadie and I were just talking about how miserable we were during the storm. Confined, bored." Lillian shook her head. "We're both glad it's all over."

"I didn't say I was *bored*, though," Sadie rushed to say. She looked back and forth between Kade and Lillian. Kade smiled. Lillian looked confused. But Lillian was quick, and she didn't stay confused for long.

"No, Sadie didn't say she was bored," Lillian said. Then she grinned. "I did all the talking. Sadie didn't say much at all."

"I was by myself, in the house . . . in the night hours. *Ya*, in the house by myself most of the time." Sadie took a deep breath. "Except for playtime. I mean, card time. Or talking time. And we played in the snow once, and . . ." She couldn't seem to stop herself. She took another deep breath, and then glanced back and forth between Lillian and Kade. Lillian was grinning from ear to ear. Kade was a gentleman.

"Well, ladies, we wanted to see your shop and say hello. Lillian, it was a pleasure to see you again." He turned his attention to Sadie. "And Sadie, this is a great place you have here."

"*Danki*," she whispered. Lillian was going to get hold of her the minute Kade and Tyler were out the door. This Sadie knew.

"Oh, and Sadie, I wanted to let you know—Tyler and I are going to venture out this afternoon. I think it's time we see Lancaster County." Kade pointed toward the barn. "My car is back. I arranged for some men to dig it out of the snow and bring it back, but Tyler and I are going to take a cab. Not only do I not drive very well in the snow, but I think that driving, reading a map, and Tyler in the car . . . well, it might be a little much."

"Here, take this." Lillian handed Kade a pamphlet they kept on the counter. "It's an off-the-beaten-path map. It'll take you away from the touristy places to real Amish shops, bakeries, and such. We like to share this with our customers."

Kade accepted it and waved as he headed out the door.

It took every ounce of Sadie's willpower not to say, "Will I see you for supper?" but she reminded herself that things had changed now that the blizzard was over. And she found that thought most depressing.

The bell on the door was still ringing from Kade and Tyler's exit when Lillian said with a grin, "Oh, my. What has my best friend been up to?"

It was early afternoon when Sarah Jane, Katie Ann, Mary Ellen, and Rebecca showed up at the shop, each telling stories about their confinement during the storm. Sadie kept quiet. She had told Lillian about her past few days, but only sparse details. Of course, Lillian filled in the blanks on her own, and there'd been no doubt that Lillian, worldly as she'd once been, was worried about Sadie. "Be careful, Sadie," she'd said. "Kade Saunders is a powerful man who comes from a world you know nothing about."

While that might be true—that she knew nothing of Kade's world—she knew *Kade*, the man. But she realized Lillian had every reason to be concerned.

"Ivan found it to be *wunderbaar gut*, staying in the *haus* for all those days," Katie Ann huffed. "Said it was like a vacation." She shook her head. "A vacation for him maybe. But he was making me *narrisch!*"

Sarah Jane laughed out loud. "I'm sure you girls all had a rough time, but please remember that I was cooped up for six days with Pop."

"*Ach,*" Rebecca said. "That's true. I reckon you were more *narrisch* than the rest of us."

They all laughed, picturing six days trapped inside with the lovable, yet mischievous Jonas.

"Do you know that Pop and Lizzie have been communicating with walkie-talkies?" Sarah Jane told them all. "It's the cutest thing in the world, really. But I think if I hear 'breaker, breaker' one more time, I might snap like a twig."

"It's sweet that they are courting," Mary Ellen said.

Sarah Jane took a seat on the stool behind the counter. "I'm happy that Pop seems to have found someone he cares about. He was a wreck after *mei mamm* died."

"Irma Rose was a *gut* woman," Rebecca said.

"But having Pop in the house, in his state of mind, and courting . . . well . . ." Sarah Jane laughed again. "I think you can all imagine; I have my hands full."

"We all love Jonas so much," Sadie said.

"I'm happy to share him with all of you," Sarah Jane said with enthusiasm. "There is enough of Jonas to go around, that's for sure."

"*Wunderbaar gut* to see the sun out," Katie Anne said. She walked to the window that faced Black Horse Road. "And to see the snow-plows out. I've even seen a few cars on the road."

"We had two visitors here in the shop earlier," Lillian said.

"They didn't buy anything, but it's *gut* to see people are getting out and about."

"Is that your *Englisch* renter pulling into the drive in the yellow taxi?" Katie Anne asked. She pointed out the window at a cab turning into the driveway.

"*Ya*, I reckon so," Sadie said. She joined Katie Anne at the window. *And he's in time for supper later.* They hadn't discussed it, but Sadie knew she'd make the offer, bishop or no bishop. Right or wrong. Her time with Kade and Tyler had been some of the best she'd had in years. All the warning bells in the world weren't going to stop her from a night of supper, maybe some conversation, and a goodnight hug. They were simple pleasures, harmless. And maybe if she kept telling herself that, she'd reconcile her guilt.

They all huddled around the window and watched as the cab stopped near the farmhouse instead of the cottage. Then a man stepped out of the car, one tall, lanky leg at a time.

"That isn't the *Englischer*," Rebecca said assuredly. She shot a questioning expression Sadie's way.

She pressed her hand to her chest and pushed the others gently aside. She watched the man turn their way, and she took a deep breath to calm her pounding chest.

"Who is it, Sadie?" Lillian asked.

"Sadie?" she heard Rebecca say. "Are you all right?"

The others chimed in, but their voices were echoes in a tunnel, tuned out by Sadie's own thoughts, fears, anticipation.

There was no way for Sadie to know for sure, yet she did.

It was Milo.

14

Tyler and Kade toured the towns of Bird-in-Hand, Paradise, and Intercourse, stopping at places recommended in the pamphlet from Sadie and her friends. Tyler's highlight of the day had been a buggy ride in Paradise. He clapped his hands throughout the entire ride. Kade knew the clapping was self-stimulatory behavior, as per Monica's notes, but it was the smile on Tyler's face that Kade would remember from this special day with his son. Kade had hoped to take such a ride with Sadie, but when Tyler saw the horse hitched to the buggy on the side of the road, he couldn't resist the massive animal. For fifty bucks, they explored the back roads in Paradise, to Tyler's delight. And the cab driver seemed thankful to be carting Kade and Tyler around for most of the day.

During the taxi ride back to the cottage, Kade admired Amish homesteads cloaked in white along the winding roads, each with a silo and several outbuildings. They passed other buggies along the way, the occupants bundled in thick blankets, the same as Kade and Tyler had been during their ride. Tyler had laughed and pointed at the passersby, sometimes waving. It was their first outing as father and son, and it felt good. Kade was eager to get to know his son better. His fears had subsided, and

Sadie had played a big part in that. She'd been so good with Tyler from the very beginning, so natural. For Kade, it hadn't come easy, but watching her gave him confidence that he could do the job—maybe even do it well.

Kade had been all over the world, but something about Lancaster County provided an elusive sort of peacefulness that Kade hadn't felt anywhere else, as if the Amish held the secret to true contentment, tucked away in their own world detached from modern society—a world Sadie had given him a glimpse of. He thought he'd head back to L.A. once the storm let up. He needed to prepare for Tyler, and he had thirty-six business-related messages on his cell phone that he'd been putting off. And at some point, he knew he needed to talk to Val.

But at the moment, only one thing was on his mind. Actually, two. The bright-eyed boy sitting next to him in the cab, and Sadie. Everything else seemed distant and unimportant.

The driver made his way back toward Sadie's place, and Kade recalled the past few days in vivid detail, zoning in on their good-night hugs. Never before had a simple gesture of affection moved him in such a way. It wasn't just the feel of her in his arms, her fresh aroma and soft skin—although those things kept him up at night—it was Sadie, the woman. She made Kade want to be a better man.

Kade also felt a new level of responsibility. He was accountable for a lot of people's livelihoods, for billion-dollar business deals, and a host of other things that, at the moment, didn't compare to the job he'd been handed—raising his son.

"Sadie's house," Tyler said when the driver pulled into the driveway.

"Yes, it is. That's Sadie's house." Kade watched his son's face light up and knew that Sadie had the same effect on Tyler as she did on him.

"Tyler loves Sadie," Tyler said.

Me too. The thought hit Kade like a jab in his chest, pushing him to a place he hadn't expected. Did he love her? Was that even possible? The idea had certainly popped into his head as naturally as Tyler had said the words. It was an idea too complicated to explore right now. The end result may not be what Kade wanted, and he was too caught up in the time he had left to worry with what the future might bring. Life was good today, and he planned to live in the present.

"Thank you." He handed the driver a wad of cash, anxious to see Sadie. The driver responded with an enthusiastic "Thank you!" before he drove away.

"Do you want to go say hello to Sadie?" Kade asked Tyler.

Tyler nodded and reached for Kade's hand. It was a first. And Kade knew that at this moment, on this day, he was exactly where he needed to be. Everything else could wait.

They walked toward the farmhouse and eased their way up the icy steps.

Kade heard voices inside. Sadie's voice and . . . a male voice.

"Are you sure?" Lillian had asked Sadie. "How do you know it's Milo? You've never seen him. How could you possibly know?"

But Sadie did know, sure as she'd known anything in her life. Milo's tall stance, his questioning eyes as he scanned his sur-roundings—yes, it was him. She was sure. And she didn't move.

The ladies turned their attention to her. "He's heading up to the farmhouse, Sadie," Rebecca said. "Aren't you going to go find out for sure?"

"I bet you can hardly contain your excitement!" Mary Ellen squealed.

Lillian's mother nudged the others aside and cupped Sadie's cheek in her hand. "Sadie, dear, it's only natural for you to be *naerfich*," Sarah Jane said. "You've been writing letters to Milo for a long time. And now he's here."

Sadie's feet were rooted to the floor.

"If it's even him," Katie Anne said in a skeptical voice. She poked her head around the others and stared toward the farmhouse. "Sadie, he's knocking on the door. You better go see if it's him." She eased Sadie toward the door, even though Sadie's feet fought to stay where they were.

"It'll be fine," Lillian said as Sadie turned the knob.

The bell on the door clanged as she closed the door and looked toward the farmhouse. She began the long trek to what she had presumed for a long time would be her future. Milo. But her head was abuzz with doubt, fear, worry—and, most of all, Kade.

She was within a few steps of the porch when he turned around. Sadie stood perfectly still, studying him. Handsome. Very handsome. Dark hair and a short beard, and tall, just like he'd described himself. Although he left out that he had stunning, bright-blue eyes, and a smile that stretched wide above a square jawline. Milo, if indeed it was him, had been much too modest about his appearance. Looks were not everything, but there was no denying that Milo's attractiveness caught Sadie's eye.

"Sadie?" His voice was deep.

"Milo?"

His smile widened, and he headed down the porch steps toward her. After stopping for a moment in front of her, taking in her appearance as well, he wrapped his arms around her in what should have been the happiest moment of her life.

She closed her eyes tight. Milo didn't smell like Kade. He was taller than Kade, towering over her by almost a foot. *He isn't Kade.*

"Sadie," he whispered. He held her tighter. "I couldn't wait until spring." He pulled away from the hug, but kept his strong hands on her arms. "I began my travels two weeks ago, but a blizzard kept me away for almost a week. I haven't been able to phone you . . ." He paused and fused his eyes with hers. "Sadie, you are more beautiful than I could have pictured in my mind."

"*Danki.*" She looked away, blushed. "Let's go in out of the cold," she said.

Milo followed her up the porch steps, and Sadie felt as though she were in a dream. She should have been walking on clouds in this dream she'd harbored for two years. But instead, the fantasy of Milo and the reality of him faced off like competing emotions, confusing Sadie so that she wasn't sure what she felt.

Sadie prepared some hot cocoa, then sat down on the wooden bench at the kitchen table across from Milo.

"It's so *gut* to finally be here." Milo's eyes shone. He was everything she imagined him to be. "I reckon that after all this time, you might have been thinkin' I wasn't coming."

Sadie shook her head, though it had been exactly what she'd been thinking. "I knew that someday we would meet." She sipped her cocoa. This man was a stranger, despite all their correspondences. It felt odd for him to be sitting here at her kitchen table.

But now that he was here, Sadie tried to reconcile her thoughts and recall how much she'd longed for this day. *Everything will be fine now.* She planned to continue telling herself that for as long as necessary, until things were as God intended them to be.

"You have a fine homestead," he said. "I'm anxious for you to travel with me to Stephenville. I read much about Lancaster County in the *Budget* and the *Die Botschaft.* And from what little I have seen of your fair county, it has much more population than where I come from. As I wrote in *mei* letters, our Order is small compared to Lancaster County."

How much smaller? She took in a breath and exhaled slowly as she thought about the possibility of living somewhere else.

"I will need to talk with Katie Anne and Ivan to make arrangements for you to stay with them while you're here. They have been expecting for you to be their guest whenever you arrived." Sadie hoped the last-minute notice would be all right with Katie Anne. "Katie Anne is at my shop right now." Sadie pointed out the window, where she could see in the distance all the women still peering through the window toward her farmhouse. She was tempted to close the blind, but instead, she smiled to herself.

"I don't want to be a bother for anyone, and I don't mind getting a room in town or—"

"*Ach*, nonsense. Katie Anne and her husband, Ivan, will love to have you in their home. They haven't been blessed with *kinner* yet, so it's just the two of them."

"Sadie, I feel like I know you so well." He smiled at her, the way a man does when he's smitten. She smiled back, but she wasn't feeling like she knew Milo very well at all. She knew the voice on the other end of the phone, the penmanship in the letters she'd received. But the man before her seemed like a stranger, familiar yet unreal.

"*Ya.* It is so *gut* to finally meet you in person," she said. *Very handsome,* she thought again, as her eyes met his. "How long will you be staying?"

Milo's forehead wrinkled. "Not as long as I'd hoped. Due to *mei* delays with the weather, I will need to leave in a few days. On Saturday."

"That's only three days from now." After all this time, after two years, and he could only stay for three days?

He reached over and placed his hand on hers, which rattled Sadie a bit, but she didn't move her hand. "Come to Texas with me on Saturday. I have two bus tickets for us to travel together. You can come before the harvest begins, and we'll have time to get to know each other."

It was so sudden. Sadie had never been out of Lancaster County before, much less across the United States to Texas. "Can't you stay here a bit longer?" she countered.

"I would love to stay in your community, get to know your family and friends, but I must prepare the fields for harvest. We only have a small family harvest, and I work at my carpentry. *Mei* sisters and *mamm* will keep you company when I'm not able to, and they will introduce you to members of our community, in hopes that you will want to stay." He paused, then smiled. "In hopes that you will want to stay with me and become *mei fraa* someday."

They'd talked about it on the phone many times, and corresponded about it in letters as well, but hearing Milo recite their plans right here at her kitchen table was almost overwhelming. This was her home. There was her shop, her friends . . .

Milo's expression was kind, sympathetic. He still had his hand atop hers, and Sadie feared her hand was growing clammy at the thought of leaving. "I know how hard it would be to leave your community, the only place you've ever known. Don't think I would take that lightly, Sadie." He gave her hand a gentle squeeze. "But our life will be *wunderbaar gut*, and *mei mamm*, sisters, and the rest of the district will welcome you with their arms and hearts open. Leave with me on Saturday, Sadie? Stay as long as you like." He smiled. "Perhaps, forever."

Sadie couldn't help but smile. He was offering her everything she'd dreamed of. But yet, she felt almost relieved to have an excuse not to go. "I would love that, Milo. But I have a renter in the cottage. He will stay through March, and he has his young child with him."

Milo's face sank, and he took a deep breath. "I understand." Then he forced a smile. "Then we shall enjoy the time we have while I'm here." He gave her hand another squeeze.

"*Ya.* For sure we will have a *gut* time." But all Sadie could think about was whether or not he would be leaving in time for her to prepare supper for Kade and Tyler.

She heard footsteps coming up the steps. And then a knock.

"Excuse me." She pulled her hand from beneath Milo's and walked to the door. When she opened it, she wondered if her face lit up the way her heart did. "Kade, Tyler, come in." Sadie stepped aside and motioned them into the kitchen. "You two come in here out of the cold."

Milo stood up when Kade and Tyler walked into the kitchen. "Milo Troyer," he said, extending his hand to Kade.

"Kade Saunders." Kade returned the handshake, but his eyes cut to Sadie's, his expression reserved.

"Hello there," Milo said to Tyler. As was his way, Tyler's eyes were all over the place, until they landed on Sadie.

"Tyler loves Sadie." He ran to her. "Hug."

Sadie wrapped her arms around Tyler. "Sadie loves Tyler too." She looked up at Milo. "And this is Tyler," she said proudly. "Sit down, everyone." She ushered Tyler to the bench and helped him get situated.

"Uh, no. We can't stay," Kade said. "We came to say thank you for telling us about the off-the-beaten-path tour. We had a great time."

He doesn't look like he's having a great time, Sadie thought, as she tried to catch his eye. But Kade refused to look at her. And his tone hinted that he'd returned to the man who arrived a few weeks ago—cold, aloof.

"I'm getting ready to make supper." Sadie smiled. "Beef stew. Please stay." Her eyes were pleading with Kade, and she couldn't help but wonder if Milo noticed.

"No, I know you've been waiting a long time to meet Milo, so Tyler and I are going to excuse ourselves." Kade walked toward Tyler. "Tyler, let's go to the cottage so Sadie and her friend can spend some time alone."

"No, that's not necessary. I have plenty . . ." Sadie was feeling desperate.

"Sadie's right. Please stay," Milo said. "I was just telling Sadie how I'd hoped she would be able to travel with me to Texas on Saturday, but she explained that she had a renter. It's nice to meet you."

But Kade didn't sit down. He stared hard at Sadie and then looked at Milo. "There's no reason Sadie can't go to Texas with you. Tyler and I will be fine. As a matter of fact, Sadie, maybe you should take this opportunity to go while we're here. I can take care of your animals."

"But you know nothing about taking care of animals," Sadie said. *Why is he doing this?*

"I'm sure Milo can give me a lesson or two before you leave." Kade smiled and arched his brows toward Milo.

"I would be happy to. *Wunderbaar* news!" Milo glanced at Sadie. "Isn't it, Sadie?"

"*Ach*, no. It wouldn't be right." Sadie shook her head with determination. "I provide Mr. Saunders with groceries, and it's not his place to tend to my farm while he is leasing the cottage. I won't hear of it. No. It wouldn't be right." She continued to shake her head.

"No, no. You take this opportunity," Kade said. "Tyler and I will be fine. We are quite capable of getting our own food and taking care of ourselves." He paused. "Unless, you don't trust us here or—"

"Of course I trust you," Sadie snapped.

"Then that settles it." Kade extended his hand to Milo. "Milo, a pleasure to meet you. Enjoy your time with Sadie. She seems like a fine woman. You two go to Texas, and I'll keep an eye on things here."

"You know nothing about a farm." Sadie folded her hands across her chest.

Milo stood up to shake Kade's hand, and as if Sadie wasn't even in the room, he said, "*Danki*, Mr. Saunders. Sadie and I have been waiting for this for a long time."

"As much as I would love to go, I'm afraid Mr. Saunders had a tragedy recently, and he probably has to leave soon. When he leaves, I can come to Texas then."

"No. I'm not leaving. In another six weeks, perhaps I'll be ready to go back to L.A., but for now, Tyler seems to like it here, and I can conduct my business via conference calls." Kade helped Tyler to his feet.

"Milo, will you be staying here with Sadie?" Kade still refused to look at Sadie.

Milo looked as shocked as Sadie. "Uh, no," Milo said. "I will be staying with friends of Sadie's, of course."

"Ah, yes. I suppose anything else would be *inappropriate*." The way Kade said the word *inappropriate* made Sadie want to swat him, a feeling she'd never had before.

Sadie stood dumbfounded as Kade and Tyler walked out the door. "Have a good evening," Kade said.

As he closed the door behind them, Milo said, "What a nice man to offer to tend to the place so you can join me." He sat down across from her. "Sadie?"

"*Ya?*"

"Are you sure you want to come with me to Texas? You seem to be puttin' up quite a fight."

Maybe it was the kind, honest way he directed the question to her, but Sadie said, "Of course I want to come."

He put his hand on hers again. "I know you're nervous. I'm nervous too. But I feel like this is God's plan for us. Everything will be fine."

"*Ya,*" she said, forcing a smile. "I should start some supper. Why don't you go rest in the den, warm yourself by the fire."

"I am a mite tired from my travels," Milo said. He stood and walked toward the den, but he turned around before he rounded the corner. "Sadie, you really are a vision. I'm glad I came."

"Me too." She smiled back, although at the moment, Sadie wasn't glad about one single thing. And she'd like to get her hands on that Kade for pushing her into a situation that she didn't have time to think on.

Her eyes were filling with tears, and she was glad Milo was resting on the couch and not insistent on helping her in the kitchen, the way Kade had. No need for him to see her with such worry in her heart. And anger. And hurt. She had thought there might be something between her and Kade. Clearly, she was wrong. He'd practically insisted that she leave with Milo. If he cared one bit, he wouldn't have done that.

<hr />

The pain in Kade's heart was immeasurable. It was one thing to hear Sadie talk about her past with Ben, but entirely another to envision her with Milo. The thought of her running off to test a potential new life with him was a concept Kade had trouble comprehending, but if he'd learned one thing from Sadie, it was that he wanted to be a better man. Holding her back would be a selfish thing to do. She had an opportunity with this man, a chance at happiness with someone of her own kind. Offering to stay here, alone with Tyler, and pushing her to go with Milo was indeed the most unselfish thing Kade had ever done. She was going to go eventually; might as well be now.

The truth was, he should be going back to L.A., but with or without Sadie here, he wasn't ready to face the real world yet. He planned to use this time to get to know his son. As he watched Tyler rolling across the floor in the den, giggling, Kade thought about how much things had changed between him and his son since Monica had dropped him off. They still had difficult moments, but he was learning about Tyler, finding out the things that made the boy laugh, things that made him sad. Tyler had his own personality, despite his challenges.

His thoughts returned to Sadie. The immediate connection she'd made with Tyler, the conversations she and Kade had shared, the way she felt in his arms, the smell of her. Yes, it was best that she go. If she didn't go now, Kade might say something to try and convince her to stay, or worse, tempt her away from a faith and place that she belonged. And even Kade didn't have the heart to do that.

After Tyler's bath, Kade tucked him into bed and said prayers with him, something they had started doing a few days ago. Tyler repeated each prayer along with Kade. This was a special time for Kade, but he had to admit, he was still waiting for another message. He wasn't willing to write it off as a coincidence, nor was he willing to accept it as divine intervention from God. Either way, he always waited anxiously, just in case.

Tyler had been tucked into bed for about an hour when Kade heard a pounding on the front door. He closed the book he was reading and edged off the couch in his socks and sweat pants. He pulled the door open to find Sadie standing on the porch, her cheeks red and her teeth chattering.

"What are you doing here? It's freezing! Get in here." Kade grabbed her by the arm to drag her inside.

"Not until you dress properly," she said, freeing herself of his grip. Sadie lifted her chin and looked away from him.

"This is ridiculous." But Kade walked into the bedroom and threw on a sweatshirt. He'd barely gotten it pulled over his head when he returned to the door. "Better?" he asked. He motioned her inside.

"What do you think you're doing?" she asked once he'd closed the door behind her.

"Would you like to take your coat off and stay awhile?" It was sarcastic, and she didn't find it amusing.

Sadie walked up to him with a fire in her that Kade hadn't seen before. "You cannot boss me about my life, Kade Saunders."

"I didn't realize I was *bossing you*, Sadie Fisher." He smirked, amused at her angry display and choice of words, then crossed his arms. "You'll have to be more specific."

"Don't play with me, Kade." Sadie actually stomped her foot. "Couldn't you tell that I didn't want to go to Texas right now? I was trying not to hurt Milo's feelings. Now I have to go, because you made it so very convenient for me to do so."

"I thought I was doing you a favor. You said you've been corresponding with Milo for over two years. I thought my staying here to watch the place would give you an opportunity to get to know this man. I thought you'd be happy."

"No, you didn't." There was a lethal calmness in her blue eyes. "You were just trying to be powerful, because that's the way you do things in your world."

"Sadie, who am I to tell you what to do? If you don't want to go, don't go." Kade shrugged. "I don't know what the big deal is."

"Evidently, you do not." She turned to walk away, but Kade gently grabbed her arm.

"Hey, hey. Come back here. Talk to me, Sadie."

She shook free of his hold. Kade watched her backing away, tears in her eyes. It was breaking his heart. Now was his chance.

She was feeling something for him too. If he was ever going to tell her how much he cared for her, now was the time—and he would probably screw up her life in the process. Kade took a deep breath.

"What do you want me to say?" she asked.

Kade walked toward her, but she backed up a safe distance. "Come here, Sadie." He held his arms out to her. He couldn't help it. God forgive him, he couldn't stand to see her like this. So torn. She looked shattered, as shattered as he felt. "Come here," he repeated, stretching his arms out further.

"I can't," she said.

"Then why did you come here?" Kade took a step forward. She didn't back up.

"To see . . . to know if . . ." A tear spilled over, and Sadie let it run the length of her cheek without taking her eyes from Kade's.

I love you, Sadie. He wanted to tell her so much that it physically hurt. But he said nothing. *It's the right thing to do.* But couldn't he at least hold her, comfort her, one last time? Soon she would grow close to Milo, as it should be, and Kade would lose her forever. He moved toward her again.

"To know if what?" he asked. "Why are you crying?"

She looked embarrassed all of a sudden and turned her eyes away from him. He grasped both of her arms and pulled her toward him, and then he lifted her chin and forced her to look into his eyes, eyes longing for the same thing hers did. Then Kade did the hardest thing he'd ever done in his life.

He readied himself, stood tall, and firmly said, "Go be with Milo. Go to Texas, Sadie."

She jerked free of his hold, turned, and ran for the door. And she never looked back. If she had, she would have seen the tears filling Kade's eyes.

What have I done?

15

LIZZIE WAS AS NERVOUS AS ANY A PERSON COULD BE. She fumbled with her *kapp* as if she hadn't been wearing the prayer covering for the past sixty-plus years, poking at loose strands of gray hair that kept falling forward. She had known Samuel Stoltzfus since he was a baby, and she'd taken a liking to his wife, Lillian, right away. And Jonas's daughter, Sarah Jane, had always been mighty good to Lizzie. There was no need for all this fuss just because she was going to supper at Jonas's house.

She was honored when Jonas invited her on behalf of them all. It was a big step for Jonas, and Lizzie suspected it might mean that Jonas was ready to take their friendship to the next level. She wanted to make a good impression. *So silly*, she thought. These were all fine people whom she'd known for years.

The sound of a buggy approaching gave her the push she needed to tame her unruly tresses. A final poke beneath her prayer covering, and she was ready. She bundled up in her heaviest coat and pulled on her boots, glad she'd worn two pairs of thick, black tights beneath her best blue dress. She molded her black gloves around her tired old hands and pretended for a moment that she was a young woman. Lizzie closed her eyes and imagined what it would be like to live the next fifty years with Jonas—that she was a woman in her youth, vital and strong.

She sighed, smiled, and realized she would be happy to take what she could get where Jonas was concerned. A week, a month, a year, or twenty years, she wanted to live out her days with Jonas by her side, caring for him, doting on him, playing chess with him, and loving him. She waited on the front porch for him to halt the buggy and come help her down the porch steps, which he insisted on. Her kind, chivalrous huggy bear.

"Sarah Jane's got a mighty fine meal planned for you," Jonas said, his shoulders squared and his chin held high. He met Lizzie at the top of the porch and offered her his arm, which she gladly latched onto. "She's lookin' forward to having the *kinner* and you all over for supper. Lillian said to apologize to you that we're eatin' so late. She had a doctor's appointment this afternoon in the city, and it ran a bit late."

"Is everything all right?" They took the porch steps slow and steady, each holding a handrail, and each other.

"*Ya, ya.* One of those regular checkups 'bout the baby. Everything is *gut.*"

Jonas helped Lizzie into the buggy and handed her a thick, brown blanket.

"*Danki,* Jonas," she said.

A short ride later, they rounded the corner at Jonas and Sarah Jane's house.

"I reckon the whole bunch is already here," Jonas said. He parked the buggy and helped Lizzie down. "Now, don't you be nervous, Lizzie. They all love you." He winked.

But do you love me, Jonas? She nodded.

Samuel and his son, David, were already sitting at the table when Lizzie and Jonas entered the kitchen from the porch. Anna was snacking on crackers in a high chair while Sarah Jane and Lillian scurried around the kitchen.

After the greetings, Lizzie asked, "Can I help with anything?"

"No, Lizzie, *danki*. You sit down and visit while we finish up here," Sarah Jane said. She stirred a pot on top of the stove.

"David, how are you feeling?" Lizzie asked. Samuel's son had undergone a kidney transplant this past year, and the boy looked like he was doing well, a healthy color in his cheeks.

"I feel *gut*." The fifteen-year-old smiled.

"And I see little Anna is growing like a weed." Lizzie reached over and tenderly touched the child's cheek. "So precious." What a lovely family. Lizzie wanted to be a part of it.

Jonas sat at the head of the table and instructed Lizzie to sit at the other end. It felt strange to sit in Irma Rose's spot, but she was honored to do so. Samuel and his wife sat on one side, and Sarah Jane took a seat beside David after she placed the stew in the middle of the table.

"Let us pray," Sarah Jane said. They all bowed their heads. Lizzie had so much to be thankful for.

"Now, let's eat," Jonas said when he felt they'd prayed for long enough. He smiled at Lizzie and winked, and she knew everything was going to be fine.

"This stew is *wunderbaar*, Sarah Jane," Lizzie told Jonas's daughter. "I'd be honored to have this recipe."

"Remind me after supper, and I'll be happy to jot it down for you," Sarah Jane said. "There's a secret ingredient in it."

Lillian laughed. "There's no secret about it, *Mamm*. I know what's in it, it's—"

"*Ach!* Don't say," Sarah Jane interupted. "These boys will tell everyone."

"Sarah Jane, you think you be havin' a secret, but I know your special ingredient," Jonas said with a wink. "Pickle juice." He paused to chew a piece of meat in the stew. "You put a squirt of pickle juice in everything. Irma Rose, you taught her that, didn't ya, now?"

The room went silent, and Lizzie could feel all eyes on her. Just for this one day, in front of his family, Lizzie had hoped Jonas could remember that she was Lizzie. She could feel her face reddening, and her hands began to tremble, making it difficult for her to hold on to her spoon. Then she dropped the utensil, full of stew, and made a mess on the floor, like a small child.

"I'm so sorry, I—" She choked back tears.

"Don't you give it a second thought." Lillian was on her feet right away and retrieved the spoon. She had a fresh one in Lizzie's hand in no time. "Anna makes a mess all the time. We're used to it."

Lizzie forced a smile. She knew Lillian's intentions were good and her words said in the spirit to make Lizzie feel better. But Lizzie wasn't a baby, and she should be able to hold her own spoon and carry herself at supper, for goodness' sakes.

"Lilly, how did Sadie fare out there during the storm with the *Englischer* renting that cottage of hers?" Jonas asked. "I don't trust that fella."

"Now, Grandpa, that *fella* helped us the night you were— the night we couldn't find you," Lillian said. "He seems nice enough."

"A man like that might try to steal our Sadie away from here." Jonas sat up a little taller. "You want your best friend to be leavin' us?"

"Didn't you hear?" Lillian's eyes grew wide, and then she turned toward her mother. "Didn't you tell Grandpa, *Mamm?*"

"Tell me what?" Jonas stopped chewing and eyed his daughter. Lizzie was glad the focus was not on her.

"*Ach.* I guess I forgot. Milo showed up."

Even Lizzie had heard of Milo, and she thought Jonas might drop *his* spoon at the mention of this news. "The pen pal from Texas?" he asked.

"*Ya.* And if you're going to worry about anyone stealing Sadie away, you better worry about him."

Jonas grunted. "At least he's Old Order. Sadie wouldn't be veering from her faith and facing a shunning."

"I don't think you have anything to worry about," Lillian said.

But something in Lillian's tone made Lizzie suspect that maybe there was something to fear.

"Irma Rose, pass those rolls over here, can ya, please?"

Lizzie took a deep breath. Sarah Jane reached over and clutched Lizzie's free hand as she looked at her father. "Pop, this is Lizzie," she said in a firm voice.

Jonas looked up and seemed to realize what he'd done. "I'm sorry, Lizzie," he said, regret in his voice. And then he kept staring at her.

Lizzie grasped her spoon extra tight and said, "It's all right, Jonas."

But Jonas didn't look all right. His gaze lowered, as did his voice. "No, it's not all right," he said.

Everyone was quiet again for a few moments, and Lizzie knew she was trembling. It happened when her nerves got the best of her.

But then Lillian began to talk about her visit at the doctor's office, the mood lightened, and they all finished supper without incident. When it was time for Jonas to take Lizzie home, each one of his family hugged her neck and thanked her for coming. Given the circumstances, she figured things had gone rather well.

Jonas was quiet on the drive home.

"*Danki* for having me to supper with your family, Jonas," Lizzie said.

He nodded as he turned onto Lizzie's driveway, but he said nothing. Something was terribly wrong. Maybe it was a bad idea to have supper where he'd dined with Irma Rose for most of his life. Or perhaps she was being her normal worrisome self. She sat up a little taller. "Will I be seeing you for chess tomorrow? I think we have a rematch to play." She offered him a hopeful smile.

Jonas didn't answer and pulled the buggy to a stop. "Whoa, Jessie."

Lizzie fought the tears building in the corners of her eyes, and her heart was thumping madly. *Please, Jonas. No.*

Jonas hung his head. "Lizzie . . ." He gazed in her direction, and even in the darkness, his eyes told the tale. "Let's get you in out of this cold, and we'll talk inside."

He walked around to her side of the buggy and helped her down. And as she'd done before, she locked her arm in his and they headed up the porch steps. Lizzie held on extra tight.

"A game of chess before you go?" She tried to sound as cheerful as possible, even though her heart was breaking.

Jonas's eyes narrowed as he walked Lizzie to the bench at her kitchen table and motioned for her to sit down. He took a seat beside her.

"You don't have to say anything, Jonas." Lizzie lowered her eyes.

Jonas reached over and held her hand. With his other hand, he lifted her chin and gently turned her face toward him. "Lizzie, you are a special woman. A *gut* woman." She began to cry, and Jonas brushed away a tear with his thumb. "But I can't do this."

Lizzie pulled her hand from his and wept into her palms, not wanting him to see her like this, but unable to control the grief of not having him in her life.

Jonas stood up. "I'm sorry, Lizzie. I've only loved one woman. And it might be my silly way of thinking, but I feel like I'm betraying Irma Rose. I'm sorry. I think it'd be best if I not be comin' around anymore like this, and—"

"No, Jonas." She cried harder. "Please don't do this. We've enjoyed each other's company so. Surely, we can continue on in a friendly manner. We can still play chess, and you can still be my huggy bear, and—"

"Good-bye, Lizzie."

Lizzie followed him onto the front porch. "Jonas?"

He stopped, and then slowly turned around. "*Ya?*"

Lizzie wiped her eyes and caught her breath. "You can always come back, huggy bear."

He gave a sympathetic smile, and then he was gone.

Lizzie clutched her sides and wept, watching until he was out of sight.

———

Kade dressed Tyler the next morning and indulged his son by letting him lick the bowl clean of the tapioca pudding. "That might be all the pudding we have for a while," he said to Tyler. But then added, "Until I get things fixed with Sadie."

He'd had a sleepless night. Sadie's tearful face, her pleading eyes. He couldn't let her leave for Texas, not like this, anyway, with so much unsaid. It was a mess, and he wasn't sure how he was going to fix things, but her leaving because he forced her to go didn't seem to be the answer.

"Let's go, buddy." He helped Tyler get his warm clothes on, although it was a sunny day outside. Maybe they would be able to shed some of this winter gear later this morning.

First stop, a flower boutique. It had been a long time since he'd given a woman flowers, but it was the thing to do when you'd made one cry. "Let's go get Miss Sadie some flowers. What do you think about that?"

"Love Sadie." Tyler smiled.

"Me too, buddy. Me too."

Kade pulled his car out of the barn for the first time since the blizzard, and he found a flower shop on Lincoln Highway.

He knew that extravagant would not impress Sadie. Quality of the bloom itself would. He had heard her talk more than once about how the Amish prided themselves for toiling the land and producing quality products. Roses. Elegant and traditional. He chose two dozen, realizing when he left that a dozen might have been more appropriate. "We'll just say a dozen of them are from you," he told Tyler.

His son had behaved so well in the flower shop, Kade decided to stop at the bakery and reward the boy with a whoopie pie.

"Tyler, you do realize that you won't always be able to eat tapioca pudding and whoopie pies, right?" Kade smiled. Tyler shoved the last bite in his mouth, and then grinned back at his father.

"Let's head to Sadie's and see if we can fix things somehow."

It was close to lunchtime when Kade pulled into Sadie's driveway. He wasn't sure if she'd be at her shop again today. Even when it wasn't a scheduled day to work, the ladies seemed to gather there. Kade would stop there on the way to the farmhouse.

"Hello, Kade," Lillian said when he and Tyler walked in. "Is everything all right?"

"Yeah. I was looking for Sadie. I figured I'd stop here on the way to the house."

"Actually, she told me to help you with anything you might need while she's away."

Kade took a step forward. "What do you mean, *away?*"

Lillian set aside some sort of knitting project she was working on. Her eyes grew serious. "Kade, she left for Texas this morning with Milo."

Despair gnawed at Kade's heart. "For how long?"

"I don't know. Possibly a few weeks. Maybe longer." Lillian didn't seem surprised by Kade's reaction to the news.

"I thought she wasn't leaving until Saturday. Why'd she leave today?"

Lillian's questioning eyes met with Kade's. "You tell me."

Kade realized that Sadie must have confided in Lillian, but he was unsure how much she knew, and he didn't want to get Sadie in any trouble with her friend. "I'm guessing maybe she was upset with me?" Kade posed the question as if he might already know the answer.

"This is an opportunity for her to find happiness, Kade," Lillian said. "I don't want Sadie to leave here. She's my best friend. But I want her to be happy."

He shoved his hands in his pockets and sighed heavily. "That's exactly why I told her to go."

"I am sensing that was hard for you to do."

"How much did she tell you?"

"Enough."

Kade needed a spark of hope. "Can you maybe throw me a bone, here? I mean, does she care about me in the least?"

Lillian smiled. "I think you know the answer to that."

Tyler walked up to Lillian and touched her on the leg.

"Well, hello there, Tyler," she said.

"Kade loves Sadie." He smiled broadly.

"Wait! No. I mean, I never said that," Kade said. He turned to Tyler. "Tyler, why did you say that?" Then Kade remembered— Tyler had told him earlier that he loved Sadie, and Kade had said, "Me too, buddy." He couldn't make his child out to be a liar. "Okay, I might have sort of said it."

Lillian cocked her head to one side. "And how does one *sort of* say it?"

Kade put his hands on his hips, paced around the room. "I thought I was doing the right thing."

"You did do the right thing," Lillian said.

"Then why do I feel so crummy?"

"Kade, what did you think would happen if feelings continued to develop between the two of you? That Sadie would leave everything she loves, her friends, her family, and travel to a life that is foreign to her?"

"Didn't she just do that?" He was sure his hurt shone through in his sarcastic tone.

"You know what I mean. Or, even a further stretch, were you willing to give up all you know to be a part of Sadie's life here? If the answer to both those questions is no, then you did the right thing by letting go of Sadie, no matter your feelings for her."

Lillian was right. It was the reason Kade told Sadie to go to Texas in the first place. He just didn't realize it was going to hurt so much. "You're right." He had no one to blame for his defeat but himself. A knot churned his stomach.

"But if there is anything you need, one of us is here at the shop during the day. I'm filling in for Mary Ellen today, as she has a sick child. We mix things up a bit, but one of us will be here—short of a blizzard." Lillian smiled.

The only thing Kade needed was Sadie.

"Thanks," he said. He motioned Tyler toward the door.

"What do you mean you won't be seeing Lizzie anymore?" Sarah Jane asked her father over lunch a few days later. "I thought the two of you enjoyed each other's company, enjoyed playing chess together."

"*Ya*, we did." Jonas opened the *Budget* and scanned the pages. It didn't appear that he felt the subject warranted further conversation, but Sarah Jane suspected it did.

"What happened, Pop?" She folded the kitchen towel over her arm and stood beside her father, who was seated at the kitchen table.

He peered above the paper and cut his eyes in her direction. "I reckon this is not conversation for a father to be havin' with his daughter."

Sarah Jane chuckled. "Pop, I'm a middle-aged woman, not a child. And you sure did seem happy when you were spending time with Lizzie." She paused and recalled the way Lizzie gazed at Jonas during supper the other night. "And Lizzie sure is crazy about you."

Jonas folded the newspaper, blew out a breath of frustration, and looked up at Sarah Jane. "Lizzie is a *gut* woman. But it seems rather silly to be courtin' at my age." He took a sip of the sweet tea Sarah Jane had prepared for him.

"Why? Why is that silly, Pop? I think you should do whatever makes you happy." She walked to the counter and finished preparing a turkey sandwich for him. When he didn't answer, she took him the sandwich, then took a seat across from him. "Why is it silly, Pop?" she asked again.

Jonas took a big bite, chewed it, and thought over his response. "She's not my Irma Rose. Sometimes I might think she is." His face twisted into a scowl. "I know I get a bit confused sometimes, and I reckon it ain't fair to Lizzie." Her pop held his head high. "I've only loved one woman, Sarah Jane. My Irma Rose. Your *mamm*."

"Pop, I know how much you loved *Mamm*. But that doesn't mean you can't be happy with someone else too. I think *Mamm* would want that, and she thought the world of Lizzie. It just makes me sad, because the two of you seem to get along so well."

He took another bite of his sandwich, mulled it over some more. Then he swallowed and shook his head. "Something 'bout seeing Lizzie sitting there in Irma Rose's chair just—"

Sarah Jane reached over and touched her father's hand. "Go on," she said.

"It didn't seem right, I reckon. And it can't be *gut* that sometimes I think Lizzie is Irma Rose." Jonas pushed back his plate, half a sandwich still left. "I choose not to talk about this anymore, Sarah Jane."

She was clear on the rules. When the man of the house said a topic was not up for discussion, it was not to be debated. But Sarah Jane had spent a large part of her life living with the *Englisch*, and she tended to push when she shouldn't. "All I'm saying, Pop, is that—"

Jonas spun around. "Sarah Jane, did you not hear me?"

"*Ya*, Pop." His face was fire red, and Sarah Jane didn't want his blood pressure to get any higher. Between her father's cancer and the onset of Alzheimer's, they had enough to deal with. Maybe there would be a better time to talk about this, when her father wasn't feeling so sensitive. He'd been sulking for the past several days.

"I'm gonna go over to Sadie's place, check on that *Englisch* fella. He oughta not even be left alone out there. Might steal everything Sadie's got." Jonas put on his straw hat and grabbed his long, black coat from the rack.

Sarah Jane grinned. "Pop. Surely you're not serious. That man is filthy rich. He's not going to steal anything from Sadie. That's ridiculous." She cleared the plates from the table.

Jonas grumbled, and Sarah Jane couldn't make out what he said. "What?" she asked.

"I said I think I heard the word *filthy* in there somewhere." He pulled his coat tight. "I'll be back later, Lilly."

Sarah Jane watched him walk out the door and hoped he would be safe in the buggy, realizing he had just called her *Lilly*.

———————

Jonas headed down Black Horse Road toward Sadie's place. He slowed down and hesitated at Lizzie's driveway. She'd been pretty torn up when he last saw her, and the vision haunted him. But he sped up again and passed her house. No good could come of his spending time with Lizzie. Jonas was sure she wanted to marry him, and that was something he wasn't about to consider. Irma Rose would be throwing stones at him from heaven.

But he couldn't help but wonder how Lizzie was and what she might be up to right now.

Jonas pushed the thoughts about Lizzie aside and turned into Sadie's driveway. He stepped out of the buggy onto the packed snow, glad the sun was out and warming things up a bit. Jonas knocked on the door of the cottage.

To his surprise, a small person answered. A cute youngster. Must be the slow child he'd heard the others talking about. "Hello. Where is your pop?" Jonas asked.

"Pop, pop, pop!" the boy yelled, but he didn't move from the door. "Pop, pop, pop!"

Jonas couldn't help but grin. The young lad was beaming and cute as he could be.

He heard footsteps approaching and saw the *Englischer* coming up behind his son.

"Jonas." The fella looked surprised, ran his hand nervously through his hair. "What brings you here?" Then he looked down at the boy. "Did you meet Tyler? Tyler, this is Mr. Jonas."

"Just *Jonas* will be fine," he said. "Hello, Tyler." He tipped his hat in the child's direction. "I'm just checkin' on you." Jonas lifted his chin, eyed the *Englischer*. "Why are you still here? I understand the boy's mother passed. Don't you need to be gettin' back to the city?"

"I probably do." Kade shrugged. "But I'm not ready to face my life back there, plus I told Sadie I'd take care of things around here while she's gone, which reminds me . . ." He put his hands on his hips. "Her *friend* forgot to show me how to take care of these animals."

"*Ach*, you mean Milo, her future husband?" Jonas asked. Then he laughed. "I reckon to venture that you don't know a thing 'bout tending to Sadie's animals."

"I don't believe I've heard anyone say that Milo is her future husband."

Jonas was enjoying the *Englischer's* irritation, which he knew was wrong in God's eyes. But he couldn't help himself. "They'll be wed soon enough, I reckon."

"Whatever." Kade rolled his eyes. Jonas grinned. "Is there

something you need, Jonas? Tyler, why don't you go play with your letters." Kade motioned for Tyler to step into the house, and the boy did so.

Jonas pushed back the rim of his hat. "Just checkin' on things." He paused, then sighed. "But I reckon since I'm here, I'd best show you how to tend to Sadie's animals since you said you'd take care of that, which was probably a silly thing to do."

"It can't be that hard. Let me throw on my shoes and coat, and get Tyler dressed. We'll be right back." He paused at the door. "Do you want to come in, out of the cold?"

Jonas shook his head. "I'm plenty fine right here."

"Okay." Kade closed the door.

It just didn't make no sense to him why the *Englischer* didn't go back to where he came from, unless he had some pretty strong feelings for Sadie. After a couple of minutes, Kade and the boy were back.

"Come on, Tyler." Kade escorted Tyler through the doorway and closed the door behind him. "We're ready."

When they got to the barn, the boy's eyes lit up at the sight of Sadie's two horses. He ran to the stall and climbed up on the first notch of the gate.

"You like the horses?" Jonas asked. He patted the boy on the head. The child jerked away from him like Jonas had hurt him.

"He doesn't like to be touched," Kade said. "Well, I mean, he does. He likes to be hugged, but he sort of lets us know. He doesn't like to be touched otherwise."

Jonas nodded, although he wasn't sure he understood what Kade meant by that. "This here is Sugar, and that one is Spice. Silliest names I've ever heard for horses." Jonas shook his head.

"Sugar!" the boy echoed enthusiastically. Jonas couldn't get over what a handsome youngster he was. He had to admit, if he was fair, the boy did get his looks from his father.

"They like to have their noses scratched. See here." Jonas showed the boy how to scratch Sugar's nose, then Spice's. Then he walked around the barn and showed Kade where everything was kept. Feed, supplies to clean the stalls, horse grooming brushes. "You'll be needin' to tend to the pigs as well." Jonas stopped and studied Kade's fancy clothes. "You gonna be able to handle all this?"

"It doesn't look like all that much. Feed the horses, clean the stalls, brush them. Check their water. Feed the pigs. Did I miss anything?"

Jonas narrowed his brows. "I reckon not." He had to admit, it warmed his heart to see Tyler having such a good time. "He seems to have taken a special liking to the horses." Jonas pointed to Tyler, who was still scratching the horses on their noses.

"Yes, he does. I'm still trying to learn the things he likes and doesn't like. He's autistic. Do you know what that means?"

"I reckon I don't much." But Tyler looked to Jonas like he was just being a normal little boy at the moment.

"Well, for example, he can read. But he doesn't understand what he reads. I guess you could say he has a limited understanding about some things."

Jonas could see the worry in the *Englisher*'s heart for his boy. "He looks like he's having a mighty *gut* time right now."

Kade smiled, donning the proud look of a father. "Yes, he does look like he's having a *gut* time."

"*Ach*, you speaka *da Deitch?*" Jonas grinned at Kade's attempt.

"No, not much. Only what I've picked up from Sadie." Jonas watched Kade staring at the boy, as if worrying about the fact that he was different.

"Children like Tyler are a special gift from God. There's a special place in heaven for them," Jonas said.

"That's what Sadie said." Kade didn't look up though. He kept staring at the boy.

"Sadie is a smart woman."

"Yes, she is."

Jonas wasn't sure about this *Englischer*, but one thing was for certain—he appeared to be hurting about several things. Mostly his son. And Sadie being gone. Jonas knew what it was like to be detached from a child. Sarah Jane had left them when she was eighteen to live in the *Englisch* world. They'd only been blessed by her return a few years ago. And Jonas also knew what it was like to love someone you couldn't have. He'd been in love with Lizzie for a while now, even though it was a dishonor to Irma Rose. Jonas could tell that Kade was in love with Sadie—something about the way he spoke her name. And Kade certainly had worry in his heart about the boy.

"How would you boys like to take a ride in my buggy into town? I wonder if Tyler would like that."

Kade looked confused. Rightly so. Jonas had given the man a rather hard time since he'd arrived in Lancaster County. "Seriously?"

"*Ya, ya.* We best enjoy the sunshine. We can have coffee in town." Jonas figured it might keep his mind off Lizzie. He didn't have anything else to do anyway.

"That would be great. Tyler, you ready to go for a ride in the buggy?" He turned toward Jonas. "Thanks, Jonas. This will be fun for Tyler, and there is something important I want to ask you."

Jonas couldn't imagine what Kade wanted to talk about, so he shrugged. "Let's be on our way, then."

16

I T W A S T W O W E E K S B E F O R E L I L L I A N R E C E I V E D A L E T T E R from Sadie. She'd reprimand her friend later for not checking in sooner, but for the moment she was thrilled to pull a letter from her mailbox.

"Look, Anna, a letter from Sadie," she said to her little one. Anna was cutting another tooth and a bit fussy, so Lillian set the letter aside and gave Pete a flick of the reins. "We'll read the letter when we get to *Mammi* Sarah Jane and *Daddi* Jonas's *haus*. How's that?" Lillian pushed back Anna's soft hair from her face and checked the buckle on Anna's car seat. Many of the Amish carry their babies on their lap, but Lillian wasn't comfortable with that. Maybe it was the time she'd spent in the *Englisch* world, where car seats were a necessity, but she wanted Anna safely strapped in, even in the buggy.

Lillian reached down and rubbed her expanding belly. *Less than two months to go*, she thought, as she pulled onto Black Horse Road. The weather had warmed to a cool thirty-eight, and the sun was making a regular appearance. Still cold, but a welcome relief following the nasty blizzard they'd recently gone through. Lillian was looking forward to spending the day baking and chatting with her mother. And she was looking forward to reading Sadie's letter. She couldn't imagine what adventures Sadie must be having, since she'd never been far from Lancaster County. Since Lillian had lived in Texas prior to converting to the Old Order Amish in Pennsylvania, she was anxious to hear what her friend thought about the Lone Star State, and more important, how things were going with Milo Troyer.

But as Lillian headed down the road, she felt compelled to make a stop along the way. She knew her grandpa wasn't spending time with Lizzie any longer, and Lillian thought she'd check on her. The first few days after their initial breakup, her mother said Grandpa had been a bear to live with, moping around the house, complaining that Sarah Jane didn't play chess with him enough, and even complaining about the food her mother was cooking. But then, her mother had told her that an unlikely friendship had developed. Grandpa had been spending his free time with *Englischer* Kade Saunders, who as it turned out, proved to be a challenging chess partner.

It didn't make any sense to Lillian, though. What could those two possibly have in common outside of chess? Grandpa had bordered on being mean to Kade since the moment they met, citing his distrust for the man on more than one occasion. Lillian guided Pete down the drive to Lizzie's house. She unstrapped Anna and grabbed a loaf of banana nut bread she'd made, along with a container of chicken soup. Balancing Anna on her hip, she struggled up Lizzie's porch steps.

"Lillian, how *gut* to see you," Lizzie said. "Come in, child. Come in."

"Hello, Lizzie. I brought you some banana nut bread and some chicken soup." She set Anna down on the wooden floor once they were inside.

Lizzie squatted down to Anna's level. "You are getting so big."

Lillian set the soup and bread on Lizzie's table. "I hope you don't mind us stopping by. I was worried about you."

Lizzie stood up. "*Ach*, I be fine," she said. "And you stop by for any reason, anytime. And, oh, how I'll enjoy this bread and soup."

"No, Anna," Lillian said when Anna reached for an apron Lizzie had hung on a nearby rack. Lillian turned toward Lizzie. "She's a handful these days."

Lizzie walked to her cabinet and pulled a box of crackers down. "Can she have some of these?"

"Sure." Lillian set Anna in the wooden armchair at the end of Lizzie's table. Once Anna was settled, both women sat on either side of the table. Lillian glanced around the kitchen and saw a frightful mess—dishes in the sink, open containers of food left unattended on the counter, and the floor didn't look like it had seen a broom in weeks. "Lizzie, are you doing okay these days?"

"*Ya, ya*. I do just fine." Lizzie smiled.

Lillian was wondering how long it had been since Lizzie's nieces, or anyone, had visited.

"How about a glass of sweet tea?" Lizzie stood up and walked toward the counter. She pulled two glasses from the cabinet.

"That would be *wunderbaar*," Lillian said. She continued to study Lizzie's kitchen. There were several pill bottles to one side of the sink. Two of the bottles were knocked over and empty. Lillian stood up and walked to the sink. She picked up one of the bottles. "Lizzie, do you need me to get these filled for you?"

"No, no. Those are old bottles. I have *mei* refills upstairs by the bed." Lizzie placed two glasses of tea on the table, along with a glass of milk for Anna. "Can she drink from a glass?"

"*Ya*, she does, with some help. Sometimes she still takes a bottle, but we're trying to wean her from that." Lillian took a sip of tea and struggled to gulp it down. Sweetest tea she'd ever had, and she wondered how long that pitcher had been in Lizzie's refrigerator. She grabbed Anna's plastic glass filled with milk before Anna had a chance to get it to her lips. "Actually, Anna had a bottle before we left. Maybe just some water for her?"

"*Ya, ya*." Lizzie smiled and went to retrieve a fresh glass. As Lizzie pumped water from the sink, Lillian sniffed the milk. Then grimaced and set the glass aside, confirming what she'd feared.

Lizzie returned to the table and handed Anna the glass. "Oops," she said when water trickled down Anna's chin.

"She's still a messy drinker when it comes to cups," Lillian said. She wiped the water from Anna's chin with her thumb. "Lizzie, is there anything you need?"

"No, I have all that I need. But *danki*, Mary Ellen, for bringing me the bread and soup. Is for sure I will enjoy it."

Lillian decided not to correct her on the name. Instead she smiled. "You're welcome, Lizzie." Lillian stood up. "I best be off. *Mamm* is expecting me. But Lizzie, I'd be glad to pick you up anything you might need from town."

"No, dear. I'm fine." Lizzie stood up and patted Anna on the head. "You take care of this little one and tell your *mamm* and Jonas I send my best."

Lillian nodded, unsure whether to tell Lizzie how much she knew her grandfather missed her. But Lizzie was smiling and seemed glad she'd stopped by. She didn't want to cause any upset for Lizzie.

<hr />

"Whoa, Pete," Lillian instructed the horse. She pulled off on the side of Black Horse Road to read Sadie's letter before she arrived at her *mamm's*. Anna had dozed off in her carrier, and Lillian wanted to enjoy a quiet moment reading what Sadie had been up to. She pried the envelope open and pulled out the letter. Lillian took a deep breath and unfolded the white paper. She wanted Sadie to be happy, just not so far away in Texas.

Dear Lillian,

I am sorry it took so long for me to pen this note. It was a long travel on the bus from our home to Texas. But there was much to talk about with Milo during our trip. He is a kind man and everything I had hoped he would be. Milo's family has made me feel welcome. He has three sisters—Ellen, Hannah, and Lavina. Between them, they have twelve children. Milo's mamm, Martha, is a gut woman, and I like her very much. His daed, John, I don't see much. He is a hard worker, always busy making furniture or tending to chores around the farm. I am staying with Martha and John while I am here.

Milo is a hard worker too. He stays busy at his farm and with his woodworking projects, and he comes to his folks' haus in the evenings to pick me up, just like if we were young and courting. We even attended a Sunday singing, although I felt a mite silly at my age.

I'm not sure if this is an Old Order District, or just a gathering of Old Order families. There are only a few families left, and almost everyone works in the city. Milo is one of the few who farms his land, but he also must hold a construction job in town to make ends meet. Their ways are different than our ways. Shunning is almost unheard-of, and the supper hour is at 6:00 instead of four. They sleep later too, until 6:30. I like that part.

I miss you, Lillian. And Rachel, Mary Ellen, Katie Ann, and Sarah Jane. And I miss Jonas, his protective ways of me. I must tell you, in confidence, I miss the Englischer and his boy very much. Can you please write to me and tell me how they are doing?

Lillian, I will need to sell my farm to have a life here with Milo. We discussed him moving to Lancaster County, but it seems to make more sense for us to live amongst his large family. I will continue to live with his folks until a time when we see fit to marry, which most likely will be after the fall harvest in November. As our Order has done in the past, please offer my land to someone in the Amish community first. I'm sure Bishop Ebersol can handle the arrangements.

I will be back on April 1 to gather my things. Kade and Tyler will be gone by then. I hope that my renters have not been too much trouble. The boy loves tapioca pudding, and Kade eats just about anything, but I don't think he knows how to cook much. And Lillian, Tyler likes to read books. He doesn't really understand them, but I have a big box of books suitable for him in my bedroom. I collected them over the years for a child of my own, but please give them to Tyler. Milo's family has many books here, if God should ever bless me and Milo with a child.

If it's not too much trouble, can you please show Kade how to make tapioca pudding so he can make it for the boy when he returns to his home in Los Angeles? Or maybe he can give the recipe to whoever might be tending to Tyler.

I must go, Lillian. Please write to me very soon.

Em Gott Sei Friede,
Sadie

"God's peace to you, too, my friend," Lillian whispered. She folded the note and put it back in the envelope, most disturbed by the tone of Sadie's letter. It seemed to Lillian that Sadie was masking sadness, not once mentioning that she loved Milo, and focusing instead on the needs of the *Englischers*.

Lillian whistled Pete into action and continued down Black Horse Road to her *mamm*'s house. She headed down the long driveway and fought the worry in her heart about Sadie. But what a surprise she had when she pulled near the house.

Grandpa, Kade, and the boy were busy making a snowman in the front yard. It seemed strange to Lillian on several levels. One, she'd never seen her grandfather frolicking about in such a playful way. Two, Kade Saunders was laughing and playful as well, a far cry from the stuffy *Englischer* who had shown up several weeks ago. And most of all, she couldn't get past what good friends Kade and her grandpa had become.

She headed toward the house with Anna on her hip. "Hello," she hollered to the trio as she made her way up the porch steps.

"Hello, Lilly." Grandpa packed another mound of snow on their structure, and then held Tyler in his arms so the boy could place a carrot nose on the snowman. Kade waved, but quickly refocused his attention on his project.

"What have I told you about carrying that baby when you are this pregnant?" *Mamm* met Lillian at the steps and pulled Anna from her arms. "It's still slippery out here, and last thing we need is for you to fall with this baby in your arms."

"I'm fine, *Mamm*," Lillian mumbled. She turned to have a final look at her grandpa, Kade, and Tyler. "What are Kade and his son doing here?"

Sarah Jane put Anna in a high chair and offered her some crackers. "I told you, your grandpa and Kade have developed quite a friendship. Pop is either there, or Kade and the boy are here." Her *mamm* paused, raised her brows. "Want to hear something even more shocking?"

Lillian sat down on the bench in the kitchen. "I don't know," she said hesitantly.

"Your grandfather is teaching Kade the *Ordnung*. Kade asked him to."

"What? Why?" Lillian paused for a moment. "Kade Saunders can't possibly be thinking of staying here. That's ridiculous, a man of his stature and wealth. I mean, why would he do such a thing?"

Her mother shrugged. "You tell me." Her mother walked to the refrigerator and pulled out a tub of chicken salad. She began to spread the mixture on slices of bread she had laid out.

"*Mamm*, if he's staying because of Sadie, that is the wrong reason to join the community." Lillian shook her head.

Sarah Jane placed her hands on her hips and faced Lillian. "Are you sure you are one to speak against this?"

Lillian's jaw dropped. "I didn't convert to Amish to be with Samuel, *Mamm*, and you know that."

Her mother didn't say anything, but continued to spread chicken salad on the bread. She topped each mound with another piece of bread. Then she turned around and winked at her daughter. "I never said you did."

Lillian always believed that she would have converted to the Amish faith, with or without Samuel by her side. But was she being honest with herself?

"A man like Kade doesn't leave the *Englisch* world, *Mamm*. He's been on the cover of *Forbes*, for goodness' sakes. He's a millionaire. A person like that doesn't give it all up to become Amish, for a woman or otherwise."

"I approached this very subject with your grandfather. He said Kade is a miserable, unhappy man in search of the same peacefulness that you came here looking for."

"It's not the same!" Lillian insisted. "He has a life. Millions of dollars, people counting on him, probably lives in a mansion. People like him don't do things like this." Lillian folded her arms across her chest.

"Lillian, you know it's not our place to judge Kade's heart in this matter." Her mother reprimanded her with her eyes, and Lillian recalled being on the other side of this conversation with Sadie recently. Lillian had accused Sadie of this very thing where Kade was concerned.

"I know, *Mamm*," she said, then sighed. "But how in the world did Kade and Grandpa become friends in the first place?"

"I think your grandpa took a liking to the boy first and then got to know Kade." She twisted around and smiled. "And it didn't hurt that Kade turned out to be quite the chess player. To tell you the truth, Lillian, I'm relieved your grandpa has someone else besides me to play chess with. I don't have time to always be indulging him. Kade seemed to take over where Lizzie left off."

Lillian sighed. "We need to talk about Lizzie, *Mamm*. I think—"

"You think what?" Her grandpa burst through the kitchen door, followed by Kade and Tyler. "Is lunch ready?" he asked next. "We done worked up an appetite." He hung his straw hat on the rack and sat down at the head of the long, wooden table, and then turned toward Lillian, his face as serious as she'd ever seen it. "What about Lizzie?"

"Hello," Lillian said to Kade; then she turned to Tyler. "Hello, Tyler. Did you have fun making a snowman?" The boy's eyes jetted around the room, but he smiled for an instant in Lillian's direction.

Grandpa grunted. "Tell me about Lizzie," he demanded.

Lillian pursed her lips together for a moment, then said, "She doesn't seem like she's doing very *gut*."

Grandpa sat up a little taller and narrowed his eyes in Lillian's direction. "What do you mean?"

"She's just—just out of sorts a little." Lillian paused. "I mean, Lizzie's house has always been so tidy, but today when I stopped by there, dishes were piled in the sink, the milk she offered Anna was sour and smelled as if it had been in there for weeks, and . . ."

"And what?" Grandpa asked.

"She called me Mary Ellen when I left." Lillian turned toward her mother. "*Mamm*, I think we need to go over there later and help Lizzie clean up. I would have done it while I was there, but I had Anna, and I'm limited by what I can do with my big belly and all. Maybe we can—"

Grandpa was on his feet. "Sarah Jane, I'm taking the buggy out for while."

"Don't you want lunch?" she asked. "I have your sandwich ready." Her mother held a plate toward him but was left standing there as Grandpa scrambled out the door.

There was no doubt in Lillian's mind where Grandpa was

headed. And since she'd already stirred things up in one couple's tattered love life, why stop there? "I received a letter from Sadie today," she said, trying to sound casual.

"What?" Kade asked, his eyes wide. Then he tried to readjust his excitement. "I mean, how is she doing?"

Kade didn't fool her for a minute. "Fine," Lillian said. Selfish thoughts plagued her mind—*if Kade were to convert to the Amish faith, Sadie might come home.* "Well, I *guess* she's fine," she added.

"What do you mean, you *guess*?" Kade accepted a plate from Sarah Jane. "*Danki,*" he said smoothly.

Lillian laughed.

"What's so funny?" he asked.

"I'm sorry." She laughed again. "It sounds funny to hear you speaking Pennsylvania *Deitsch.*"

"Lillian," Sarah Jane began in a tone that Lillian was familiar with. "I don't think anyone laughed at you when you were learning the *Deitsch.*"

But Lillian didn't apologize. She tapped her finger to her chin, eyeballing Kade.

"What do you mean you guess Sadie is fine?" Kade asked again.

"She wants us to have Bishop Ebersol take care of selling her farm."

"What? Why?" Kade's voice rose in surprise. "Why would she sell her farm? To move to Texas? She doesn't even *know* that Milo person. I thought she was just going for a visit?"

Sarah Jane sat down at the table with her own plate. "It does seem a little fast," she said.

"Evidently she is going to stay in Texas. She and Milo are

talking of marriage, maybe in November," Lillian said. She looked at Kade. "So, I guess you won't need to be continuing your studies of the *Ordnung.*"

Kade reached over to wipe chicken salad from Tyler's chin. "Why is that?"

"I guess I figure, what's the point?" Lillian shrugged, then took a bite of her sandwich.

Her mother glared in her direction. "It's probably none of your business," Sarah Jane said.

"No, it's all right." Kade took a deep breath and stared hard at Lillian. "I guess you think I have alternative motives for learning about the Amish ways?"

"It crossed my mind." Lillian smiled.

Kade took a bite of his sandwich. "Hmm," he mumbled.

"I can't imagine, in my wildest of dreams, why a man of your stature would be so interested in our ways. I can't help but wonder if it's because—" Lillian could feel her mother's glare blazing into her skin, but she went on. "Because of Sadie."

"It is exactly because of Sadie." Kade's expression challenged her to argue.

"Well, that's the wrong reason to—"

But Kade interrupted her. "Sadie represents the kind of person I want to be, a Christ-centered person, a person of faith. I want to be a good father, a good man . . ." He paused, his eyes filled with hope. "Sadie makes me want to be a better person. So, yes, my decision to study the *Ordnung* is because of Sadie."

"She's not coming back," Lillian stated emphatically.

"Does that mean I can't stay, in search of my own peace? It

seemed to have worked for you. Or did you convert to be with Samuel?"

"I did not convert just to—" Lillian's voice rose, bristling with indignation. "You don't know what you're talking about anyway, and—"

"You don't know what you're talking about either." His angry gaze swept over her.

"Both of you, stop it!" Sarah Jane interjected. "You sound like two bickering children." She shook her finger at Lillian. "You are in no position to judge what Kade is doing." Then she pointed the same crooked finger in Kade's direction. "And you are in no position to judge Lillian's actions. That is for God, and God only. So both of you settle down."

Tyler began to slam his hands on the table, as if sensing the upset in the room, which caused his tea to spill. Then Anna began to wail.

"See what you both have done," Sarah Jane said. She picked up Anna and paced the kitchen, while Kade attempted to comfort Tyler.

"Hey, buddy," Kade said. "Everything is okay. Let's don't do that." He looked up at Sarah Jane. "Sorry about the mess."

"It's no problem," Sarah Jane said. "I'm going to go take Anna upstairs and see if she needs a diaper change.

Kade began to sing "Itsy Bitsy Spider" to Tyler, and Lillian bit her bottom lip to stifle the giggle she felt. Kade seemed so incredibly out of character.

There she went—judging again.

Tyler stopped slamming his hands against the table and refocused on his sandwich. Kade smiled. "Go ahead. Laugh. I know you're dying to, but it's the only thing that seems to calm Tyler down." He reached for a nearby towel and began wiping up the spilled tea.

Lillian grinned. "I'm not making fun. Really. I think it's sweet the way you sing to him."

Kade's face turned red, and he shrugged. "It's a far cry from a high-profile life in Los Angeles, huh?"

He sounded almost embarrassed as he said it, and there was something touching in his voice, combined with the way he tenderly smiled at his son. "*Ya*, it is," she said softly, wondering if perhaps he was telling the truth. Maybe even a wealthy, influential man like Kade Saunders was simply seeking contentment, the way she was when she came to Lancaster County.

"I came here to get away from life. It was never my intention to stay here, far from it." He smiled. "Then I got to know Sadie, particularly during the blizzard, and—and something about her, the calm, the goodness." He shrugged. "I'd like to see what it's all about, that's all."

"Fair enough," Lillian said. She knew what it was like to feel lost, detached from God. She also knew what a miraculous thing it was to reconnect with God and to trust in His will. "Grandpa is a *gut* teacher, I'm sure."

Kade smiled. "I don't think he cared for me too much at first, but Tyler seems to have stolen his heart, and we're sort of a package deal."

"Grandpa seems to like you just fine," Lillian said.

"He's quite the chess player." Kade paused. "Quite the *man*, actually. I'm honored to know him."

Lillian smiled. "We all are."

Jonas removed his straw hat and stared at the simple tombstone
in front of him, no different from the other plain markers in
remembrance of those who'd passed—except this stone marked
the spot where his beloved Irma Rose was laid to rest. He bent
to one knee, his tired old bones cracking in opposition, and he
bowed his head to thank the Lord for the life he'd lived, for the
blessing of living so much of it with Irma Rose.

He folded his arms atop his knee, his hat dangling from one
hand. His heart was heavy, not so much for Irma Rose as for
another in need.

"Irma Rose," he began, "I don't want a lashing from you when
I get to heaven, so I reckon I'll run somethin' by you." He paused,
scratched his forehead. "It's Lizzie, Irma Rose. I think she's in
trouble, and I reckon I'm 'bout all she's got, and—"

Jonas shook his head. That wasn't the truth. Not all of it
anyway.

He glanced around the small cemetery, sprigs of brown
poking through the melting clumps of snow. Sunshine beamed
across the meadow in delicate rays, as if God were slowly cleaning up after one season, in preparation for the next. Soon·it
would be spring, Irma Rose's favorite time of year, when new
foliage mirrored hope for plentiful harvests, when colorful
blooms represented life, filled with colorful variations of our
wonderment as humans.

"I love you, Irma Rose. I've loved you since the first day I saw
you, sittin' under that old oak tree at your folks' house, readin' a
book. You musta been only thirteen at the time, but I knew I'd

marry you someday." Jonas smiled at the recollection of that young girl, so long ago. "And we had a *gut* life. I miss you every single day." He swallowed back emotion. "But I've grown to love another woman, Irma Rose. Lizzie. She's a fine woman, and I'd like to do right by her and love her openly the way she loves me. But I've been holdin' back, out of my loyalty to you, my wife."

Wet snow was soaking through the knee of his pants, numbing the joint to a point he feared he wouldn't be able to hoist himself up. But it didn't seem right to speak about such things towering over her, so he endured, and went on. "I'm gonna ask Lizzie to marry me, Irma Rose. And I reckon I've come here for your blessing."

17

SADIE HELPED MILO'S MOTHER, MARTHA, CLEAN THE breakfast dishes. Daylight shone through the kitchen window as the clock on the wall chimed seven times. It still seemed odd to Sadie that breakfast was served so late in the morning. At home, she would have already had breakfast, done her baking, given the house a once-over, and tended to the animals.

She glanced around Martha and John's kitchen, not unlike her own, except dark-blue blinds covered the windows instead of green. And Martha had a few decorative trinkets placed about the room, items Bishop Ebersol wouldn't have taken a liking to—a colorful fruit print propped up against the counter backdrop, a stained-glass picture hanging in the window, and three ceramic dogs grouped together on the hutch. All items that served no purpose, but gave the room a certain luster. Even though this house was simple in nature, Sadie knew she was a long way from home.

In the den, Martha and John's furniture had decorative carvings etched into the wooden rocking chairs, and multicolored throw pillows lined a long, tan couch. A colorful rug was the focal point in the room. Milo's community abstained from electricity, owning cars, having a telephone in the house—most of the other rules that Sadie's district adhered to—but things seemed more

casual, lacking the discipline Sadie was used to. Even church service was only an hour and a half, as compared to the three-hour
worship she was accustomed to. Although, truth be told, that was
okay by her.

She placed a plate in the cabinet and stared out the window
toward flat, brown land that stretched as far as she could see. No
dips or meadows, just barren land waiting for spring to arrive.
And it was warm in Texas. It was the first week in March, but the
thermometer on the tree outside the window read seventy-two
degrees. She wondered if snow still covered the ground at home.

Homesickness set in right away, but Sadie did her best to push
through it, basking in her time with Milo and getting to know
what would potentially be her new family come fall. It was all
lovely. Milo's family was wonderful, and Milo was a gentleman
in every way. He was perfect for her, just as she'd hoped.

Milo lived on the adjoining property. Sadie could see his
house from the window. She'd had supper there several times,
always with Martha and John present, or with other members of
Milo's family, as it should be. But she and Milo still found plenty
of time to be alone and get to know each other.

He was quieter than Kade and didn't seem to possess the same
playfulness. Somehow, she couldn't picture Milo rolling around in
the snow or making a snowman. Come to think of it, she'd never
thought Kade could be capable of such behavior. The memory
always brought a smile to her face.

Milo didn't seem to enjoy deep conversation the way Kade did
either. Twice, she'd tried to talk to Milo about Ben, how she felt
after his death, and the struggle to move forward. He'd seemed
very uncomfortable and changed the subject both times. Once,

Sadie had tried to spark up a conversation about faith. She hinted at her own need to understand God's will sometimes, but she was careful not to say too much. Rightly so. Milo didn't want to hear of such questionings when it came to the Lord. And she knew he was right to feel that way, which added another layer to her guilt. She had no reason to doubt, after all. God had sent her the perfect man to spend the rest of her life with and blessed her with an opportunity for a new beginning. She knew there was nothing to gain by comparing Milo to Kade.

Her *Englisch* friend had aroused feelings in Sadie she thought were long gone and had awakened her to the fact that she was still a woman—a woman who longed to be held, touched, and loved. But he was not the right man for her. Her place was here, with Milo. To consider anything else would only cause heartache. She should have never allowed herself to get close to Kade or Tyler.

It wasn't only Kade and Tyler that Sadie missed—it was also Lillian, Mary Ellen, Rebecca, Katie Ann, Sarah Jane, and Carley. Hopefully, one of the women would be able to continue to run Treasures of the Heart, even after the farm was sold, a thought she chose to push aside, knowing Lillian most likely had begun that process. She had worked so hard to get the shop up and running. How Ben had loved that farm.

Surely, over time, she wouldn't feel so homesick.

"What is it, dear?" Martha touched Sadie lightly on the arm. "You look a million miles away."

"I guess I was just thinking—" Sadie wasn't sure how much to say. Martha and her entire family had been more than hospitable; they'd welcomed her as part of their own family.

"Let's sit a bit." Martha motioned toward the den. "It's normal for you to be feelin' homesick, ya know?" Martha said when they sat down in the rockers.

Sadie nodded, but there was a catch in her throat as she opened her mouth to speak.

"This is all very new to you. A new place. New folks to get to know."

"*Ach*, I'm fine. Really." Sadie smiled.

Martha pursed her lips, folded her hands in her lap, and then took a deep breath. "Sadie, I know that your parents have passed. And I'll not try to assume the role of your *mamm* . . ." Martha paused, her hazel eyes radiating with kindness. "But if ever there is a time when you need to talk, for certain you can come to me. Milo is my son, and you seem to make him very happy. But you must feel right in your own heart too."

"Milo is wonderful," Sadie said, surprised Martha would doubt her intentions. "I care for him very much. It's just that—" She couldn't tell Martha that her own heart belonged to another, someone she could never be with. "I am a bit homesick. I mostly miss *mei* friend, Lillian, and several other ladies in my district." She smiled. "And Lillian's grandfather, Jonas, is also very special to me." Sadie lowered her head. She was telling the truth, just not the entire truth.

"*Mei* daughters all care for you very much, and with time, you'll make lots of new friends here." Martha reached over and patted Sadie's hand. "Will just take some time."

Time. Yes, time, Sadie thought. She was exactly where she needed to be.

Kade tucked the quilt up around Tyler's neck, thankful his son was taking a nap. Kade needed time to think. In nine short weeks, he'd had a life overhaul. Monica's death. Full custody of Tyler. His friendship with Sadie. And now, he was learning the ways of the Plain people of Lancaster County from a kooky old man he'd grown to love. Jonas was completely opposite from his own father, yet they were each independent keepers of great knowledge. Kade's father was wise in ways of the world—an innate ability to turn a buck into a million, a way with people that had earned him trust by unlikely parties, and Kade respected him more than any man he'd ever known. Yet Kade couldn't deny that his relationship with his father consisted of a detached type of love that ran both ways.

Jonas's distrust for the *Englisch*, as he called them, had shone through from the beginning—particularly a wealthy *Englisch* man with a past far more complex than Jonas could imagine. But once the elderly man saw past the image of Kade and his wealthy lifestyle, Jonas dove deep into Kade's spirit, got him to think about deeper questions. For reasons Kade didn't understand, Jonas had allowed himself to become both mentor and friend to Kade.

Repeatedly, Jonas had told Kade that a life among the Amish would never work for Kade. And it sure seemed that way. Every reason Jonas cited made perfect sense, yet Jonas continued to teach Kade, almost as if he was testing his will. And Kade continued to soak up Jonas's teachings with an insatiable thirst that he couldn't quench, although logistically it made no sense.

Kade's search for real contentment had been unattainable for his entire life, and Jonas seemed to hold the key that was opening up possibilities for Kade, possibilities for happiness that had nothing to do with money or material possessions—things Kade already knew could not bring the type of fulfillment he was looking for. Jonas spoke about God so passionately and with such ease, Kade felt compelled to learn more. Eventually, Kade opened up to Jonas in a profound way; Jonas had nudged him to feel things he'd never felt before. Once he even cried in front of Jonas, who merely said, "Welcome the Lord, Kade."

Some days, Jonas checked out for a while. Sarah Jane said the doctors were not completely sure whether it was his cancer medications or the progression of Alzheimer's that made him mentally lapse. Kade believed it to be the latter. He recognized the symptoms. He'd been through it with his own father, and as distressing as it was to relive, Kade guided Jonas back to reality as best he could. He needed Jonas. And in some way, Kade felt like Jonas needed him too.

Sadie. He thought about her constantly, wondered how her new life in Texas was working out. He constantly fought to keep his heart from turning bitter. Why would God introduce him to such a woman if she was destined to love another man? He often fantasized about having a life with Sadie in this wonderful Amish community, but it seemed so far-fetched that his mind wound in circles and always came back to the most prevalent question, *what am I doing here?*

Kade picked up his cell phone from the coffee table, the flashing red light indicating a message. He'd been avoiding the link to his previous life for days—but he knew that to move forward, he had to take care of what was behind him. He dialed his voice mail. Forty-two new messages. His heart raced, not from anticipation but from dread. To go back to his house, his money, his friends—a term he now used loosely—seemed like a prison sentence. He couldn't go on living the way he had been. Something had been so amiss in his life, and that something was God.

The heart of the people in Lancaster County was unlike anything Kade had known, and he clung to their beliefs like a drowning man to a life preserver, clutching the one thing that could carry him to safety—a relationship with God and His Son, Jesus Christ. And yet the logical side of his brain continued to reprimand his choices, begging him to rethink this absurd behavior.

Seventeen voice mails were from Monica's mother, checking on Tyler. He owed Andrea a call and regretted not calling her before now. Plus, he'd never returned Val's first batch of messages, and now there were eight more from him, all pleading with Kade to call him—once stating that he had something important to talk with Kade about. The rest of the messages were from board members, business contacts, and people representing Kade's interests on various fronts. He knew he'd shown the irresponsibility of a young teenager, off on a *rumpschpringe*, as Jonas would call it. And yet, he listened to all the messages, placed the phone back on the table, and chose to talk to no one.

No one on that phone list anyway. He wanted to talk with someone else. "Dear heavenly Father . . ." he began.

———

Jonas knocked at Lizzie's door for the third time—resolved that if she didn't answer, he was going in anyway. To worry was a sin, but it pulled at Jonas like a weight, dragging his spirit down. He needed to know if Lizzie's current state was his fault. He'd thought he was doing right by Irma Rose not to act on his feelings for Lizzie, but when Lillian said Lizzie wasn't doing so good, he knew he'd been wrong to abandon her the way he had.

Finally, the door opened, and Jonas was shocked at what he saw. Lizzie's long gray hair cascaded down around her shoulders. So silky and smooth, Jonas resisted the urge to stroke it with his hand. She looked like she'd been in her blue dress for more than a day or two, and as Lillian had said—the place was a mess. As improper as it was to behold Lizzie's hair, unbound and flowing freely without the confines of her prayer covering, Jonas suspected there might be bigger issues at hand.

"Lizzie, you all right?" he asked hesitantly from the front porch.

Lizzie stepped back and motioned for Jonas to come in. "*Ya*, I'm *gut*, Jonas. Just a bit tired, that's all." She sat down on the bench at the kitchen table. "Please, sit down, Jonas."

Jonas removed his straw hat and hung it on the rack inside the door and studied her for a moment. Didn't she realize she was missing something? He tugged on the full length of his beard, clamped his lips tight. Then he asked, "Lizzie, do you know that you don't have your *kapp* on?" Right away, he wished he hadn't mentioned it.

She jumped up, bumped her knee on the table, and brought both hands frantically to her head. "*Ach*, no." Tears welled in the corner of her eyes. "I'm so embarrassed. I'm so—How could I not know that?"

Jonas wasted no time moving around the table. He placed his hands firmly on each arm and gazed into her eyes. "We won't tell a livin' soul 'bout this, Lizzie. I reckon it is just fine."

"It's not fine." She cradled her face in her hands, and Jonas could feel her trembling.

He wrapped his arms around her and pulled her close. "Lizzie, don't cry." She felt so tiny pressed against his lanky, thin build. What a pair they made. "I've missed you, Lizzie. I'm sorry that—"

She eased him away, turned, and walked out of the room. When she returned, her hair was tucked beneath her prayer covering, her head held high. Jonas wanted to take her in his arms again, but her expression was solemn, and Lizzie didn't seem excited to see him, the way he'd hoped. But Jonas knew something that would cheer her up. He cumbersomely dropped to one knee and balanced his weight by holding on to the kitchen table.

"Jonas, I think I've had a stroke," she said matter-of-factly, with no regard for Jonas's obvious intentions. "Maybe you ought not be thinking what you're thinking, and stand up," she said in a bossy tone he hadn't heard from her before. Jonas wasn't sure he could stand up. His old joints had had one too many trips to the bended-knee position today. "Get up, now," she demanded.

He eyed her with amusement. Lizzie was trying her best to look tough, but she looked downright silly to him. "Lizzie, what do you think you're doing?" he said, still on bended knee, one hand resting on the kitchen table.

"What do you mean?" She cupped her small hips with her hands.

"Why are you trying to be all tough and mean when you ain't got a mean bone in that tiny body of yours?" He grinned.

"Did you hear what I said, Jonas? I think I've had a stroke. I'm not sure, but somethin' ain't right in my mind." She took a deep breath, then lifted her head a little higher. "I reckon that's what happens when a person has a stroke. I remember when it happened to Anna Mae last year. She got all crazy in the head."

"What's all that got to do with me being down here on this floor like this, and you trying to be all . . . whatever it is you're trying to be?" He groaned a bit, but kept himself in proposal position.

She shook her head. "I never want to be a burden on anyone."

Jonas bellowed out a hearty laugh.

"Do you find this funny?" She pressed her thin lips together.

"Lizzie," he began, "I don't know what's goin' on half the time, so I reckon it'd be a fair shake as to who'd be a burden to who. Don'tcha think?" He groaned.

"Jonas, maybe you should get up from there."

"I'll get up when I'm *gut* and ready, when I've tended to my business," he grumbled.

Jonas straightened his back as best he could and gazed into her eyes. "Lizzie, I want you to marry me, move in over with me and Sarah Jane, where we can tend to ya."

Her big, brown eyes went wild with fury—almost rabid, like his old hound dog years ago. She was as frightful a woman as he'd ever seen. "Is that a yes?" He cowered backward a smidgen.

"I don't need no one tending to me!" she hollered. "Why would I want to marry a man just so he could *tend* to me? That's as wrong a reason as I can think of, and—"

"Lizzie!" he snapped.

She closed her mouth and waited for him to speak.

Jonas drew in a deep breath. "Woman, don't you know how much I love you? After Irma Rose died, I never expected to love another, Lizzie." He paused, seeing her eyes soften. "But I do, Lizzie. I love you. I love the time we spend together. I'm at my best when I'm with you. And you'd do this old man an honor by becoming *mei fraa* and growing old with me."

"We're already old," she said smugly. "And what if I've had a stroke? What if my mind is going? What if it's something else?"

Jonas snickered. "Lizzie, I'm not even sure I can get up off this floor of yours, and who knows if I'll drop dead tomorrow. I got the cancer, ya know. And we already know I don't be remembering things so *gut* these days. But I say we go nuts together and make the best of it."

It warmed his heart to hear Lizzie laugh. "You're a silly old man, huggy bear."

"That's what they tell me, that daughter and granddaughter of mine. So what do you say? Wanta get married to this silly old man?"

"Oh, Jonas. Yes." Her voice bubbled with joy.

He was tickled by her reaction, but there was another issue at hand. "Lizzie."

"*Ya?*"

"I can't get up." Jonas tried to push his weight upward, but the pain in his legs was unbearable.

"Here, let me." Lizzie wrapped her arms underneath his and pulled with all her tiny might.

Slowly, Jonas rose to his feet, amid all the crackling in his joints and bones. "And I don't see no reason to wait until November to get married either."

"Folks will expect us to wait till after the fall harvest," she said.

Jonas grinned. "I don't know 'bout you, but I ain't got a fall harvest."

"Oh, Jonas," she said again, her eyes twinkling.

"Now, that's my Lizzie," he said, and then wrapped his arms around her.

"And you're my huggy bear."

She pulled back a little and looked up at him. "Who will you have to stand with you?"

Jonas thought for only a moment. "I reckon it should be Samuel."

"That's lovely, because I am going to ask Lillian to stand with me. How sweet to have husband and wife!"

He couldn't help but smile at Lizzie's girlish enthusiasm. He was feeling a tad giddy himself. "Not one of your kin?" he asked after a moment.

"They are *gut* girls, my nieces, but I hardly ever see them. Your granddaughter has always checked on me regularly, her and Sadie both." She paused. "I hope Sadie finds happiness in Texas, but I'll sure miss having her here in Lancaster County. Such a *gut* girl."

"Sadie is special," Jonas said fondly.

"Jonas?" Lizzie's enthusiasm floundered a bit. "Do you reckon I'm losing my mind? I've never forgotten to wear *mei kapp*." She lowered her head.

Jonas lifted her chin gently with his hand. "Lizzie, there ain't no shame in gettin' old, and I don't think you're losin' your mind." He chuckled. "No more than I am. But I do think we need to have Noah take a look at you. If you be forgettin' things, might be easy to fix."

Lizzie glanced around at her house, and Jonas felt sorry for her, knowing she was embarrassed, but not wanting to say anything.

"I've been so tired, Jonas," she said softly as she eyed the dishes in the sink.

He pressed his palm to her cheek. "We'll help each other grow old. We'll do it together."

Lizzie smiled and molded herself into his arms.

⸻

Kade looked at the calendar hanging on the kitchen wall. One more week. That's all he'd signed on for—three months. Jonas told him that Bishop Ebersol sold Sadie's farm right away to Lester Lapp, who'd agreed not to take possession until Sadie returned to collect her things, which wouldn't be until he and Tyler were gone.

Sadie loves this place, Kade thought, as he stood staring at the calendar. *But she must love Milo more.* He fought the bitterness that continued to creep into his soul when he thought of Sadie playing house with Milo in Texas.

Tyler was on the floor, playing with his letters, so Kade allowed his mind to drift into a world where his thoughts were clean and pure, a place with no worry, no deadlines, no distrust, fear of failure, fear of death, fear in general—a world where God sat beside him as a good friend and mentor. A world like he'd found here in Lancaster County.

But he had a home, and soon he'd be leaving to go there. Somehow, he needed to bottle up everything he felt here and take it with him. He and Tyler were certain to have great challenges when they returned. Tyler seemed to have settled into the routine of life here. His tantrums were still a daily occurrence, but Kade was learning, and together they would make it through the transition. Guilt at his own absence from the boy's life still stabbed at his heart, but that was slowly being replaced by a love that Kade had never known.

His thoughts were interrupted by a pounding on the door. Tyler beat him to the door and wrapped his arms around Jonas's legs.

"Here's *mei* boy," Jonas exclaimed like a proud grandfather. Kade knew Jonas was going to miss Tyler.

Jonas walked in the door, the way any good friend does, and helped himself to a seat on the tan chair next to the couch. A light jazzy mix resounded from the small radio. "Sounds like craziness, that music." He removed his hat and looped his thumbs through his suspenders.

Tyler resumed his position on the floor, and Kade sat down on the couch and propped his white socks on the coffee table. "It's jazz," Kade said. Then he shook his head. "That's one thing that would be difficult to give up if I stayed here."

"We both know that ain't possible," Jonas said with conviction.

"Why do you do that, Jonas?"

Jonas innocently raised his brows. "What's that?"

"You act as if I could never make the necessary sacrifices to conform to your life. How do you know that? After all the conversations we've had, you know me pretty well, and you know what a mess my life has been. Why do you assume I could never be happy here?"

"Could you be? Happy here, that is."

Kade was suddenly stumped. Usually, Jonas held firm to the

conviction that Kade's staying was not an option. "I'm happy here now."

"Because you're on vacation," Jonas said. "But a man like you doesn't exchange the things you have for our way of life."

Kade thought long and hard before he spoke. "Jonas, I've been a wealthy man my entire life. Money, possessions, great business success—I've had it all. And yet, I don't have an ounce of the peace of mind you have. And those material gains are no longer alluring to me, and to tell you the truth, I'm not sure they ever were. It's all I ever knew. Had I not come here for a reprieve from my life, I'd have never known this way of life even existed. So, I really don't think it's fair for you to judge my intentions."

"Is that what you think I'm doing? Judging you?"

Kade eyed Jonas curiously. This was the wise man he'd grown to love, pressing him in ways that often confused him. "Yes, I think you're judging me."

"Then stay," Jonas said, his face somber.

"What?"

"You heard me, my *Englisch* friend." Jonas remained serious, his eyes fused with Kade's. "Just stay."

It became apparent: Jonas was going to miss Kade as much as Kade was going to miss the old man. "But I—" It was a fantasy to think about living here, and the reality didn't align with the dream. Although he feared leaving Paradise might kill him, he knew he didn't have a choice. "I have responsibilities that I've ignored for too long," he finally said.

Jonas was quiet for a moment. "Kade, I reckon you're gonna find that you're not the same man you were when you arrived here." He paused, stroking his beard. "But the things you have learned here, along with your renewed relationship with our Lord—this feeling of wholeness—you can have it anywhere. There is no reason you can't live your life among the *Englisch* with a new sense of freedom. You'll take it all with you, Kade. God is not geographically prejudiced, presenting Himself more to us than those out in the rest of the world. You can seek Him out from anywhere. His Holy Spirit dwells within you."

Why was it, when Jonas spoke to him like this, that Kade had a hard time controlling his emotions? "You don't know how much I'd like to just never go back, Jonas." He paused and fought the unwelcome tremor in his voice. "I'm afraid, Jonas—I'm afraid that the world out there"—Kade swung his hand toward the door—"will suck the life out of me again—will steal my will and all that I've gained here."

"You still have much to learn," Jonas said. "Fear hinders a man. Once you stop being afraid, your life will change in ways you've never imagined. Fear keeps your heart closed and prevents the Lord from reaching you."

"Are you scared, Jonas? I mean, the cancer and all."

"I'm human, Kade. I'd be lying if I said that leaving my loved ones didn't cause me pain. Chances are, I'll never see the child that Lillian carries grow much past a toddler, if that much. I worry about leavin' Lizzie, how she'll be when somethin' happens to me. It worries me to leave Sarah Jane, Lillian, and the rest of the people I care about, even though worry is a sin." He paused. "I am human. But am I afraid of death? The answer is no."

They sat quietly for a few moments. Then Jonas said, "I came here to tell you some news." He grinned. "Me and Lizzie are getting married."

Kade shot Jonas an instant look of approval. "Jonas, I think that's great."

"We ain't farmers with harvests to tend, so I reckon we'll be gettin' married next month. The twentieth of April is the day we picked. Sure would mean a lot to us—to me—if you could be here."

Kade was deeply touched. "I wouldn't miss it," he said.

"I know it's a long way to travel, but sure would be *gut* if you could bring Tyler."

"We'll do our very best to be here."

Kade's cell phone began to ring. "The closer it gets for me to leave, the more this thing rings." He reached for the phone, pushed the End button, and tossed it back on the table. "That cell phone is one thing I wouldn't miss if I lived here."

Jonas stood up. "See you for supper? Sarah Jane is makin' meat loaf."

"That sounds great." Kade walked Jonas to the door.

Sadie hung up the phone in Martha and John's barn. She didn't leave a message. She wasn't even sure what she would have said if Kade had answered. But she felt compelled to make the call, hoping that Kade would say something, anything, to cause her to return to her home, to a place in his arms, to the fantasy world she created of them sharing a life together.

In reality, if he had answered, she would have probably told him that she was happy in Texas, and that she was merely calling to check on Tyler.

But happiness was not the emotion that overflowed from

Sadie's heart, particularly after what Milo had told her, "Bishop Ebersol left a message, Sadie. Good news. Your farm has been sold."

She fought back the tears building in the corner of her eyes, looked up to heaven, and begged God to give her the strength to stay on the path He has chosen for her.

Sadie knew she should be counting her blessings, but Milo's words kept ringing in her head like gongs of forthcoming doom.

18

KADE'S RETURN TO HIS OLD LIFE LOOMED OVER HIM like a dark cloud, and in a mere two hours, he'd be home, back to a world filled with shrewd business deals, high-powered luncheons, and enough vanity to choke on. And beautiful women—lots of beautiful ladies interested in a place on Kade's arm—all with the same selfish pursuits of furthering their own social status. Then, of course, there was Val.

The captain's voice sounded through the plane, something about arriving in Los Angeles early, but Kade's mind was elsewhere. He thought about Monica and how her life was cut tragically short. He reached over and stroked Tyler's head while he slept, knowing that change was not easy for his son. *I wonder if Penelope knows how to make tapioca pudding.*

The flight attendant stopped her cart in the aisle. "Cocktail, sir?"

Kade shook his head.

He constantly thought about Sadie and how much he missed her—the sound of her laughter, her loving ways with Tyler, and, of course, their hugs at the end of the evenings. And even the firm way that she kept Kade in line. He recalled the way he'd almost lost his cool about Val, but Sadie warned him with her eyes when unsuitable language threatened to spew from his mouth. And she'd always kept a safe distance from Kade, even though Kade often saw the longing in her expression to do otherwise. He smiled as he thought about the way she'd scolded him about his dismissive hand gestures, a habit Kade had just about kicked. Memories of her calmed him, but also tormented him. Sadie could never be his, and that badgered his heart unmercifully, testing his resolve to quiet his troubled spirit.

Kade rested his head against the back of his seat, closed his eyes, and pretended he was back with Sadie in the middle of the blizzard, back in the warmth of her company. There was no sex. No false promises. No pretending. No lies. Just Sadie being herself—honest and pure, loving and kind.

Now he was homeward bound and feeling more destitute than he'd ever felt, with each passing mile putting more distance between the place and the people he'd grown to love.

But knowing he'd go back for Jonas and Lizzie's wedding gave him a tiny bit of comfort, and he wondered if Sadie would be back for the wedding, and if she'd have Milo with her.

Sadie kept hearing the words pounding in her head. "Your farm has been sold. We can travel to Lancaster County and collect your things soon."

Milo hadn't formally asked her to marry him. It was an assumption, and Sadie hadn't done anything to dispel or confirm it. They spent time together, and Sadie had laughed and carried on as a young girl during courtship. But Kade and Tyler were always in the back of her mind. She knew it would be a sin to marry Milo when her heart belonged to another man. But now her farm was gone.

Sadie waited until Martha and John traveled to a neighbor's house for supper, declining the invitation because of a terrible headache. She made her way to the barn and prayed silently that someone at Lillian's house would hear the phone ringing in the barn. She'd never needed a friendly voice more than now. But when there was no answer, she dialed the number to Jonas and Sarah Jane's house.

The phone rang six times, and Sadie was about to hang up when the ringing stopped. She heard a raspy voice say hello.

"Jonas, is that you?" she said. "Jonas?"

"Who be callin', please?"

"Jonas, it's Sadie!"

"Sadie, it's *wunderbaar gut* to hear your voice. How are you, my child?"

And that was all it took. She yielded to compulsive sobs.

"Sadie?" His voice was comforting, compassionate. "Tell me your troubles, dear Sadie."

"My farm is sold," she babbled while wiping her eyes.

"*Ya*, it is. Isn't that what you wanted?"

"Yes," she lied softly. "I'll be coming to collect my things soon."

She heard a sigh on the other end of the line. "So, you will be staying to make a life with Milo in Texas?"

"*Ya*." She bit her lip.

"And this makes Sadie cry?"

"*Ach*, I'm being silly." She sniffled, dabbed at her eyes. "Milo is a wonderful man, and he'll make a fine home for me here in Texas.

I'll be traveling back by bus in two days. I reckon I'm homesick, and it will be *gut* to see everyone, especially Lillian and you."

"We all miss ya, Sadie. But we want you to be happy. A *gut* girl like you deserves to be happy." He paused. "Are you happy, Sadie?"

"*Ya*," she said as convincingly as she could. "Milo is wonderful. He'll make a fine home for me here in Texas."

"*Ya, ya.* You just said that." Jonas paused again. "Are you *in lieb* with him, Sadie?"

She couldn't lie to Jonas, but she couldn't quite tell him the truth either. "He's a fine man. It's all happening so fast, I reckon."

"Sadie . . ." She could hear Jonas inhale deeply on the end of the line. He took his time releasing the breath. "We can't force God's will or try to guess what His plan is for us. It is important that you not let your own wants and needs block out His voice. Listen to Him, Sadie."

Sadie sighed. "I know you're right, Jonas." What a wonderful bishop Jonas would have been. So wise and kind. But Sadie knew Jonas lacked the harsh discipline to enforce the rules, as was expected by the bishop. His heart, though, was always in the right place. She was glad he answered the phone today.

Silence stretched the distance between them, and she waited for Jonas to speak. "I have news, Sadie."

"About Kade and Tyler?" she asked.

"Uh, no. 'Tis 'bout me and Lizzie."

"Oh."

"Ain't no need to sound so disappointed. My news might shed some light on Kade and Tyler as well. I've asked Lizzie to marry me."

"*Ach*, Jonas! That's so *gut*, so very *gut*. Lizzie is a fine woman, but . . ." How did this shed any light on Kade and Tyler?

"I know you're coming home in a couple of days, but I'm sure hoping you'll somehow be able to be at my wedding. It'll be a few weeks from now. The twentieth of April is when I'll take Lizzie as *mei fraa*, and we'd be mighty glad if you could be here. But I understand if that's too much traveling too close together."

"That is a lot of traveling. Texas is a long way from Lancaster County." Her heart was breaking. "But I want so very much to be there, Jonas."

"Kade and the boy will be here to see me and Lizzie wed." Jonas tempted her with his tone.

"I'm surprised," she said. "I mean, I received a letter from Lillian telling me that the two of you had become friends, but—"

"He's a fine man."

"*Ya*," she said softly. "How is Lillian and everyone else?" She clamped her mouth tight and fought the tremor in her voice as she wiped another tear from her cheek.

"My Lilly is doin' fine." He paused for several long moments. "Come home, Sadie," Jonas finally said. "Just come home."

Penelope was standing in the front yard when the cab rounded the circular drive in front of Kade's house. And so was Val.

Kade sighed from the backseat. Tyler had been restless, fussy, and downright mean during the taxi ride from the airport to Kade's home in Los Angeles, trying twice to bite Kade. But Kade knew Tyler was rattled by the plane flight, change in schedule, and new surroundings. His son needed stability, and the day had been void of a normal routine.

Kade was exhausted, stressed, and not in the mood to face Val.

"Welcome home," Val said when Kade stepped out of the cab with Tyler.

Ignoring Val's extended hand, Kade reached in his pocket for his wallet and handed the driver a hundred-dollar bill. "I'm really sorry about the ride."

"No problem." The driver accepted the generous tip, but Kade saw him roll his eyes.

"How big he is!" Penelope rushed to Tyler. "Hello, Tyler."

Tyler's eyes grew wide and fearful. "Hug," he said to Kade. Tyler wrapped his arms around Kade's legs, and that one small gesture made up for the entire day. Kade scooped Tyler into his arms. "He's had a hard day. Hello, Penelope." He hugged his longtime house-keeper as he balanced Tyler on one hip.

"So good to have you both home," she said.

Kade took a deep breath and extended his hand to Val. "Hello, Val." He set Tyler down beside him and grabbed their suitcase. "I need to get Tyler something to eat and introduce him to his new surroundings."

Val followed a few steps behind. "Penelope found a school for Tyler, but he would have to live there most of the time. It's the best school for autistic children in the area, and—"

"Tyler will be living here with me." The thought of anything else caused Kade's stomach to churn.

"I've prepared your favorite meal, Mr. Saunders. I've made ratatouille."

Kade recalled the eggplant casserole with tomatoes, zucchini, and onions. It was one of Penelope's specialties. As they all continued up the walkway to the front double doors, he said, "That sounds fine, Penelope." Then he turned toward her as she walked alongside him. "But feel free to tone things down in the future. Even meat loaf and stew would be fine with me." He thought about the fabulously simple meals Sadie prepared for him.

"Oh, and Penelope—" Kade walked ahead of her and through the front door with Tyler. "Call me Kade from now on."

He glanced over his shoulder in time to see Penelope give Val a confused look. Kade didn't comment. He motioned Tyler ahead of him on the spacious, tiled entryway—an entryway as big as Sadie's entire den. It felt unusually cold and distant here now.

"Tyler, this is your new home." Kade watched his son eye the massive room ahead of them. And then Kade began to examine the room himself, making a mental note of all the things that had to go, things that could hurt Tyler—like the abstract sculpture atop a marble stand to the side of the fireplace. Spiked, fluted spurs extended from a solid bronze base and shimmied aimlessly into the air about three feet. Once considered his most prized possession, he now regarded his first piece of fine art as a danger for his son. If Tyler pulled on the marble base, and the sculpture were to fall with all those spikes . . .

Kade surveyed the rest of his house. More sculptures, exotic finds, rare collections, priceless vases, glass tabletops with sharp edges, and the list went on.

"Penelope, we are going to make some major changes around here. There are many things in this house that can hurt Tyler. I want to start selling some of these items, tone things down a bit, provide a simpler atmosphere, one safer for my son. No sharp edges, dangerous sculptures . . ." Kade pointed to the sculpture a few feet ahead of them. "Objects like that."

"Yes, Mr.—I mean, Kade."

Mr. Saunders may have been the man who left three months ago, but Kade was the man who came back. He didn't want to remember the person he used to be. "Penelope, I have some issues to discuss with Val. Would you take Tyler into the kitchen and get him something to eat? If you have any problems, call for me." He paused. "Do we have any pudding?"

"No, Mr. Saunders." Penelope blinked her eyes closed, then opened them. "No, Kade."

"Tyler loves tapioca pudding. Maybe you could make him some soon. But for now, he seems to like bread with peanut butter, and maybe some cheese spread on it. Do we have anything like that?" Without waiting for an answer, Kade said, "Nothing that requires a fork, only a spoon. He likes mashed potatoes also."

"Yes, Kade." Penelope held her hand out to Tyler. "Come with me, Tyler."

"Oh, he doesn't like to be touched," Kade said. "I mean, not unless he asks for a hug. And that lunch box he's carrying, he takes that everywhere. I have a list of his likes and dislikes, Penelope, that I can go over with you later. But no worries. Tyler will be spending most of his time with me."

"What?" Val asked.

"Tyler, go with Ms. Penelope, and I'll see you in a minute."

"Tyler go with Ms. Penelope," Tyler repeated.

"He knows my name." Penelope sounded proud as she guided Tyler toward the kitchen.

Kade waited until they were out of the room before he turned to Val and wasted no time getting to the point. "I'm sorry for your loss, Val. About Monica. She was a fine woman, and of course, she's Tyler's mother. So my grief and sympathy span several levels." He paused to see Val's jaw drop. Clearly, his friend was expecting a verbal lashing. And a couple of months ago, that's what Kade would have done. "My preference would have been for you to trust our friendship enough to tell me that you were seeing her, but what's done is done. Moving on, though, I know you have stock in Saunders Real Estate and Development, and a vested interest since your company has done several deals with us. So, I want you to know that I am addressing the board tomorrow, resigning as CEO, and putting my shares up for sale." Kade fused his eyes intently with Val's. "I'll trust you to keep this information confidential until I speak with the board tomorrow."

Val nodded, and his jaw dropped even further.

"I'm stepping out of the rat race, Val. I want to spend time with Tyler." Kade began sorting through the pile of mail on the counter at the bar.

"May I?" Val asked. He rounded the corner of the wet bar and helped himself to a glass. "I think I need a drink." He paused, narrowed his eyes at Kade. "Don't *you* need a drink? Scotch?"

Kade realized he hadn't had a cocktail since he'd been gone. "No, thanks. But help yourself."

"What happened to you in Lancaster County?" Val filled the small glass and took a giant swig.

"My priorities have changed, that's all."

"I'll say." Val chugged the drink. "Kade, about Monica . . . I was going to tell you."

"It doesn't matter at this point, does it?"

"I suppose not." Val walked around the bar to where Kade was standing. "Your father started Saunders Real Estate and Development, Kade. How can you give it all up?"

Kade looked up at him. "Just doesn't seem important anymore." He motioned around the room. "None of this seems important."

Val shook his head. "Kade, I can understand you wanting to be a good father to Tyler, but I hate to see you start making rash decisions because you've spent a few months with the Amish. What? They brainwash you or something?" Val grinned.

"Yes. That's it, Val. They brainwashed me." Kade rolled his eyes. "If you don't mind, Val, I want to check on Tyler, and I have mounds of mail to go through. I have a lot of lifestyle adjustments to make." He extended his hand to Val. "No hard feelings."

Val was slow to grasp Kade's hand. "I'm glad about that, Kade."

When Val was out the door, Kade headed to the kitchen to spend some time with his son. He wanted to show Tyler around the place and start making the changes he knew were necessary to accommodate Tyler's needs.

Sadie and Milo sat quietly at the train station, tickets in hand. As planned, they would travel to Lancaster County, where a moving van would meet them at Sadie's farm, or the farm that used to be hers. Her things would be loaded and hauled to Texas. She sat thinking out how this had gone from a visit to a full-blown move so fast, and with a wedding planned for November. She hadn't argued against any of it, going along with each of Milo's suggestions. It was, after all, her chance at happiness.

However, waves of panic surged through her, threatening to suffocate her. She tugged on the neckline of her dress and endured stares from the *Englischers*. She'd never felt more on edge. She was overcome by an urge to run, and she knew if she didn't speak up now, it would be too late.

"Milo," she said softly.

He reached over and grabbed her hand. *"Ya?"* His profile was strong and rigid, his blue eyes kind, but questioning. A muscle flicked in his jaw, as if the expression on her face brought forth worry.

What a wonderful man, she thought. *What a wonderful father he would make.* Indeed, he was everything she asked God to provide for her.

She inhaled a deep breath and blew it out slowly.

"There's something I need to tell you," she finally said.

19

SADIE WALKED ACROSS HER YARD, NO LONGER COVERED in snow like when she left. She stumbled up the porch steps, toting the cumbersome suitcase, and walked into her den. Actually, Lester Lapp's den. She set the luggage down and looked around. Her first order of business would be to visit with Lester and see about buying the farm back. Lester was a kind man, and Sadie felt sure he wouldn't hesitate to sell back the property that had been in Sadie's family for generations. She tried to shake the forlorn expression on Milo's face when she explained that she wouldn't be moving to Stephenville.

She'd been home about fifteen minutes when she heard a buggy coming up the driveway.

"Lillian!" Sadie yelled as she ran down the porch steps. "I missed you so much," she said when Lillian got out of the buggy.

"We all missed you too."

Sadie could barely get her arms around Lillian. She pulled back from the hug and said, "You are huge."

Lillian groaned. She took hold of Sadie's arm and motioned toward the porch. Then her friend lowered herself onto one of the rockers. "I know. The doctor said it should be any day. And I'm miserable." Then she smiled. "But I sure am glad you're home. I have to admit, I wasn't all that surprised when you left word that you were coming back—alone—to stay."

"Why do you say that?" Sadie wondered if Lillian knew her secret.

Lillian shrugged. "I don't know. Maybe because this is your home. Or maybe because I wasn't sure Milo was the right one."

"But you only met him briefly before I left for Texas. How could you possibly suspect that he wasn't the one for me?"

Again, Lillian shrugged. "You didn't have that look. You know. The look a person has when she is *in lieb*."

"I wasn't in love with Milo, but I guess I thought I could be. His family was so wonderful, Lillian, and you should have seen the look on his face when I told him I would be traveling alone and not returning to Texas." She shook her head. "In so many ways, he was perfect. I hope I haven't made a *baremlich* mistake."

"What are you going to do now?" Lillian twisted uncomfortably in her seat.

"I'm going to go right over to Lester Lapp's house and buy back my farm. I'm sure he'll sell it back to me, and—" Sadie stopped when Lillian's face went white. "What's wrong?"

"Didn't anyone tell you?"

"Tell me what?"

"Lester Lapp closed on the farm, and the very next day, he sold it to someone else—an *Englischer*."

"What?" Sadie grabbed her chest with both hands. "Who?"

Lillian shrugged. "I don't know. I heard the news from Mary Ellen, who found out from Rachel. And evidently, Rachel got word of it while she was at the farmer's market."

"*Ach!* It's Dale Spalek—that *Englisch* fella in town. He's been try- ing to purchase property along our road for years. Remember when he tried to purchase the Lantz place? But Amos Lantz wouldn't sell to him." She gasped. "Probably for tourists. They will want to use my shop out front to sell overpriced things to tourists! Mr. Spalek has two stores in town already. He doesn't need my family farm." Sadie looked at her friend. "Lillian, what am I going to do now?" She covered her face with her hands. "I've made such a mess of everything."

After several moments of silence, Sadie uncovered her face and stared at Lillian. Something was wrong.

"Uh-oh. It appears I've made a mess too." Lillian's eyes were wide as she slowly focused on the water seeping over the edge of the chair.

Sadie tucked her chin to her neck. "Did you wet yourself, Lillian?"

Lillian scrunched her face up. "No, silly. My water just broke!"

"Pop!" Sarah Jane yelled throughout the house. "Pop! Sadie left a message on the barn phone! Lillian is in labor, and Carley is taking them to the hospital. Pop, where are you?" She ran upstairs and checked every room, then checked each room downstairs again. "Where is that man?" she grumbled. "Pop!" she yelled again. "Barbie is on her way to get us."

Twenty minutes later, Barbie was in the driveway. Sarah Jane made one last scan of the house and then hurried down the porch steps.

"Where's Jonas?" their *Englisch* friend asked when Sarah Jane climbed into the front seat.

Sarah Jane pulled on her seat belt. "I don't know. I reckon he must have gone to Lizzie's without telling me. He still does that, sneaks off." She blew out a sigh of exasperation. "Sometimes I think he enjoys the thrill of sneaking around, when there is no need to. All he does is worry me when he does that."

"Do you want to swing by Lizzie's house and see if he's there?"

"No. I don't have time to be chasing him around today. Lillian is in labor, and I want to be there. I'm sure he's all right. He always is. Pop is so mischievous, like a child sometimes. He frustrates me. But I'm hoping once he and Lizzie get married, he will stay close to home where I can keep an eye on him."

"How's his cancer?" Barbie asked. She turned off of Black Horse Road onto Lincoln Highway.

"Most days he does fairly well, although he gets confused sometimes." She paused and thought for a minute. "The doctors say he might have a touch of Alzheimer's, but honestly, I think sometimes it's his medications. I think they make him a tad loopy."

"Jonas is such a dear. You know, everyone who meets him loves him."

Sarah Jane laughed. "I think Pop scares some people when they first meet him. It isn't until people get to know him that they realize what a big teddy bear he is. You know, he'd do anything for anyone. Pop has a huge heart."

"I guess you're right. Years ago, I suppose it did take Jonas a while to warm up to me. That seems like such a long time ago."

"You've been a *gut* friend, Barbie. Pop loves you. So do I." She smiled at her friend as they made their way toward Lancaster General. "I can't wait to see if Lillian has another girl or a boy!"

The plan was simple, Jonas thought, lying out in the field halfway between his house and Lizzie's farm. Strap on his walkie-talkie, sneak across the field between their farms now that the snow had cleared, then call her on the walkie-talkie and tell her he was sitting on her front porch. She would have been tickled pink at his playfulness.

Instead, he had tripped and stumbled, then landed flat on his back. Now he couldn't seem to move. It had been downright frustrating to hear Sarah Jane hollering for him, and even more so, to watch his daughter ride off with Barbie. *And where are they going anyway? It's almost my lunchtime.*

He unclasped the walkie-talkie from the clip on his suspenders and groaned from the pain in his back. "Breaker, breaker," he rasped. "Lizzie, you there?"

"Is this my huggy bear?"

"Lizzie, I got myself in a bit of a predicament." Jonas tried again to shift his weight.

"You all right, Jonas?"

He noticed his straw hat about a foot over, reached to grab it, but the pain was too much. "Lizzie, I took a fall, and I'm laid out here in the field between your *haus* and mine. Ain't a thing you can do either."

"I'm comin', huggy bear."

"You ain't comin' out here, Lizzie. It's too far for you to walk.

Nearly half a mile, I reckon." *She'd never make it,* Jonas thought, hoping she would have the good sense not to try. Lizzie could barely get up and down her own porch steps and around her house. "Lizzie," he said again when there was no response. "Don't you leave your house. Someone will be by to check on you. Just tell whoever it is to come fetch me out in this field."

"That could be hours from now. Or days, Jonas. I'm on my way," she said.

Hardheaded woman! "Lizzie, don't you dare. I'm ordering you to stay there. Do you hear me?"

"I'm not your *fraa* yet, Jonas Miller. I don't reckon you can be ordering me to do anything."

Jonas sighed, and even that small gesture sent a ripple of pain throughout his body. His pain from the cancer had gotten worse lately. His doctor wanted to put him on medication to manage his discomfort, but had also said it would make him out of sorts. He figured he'd live with the pain, as he was out of sorts enough as it was. Plus, he needed his mind in the right place if he was going to take care of Lizzie.

"*Ach.* No, Lizzie," he whispered to himself. He saw her tiny frame, a dot in the field, moving his way. He pushed the button on the walkie-talkie. "Lizzie, you go on back to the house. You'll catch a chill, and it's too far for you to come out here."

Silence for a few moments. Then Jonas heard her on the walkie-talkie as he watched her taking baby steps across the field. "I'm comin', Jonas."

He didn't have the strength to argue.

"It's a girl," Samuel told the crowd in the waiting room of Lancaster General. "We will be calling her Elizabeth."

"Wonderful news," Sarah Jane said. "How's Lillian?" It had been a short labor and delivery, barely four hours.

"She's *gut*. You can go see her." Samuel couldn't wipe the grin from his face, and Sarah Jane was a proud grandma yet again.

She stood up, hugged Samuel, and headed toward her daughter's room.

"*Mamm*," Lillian whispered when Sarah Jane walked in. She was holding little Elizabeth in her arms. "Isn't she beautiful?"

Sarah Jane held back tears of joy. "Oh, Lillian. She certainly is. Just beautiful." She gently touched the baby's cheek, and then cupped Lillian's face. "She will be a fine baby sister for Anna and David. I think David will want to come in. Is it all right if I go get him?"

Lillian nodded, but her eyes were fused with the new bundle in her arms.

Sarah Jane thought for a moment. "As a matter of fact, sweetie, I think I better go. I couldn't find your grandpa before I left. He probably snuck off to Lizzie's, but he'll be hungry and sorry that he missed all this."

"It's fine, *Mamm*. Send David in. You go find Grandpa."

Sarah Jane kissed her daughter on the forehead. "Do you need anything? I will be back first thing in the morning."

After Lillian assured her that she and the baby were fine, Sarah Jane excused herself, wishing she could stay, and trying not to be irritated with her father.

Lizzie fell for the second time, and she heard her hip pop. As she lay in the field, new spring growth poked her legs and back.

"I'll be there soon, Jonas," she said into the wind. With every ounce of strength she possessed, Lizzie pulled herself to a standing position. She stifled a cry of pain as she edged forward, almost dragging her right leg behind her. Her heart was racing much too fast, and it was difficult to breathe. But her huggy bear was in trouble. She could see him up ahead, sprawled out and not moving.

"Please, Lord," she prayed, "let me make it that far."

She pressed forward, not knowing what she would do when she reached him. But something inside her drove her onward, to Jonas, to her love. "I'm coming," she whispered. And with each painful step, she held her chin high and fought the urge to quit, to lie down, to rest.

But she fell again, and this time the pain in her hip caused her to cry out. It felt dislocated, completely out of joint. She closed her eyes, grimaced, allowed herself to feel the pain, and then she struggled to stand up again. "Please, Lord," she said. "Just let me lie beside him, hold his hand."

Her legs wouldn't lift her, and Lizzie feared she had gone as far as she could. She'd lie here in the field, within only a few yards of him, until someone found them. "Jonas!" she cried with all her might. And then she laid her head back, tears flowing down her wrinkled face. "I can't do it," she cried. "I'm sorry, my love." And she closed her eyes.

It was a few moments later when the breeze carried the sound of his voice. "Lizzie?"

"Jonas?" She struggled to lift her head. "Jonas?" she asked louder.

"I'm here, Lizzie. But I can't move."

Lizzie pushed herself up onto her elbows and realized something. Her upper body was working far better than her lower body. She inched along on her elbows, dragging her legs behind her. "I'm coming, Jonas."

"Stay there, Lizzie. I'll come to you," Jonas said.

She fell onto her back and waited. But nothing.

Lizzie lifted her head. "Jonas?"

But there was silence. "Jonas!" she yelled. "Jonas! Answer me, you silly old man!"

She propped herself back up on her elbows and dragged herself forward through the tall weeds, a few inches at a time, not sure she'd ever felt such pain or determination. Then she saw him—inching toward her, his face filled with pain, but with the same determination she had. "Jonas," she whispered. She continued to pull herself toward him.

"Lizzie." His voice was low and hoarse. "Wait. I'm almost there."

But Lizzie pressed forward, her heart pounding through her chest, both hips preventing her legs from assisting with her efforts. And finally . . . she was within two feet of him. She lay on her stomach and reached her hands as far as they would stretch. Jonas did the same.

"You silly woman," he breathed as his fingers met with hers.

"You silly old man." She intertwined her hand with his and stared into his tired eyes. "I'm so tired, Jonas."

"I know. I'm tired, too, Lizzie."

"Maybe we should rest for a bit."

As they both closed their eyes, Lizzie felt the crisp winds

swirling, heard the rustling weeds swooshing to and fro around them. A tiny insect buzzed in her ear, but she was too exhausted to wave it away. Jonas clutched tightly to her hand, and Lizzie could hear his labored breathing. She would figure out what to do after a little rest.

"I think little Elizabeth looks like Anna," Sarah Jane told Barbie on the drive back to the farm. "They both have those incredible blue eyes like Samuel."

"I can see Lillian in both the girls too, though." Barbie turned toward her and smiled. "Beautiful children."

"I'm so thankful this was a short, easy delivery for Lillian. You know, she had quite a time when Anna was born. Twenty hours of difficult labor."

Barbie nodded as she turned onto Black Horse Road. "I remember. We thought Lillian would never have that child."

"*Danki* for taking me to the hospital, Barbie. I have a fresh batch of cookies I'd like to send home with you for Thomas and the boys."

"That's not necessary, Sarah Jane. I wanted to go." She snickered. "But I'll still be glad to take those cookies off your hands. Do I dare ask if they are my favorite?"

"Raisin puffs. Your favorite." Sarah Jane unclasped her seat belt. "Come in. Let's have a cookie. Hopefully, Pop is home and found himself something to eat."

"Well, the buggy is here," Barbie said. "Your dad didn't get far. If you'd like, I can swing by Lizzie's on my way home."

"I might have you do that, if he's not inside. He could be

napping by now, though. He usually lies down about this time of—"

Barbie grabbed her forearm hard. "Sarah Jane!" She pointed toward the wide-open meadow spanning the space between their farm and Lizzie's house.

Sarah Jane's heart pounded violently. "Oh no," she said. "Pop!" she yelled. "Pop!"

Her legs were already moving toward the field when she realized there were two people lying amid the tall weeds. She broke out in a run, praying aloud. "Please, God, please, God, please, God . . ."

"I'll call 911!" Barbie yelled.

Sarah Jane ran as fast as she could across the meadow. "Pop!"

20

SADIE LEFT THE HOSPITAL, ELATED FOR LILLIAN AND the birth of Elizabeth. But she also felt a profound sense of panic at her own situation. Her farm was gone. And somehow, she was going to have to buy it back.

She thanked Carley for bringing her home, although she'd never felt more homeless or unhappy in her life. God presented her with an opportunity at happiness, with Milo and his wonderful family in Texas, and she had ungraciously walked away from all He offered. She hung her cape on the rack and sat down on the bench at the kitchen table. Maybe she'd made a terrible mistake by not giving things more time between her and Milo.

But every time she'd start to get close to Milo, Kade's face would pop into her mind. She wished she had never met Kade Saunders. Then she would have fallen happily in love with Milo and lived the life she was meant to live. Now, the familiar bitterness she tried so hard to steer away from crept back in. Why would God show her a glimpse of true love with a man she could never be with? Questioning Him was driving her right back to a place she didn't want to be.

Her thoughts were interrupted by the sound of horse hooves coming up the drive. She pulled herself up and went to the door, although she was not in the mood for visitors. After a few moments, she recognized her guest, and this was the one person she was glad to see on this gloomy afternoon.

"Hello, Lester," she said to Lester Lapp. The elderly man hobbled up the porch steps and tipped his straw hat in her direction.

"Sadie, it's *gut* to see you home."

"From what I understand, I don't have a home. I was hoping to buy back my farm from you, but I heard it's already been sold again."

Lester pulled off his hat, scratched his head. "Ya know the only reason I bought this place so quickly, Sadie, was so the property wouldn't go to an *Englischer*. Bishop Ebersol had your power of attorney, so I snapped it up." He paused. "And I'd have sold it right back to you if I'd known you were comin' back."

"Then why did you sell it?" She knew her tone was accusing, but he just said he didn't want the property to go to an outsider.

He took a deep breath and walked to the rocker on the porch. He eased onto the seat, but Sadie kept standing. She folded her arms across her chest and waited for an answer.

"Mary has the cancer," he said. "I'm sure you know that."

Sadie softened her look and voice. "*Ya*, I do. I'm so sorry, Lester. How is she?" She genuinely cared for Mary and Lester, but Mary had been diagnosed with breast cancer months ago. What did this have to do with her farm?

"The city doctors are trying an experimental medication on Mary, and the cost is two thousand dollars a month. I know the community would draw from our fund to cover it, Sadie, but it puts a huge burden on our district. When someone offered me double what I paid for your farm, I reckon I didn't see past the fact that the fella was *Englisch*. That money will go a long way toward Mary's care." He shook his head. "I'm real sorry, Sadie. I figured you to be stayin' in Texas, making a life there."

"So did I," she mumbled.

"Maybe you can buy it back from the *Englischer*? I'll give you the profit I made to do just that."

Sadie knew the sacrifice Lester was making by extending such an offer, but she also knew that the community would cover Mary's medical expenses, one way or the other. If she didn't get her farm back, she was homeless.

"Why would anyone offer twice what the property is worth?" she finally asked. "I don't understand. Mr. Spalek is very greedy to snatch up my property from you, offering to pay such a ridiculous—"

"Whoa, there," Lester interrupted. "It ain't Dale Spalek who bought the property. It was your friend . . ." Lester ran a hand through his long beard. "What was that fella's name?"

"What? Who?" No one Sadie knew had that kind of money or intentions.

"Why, it was that Saunders fella. Kade."

"What?" she asked again. Her blood was starting to boil as she realized that Kade was indeed the only person she knew with the means to purchase her farm at double the value. "Evidently, he is not my *friend*. Why would he want my farm?" she demanded.

Lester shook his head. "I don't know, Sadie. But yours wasn't the only place he bought. He bought the old King place too. Isaac had that place priced way too high, and that's why it's been sittin' there for almost two years. But Mr. Saunders paid top dollar for all ninety-eight acres."

"I don't understand." Sadie folded herself into the rocker. "Why would Kade Saunders be buying up property in the middle of our community?" Then a thought hit her. Maybe he was coming here to live. Seemed a far-fetched idea, though.

"That ain't all," Lester said. He lifted his chin, challenging her to question him.

"What do you mean?"

"That twenty-acre tract right next to Noah's clinic. It's been for sale nearly six months. Saunders bought that too."

Sadie's eyes grew wild. Kade wasn't moving here. He was just buying up all their property for some commercial use, because he had the money to do it. She'd never been more furious. How wrong she'd been about him. *Greedy, greedy.* He'd gotten a taste of their quiet community and decided to profit from it.

"Is there any more? Did he buy anything else?"

Lester stood up. "Not that I know of, Sadie. I'm real sorry. But you take the money I made on your place so that you can purchase you somethin' else."

Sadie wanted to tell him that this was her family property and that she didn't want anything else, but Lester looked tormented, and she knew he had plenty to worry about with Mary.

"I'm going to talk to Mr. Saunders," she said. "And when I get done with him, he's going to sell me back my farm for what I sold it to you for, and you're going to keep that extra money to tend to Mary's medical needs."

"Why would he sell it back to you for such a loss?"

"Because he can afford to."

And with that, Sadie bid Lester good-bye and stomped toward the phone in her barn. Kade Saunders was about to get a piece of her mind.

It amused Kade to see the stunned looks on the board members' faces when he announced his resignation from Saunders Real Estate and Development. As he stared at the twenty dropped jaws, he decided to give them a moment to let the news sink in. He supposed that three months ago, if anyone had predicted such a maneuver, he'd have laughed. But he wasn't the same man he had been three months ago.

"What happened to you during your hiatus?" Larry Paulson bravely asked when no one else spoke up.

"Nothing happened to me, Larry. My situation has changed, that's all. As I'm sure you are all aware, I have full custody of my son, Tyler, following the death of his mother. Tyler has special needs, and I choose to be a hands-on father."

Mouths were still agape, and Kade's colleagues couldn't seem to grasp the concept. All except for one, Sheila Burns. A mother of four, her eyes were sympathetic, and she had a slight smile on her face. "I think it's a wonderful thing you're doing, Kade," she said.

Sheila wasn't the only female, or mother, in the room. However, the other four women present didn't seem to share Sheila's understanding.

"Kade, we all have children," Carol Watkins said. "And some of our children have special needs as well. But we don't give all this up, everything we've worked hard to achieve. Are you sure you've thought this through?"

Kade looked at Carol, then at Larry, Sheila, and continued around the room until he'd made eye contact with each and every one of them. Then he said, very simply, "Money will not buy any of us happiness. Everyone in this room has more money than they will ever spend in a lifetime. And how many of you can say, in all honesty, that you are truly happy and at peace with yourself and your life?"

While Kade might not have made such a comment several months ago, strangely enough, his colleagues seemed to consider his statement. No one said anything.

A knock at the conference room door pulled them all from their musings.

"I'm sorry to interrupt, Mr. Saunders," Mindy, the receptionist, said. "But there is a woman on the phone who insists she must talk to you. I told her repeatedly that you are not available, but she said it's urgent."

"Who is it?" Kade asked.

"She said her name is Sadie. She said you rented a cottage from her?"

Kade's heart thumped anxiously. "Put her through to my office." Then he turned to the board members. "Please excuse the interruption. I need to take this call." He left the room and walked a few paces to his office down the hall.

He answered on the first ring. "Sadie, is everything all right? How are you? Where are you? It's so good to hear—"

"How dare you!" she yelled into the phone, startling Kade.

"How dare I what?"

"You bought my farm from Lester Lapp for a ridiculous amount of money. And now, I need you to sell it back to me for what Lester originally paid for it. That is my family farm, Kade!"

Kade couldn't help but smile. "So, you are in Lancaster County, not Texas?"

Silence for a moment. "*Ya.* Now, will you sell me my farm back?"

"Of course. Why aren't you in Texas?"

He heard her sigh on the other end of the phone. "*Danki, danki.* I was feeling homeless."

"Sadie," he said soothingly. "I'll draw up the papers and get them to you. And, of course, for the same price you sold it to Lester Lapp. Now, why aren't you in Texas?"

"Why did you buy so much property in Lancaster County, Kade?"

"Why do you keep answering a question with another question?" It was wonderful to hear her voice. He could visualize her face, the way she bit her lip and twisted her face into a scowl when she was angry.

"Are you planning something? Something bad? Are you trying to bring your *Englisch* business into our community, Kade? Because we won't hear of such a thing, and—"

Kade smiled. "I sure have missed you, Sadie Fisher. I have missed you a lot. Now again I'll ask, why aren't you in Texas?"

A moment of silence, and then she said, "It wasn't right for me."

"*It* wasn't right for you, or Milo wasn't right for you?"

"Both," she conceded.

Kade wasn't sorry in the least to hear that news. It was a huge bonus to his already developed plan he'd put into action.

A huge perk, indeed. "I'll be coming to Lancaster County for Jonas and Lizzie's wedding in a couple weeks. It will be wonderful to see you."

He waited for her to reciprocate, but he only heard silence. "You still there?" he finally asked.

"*Ya*, I'm here." Her tone seemed laced with skepticism, and Kade felt the need to make her understand how much he missed her.

"I meant what I said," he began. "I've really missed you. I've wanted to contact you, but I didn't want to interfere with the new life you were pursuing." He waited again. Then he grinned. "You missed me, just a little, didn't you?"

He waited, then was elated to hear her say, "Just a little."

And that would be enough for now.

"How is Tyler?" she asked.

"He is adjusting, but he misses your tapioca pudding. Penelope, my housekeeper, made him some, but he doesn't eat it by the bowlful the way he does yours."

She chuckled, music to Kade's ears. "Are you bringing Tyler to Jonas's wedding?" she asked.

"Jonas would kill me if I didn't bring Tyler. I think he likes Tyler more than me."

"*Ya*, I understand that you and Jonas formed quite a friendship while I was away."

"Shocking, huh? We got off to a rocky start." Kade paused. "He's a fine man, Jonas."

"The best," she said.

Mindy's voice came across the intercom. "I apologize again, Mr. Saunders. It seems there is another call from Lancaster

County coming in. And the woman also says it's urgent. Do you want to take a call from Sarah Jane Miller?"

"Yes. Put her on hold. I'll pick it up," Kade said.

"I heard what that woman said," Sadie said, sounding alarmed. "Why is Sarah Jane calling you?"

"I don't know. Do you want to hold on while I find out?"

"*Ya.*"

"Okay, sit tight." Kade pushed the hold button and clicked over. "Sarah Jane? What is it? Is everything all right?"

Kade listened intently, and a minute later, hung up the phone.

He clicked back over to Sadie. "Sadie, it appears I will be traveling to Lancaster County sooner than I thought."

21

As the cab pulled up in front of Jonas and Sarah Jane's house, Kade counted the buggies. Twelve. A small crowd, but that's the way he understood they wanted it. He helped Tyler out of the taxi and paid the driver.

This trip to Lancaster County had consumed Kade's thoughts for the past three days, since Sarah Jane's phone call. Tyler didn't do very well on the plane last night, and an unfamiliar hotel room only added to the mix, rendering them both without much sleep. Then more problems this morning when Kade realized he forgot Tyler's favorite breakfast cereal. You would think a hotel could round up some Honey Nut Cheerios.

He hated to be late to anything, particularly an occasion such as this. He glanced at his watch. Eight thirty. They were a half hour late.

Sarah Jane warned him on the phone that the service would last from three to four hours, and Kade had considered just showing up for the last hour. But somehow, that seemed disrespectful. It would be a long morning with Tyler, but Kade figured he could slip outside with Tyler from time to time, if necessary.

"Tyler, we need to be very quiet inside," Kade told his son.

They headed up the porch steps, and Kade decided it would

be best to enter through the kitchen. He quietly pulled the screen door open and tiptoed in with Tyler by his side. Kade handed Tyler a candy sucker, saved for this very moment. It wasn't the recommended parenting tip, but Tyler smiled and began licking the lollipop. They walked around the corner and into the den.

Everyone was seated on wooden benches that had been lined up and angled toward the front of the room. Women were on one side and men on the other side, except for a few who were huddled around Jonas and Lizzie. Kade swallowed hard. The small congregation was singing a song in German, slow and without any musical accompaniment. Kade and Tyler slipped into the back row on the men's side of the room, the song filling the room with enough sound to cover their movements.

Tyler seemed mesmerized by his surroundings, and his eyes darted about in every direction. But the minute the music stopped and the bishop began to speak, Tyler made their presence known.

"Good!" he yelled.

Kade wasn't sure if Tyler meant the candy, the singing, or something else, but every person in the room turned around to look at Kade and his son. Sheepishly, Kade smiled and waved to his friends. Some returned the gesture, and Bishop Ebersol continued on with the service. Kade took a deep breath and hoped that Tyler would be able to refrain from any more outbursts. Then he saw Sadie in the front row.

She stared at him and smiled faintly. It was torture for him to be only a few yards away from her and not be able to talk to her. He desperately wanted to tell her how much he missed her. But there would be time for that later. Kade was glad to be back in

Paradise for a few days. He planned to have Sadie's property transferred back into her name and get his other plans rolling. But mostly, he was looking forward to spending time with Sadie.

Bishop Ebersol began to speak in German or Pennsylvania *Deitsch*. Kade couldn't tell the difference. The German language and the Pennsylvania *Deitsch* dialect sounded a lot alike to Kade. Twice, the bishop translated, seemingly for Kade's benefit, the stories of the Old Testament. Tyler yelled, "Good" two more times, but the bishop merely went on, and the attendees smiled.

Anywhere else, Tyler's interruptions might not have been so well received, but here—in Lancaster County—things were different. Kade's eyes shifted to Tyler, who was now reading the Bible he'd brought with him, his finger running along each line of fine print. Right away, Kade recalled Tyler's past Scripture quotes to both him and Sadie. Each time Kade saw his son pick up the Bible, he still felt a level of anticipation at the possibility of another revelation.

About an hour later, Kade and Tyler slid from their places on the back bench and went outside. Kade was shocked that Tyler had made it that long, and Kade had to admit it felt good to stretch his legs. As much as he respected, admired, and often longed to be a part of the Amish community, he couldn't quite get used to the lengthy worship services. Twice, he'd attended with Jonas before he returned to Los Angeles. Jonas had said, "Ya get used to it." Kade knew it was an honor to be invited to an Old Order church service, not something most of the outside world would ever have the privilege to experience.

He smiled as he recalled times spent with Jonas. And with Sadie.

Fifteen minutes later, Kade told Tyler it was time that they headed back in. Kade was worried he'd miss the main event, but they came back just in time. He helped Tyler to his seat and scooted in beside him. Kade smiled when Bishop Ebersol began the part of the service he was looking forward to the most.

"It is a blessed day," Bishop Ebersol began. "We are gathered together for this joyous occasion, to unite Jonas Ivan Miller and Elizabeth Mae Esh in holy matrimony . . ."

Jonas glanced Kade's way and smiled, then focused on his bride-to-be. What a scare those two had given everyone. Sarah Jane had told Kade on the phone about the adventure that had landed both Jonas and Lizzie in Lancaster General a week earlier. Luckily, neither was injured seriously. Following their one-night stay at the hospital, both Jonas and Lizzie wanted to push the wedding up. Sarah Jane had laughed, saying they'd both be safer if they were together.

Kade gazed at the couple. Jonas stood tall and proud, and Lizzie was a glowing bride, clothed in a blue dress, white apron, and white prayer covering, her face radiant as she smiled at her husband-to-be. He remembered Sarah Jane saying that when Lizzie and Jonas had split up for a short while, Lizzie'd had a bout with forgetfulness. They worried that she might have had a stroke, but Lizzie had been so depressed, she'd forgotten to take some of her medications. There was no evidence of a stroke.

Kade could hear sniffles throughout the room, and he struggled with his own building emotions. It was a glorious day, and Kade was honored to be included.

Everyone seemed to breathe a sigh of relief once Jonas and Lizzie had repeated their vows to each other. *What a blessing this day is,* Kade thought with a smile.

When Bishop Ebersol closed the service, Jonas and Lizzie made their way through the small crowd. It was heartwarming to see Jonas practically pushing past everyone to get to Kade, extending his hand two feet before he arrived. "I was worried you might not make it."

Kade latched onto his friend's hand, but then pulled him into an embrace. "I wouldn't have missed it, Jonas."

Lizzie joined her husband. "It's so *gut* you and the boy are here, Kade." She leaned in to hug Kade.

Kade's eyes scanned the room. "Where's Tyler?"

Jonas pointed to the far corner. "With Sadie. We see who's number one on his list." Jonas chuckled. "And I thought it was me."

Sadie hugged Tyler and caught Kade watching her. Kade took a deep breath. Being here—with Jonas, seeing Sadie, the feel of the place, the fellowship, the spirituality in the room—Kade felt almost overwhelmed. And to think that these people have this every single day.

He couldn't take his eyes from Sadie, who was now holding Tyler, laughing, and whispering something in his ear. There were so many things Kade wanted to say to her. But just then, Jonas spoke to him.

"Kade, me and Lizzie have something to give you, later, when things calm down a bit. Just don't run off until we're able to talk with ya for a few minutes."

"I'm not going anywhere, Jonas. I can't think of anywhere

I'd rather be. And I'll be staying for several days. There are some things—"

"Kade! Wonderful to see you," Noah Stoltzfus said. The doctor extended his hand to Kade.

"Great to be here," Kade responded. "It was a beautiful ceremony."

Jonas and Lizzie excused themselves to mingle with the other guests. "Just remember what I said, Kade," Jonas reminded him. He tipped his black hat as he walked away. Kade nodded in acknowledgment.

"I'm very excited about our project, Kade," Noah said when Jonas and Lizzie were out of earshot. "What you're doing is a wonderful thing, a great thing for the community. I think it will be wonderful for Tyler too."

Kade turned back toward Noah. "This place, and everyone here, will be good for Tyler."

"I agree," Noah said. He rubbed his chin for a moment. "Listen, I don't want to be overstepping my bounds—"

"What is it?"

"Well, as we discussed, I haven't mentioned your plans to anyone. But I was wondering if Sadie knows?" He paused. "I mean, people talk, even here, and word around the community is that perhaps something is going on with you and Sadie, and—"

"What?" Kade frowned. "I'll do whatever I have to do to protect Sadie's reputation. We're just friends, and Sadie has been very good to Tyler and me. If people are talking—"

"Wait, wait. Hold on, there, buddy," Noah said. "That's how we in the *Englisch* world think, but that's not what I meant. Sadie's reputation isn't being questioned. That would never occur to anyone here. What I meant was—in the words of the Amish—there is talk that a courtship is going on, even perhaps long-distance. I think that got started when Sadie returned from Texas, with no plans to marry Milo. I'm mostly wondering if you are considering converting?"

"I know people will probably think that, especially when we move here to stay. But God led me here, and this is where Tyler and I will stay." He paused for a moment. "Do I fantasize about what it would be like to convert, to be with Sadie as a family? Yes, I do. We became very close while I was here, and I care about her a great deal. But Noah, I'm wise enough to realize that a decision like that must be carefully weighed, and a change in faith of that magnitude would require more time, and a better understanding of the *Ordnung.*"

"I'm glad to hear you say that. Because an Amish woman would never allow a man to convert to the Plain ways just so he could be with her." Noah smiled. "Listen, I grew up Amish. If I can help you with anything, let me know. But I am thrilled that you and Tyler will be moving here, and I'm very happy about our project."

"So am I."

Kade looked across the room at Sadie walking toward him, holding Tyler's hand, and he wondered if he was being honest with himself. A large part of his intent in coming to Lancaster County was to be with Sadie, in some capacity. Could he really be happy being just her friend? Could he overhaul his life to that extent that he could claim a place in this fine community, a place with Sadie?

He looked around the room and smiled. *Maybe so.*

Sadie had tried to stay focused on Jonas and Lizzie during the ceremony, but she couldn't stop thinking about Kade and Tyler in the back row, so close. Sarah Jane told her they would be staying for a few days. Kade's words—*I've missed you*—resounded in her head.

Now she was anxious to get to Kade, when Lillian grabbed her arm.

"Thank the good Lord this all went well today," Lillian said. "Grandpa and Lizzie are so happy, and both of them know *who* they are and *where* they are today." She smiled, then spoke to Tyler. "Hello, Tyler."

"Hello, Tyler," the boy repeated to Lillian.

"It's a *gut* day for everyone," Sadie said. She fought to keep her eyes from drifting in Kade's direction.

"You know," Lillian said with a twinkle in her eye, "there is a rumor circulating around the community."

"Gossip and rumor are sins," Sadie said as she winked at Lillian. "But tell me."

Lillian leaned in close. "Rumor has it that Kade is staying here."

"I know that," Sadie said. She was somewhat disappointed Lillian didn't have anything juicier than that. "He'll be staying for three days."

Lillian grinned. "Uh, no, my friend. That is not what I meant." She folded her arms across her chest. "Rumor is that he will be *staying*. Moving here."

Sadie twisted her mouth from side to side, thought for a minute. "I wondered why he was buying so much property here."

She paused. "But I can't imagine what kind of business he would conduct in our Amish community."

"Maybe it's not business," Lillian said. "Maybe he's moving here to be with you!"

Sadie narrowed her eyes. "Lillian, that is ridiculous! He's not Amish." *But oh, how I wish he was.*

"People convert. Look at me. I did." She smiled.

"I know, Lillian. But people like Kade don't do that. Besides, we don't have that kind of relationship, nor would I ever hear of a man converting to our faith for the wrong reasons. I'm sure Kade's motives are—"

"Did I hear my name?"

Sadie had gotten so caught up in the conversation that she didn't realize Kade was standing beside them. "Kade," she said, her cheeks flushing. She felt like she might cry all of a sudden.

"I missed you," he whispered in her ear, and Sadie allowed herself to bask in the feel of his closeness.

But she pulled back, unsure what Lillian would think, and wondering if Lillian had heard what Kade said. "It's so *gut* of you to come to Jonas and Lizzie's wedding," she said.

"I wanted to be here. For a lot of reasons." He smiled.

"I better go find my family," Lillian said. "*Mamm* is proudly toting little Elizabeth around. And David has Anna. As much as I'm enjoying this break, I'll let you two talk." She grinned at Sadie, which caused Sadie to blush again.

"It's good to see you, Sadie," Kade said when Lillian was gone.

He seemed so familiar, as if no time had passed. Sadie gazed into his eyes, wondering, speculating. Then the words flew from her lips. "Are you moving here?"

Kade didn't seem at all surprised by the question. "Yes," he said smoothly.

People were bustling past them, particularly the womenfolk, and Sadie knew she needed to head to the kitchen and help prepare the meal. But she had so many questions. "Why? Why are you moving here?"

Kade's eyes darkened a bit. "I thought you might be glad I was moving here." He touched her arm. "Can we go outside for a minute to talk?"

"I need to help with the food, and—"

He tugged at her arm and guided her to the door in the den, which led outside. "Just for a minute." Tyler had taken a seat on the bench with Jonas, and Kade called Jonas's name. "Will Tyler be all right with you for a few minutes?"

Jonas looked up and nodded.

Sadie glanced over her shoulder, but everyone was busying themselves.

Once outside, Kade practically dragged her around the corner of the house, out of sight.

"Kade, stop it." She wiggled free of his hold on her arm. "What if someone sees us? Why are we hiding back here? I need to be inside helping with—"

"I missed you, Sadie," he said again. Kade pulled her close, and she gasped unexpectedly, afraid to stay in his arms, and yet not wanting to push him away either. His lips were so close to hers, she could feel his breath. He was going to kiss her, and what a mess that would make of things. Sadie knew she didn't have the strength or desire to stop him. *God, forgive me.*

But he didn't kiss her. Instead, he spoke softly, but intently, gazing steadily into her eyes—eyes Sadie knew reflected the fear in her heart. Fear he'd stay, fear he'd go.

"I'm not the same man I was before I came here, Sadie. Call it a spiritual awakening, or a spiritual cleansing of sort, but I'm not the same. I want a different life for both Tyler and me. I want that life to be in Lancaster County. I think the world of Jonas . . ." He paused. "And you. I don't have any expectations past knowing that I need to leave the city, my life as it was, and to start fresh. Basically, I'm taking the steps I feel comfortable with, based on what I believe is God's will for me. I plan to take things one step at a time. I hope I can count on your friendship."

It should have been what Sadie wanted to hear. But she was disappointed and wondered why. She already knew that men like Kade didn't give up their lives to become Amish. But that thought only brought up more questions. Her mind was buzzing, and she was having trouble thinking straight.

"I know you need to go inside to help with the meal," he said. "Could Tyler and I come by this evening?"

Sadie nodded mechanically. Saying no was not an option, this much she knew. "I'll cook supper," she said.

"Wonderful," he whispered. And then he was gone.

It was later in the afternoon when Kade asked Sadie if she could keep an eye on Tyler while he joined Jonas out by the barn, away from the others. Inside the barn, Jonas retrieved a metal box from the corner of his workbench, although Kade could tell there hadn't been any actual projects going on for quite a while. Cobwebs covered the vise grip bolted to one corner of the long, wooden table, and sandy dirt covered most of the surface. Jonas pulled an envelope from the metal box and motioned for Kade to sit down on a nearby bench. Jonas sat down on a wooden chair across from him.

"Kade, between my medications for the cancer and this Alzheimer's disease, my mind is a mess," Jonas began. "Some days I reckon I do real *gut*, but some days, I'm not sure who's who or where I'm at. Before things got too bad, I decided I wanted *mei* kin to know how I felt about them, how they added to this *wunderbaar* life the Lord blessed me with. So, I scribbled some letters to *mei* family, telling each one of them my most private feelings, things I might not be able to say in person." Jonas pressed his lips together. "We feel things just like other folks, Kade. But as Amish men and women, we know it's not always proper to say what's on our minds."

Kade listened intently, not sure where Jonas was going with this.

"These are the letters." Jonas held up the envelope. "Lizzie made a promise to me that she'd make sure to give each letter to each person if I die, or if I just go nuts." He lightly tugged at his long, gray beard. "And Lizzie has letters, too, to her kin. I'd promised to give them to each person." Jonas shook his head. "But we recently combined all our letters in this envelope. We fear that we could both not have our right minds at the same time, and no one would find the letters, or at least not for a while. And we reckon it might help our loved ones know what they meant to us, to help them durin' a time of grief, or even worse—if we were still on God's earth but not in our right minds."

"I think that's a nice idea, Jonas."

Jonas handed Kade the envelope. "I'd like for you to make sure everyone gets these letters at the right time. I reckon if somethin' happened to Lizzie, my mind would be like slosh, and I'm worried I'd forget where I put them."

"I'd be honored, Jonas." Kade accepted the envelope. "I will take care of this, if ever there becomes a need."

"*Ach*, there will come a need." Jonas chuckled. "Just ain't sure when."

"Can I ask you . . ." Kade hesitated. "Why me?"

"Why not you?"

Kade smiled. That was Jonas's way, and as Jonas had stated before, he wasn't comfortable being open with his feelings. But Kade knew it was an honor to be asked to do this on behalf of both Jonas and Lizzie.

"I feel better we've handled this, Kade. I trust you to take care of it." Jonas took a deep breath. "But now I reckon I need to talk to you about something else."

"What's that?" Something in Jonas's tone worried Kade.

"You ain't gonna like it, but I'm gonna speak the truth."

"Okay," Kade said.

Jonas took another deep breath. "I know you're planning to move here, Kade, and I'm pleased by this. I also know that you gave Noah a large amount of money to open a school next to his clinic, a school for special children, like Tyler and some of the others in our community. This pleases me also."

Kade opened his mouth to ask how Jonas knew this, but Jonas flashed his palm forward.

"And I know you plan to live on the other farm you bought, the King place." He paused. "'Tis *gut* as well."

Kade heard the *but* coming, loud and clear.

"But until you know if you plan to convert yourself to the Amish faith, renounce your worldly ways, and live as one of us by putting your faith in all that is God's will—then you need not be courtin' Sadie in any manner."

Kade wasn't sure he understood what Jonas was telling him. "But we can be friends, right?"

Jonas took off his hat and placed it on his knee. His eyes shone with implacable determination as he spoke. "If you have any thoughts of comin' here to test the waters, spend time with Sadie, and then make a decision one way or the other, it ain't right. You kids spent a lot of time together durin' the blizzard, and I looked the other way. But with you comin' here to live, it's only right that I tell you how I feel."

"I'm not sure I understand." Kade tipped his head to one side.

"I believe the *Englisch* say, 'You can't have your cake and eat it too.' And what I mean 'bout that is, you find your way *first*, Kade. Don't be courtin' Sadie without having made a commitment to the faith. Ain't fair to her."

Kade sat quietly for a moment.

"Can you say with certainty that you are going to leave all your worldly ways behind you and become a true member of our community through baptism?"

"Well, no, not yet. But I'm selling most of my personal possessions, donating them to charities, downsizing my life, all in an effort to see—" He stopped. Jonas was right. He was reducing his material baggage, and he was trying to turn his life over to God. But he hadn't made a final decision to commit to the Amish ways.

"When you can look me in the eye and tell me that you are ready to live as an Amish man, then, and only then, would it be appropriate to court our Sadie. You may think that you might want to be Amish, but more time is needed. I reckon I will continue to teach you the ways of the *Ordnung* as long as my mind allows me to, if you'd like."

Kade considered Jonas's comments. "I want to learn everything I can. I guess I thought that I could still spend time with Sadie while I was doing that, and—"

Jonas was shaking his head. "It's not right, Kade."

"But Bishop Ebersol wouldn't have to know," Kade said.

Jonas's expression was solemn and reprimanding. "But you will know. God will know." Jonas stood up. "I will leave you to think on this."

Kade sat in the barn for about twenty minutes, thinking about everything Jonas said. With much regret, he knew what he had to do.

He found Sadie in the house with Tyler. They were smiling and laughing. It was a picture-perfect moment, and he was about to ruin it.

22

Sadie unlocked the door at her shop. Then she sprung open the windows and allowed the crisp April winds to blow in, bringing with it the sweet smell of wildflowers. She inhaled, hoping the aromas would fill her senses with the tranquillity of the season. Spring was her favorite time of year, but on this day, it was taking all her effort to enjoy the beautiful weather.

She'd heard that Kade and Tyler were settled in at the King farm, even though she hadn't heard from him since the day of Jonas and Lizzie's wedding. Following his abrupt departure from the wedding, he'd returned a few weeks later to take up residence less than a mile away from her.

Her last conversation with Kade replayed again and again in her mind, and each time her thought process concluded, she was right back where she started, wondering what her future held.

Kade had canceled supper that evening with only a vague explanation. "I want to be a better man, Sadie," he'd said. "And I think I'm going to need some time to myself, just Tyler and me, for a while. Do you understand?"

Sadie didn't understand, but she'd nodded just the same, unsure what had changed since earlier in the day. She had wanted to ask him, how much time? And why did he have to distance himself from her in such a way? But then he added, "Only God can see past this moment, so I promise to walk with Him and see where His road leads me."

And that was something Sadie couldn't argue with, no matter how much she wanted to.

Yet, after all this time, she hadn't laid eyes on him, and Sadie had decided that Kade's promise to walk with God was not leading him toward her. Otherwise, surely he would have been by for a brief visit or something. She'd also heard rumor that Kade was involved in a business deal with Noah. *It's okay for him to socialize and do business with other members of the community and not me?*

Bitterness tugged at her heart—a heart filled with holes that she was tired of plugging. First Ben. Then Milo. And now Kade. Each bringing his own heartache. Sadie was done opening her heart or praying for a happy ending. Instead, she busied herself with other things and constantly prayed that God would help her understand His plan for her—a plan that seemed destined for her to be alone. But she knew that marrying a man she didn't love would have never brought her true happiness. Better to be alone.

"It's a gorgeous day," Mary Ellen said as she walked into the shop.

Rebecca followed behind her. "*Ya.* I love this time of year."

Both women walked over to Sadie, who stood near a rack of quilts on the far wall.

"I'm just adding this quilt to the others," Sadie said. It wasn't her scheduled day to work, and she had lots to do at her house. She heaved the quilt onto a large wire hanger for such a purpose. "I've already put a price tag on it. Sarah Jane dropped it off yesterday."

"I reckon you'll be readying your *haus* for church service this Sunday?" Mary Ellen asked. She helped Sadie straighten the quilt on the hanger.

"*Ya*. I'm getting ready to head to the house now."

Sadie hadn't hosted worship service at her house in almost nine months, which was about the amount of time it took to circle back to her after other members of the community took their turns. There was much to do in order to ready the house for such a gathering, a group of almost one hundred. And she only had today and tomorrow to do so. Samuel and several other men would be by tomorrow to help line up the wooden benches she kept in the barn and to remove the panel in her den for the occasion. The wooden room divider, a common addition to most Amish homes, separated Sadie's large den into two rooms. But on worship day, the two cozy areas became one large space big enough to host everyone.

Ben had loved having church service in their home. She missed him now, more than ever. And despite her bitterness, she also missed Kade and Tyler.

How naive she had been. She'd thought that Kade was moving here to be close to her, when he was really only here for business opportunities, opportunities he only knew about because of acquaintances that Sadie had introduced him to. He didn't even bring Tyler by to see her. Nothing. Her anger at him kept dragging her down. Eventually she'd have to pick herself back up, determined not to let Kade Saunders get the best of her.

Even all these weeks later, she could still see his face, feel his arms around her, and hear the sound of his laughter. She missed Tyler, too, his gentle ways, his innocent giggle. She recalled the way he'd clung tightly to her at the wedding. If she allowed herself to think too much about the two of them, it always brought forth tears. And there was way too much to do today to allow herself the luxury of feeling sorry for herself. So, with that thought, she bid good-bye to Mary Ellen and Rebecca and trudged toward home, to begin a thorough cleaning of the farmhouse.

Kade and Tyler spent most of their time with Jonas, at his place, when they were not in their new home. Not a day went by when Kade didn't long to see Sadie. Tyler was adjusting to his schedule, and Mary Ellen's daughter, Linda, babysat him when it was necessary for Kade to be without him. Today was one of those days.

"Thank you, Linda," Kade said when the girl arrived to keep an eye on Tyler for a while. "I shouldn't be gone more than an hour or so." Tyler liked the teenager, and Linda seemed to enjoy taking care of Tyler as well. However, today, Linda had a strange look on her face.

"Is something wrong?" Kade asked.

Linda walked to the window and pointed outside. "Is that yours?"

"Yes. What do you think?"

Linda raised her brows, and her eyes were as large as golf balls. "Do you know how to drive a horse and buggy? And where did you get *that* horse?"

Kade smiled. "Jonas has been teaching me. He's been letting me drive his for about two weeks."

"Where'd ya get that horse?" Linda's eyes were still wildly curious.

"From Big Jake, down past the Gordonville Bookstore." And what a deal he'd gotten. He couldn't wait until Sadie saw him pull up in his own buggy for church service this Sunday. It would be Kade's first time to attend worship since he'd been back, and a bonus that it would be at Sadie's house, a place filled with grand memories for him. He knew enough about the *Ordnung* at this point to know that pride was an unacceptable trait, but he suspected the emotion might surface just the same.

"That's what I thought," Linda said smugly. Then she abruptly spun around and faced Kade with warning eyes. "You bought Loco."

"What?"

"We call 'im that cuz he's a crazy horse. That's why Big Jake ain't been able to sell him." She paused and tapped her finger to her chin. "But I reckon you got him all the way here, so you must know what you're doin'." Linda shrugged.

"Well, actually—" Kade scratched his forehead. "Big Jake brought Loco, as you call him, early this morning. He hitched the horse up to the buggy for me. I purchased the buggy yesterday from Lester Lapp. He delivered it."

Linda giggled. "So, you ain't ever been behind the reins with Loco then, huh?"

"Loco, loco, loco!" Tyler exclaimed from his spot on the floor where he was playing with his letters.

"That's right," Linda said. "Your Pop is loco if he gets in the buggy with that horse a-pullin' 'im." She shook her head.

Kade felt a hint of nervousness, but if he was going to give the Amish life a try, he needed to live as they did. He had been doing a pretty good job so far. No electricity, for starters. It wasn't in the King house when he purchased it. Plus, he'd come a long way with his studies of the *Ordnung*. It was all strange and new—wonderfully strange and new. He and Tyler were settling into this peaceful community, and Kade had never been so relaxed in his previous life in California. Only one thing was missing, and he was working on that.

He was probably the richest Amish wannabe in history, but he was living proof that money didn't buy happiness, and he'd spent the last few weeks spreading his wealth around to those who needed it the most. He did miss one thing—his music. He missed listening to the radio. Most of what made up his past life—the business meetings, unscrupulous deals and people, the rat race—he was glad to be rid of.

He would miss a few people at his office, along with neighbors down the street. And he'd miss Penelope. He'd even miss the doorman at his favorite restaurant. The elderly man had opened the door for Kade at the eatery for seven years and then parked Kade's car, always with a smile on his face and, Kade believed, with the Lord in his heart. In many ways, the man had shone a wealth of spirit that Kade had never possessed with all his money. Until recently, Kade only knew the man as Jerry. But Kade made sure that Jerry wouldn't need to park another car for the rest of his life, unless he chose to do so.

Since he'd been gone, several high-profile publications had offered a pretty penny for an interview about Kade's transformation, and he'd declined. He knew they would print their own version of what they would call an early midlife crisis.

"And another thing." Linda's voice interrupted his thoughts. "I don't reckon it's right for you to be driving the buggy around like that." She pointed to Kade, dressed in his blue jeans, white T-shirt, and tennis shoes. "You don't look Amish."

"I'm not Amish. Not yet."

"Then why are you wantin' to drive the buggy?"

This girl was frustrating him. "Because I need to be able to get around, and I'm trying to live—"

"I seen a car in the barn." Her hands landed on her hips.

Kade sighed. "I'm trying to live the Amish way. But I guess I'll just take my car," he conceded, deciding Linda was probably right. "I'll be back in an hour or so then."

"Take your time. Me and Tyler will be just fine."

Kade pulled into Noah's clinic about ten minutes later.

"Hello, there," Noah said when he walked in. "Perfect timing. I don't have another patient for about a half hour. That will give us time to talk." He motioned Kade down the hall and toward an office on the right. Kade took a seat in front of Noah's desk in one of the two high-back tan leather chairs.

"These are the plans I had in mind." Kade handed him a rolled sheet of paper. "I'll leave this with you to take a look at. See what you think, and we can talk next week."

Noah tapped his pencil on the desk. "Lillian told Carley that you haven't seen Sadie since you've been back. I thought . . . Well, let's just say I'm surprised."

"It hasn't been easy," Kade said. "I want to spend every waking minute with her, but Jonas made a good point when he said I need to decide if I truly want to convert to the Amish ways before I pursue Sadie. So I guess I've been trying to do that."

"Sadie's pretty upset," Noah said. "According to Carley, Sadie thinks you only moved here for business reasons, and the other girls aren't saying otherwise. They're afraid you won't make the commitment, and they don't want to see Sadie get hurt."

"Makes sense. Sounds like all those women really watch out for each other."

"They're all daughters of the promise," Noah said.

"What?"

"Each one of them has been on a journey toward faith, hope, and love—a spiritual journey. These women all have a very strong faith, even my wife, Carley, who isn't Amish."

"Noah, you walked away from being Amish. How can I be certain converting is the right thing? I mean, I want to be with Sadie, but I honestly don't even know if she'll have me. Plus, I really do want to make a decision of my own volition."

Noah shifted uncomfortably in his chair. "I'd be lying if I said I wasn't surprised that you're considering such a radical change. But I will tell you this—these people live the life they believe in. They don't just talk about it or admire what it stands for. They live it. Each and every day. And as someone who has lived it before, I can vouch for the tranquillity that such a life has to offer."

"But you left." Kade needed more.

"Yes, I did. But I have Amish roots that will never be completely severed. Part of me will always be Amish, even though I don't mention that to most folks. I'm a blessed man, Kade. I get to live among them, take care of them, and yet still follow my own calling. At one point, I turned it over to God, and He showed me my place in this grand community."

Kade didn't say anything. How was he to know if he was truly following God's plan or if he was just running away from a life that caused him heartache?

"One thing I should mention, Kade," Noah went on. "You don't have to be Amish to have a relationship with God. The kind of peace you're looking for can be found anywhere." He paused, then smiled. "I think it's just easier to recognize that peace here in Lancaster County."

"I feel better than I've felt in my entire life, Noah," Kade said. "I have hope. Does that make sense?"

"Yes. It does." Noah smiled. "But once this school is built, what are you going to do with yourself? Somehow, I don't see you as a farmer. No offense intended."

Kade chuckled. "None taken. I don't know the first thing about farming. But I guess if it's meant to be, God will open doors for me."

"Yes. I believe that to be true. When things come very easily to us, it is usually because we are taking the path God wants us to take. Too much opposition means we are straying from His plan."

Kade smiled. "This has all happened easily for me—disbursement of funds, rearranging my life, finding the King farm, all of it. Tyler has adjusted well, and he seems to like it here too."

"I will continue to pray for you, my friend. You'll make the right decision."

Kade stood up and shook Noah's hand. "Thank you, Noah."

As Kade got into his car, he knew he needed to talk to Sadie on Sunday.

"Are you sure he's coming?" Sadie asked Lillian Sunday morning.

"Grandpa said he is." Lillian set a large bag on Sadie's counter.

"There are seven loaves of homemade bread in here. But we might want to warm them a bit later."

Sadie nodded, then moved to the far corner of the room to make way for Samuel and his brother Ivan to carry another bench through the kitchen and into the den.

"I don't know why they're not carrying those things through the den," Lillian complained.

Sadie shrugged. "What did Jonas say about Kade?"

"Just that he's comin'. That's all."

Sadie's hands landed on her hips. "Why do you never want to talk about Kade? He has been here for weeks, and I know he spends a lot of time with Jonas. And yet, I reckon no one tells me anything, and—" Sadie choked back tears.

"Sadie, don't cry." Lillian hugged her friend. "I've been worried to voice my opinions just yet."

"But why? You are my best friend. You know how much I care for Kade and Tyler, and still you won't open up to me about why he's here or what Jonas is saying. Nothing. I don't understand."

Lillian kissed Sadie on the cheek, then brushed a tear from her face. "I think you will understand soon enough."

Sadie was having one of those days where she couldn't stop feeling sorry for herself, yet those emotions were mixed with extreme levels of excitement at the prospect of seeing Kade and Tyler. But if he really cared for her, why hadn't he been around?

"Well, I don't understand. That's for sure." She shook her head and began hastily unpacking the loaves of bread from the bag. "I don't understand at all."

Jonas arrived at Kade's farm at seven thirty Sunday morning, with Lizzie by his side. Kade had forgotten that he'd asked Jonas for a ride to the worship service this morning. He didn't want to drive up in a car. But that was before he'd gotten a buggy and horse.

"Good grief," Jonas said. He stepped out of the buggy and walked toward Kade, who was standing in the front yard with Tyler. "What have you done?"

"It's our clothes, huh?" Kade felt ridiculous. He'd picked up clothes for him and Tyler at an Amish-owned shop in town.

Jonas stroked his beard. "No, you look mighty fine. Yes, you do. You both make fine-looking Amish gentlemen." Jonas pointed across the yard. "But, *what* have you done?"

"Oh, I was going to surprise you. I bought a buggy and—"

"Loco. You bought Loco! Boy, what were you thinkin'?"

"Big Jake said he's a great horse, and he gave me a really good deal on him. I'm taking the buggy to church."

Lizzie walked up beside her husband. "Is that Loco over there?"

Jonas began laughing so hard that he had to lean down and put his hands on his knees. Then he snorted, and said, "*Ya*, that's Loco, all right. And Kade thinks he's gonna have Loco pull that buggy all the way to Sadie's place."

Lizzie grabbed her chest and gasped.

Kade frowned. This was humiliating. "Don't let the name fool you," he said casually.

"*Ach*, we're not!" Jonas exclaimed. "Ain't foolin' us one bit. That horse is crazy as can be. And so are you if you think he's gonna get you to Sadie's in one piece."

"I'm counting on it." Kade held his chin a little higher. "Tyler and I were getting ready to leave."

"You do what ya want, but the boy rides with Lizzie and me." Jonas shook his head. "It's your funeral."

Kade's stomach twisted. How bad could this horse possibly be?

"Kade, I think maybe you best be ridin' with Jonas and me," Lizzie said softly.

"No, I'm taking Loco, and I'm driving this buggy to Sadie's house!" It was becoming a matter of principle at this point.

"Fine. But the boy comes with us."

"Fine."

Jonas turned to leave with Lizzie and Tyler, but turned back. "*Ach*, wait. I almost forgot. I brought you something." He pulled the seat of the buggy forward and reached into the backseat. He pulled out . . . *What? A radio?*

He handed it to Kade. "I know it's not fancy, like what you must be used to, just a battery-operated device, but it'll serve its purpose."

Kade accepted the radio but eyed Jonas with skepticism. "But, Jonas, it's not allowed. If I'm going to really be Amish, then I shouldn't have it." He pushed the radio back toward Jonas.

"Hogwash. Lots of folks have radios." He grinned. "Be best to listen to it in the barn, though."

Kade folded his arms across his chest, atop his new suspenders. "If I recall, I suggested not telling Bishop Ebersol something not too long ago, with regard to Sadie, and you said, 'But you will know and God will know.'"

Jonas twisted his mouth to one side. Then he leaned in toward Kade, a twinkle in his eye. "I reckon you need this to check the weatherman's forecast, no?"

Kade grinned back at his friend. "I suppose so."

"As you grow in faith, you'll know which rules are meant to

be bent, and which ones ain't." He winked at Kade. "And there's a little something for Sadie inside that trapdoor on the radio." Kade pushed the button marked Eject, and a CD popped out. *Favorite Country Gospel Tunes*, he read aloud.

"The girl loves music."

"I know." Kade smiled, remembering how Sadie had loitered on the cottage porch, listening to his music playing, and how much she enjoyed listening to the jazz melodies in his car. So much had happened since then.

"I figured there's a chance the two of you might be seeing each other in the near future." Jonas paused and stared warmly into Kade's eyes. "You're ready, Kade. And it's truly been an honor to travel on this journey with you."

"The honor has been mine, Jonas." It was a special moment, and Kade could feel God working in his life in so many ways.

"Hope you live long enough to enjoy the radio." Jonas snorted, tipped his hat back, and headed to his buggy.

Kade shook his head, a smile on his face. Then he headed to his own buggy. And Loco.

It was ten minutes until eight when Jonas pulled up with Lizzie. Most of the people Sadie expected to attend were already there. She was surprised to see Tyler with Jonas and Lizzie. Obviously, Kade wasn't coming after all.

She hugged Jonas, then Lizzie, when they stepped out of the buggy.

"Hello, Tyler," she said, squatting down.

Tyler wrapped his arms around her neck. "Sadie, Sadie," he said, almost bouncing up and down.

"I'm so glad you came, Tyler." She looked up at Jonas and tried to sound casual. "I suppose Kade isn't coming?"

Jonas let out the silly snort he was known for. "*Ach, ya.* He's comin' all right. Just ain't sure if he'll arrive in one piece."

Sadie stood up. "What do you mean?"

Before Jonas had time to answer, all their attention was drawn to the noise coming from down the road. Sounded like a man yelling.

"I reckon that's him coming now," Jonas said.

"What's all the racket?" Sarah Jane stepped onto the porch, then eased her way to the yard where Sadie, Jonas, Lizzie, and Tyler were standing. The rest of the people who had gathered in the den made their way outside.

"Oh no!" Mary Ellen screamed. "Someone is in that buggy, and the horse is out of control!"

Dirt flew from beneath the wild animal. And the group could hear a man yelling, "Whoa! I said whoa!"

"That ain't just any horse," Jonas said. "That's *Loco*. And the crazy person in the buggy is Kade Saunders."

"What?" Sadie couldn't believe it. "How do you know? What is he doing with Loco?" She shook her head. "Surely not." Sadie grew concerned. *Please, God, don't let anything happen to Kade.*

"I told Jonas when we left Kade's *haus* that we shouldn't be lettin' that boy behind the reins with that crazy horse leading the way," Lizzie said.

"What? Jonas, how could you?" Sadie started down the driveway toward the road. The large crowd began to follow.

"Pop!" Sarah Jane said. "Why didn't you stop him? We all know that horse is crazy! And shame on Big Jake for selling it to Kade!"

Sadie's heart was thumping hard against her chest. They all continued down the driveway and were almost to the road when Kade came barreling by. The buggy wheels were lifting off the ground, and Kade was yelling at the top of his lungs. A memory surfaced in Sadie's mind—one of Ben lying on the road among the scattered fruit, the buggy toppled. It sent a chill up her arms.

Jonas shook his head. "I warned the boy."

"You should have stopped him!" Sadie yelled.

Lillian then faced off with her grandpa. "Shame on you, Grandpa!"

"You girls need to quit blaming an old man for a young man's stupidity." He shook his head. "It ain't right."

No sooner had Kade passed them by than he came barreling back by in the other direction.

Jonas snickered. "I reckon he's gettin' control of that animal after all. He got him turned around."

Lillian gave her grandpa an incredulous look. "But he passed us up again. And at warp speed, I might add!"

"This is *baremlich*! What do we do?" Sadie looked to Sarah Jane for guidance.

Samuel was already in his buggy, and preparing to go after Kade, when they heard the buggy coming back down the road in their direction. Kade was no longer yelling, and he eased the buggy onto the driveway. Everyone cleared out of the way.

Once Kade was able to stop the buggy next to the house, the crowd headed back up the driveway and watched Kade step down.

"Sorry I'm late," he said after taking a very deep breath. Then he walked toward the house, turning back once to address the group. "That's quite an animal." He arched his brows and smiled.

"That is one brave human being," Jonas said. "Brave indeed."

Sarah Jane poked her father on the arm. "Shame on you, just the same," she said.

"*Ya*, you should have stopped him, Grandpa!" Lillian brushed past Jonas.

Similar sentiments were spewed in Jonas's direction by most of the other women, including Sadie.

She heard Jonas whisper innocently to his wife, "Why they blaming me?"

Sadie was just thankful that Kade was all right.

Kade barely gave Sadie the time of day after the three-hour worship service, though, in his defense, she'd been busy in the kitchen. Kade sat with the men for the noon meal, and as customary, the women served them first, so there hadn't been much of an opportunity to talk to him. By the time Sadie sat down to eat, most of the men, including Kade, had congregated out by the barn to tell jokes. Afterward, the younger men stored the wooden benches back in the barn.

When the afternoon wrapped up around two o'clock and everyone began to say their good-byes, Sadie noticed that Kade seemed in no hurry to leave. Quite the opposite. When the den cleared, he parked himself on the floor with Tyler—in the same spot that they'd sat together so many nights during the blizzard. It was unsettling, and Sadie wasn't sure what she would say or do if he stayed. He'd been absent from her home for so long, but never from her heart.

"'Twas a *gut* day," Jonas said to Sadie on his way out the door. Everyone had left except for Jonas, Lizzie, Sarah Jane, Lillian, and Lillian's family. But as the others made their way toward the door, Jonas turned and took a few steps back into the den. "Need a ride there, little fella?" He looked at Kade and said, "I don't reckon you need to be carryin' the boy in that runaway ride you got." He chuckled.

But before Kade had a chance to answer, Lizzie spoke up. "Kade, do you think Tyler would spend the night with us tonight? We'd be glad to carry him to our house." Then Sadie saw her wink at Kade.

"What's going on?" Sadie whispered in Lillian's ear.

Lillian had little Elizabeth Mae in her arms, while Samuel stood nearby, toting Anna. David was walking out with Sarah Jane. "I don't know." She shrugged.

Kade and Jonas exchanged grins. Then Kade smiled at Lillian.

"You are not telling me the truth," Sadie whispered to Lillian. "Something is going on, and everyone seems to know but me."

Lillian kissed Sadie on the cheek. "You'll know soon enough."

Sadie looked back toward Kade. "I think Tyler would love to spend the night," Kade said. "How does that sound, Tyler? Do you want to go stay with Jonas?" Kade squatted down on the floor and started to help Tyler put his letters in the lunch box. "No promises, Jonas. I don't know how Tyler will do."

"Tyler loves Jonas," his son said.

Jonas's face lit up. "I think we'll be mighty fine."

Kade waited until everyone was out in the yard before he approached Sadie. "I thought maybe we could talk?"

"Can't imagine 'bout what," she said, shrugging as she refused to make eye contact.

"Just give me a minute to tell them a few things about Tyler." Kade whisked past her and out the door.

Sadie began to rinse the last few dishes in the sink. When she heard footsteps, she looked over her shoulder. "Hello, Tyler."

The boy had his arms outstretched. "Hug," he said.

"Oh, sweetheart. Of course." Sadie dropped the towel on the counter and walked toward him. She wrapped her arms around him, and Tyler did the same. With his head on her shoulder, he spoke softly. "Be strong in the Lord, and in the power of His might."

Tyler pulled away, then smiled.

"I see you've been reading your Bible," she said. "Ephesians 6:10. You are such a sweet boy." Once again, Tyler's quoting of the Scripture seemed to come at an opportune time. Sadie was trying hard to be strong in the Lord and in the power of His might, trusting that His will would be done.

"Tyler loves Sadie."

Sadie blinked back tears. "Oh, Tyler. Sadie loves you too."

Then he ran outside.

After a few minutes, when Kade didn't come back into the house, she walked out onto the porch to find him sitting in one of the rockers. "What do you want to talk to me about?" she asked. Everyone was gone, and he was just sitting there.

He stood up. "Let's take a walk. It's a beautiful afternoon." He reached out his hand to her.

She ignored his gesture and asked, "What do you want, Kade?"
She didn't need to take a walk. She needed to understand why
everyone was winking and snickering earlier. She needed to know
why Kade had avoided her for weeks, as if she had imagined what
they'd shared.

Kade walked toward her, and she stepped back, feeling vul-
nerable all of a sudden.

"Come here, Sadie," he whispered. He drew even closer to her.

"What do you want, Kade?" She was almost yelling. "I haven't
seen you in weeks. You just left, and you said you needed time by
yourself with Tyler, and I thought—" She hung her head.

"You thought what? That I didn't care about you?"

She glared at him. "*Ya.* You left. And you've been back all this
time, without so much as a visit." She turned away from him. "I
think you best go."

When his arms wrapped around her waist, Sadie was para-
lyzed. She could feel his breath against her neck. "Sadie," he
whispered. Then he gently turned her around to face him, holding
her out at arm's length. "Have you taken a *gut* look at me today?"

She couldn't help but grin at his use of the *Deitsch.* Then she
scanned him from head to toe. "*Ya.* I took notice earlier, and you
make a fine-looking Amish man."

"That's why I've been staying away, Sadie."

He pulled her into his arms, and his lips drew close to hers.
She began to tremble. "Why?"

"Because I needed to make a decision about my faith, my life,
and not do it based on my feelings for you. I needed to know if
this—being Amish—was right for me. And you, my dear friend
Sadie, would have only clouded my judgment." He gazed into her

eyes. "Do you remember what I promised? To walk with Him and see where His road leads me. It brought me right here, to you."

His lips met hers tenderly, and Sadie fell into the moment, as if she'd waited her entire life for him. "I love you, Sadie," he said. "And if you'd allow me, I'd like to court you properly. I spoke with Bishop Ebersol yesterday about my intentions to be baptized into the faith, and also sought his permission to court you. So, it's with his blessing that I am here."

Her knees began to fold underneath her weight, and tears threatened to spill over. Could this be happening? At last? It was as if the heavens had opened up and shined light down on the two of them. "Kade—"

He brushed the tear from her cheek. "Do you think you could love me, Sadie? Because I have this dream I've been harboring for weeks, that you, Tyler, and I could someday be a family. I needed to know in my heart that I was following God's plan for me, and—"

"I love you," she said, putting a gentle finger against his lip. "I've loved you for a long time."

Kade kissed her again. Sadie closed her eyes and gave thanks and praise to God. She wasn't going to be alone after all. She would be with the ones she loved most. "You know," she said softly as Kade gazed into her eyes, the back of his hand stroking her cheek. "I can tell Tyler has been reading his Bible, because once again he quoted a Bible scripture to me. Today, in the kitchen, before he left."

"What did he say?" Kade asked. He leaned back from her slightly, his eyes still fused with hers.

"He said, 'Be strong in the Lord and in the power of His might.'"

Kade looked down, then lifted his eyes to hers. "He told me the same thing out in the yard when I told him good-bye." Then Kade pulled her close, and she could feel him trembling. "He . . . he also told me he loves me," Kade added in a shaky voice. "It was the first time."

"Oh, Kade."

Sadie knew that she and Kade were both on the path that God had planned for them.

She glanced upward and there were just two words on her mind.

Thank You.

Reading Group Guide

1. In the beginning of the story, Sadie is convinced that Milo is perfect for her even though she has never met him in person. If Sadie had never met Kade, do you think she would have ended up marrying Milo?

2. Kade travels to Lancaster County to escape his life, but ends up finding more than he ever anticipated. What are some things that he discovered in Lancaster County? Have you ever traveled somewhere and expected one thing, only to find another? What do you think would have happened to Kade if he had never visited Lancaster County?

3. Twice, Tyler quotes readings from the Bible to both Sadie and Kade. Do you think these are coincidences, or was God trying to reach Sadie and Kade through Tyler? Has there ever been a time when you felt God was trying to reach you through another person?

4. Jonas breaks off his courtship with Lizzie because he feels guilty about Irma Rose. What factors influenced

his decision to reconsider and ask Lizzie to marry him?

5. Why do you think Tyler is able to tell Sadie that he loves her early on, but yet he doesn't tell Kade until the end of the story? Because Sadie is a woman? Or perhaps Kade wasn't ready to accept his son's unconditional love early in the story?

6. Kade lost his faith in God when Tyler was diagnosed with autism. Have you ever turned your back on God when you felt He let you down? What made Kade seek to reestablish a relationship with God?

7. The Amish adhere to the rules of the Ordnung, the written and unwritten rules of the Amish; the order by which the Amish are expected to live. Do we, as Christians, have an Ordnung? What are some of the unwritten rules that Christians are expected to live by?

8. Jonas is outspoken, but wise. He tells Kade, "Until you know if you plan to convert yourself to the Amish faith, renounce your worldly ways, and live as one of us by putting your faith in all that is God's will—then you need not be courtin' Sadie in any manner." What if Kade hadn't taken Jonas's advice? Would things have turned out differently for Sadie and Kade?

9. The Amish struggle to live a good life and be the best that they can be, but they are human. There are several instances in the story when Amish characters judge others. Can you name some of the scenes where judgment is carried through?

10. When Monica drops Tyler off with Kade, did you sympathize with her situation, or did you feel like she was only being selfish with little regard for Tyler's well-being? And, do you think Monica would have come back for Tyler if she hadn't been killed?

11. Kade's friend, Val, betrayed him, yet Kade chooses to forgive him. Have you ever felt betrayed by someone but chosen to forgive that person based on Sadie's advice to Kade? "Sometimes when we see past our own pain and into the heart of another, our own self-healing begins."

12. Kade and Jonas develop an unlikely friendship, which begins when Jonas takes a liking to Tyler. Is this another possibility that God is working through Tyler to unite two people who have something to offer each other? If so, how do Kade and Jonas help each other?

Amish Recipes

Tapioca Pudding

7	c milk
¼	c sugar
7	T tapioca
4	eggs
I	c sugar
	pinch of salt

Mix the first three ingredients in a large pot. Heat mixture on stovetop on very low heat for almost an hour. Stir regularly. Make sure the tapioca is completely clear. Then beat eggs well in a separate bowl, until fluffy. Add sugar and salt, and beat until fluffy again. Turn milk mixture to high heat and slowly add egg mixture. Cook until it is almost boiling. **Do not boil.** Remove from heat and add vanilla to taste.

Zucchini Casserole

3   c grated zucchini
¾   c Bisquick©
½   c vegetable oil
½   c cubed Velveeta© cheese
½   t salt
4   eggs
¼   t pepper
½   t garlic powder
1   small chopped onion

Mix everything together and pour into casserole dish and bake at 350° for 45 minutes.

Peanut Butter Spread

(always served at the lunch meal following Sunday worship service, along with the cheese spread on the next page)

Mix together the following:

2   c water
2   c brown sugar
2   c molasses

Bring to a rolling boil for two minutes. Let cool and then add:

2½ lbs. peanut butter
2   c marshmallow crème

Mix well and enjoy!

Cheese Spread

    1½   c milk
     2   lb. white American cheese
     1   c water
     1   t baking soda

Heat milk, water, and baking soda. Do not boil. Slowly add
cheese until melted.

Acknowledgments

I thank God every day for this blessing He has bestowed upon me. I'm incredibly grateful for the opportunity to share my stories through words that glorify Him.

This journey would be impossible without the support of my husband, Patrick, who is willing to forego dinners, live with a messy house, and put up with me when the deadlines close in on me. I love you so much. And thank you for reading everything I write, as you promised in our wedding vows. (What a guy!)

I also couldn't do this without the love and support of a very special friend. Barbie Beiler reads each of my books before they go to print, and her Amish background helps me to keep the books authentic. Barbie, I not only appreciate all that you do, but I value our friendship more and more each day.

Another special person gets tons of credit when it comes to my books. To my editor, Natalie Hanemann, you are amazing. I hope that we are on this incredible journey together for a very long time. I can't imagine anyone else by my side, teaching and encouraging me the way you do, my friend.

My fiction family at Thomas Nelson—you are all so special. I keep a picture of you all above my computer to keep you close in my heart all the time. Thank you for everything that you do.

A special thanks to my agent, Mary Sue Seymour, for being a friend as well as a great agent.

Rene Simpson, it's an honor to dedicate this book to you. Your work with autistic children is inspiring on many levels, and your hands-on experience helped me immensely during the writing of this book. Your young students are very fortunate to have you in their lives. And I am blessed to have you as one of my best friends.

Renee Bissmeyer, thank you for reading behind me as I wrote *Plain Promise*. You keep me going when the going gets tough! I will always value our life-long friendship.

Special thanks to my sister-in-law, Valarie Spalek, for testing the tapioca pudding recipe, and to my mother-in-law, Pat Mackey, for testing the zucchini recipe. You gals are the best!

To friends and family not mentioned here, please know how much I appreciate all you do to encourage and support my writing. Blessings to you all.

The Daughters
of the Promise Series

Visit BethWiseman.com

Also available in e-book formats

THOMAS NELSON
Since 1798

ENJOY THESE AMISH NOVELLAS FOR EVERY SEASON

About the Author

Award-winning, best-selling author Beth Wiseman is best known for her Amish novels, but her most recent novels, *Need You Now* and *The House that Love Built*, are contemporaries set in small Texas towns. Both have received glowing reviews. Beth's highly-anticipated novel, *The Promise*, is inspired by a true story.